THE SWINGING PENDUI

# THE SWINGING PENDULUM OF
# THE TIDE

A STORY OF SPIRITUAL AND SEXUAL REAWAKENING

CHRIS GREEN

YOUCAXTON PUBLICATIONS
OXFORD & SHREWSBURY

Printed and bound in Great Britain.
Published by YouCaxton Publications 2018
YCBN: CG-TSP-548 int v1-5

YouCaxton Publications
enquiries@youcaxton.co.uk

To my wife Sheila for her encouragement, love
and support over four long years.

*The swinging pendulum of the tide*
*has no clock:*
*the events are dateless.*

*R S Thomas*

# Forward

All the characters in this novel are fictitious and bear no deliberate resemblance to any living person. The description of sites on the mainland and Bardsey Island are as accurate as I can remember from various visits to the Llŷn Peninsular. While all the properties mentioned in the novel genuinely exist, the description of their interiors is entirely from my imagination or from what limited details I have been able to glean from property description on the Bardsey Island Trust website.

My knowledge of the island is based on three pilgrimages I made there with the Anglican Franciscans in the 1960's and a more recent day-visit with my wife. On one of these pilgrimages I met R. S. Thomas who was then Vicar of Aberdaron. I was pretty much unaware of the importance of his poetry at the time but have since become a serious devotee of his work.

Bardsey Island's connections with the Arthurian legend are somewhat tenuous but then so are many of the other claims from the Scottish Borders down to the West Country. Whether real, part-real or fictitious, Arthur was re-invented in the Middle Ages and later as a romantic hero helping to boost the concept of chivalry. It was and is hardly surprising that so many peoples should want to feel a sense of ownership of this heroic figure.

I am indebted to Liz Chave, who was the first person to read an early draft of the novel and to encourage me to continue; to my good friend David Stoll for his many helpful suggestions and support and to my daughter-in-law Lucy Dodsworth for her expert proof-reading and many helpful textual comments. Finally my thanks to Bob Fowke and his talented team at YouCaxton for their very professional approach to the publication of this novel – a first novel is a very special 'child' and requires the tenderest love and care.

*CG November 2018*

# Meilyr Brydydd

'Me, the poet Meilyr, a pilgrim to Peter,
The gate-ward who assesses qualities of perfection,
When the time to rise will come for us
All who are entombed, support Thou me.
Awaiting the call, may I be in the precincts
Of the monastery against which beats the tide,
Which is secluded and of undying fame,
With its graveyard in the bosom of the sea,
The isle of wondrous Mary, holy isle of the saints
Glorious within its resurrection to await
Christ of the prophesied Cross, who knows me, will deliver me
From a banished existence in violent hell
The Creator, who created me, will receive me
Among the saintly parish of the band of Enlli'

*(Meilyr Brydydd — early 12th century)*

# CHAPTER ONE

*T*he *two-carriage train pulled into the station with a screech of brakes and a shudder, its overheated engines, emitting a last gasp of diesel fumes. The young man who stepped out onto the crowded platform with a rucksack draped over his shoulder was tall and slim. He looked up and down the platform searching for the station cafeteria where they had arranged to meet, spotting it by the main station entrance. He hurried along the platform, biting his lower lip apprehensively. His face showed that slight look of concern that can overtake anyone who is about to meet a new group of people for the first time.*

*Inside the cafeteria it was warm and stuffy. Clearly the station authorities had made no concessions to the early August heat wave that had struck the British Isles. They had failed to open any windows or turn on the colonial-style rotating fan which hung from the ceiling. Looking around for the companions he was due to meet, he was immediately drawn to a group of a dozen or so boys and young men chattering cheerfully amongst themselves in the far corner of the room. One of them must have said something particularly amusing because all of a sudden they burst into howls of laughter. It was only then that he saw, in their midst, the rotund smiling figure of an elderly cleric garbed in the traditional brown habit of the Anglican Franciscans. 'That must be Father Beuno' he thought. Seated on either side of him were two much younger men wearing similar habits.*

*It was while he was taking this all in and considering how best to introduce himself that he felt a firm hand grip his shoulder from behind.*

*"Looking for someone by any chance? You must be Tom. We've been looking out for you. I believe that everyone else has already arrived. How was your journey?"*

*"Oh, not too bad thank you" said Tom, turning to face the fourth, tall, thin and slightly stooped brown-robed figure who had addressed him in a*

strong Welsh accent. "There was a bit of a delay at Chester but we seemed to make up most of the lost time on the rest of the journey. I'm so sorry if I've kept you all waiting."

"No problem at all. By the way, I'm Brother Ninian and my three companions seated over there are, from left to right, Brother Andrew, Father Beuno and Brother Mark... but let me introduce you."

Tom was swept into the midst of his new companions who introduced themselves one by one, and warmly shook him by the hand. Last of all Father Beuno stood up and embraced him.

"Welcome, welcome dear boy, it is so wonderful to have you with us. I have heard such good things about you from your Bishop and I have a special plan for you which I shall tell you about later. Brother Ninian, perhaps you'd be good enough to introduce Tom to the youngsters."

"Now you may already have noticed that some of our young companions are speaking Welsh. You see, for quite a few of them, Welsh is their first language" Brother Ninian explained. "Indeed, some of them struggle a little with their English. This may surprise you, but a good many of the lads come from South of Caernarvon, along the Llŷn Peninsula, where the Welsh language is still dominant. But don't worry, if you have any communication difficulties, several of the lads are bilingual. They'll be only too happy to translate for you."

"Actually I'm not all that surprised," Tom replied. "My father used to come down to North Wales on holiday over fifty years ago. He told me how the residents always used to break into Welsh the moment a stranger entered the local shop."

"Well you can hardly blame them," responded Ninian "they are naturally suspicious. They've had to live with all these English folk coming down from Cheshire and Lancashire in their smart new motor cars, with their well-dressed children, buying up local properties like there's no tomorrow and sending their value sky high, well beyond the reach of local folk. But forgive me," he said with a broad smile, "we've hardly met and here I am giving you a lecture on the rape of my homeland by your English cousins." They both laughed.

*Ten minutes later and the party had reassembled outside the station. They were soon climbing up into the coach hired to take them on the first part of their journey to the most westerly point in Wales, sitting at the very tip of the Llŷn Peninsula. The seas permitting, tomorrow they would make the crossing to Bardsey. In the meantime, Tom had the coach journey and a night in Aberdaron, plenty of time to begin to get to know his new companions.*

# CHAPTER TWO

It was an unusually bright if cool afternoon for early April. As Tom looked down on the beach, a salt sea breeze ruffled his hair and made his nose run, just as it had when he had been a small child. A sea fret had lain over the extreme end of the peninsula earlier in the day like a damp and icy shroud, but had now been all but blown away. Clambering over the rocks and heading across the sand to where the waves were breaking on the deserted seashore he felt the thrill of childhood return.

When he had unpacked his bags at the inn earlier and sat on the bed to rest his aching feet, almost too many memories had crowded into his head, certainly too many to deal with all at once. It was almost as if they belonged to another person, someone he used to be twenty-five years ago, rather than the person he had become since. But that was why he was here. He had been determined to return to this bleak and windswept landscape to try to rediscover something of that person he used to be.

Walking more quickly now, he neared the spot where the waves of were breaking in a torrent of heaving white water. He watched as they glided smoothly towards him, washing away the prints left by the few humans, dogs and sea birds who had ventured out before him. He stepped back from where the last wave had swept in, rather closer than he had expected. He smiled as he remembered how, as young boys, he and his brother, like generations of children before them, had dared the incoming tide. They had rushed in and out between each wave, shrieking with delight every time one of them had been caught in the sea's ice-cold embrace. But that was on the less rugged and more populated holiday beaches of Anglesey and the North Wales coast, not here where only fishermen, farmers and the brave pilgrims of years ago had once gathered and which now had largely become a refuge for those who truly wanted to 'get away from it all'.

Tom stepped back a little further to avoid getting his feet wet. He turned towards the far end of the beach as he watched the waves edge their way slowly but relentlessly up the shore, carrying with them fragments of tangled seaweed and the occasional broken shell. He closed his eyes and paused to savour the smell of the sea air. He held his breath for a moment and let it out with a deeply satisfied sigh. The breeze was blowing stronger now and made his eyes water. He reached for a handkerchief to wipe away the tears. It was chillier now too, so wrapping his coat tightly around him, he set off at a brisk walk towards the distant rocks at the curve of the bay. He stooped to pick up a smooth flat stone, black as graphite and streaked with white marbled strands. How many millennia of rising and falling tides had it taken for such a perfect object to be moulded, he wondered? And then with a whoop of joy he skimmed the stone flat and level over the crest of an incoming wave. He saw it bounce and fly over the surface of the sea four, five, six times before it disappeared into the next wave. Exhilarated, he picked up and threw another stone and another and another until his arm ached and his cheeks burned with the effort and the constant bite of the wind.

By now he had almost reached the cliffs at the far end of the beach. He spotted a flat shelf of dry rock, tight into the side of the cliff, which offered at least some protection from the incessant blasts of the wind sweeping across the bay. Clambering over the rocks scattered on the foreshore, he reached the shelf and sat down with his back against the wall of jagged rock which rose steeply above him to the cliff top. Looking back along the beach he could still quite clearly see the footprints he had left behind.

'Little prints in time' he thought, 'but they won't be there for long and no-one else will ever see them or know that I have been here'. And, at that very moment, the first of his prints was swallowed up by the incoming tide.

It was getting darker now. He peered into the distance, back towards the hump of the headland that stood this side of the village. He could just make out the dark-edged outline of the parish church. It lay low, tucked into the fold of the hillside, with its back turned against the sea. Its solid grey stone walls bearing witness to the centuries of protection they had offered from the wilder ravages of the wind and sea.

He chuckled when he remembered the dramatic final rehearsal that had taken place in front of the altar there on a hot summer afternoon all those years ago. For three days, he and his fellow pilgrims had stayed on the island, preparing for a series of performances of one of Laurence Houseman's *Little Plays of St Francis,* which they were due to perform in the principal parish churches between Aberdaron and Bangor. The last part of the original pilgrim route had been from the cathedral church of Bangor to the holy island of Ynys Enlli or Bardsey. However, the Franciscan brothers who were leading the pilgrimage had deliberately chosen to walk the pilgrim route in reverse from the island to Bangor, so as to end up in a 'living' centre. Apart from the four Franciscan friars who were leading the pilgrimage, most of the other pilgrims were enthusiastic church-going youngsters, a number of them training for the priesthood from the Dioceses of Bangor and St Asaph. Tom himself had been an eighteen-year-old theology student in his first year at university. He had been persuaded to direct the play.

The rehearsals on the island had gone well and the young pilgrims were jubilant, confident they were ready to put on a high-class performance for the play's 'first night' in Aberdaron. But when it came to that final rehearsal, the young man playing St Francis had suffered a severe attack of stage fright. He refused go on because he couldn't remember his lines. Despite the pleadings of the other players, he had remained adamant; there was no way he could possibly perform. In the end he had run out of the church in floods of tears. With only three hours remaining until the first performance, Tom had had to think fast to find a solution. But needs must and he had come up with the novel idea of the saint becoming a voice from off-stage, never actually appearing. Reconciled to this solution, 'St Francis' had been concealed, lying low behind the communion rail, with his script in one hand and a torch in the other. Naturally, members of the audience had been completely unaware of the circumstances that led to this decidedly original presentation of the play. After the performance, Tom had been warmly congratulated on 'that most moving production' and for having so ingeniously presented Francis as a heavenly voice rather than a physical being.

But all that was a very long time ago. Then he had been solid and secure in his faith. Indeed, like most of his young university contemporaries, he had been secure in his beliefs about most things. He had been certain that there was a better world worth fighting for and equally certain that he and his generation were capable of bringing about the changes that were necessary to achieve a fairer and more just society. Looking back now, it hardly seemed possible that he could have been blessed with such certainty. All that had once seemed so clear and straightforward — his politics, his ideals and most of all his faith — had been dashed against a massive wall of human indifference.

His thoughts returned to the last time he walked on this beach. He was not alone then but with those enthusiastic and exuberant new companions. It had been a warm sunny summer afternoon in contrast to this cold and blustery spring evening. He had rejoiced in the company of those new friends with whom he was about to share a common experience. But that was then. So, what of now? What of this dejected and disillusioned being he had become? The road he had chosen to follow over so many years had turned out to be a cul-de-sac. But while he couldn't see the way ahead, he knew that there was no going back.

# CHAPTER THREE

She felt the wind bite into her cheeks as she pulled her hood more tightly over her head. It was a chilly spring late afternoon and the wind had an icy edge. Out over the bay soft fleecy clouds hung like a curtain over the sea, parallel with the horizon, emblazoned with streaks of gold and orange by the sinking sun. The constant screeching of gulls outside her hotel bedroom window that had disturbed her tranquillity earlier had now almost ceased. All she could hear within the cocoon of her hooded coat was the breaking of the waves against the sea wall and the crunch and scrape of stones and shale in the tumble of the turning sea.

She quickened her pace towards the far end of the sea wall in the hope of fighting off the chill of the oncoming evening. From there she would be able to get a better view of the small, timeless village that had nestled in the hollow below the ancient church of St Hywyn for over a thousand years. When she reached the point where the sea wall dropped down to the beach, she gasped as a huge wave broke against the wall and showered her with a thousand droplets of icy spray. The air was so sharp that it was painful to breathe in too deeply. She raised her head to look up at the golden sky before closing her eyes and listening to the surging of the sea.

Somewhere out there, just round the curve of the headland, lay Ynys Enlli, that small island that still lay in her imagination. Weather permitting, she would soon be heading over there. But she was happy enough for the time being, content to take in this wild and swirling landscape. It contrasted so dramatically with the hills and valleys of her native Lancashire, and even more so with the stone and concrete surrounds of her university campus in London.

She opened her eyes and looked down against the sea pounding on the rocks below and then up at the last curve of the sinking sun. At times like this it was hard to understand why she had chosen to imprison herself in the dull and claustrophobic corridors of academia. She recalled only too well her mother's well-meaning warning, 'whatever you do Beth, child, don't bury yourself completely in your studies. Remember there's a whole world out there waiting to be explored!' That had been what now seemed half a lifetime ago, when she had first embarked on her academic career. Now, fifteen years later, she had a first-class honours degree and a doctorate in early medieval history under her belt. She was already establishing what promised to become a distinguished career as an academic writer and accomplished lecturer and tutor. But what modest pleasures lay in the desk-bound study of her long-dead Celtic heroes, compared to the exhilaration of being part of the living world that now lay before her?

When she came in from the college quadrangle the previous day, she was relieved to see that the corridor was empty. She was been keen to finish packing and to be on her way without further interruption. This last term had been particularly exacting following a record intake of first-year students. There had been too many poorly constructed essays to mark, too many uninspiring tutorials to struggle through, and a succession of individual student problems to attend to with a sympathetic ear. And, of course, in these days of ever-increasing bureaucratic demands, there had been a non-stop flow of paperwork to attend to. As usual, the university administrators had shown little sign of appreciation for her hard work.

Sitting at her desk on that last morning, she had felt an overwhelming sense of relief. Soon she'd be out of there, clear of the stuffy academic environment for four whole weeks. Neatly laid out on her desk were the few remaining items to be placed into her shoulder bag. An ordnance survey map of the Llŷn Peninsula lay next to the large blue notebook in which she had carefully jotted down her planned itinerary. A loose-leaf folder contained the copious notes she had prepared and printed out on her computer. Finally, there was a small pile of books: Nennius' *Historia Britonnum*, Gildas' *De Excidio et Conquestu Britanniae*, Gerald of Wales *The Journey through Wales* and *The Description of Wales*, and Geoffrey of Monmouth's *History of the Kings of Britain*. Sitting alone and as yet unopened was her latest acquisition, a Welsh-English dictionary.

A little later that same morning, she had reluctantly put up with a barrage of enquiries about her plans for the Easter vacation from Professor Anderson, her Head of Department. She put this down to the all-too-evident fondness he had for her, which she found touching if occasionally unacceptably intrusive. At least, on this occasion, she managed to get away with just a few vague hints about her plans. She would be travelling alone. She was hoping to enjoy some healthy walking along the coastal paths of the Llŷn Peninsula combined with some general sightseeing. And, oh yes, she might take a look at one or two local points of interest relating to her current studies. The well-intentioned professor, realising she was unwilling to be drawn beyond these basic facts, had concluded their conversation with good wishes for a safe journey and a quick peck on the cheek.

And now, little more than a five-hour drive from London, here she was in this remote and little-changed corner of Wales. It was somewhere so far removed from her usual environment that if it hadn't been for the bite of the wind and the taste of salt on her lips, she might have been dreaming. In the last moments before the sun finally sank below the horizon she could see a heavy build-up of rain clouds steadily making their way in towards the bay. She tried to imagine what it would be like to stand in this same spot on a midwinter's night with the sea raging below and a howling gale battering the coastline. She shivered, turned towards the village and hurried back to the warmth and safety of the inn.

# CHAPTER FOUR

As Tom hurried back across the beach towards the village, he sensed that the icy droplets blowing into his face no longer tasted of salt and that it had begun to rain. Indeed, when he was halfway between the ledge where he had rested and the edge of the village, it began to pour. It swept in from somewhere across the Irish Sea in relentless sheets that stung his cheeks and soon penetrated his inadequate outer clothing. He wished he had dressed more suitably for this first outing. He broke into a run towards the concrete road leading to the shelter of the village houses. By now he was soaked to the skin.

Shivering and out of breath, he finally arrived at the inn. An elderly couple, noting his sorry figure, stood aside and offered him a nod of sympathy as he rushed past them towards the staircase. He was shivering so uncontrollably that he fumbled with the key as he tried to unlock his bedroom door. Once inside, he tore off his wet clothes and hurried through to the bathroom to run a bath. Soon he was lying back in the hot water, gradually thawing out. He closed his eyes and luxuriated in the moment. He had long imagined the pleasure of a hot bath to be not unlike a return to the womb. After the violence of the wind and rain this seemed to be as safe and secure a refuge as he could have hoped to find.

Before the series of crises that had led to his loss of faith, it had often been moments like this that had inspired his better sermons. He thought of the doom-ridden verse in Psalm 11 "Upon the ungodly he shall rain snares, fire and brimstone, storm and tempest: this shall be their portion to drink". Well his recent return from the beach had certainly felt like it contained most of the elements of that verse. He watched the steam rise and mist over the large mirror that hung over the washbasin. He thought of how he might have contrasted that particular verse with the more reassuring words of Psalm 23 "The Lord is my shepherd; therefore can I lack nothing. He shall feed me in green pasture: and lead me forth beside the waters of comfort". "Waters of comfort', oh, how I love that phrase', he thought.

As he climbed out of the bath and reached for a towel, he caught his reflection in the mirror. He moved closer to examine his features more clearly. He had never been a particularly vain man, but the face that stared back at him now was hardly that of the once fine-featured and handsome cleric who had stirred a few hearts amongst his female parishioners. There were dark shadows under his eyes and the smooth lines that once defined his smile had lengthened into worried furrows. His cheeks seemed to have sunk deeper into his face and his nose looked narrower and sharper at the tip. The overall impression was that of a tortured soul lost somewhere between deep suffering and total despair. He was amazed at how a face, his face, could so readily reveal such inner torment.

He returned to the bedroom and looked at his watch, seeing that although the heavy rainclouds had darkened the sky, it was not yet six o'clock, a little early to go down for a drink, let alone for something to eat. 'And yet' he thought 'if I stay up here in the bedroom all I'll do is to mope around feeling sorry for myself'. He dressed quickly, putting on a warm pair of jeans and a well-worn woollen sweater. He had never been known for his good dress sense and, in any case, on an evening such as this he put warmth and comfort well ahead of any desire to impress his fellow lodgers.

# CHAPTER FIVE

When he entered the bar, Tom was surprised to find that it was already fairly busy. He assumed the inclement weather had driven people indoors. While he waited to be served, he took in his fellow customers, who it soon became apparent were mainly locals. A group of three swarthy middle-aged men at the far end of the bar were conversing in Welsh. By contrast, immediately to his left, a young couple with cut-glass English accents were loudly bemoaning the state of the weather as if, in some way, the locals were responsible for it. Not feeling sociable, he discreetly moved towards the opposite end of the bar, rested an elbow on the counter and turned his back on them.

He didn't have to wait long to be served. As soon as the cheery-faced landlord handed him his pint of best bitter, he retreated to a small table in a quiet corner. Although he had no desire to participate in the exchanges taking place around him, he was comforted by the general hum of conversation and the friendly atmosphere. He had never particularly enjoyed drinking or eating alone in a room full of strangers and was relieved to able to hide behind the copy of *The Guardian* he had brought down with him.

He flicked through the pages until he reached the crossword. It soon became apparent that this particular puzzle contained a number of anagrams. He remembered how his wife Martha, a crossword fiend if ever there was one, had depended on him when it came to working out the anagrams. She had been adept at solving literary and historical clues, but had remained mystified when it came to playing with letters and shaping them into new words. As a team, they had formed almost the perfect crossword-solving partnership. It was nearly five years now since she had been tragically killed in a car accident. But, in his mind, he could still see her, sitting next to him on their sitting room sofa, hunched over the neatly folded newspaper, taking the clues apart under the warm glow of their Edwardian standard lamp. He remembered how she would squeal with delight each time she unravelled one of the more obscure clues and how, when he had unpicked a long jumble of letters into an ingenious new word, she would squeeze his arm with encouragement and plant a light and playful kiss on his cheek. Despite the passing of the years, flashbacks like this still regularly entered Tom's head. While he had tried to learn to handle the deep emotional turmoil of his bereavement, he continued to feel just as bereft of Martha's love and companionship. He sighed and turned his attention back to the crossword in the hope of staving off the overwhelming cloud of sadness hanging over him.

When he next looked up he saw that the room had continued to fill with new customers, many of them arriving wet and bedraggled. The wind and rain had clearly not let up since he came in a couple of hours ago. From time to time there were bursts of laughter from a party of young people who appeared to be celebrating a special occasion, a birthday perhaps or an engagement? Soon all the tables were fully occupied and it was standing room only at the bar. With the continual delivery of food to tables all around him it was clear that the kitchen must be under pressure so he decided that it would be wise to place his own order as quickly as possible. He waved to a pretty young waitress in jeans and a bright red T-shirt who, with an apologetic smile, promised to return to take his order before disappearing off to the kitchen carrying a tray loaded with dirty crockery.

It was at this moment that he first noticed the young woman standing by the bar with a glass of red wine in her hand looking anxiously around the room. At first he thought she must be looking for someone. But then he saw she was clutching a stack of books under her other arm and realised that, like himself, she was probably on her own. She seemed to hesitate for a moment or two before heading purposefully in his direction. He couldn't help noticing that several of the men gave her more than a passing glance as she crossed the room. She was certainly of striking appearance, tall and slender with long black hair tied back in a ponytail.

"Excuse me" she said, approaching his table, "would you mind if I joined you, unless, of course, someone's already sitting here? It looks like it's the only empty seat left in the room and I was rather hoping to order something to eat." She smiled nervously as she hovered over the table.

"No, no, I'm quite on my own" said Tom. "You're more than welcome to join me. Here, let me move my chair round a bit to give you a little more room."

"That's very kind" she said with a further smile. "I'm Beth, by the way. If I put my books down for a moment, would you mind keeping my place while I go up to the bar to order some food?" She rather clumsily extracted the books from under her arm and put them down on the table next to her wine.

"Actually, I managed to catch the eye of one of the waitresses a moment ago and, with any luck, she should be coming over to take my order shortly. Why don't you sit down and we can both place our orders at the same time."

"Oh, that would be perfect" she said. "To tell you the truth, I'm pretty worn out after a long day's drive and a walk on the beach. The thought of fighting my way through the melee at the bar is hardly appealing."

She pulled her chair out and sat down. Tom sensed a certain awkwardness in her movements as she rearranged the positioning of her books and wine glass. He could tell she was uncomfortable conversing with strangers. For his part, he was happy to take up his newspaper again and return to his crossword.

A few minutes later, the waitress returned from the kitchen. She skilfully manoeuvred four well-laden dinner plates onto a neighbouring table before coming over to take their order. Tom noted her well-educated voice as she repeated their orders and supposed that she was probably a student working through the Easter vacation. She then somewhat inelegantly dumped place-mats, cutlery, salt, pepper and a bowl containing a wide variety of unappealing sachets of sauces in the middle of their table and hurried off to the kitchen. Tom caught his new companion's eye and she smiled back at him. "I don't think she was trained at the Ritz!" Tom said and her smile widened into a grin. "Not unless we're talking about the Café Ritz in downtown Bognor" she responded and they both laughed.

"Oh, I'm sorry" he said, "but I don't think I've introduced myself. I'm Tom."

"Good to meet you Tom. Thank you for coming to my rescue and letting me join you."

"It's my pleasure" Tom replied.

Their polite exchange came to a close when Beth picked up one of her books and began to thumb through the pages in a deliberate manner. He could see their conversation was at end, at least for the present, so he returned to his crossword. His original intention had been to grab a quick bite to eat and head back upstairs for an early night. Over recent months, as his depression had deepened, he had become increasingly reclusive and had shunned company whenever he could. Now, rather to his surprise, he found himself wanting to engage in conversation with this intensely preoccupied young woman. However, he was understandably diffident about interrupting her reading. He glanced in her direction, hoping to be able to read the title of the book she was studying so intently. But it proved to be impossible as she had it firmly grasped in both hands with its back propped up against her other books.

Somewhat to his relief, Tom spotted the waitress heading in their direction, carefully making her way between the throngs of drinkers who had now spread out from around the bar to fill half the room. She set their plates down in the same hurried manner before heading back towards the kitchen. Beth was so engrossed in her reading that, at first, she appeared not to have noticed the arrival of their food. But then she closed her book and put it on one side. Looking down at her plate of steaming hot fish pie, she said "This looks good. I'm absolutely starving. I haven't eaten a thing since breakfast."

"Yes, I nearly chose that myself," said Tom "but the pork chops won on this occasion. Bon appétit"

"Bon appétit" she replied, picking up her knife and fork and cutting into the thick potato topping with all the skill of a surgeon performing a delicate operation. Tom noted the long, slim fingers with which she held her knife and fork. He watched with fascination as she carefully dissected the potato into four equal parts before lifting one of the quartered sections to one side to gain access to the steaming fish. Then, concerned that she might be offended by his continuing interest in her operation, he turned his attention to attacking one of the two generously proportioned pork chops on his own plate. For a while they ate on in silence wrapped, up in their own thoughts.

Finally, she laid down her knife and fork with a sigh of satisfaction and, looking down at her now empty plate, said "That's better, I can't remember the last time I was so hungry."

By this time Tom, too, had cleared his plate. "Yes, that was really quite something. They certainly seem to know what they're doing in the kitchen here. That was as good a plate of pub grub as I've enjoyed for a long time."

Beth nodded in agreement, smiled again and seemed on the point of saying something. But then she looked away and started to fiddle with the binding on the book she had been reading earlier, nervously rubbing her fingers up and down the spine.

There followed an awkward silence during which neither of them knew quite what to say next. Tom glanced at Beth again and saw that she had returned to her reading. His many years in the priesthood meant that he was a good reader of other people's thoughts. It was clear that his young companion was exceptionally shy when it came to engaging with strangers. At first he had assumed she simply preferred her own company, but now he wasn't so sure.

Their silence was broken when the young waitress suddenly appeared out of nowhere to ask if they wanted anything else. They both turned down dessert but Tom ordered a black coffee and Beth asked if, by any chance, they did green tea and was pleasantly surprised to discover they did.

"I can't quite get into green tea myself, but I'm sure it's very good for you" said Tom, hoping to break the ice.

"Actually, I love coffee" Beth replied "but unfortunately it doesn't love me. I have a very busy day tomorrow and I can't afford a sleepless night!"

"I'm rather lucky" Tom said, "I can drink gallons of the stuff and it doesn't seem to have any effect at all. I know it's unusual. My wife couldn't even sniff a cup of coffee without staying awake all night." Tom stopped dead in his tracks. The last thing he wanted was to bring his dead wife into their conversation and run the risk of opening up too many unhealed wounds. He quickly changed the subject.

"I do hope you don't mind my asking, but you say you have a busy day tomorrow. It doesn't sound like you're here on holiday. I can't help wondering what brings you down to this remote corner of the Principality."

Beth began to finger the spine of her book again.

"I know it may seem rather an unusual subject for a woman, but I'm a historian and my principal area of research is the late fifth and sixth centuries, especially the legends of King Arthur and the resistance of the Britons to the Anglo Saxon invaders."

"Quite a subject, how very interesting. But I don't altogether understand. Why do you consider this to be unfeminine?"

"Well, I suppose it's because Arthur is seen as such a macho character, fighting all those bloodthirsty battles. Isn't he every man's ultimate hero? And doesn't he represent the very essence of what chivalry was all about?"

"And do you see him in those terms?" Tom asked. "I have to confess that I'm not all that familiar with the Arthurian legend."

"Well, of course, to some extent I do. But then, as a historian, I must judge my historic figures according to the standards and mores of their time. We need to understand what those early twentieth-century German theological scholars called the *sitz im leben*, or 'situation in life' of the people we're studying, and even more so of those who wrote about them."

"Are you suggesting that, somehow, King Arthur has been misrepresented and that the stories we hear about him are untrue?"

"As with most of the historical figures in the centuries following the Roman Occupation, it isn't easy to separate the truth from the mythology that's grown up around them. We only have relatively few absolute facts we have about Arthur. Some people even go so far as to suggest that he's an entirely mythological figure who never actually existed. There is more than one strand of history pointing to a historical Arthur figure. It could be that those who wrote about him later were confused by these different personae and merged the strands together to create the Arthur we know. After all, this period of history isn't known as the Dark Ages for nothing. Most of what we know about Arthur was written several centuries later and addressed to a medieval audience where kings and queens and their knights and ladies lived in magnificent stone castles. This was an age where knights entered the lists to win their lady's favour, where Kings led their armies into battle and where sacred missions, like the search for the Holy Grail, represented the ultimate expression of chivalric manhood, combined with a desire to fulfil one's true obligations to God."

Tom listened to Beth with growing interest, noting how her eyes lit up when she spoke. Such was her intense enthusiasm for her subject that she gripped the edge of the table so firmly that her knuckles had turned white. She leaned forward and looked directly at him. The words tumbled out as she engaged with her subject. Tom was fascinated, as much by the intensity of her delivery as by the material itself. He imagined how students would queue up to attend lectures delivered by this enthusiastic young woman, driven by such passion for her subject. It was hard to believe this was the same person who had first approached his table with such temerity.

Much to his disappointment, Beth was interrupted in full flow when their waitress reappeared and unceremoniously dumped their drinks down on the table before bulldozing her way back to the kitchen through the crowded bar. The interruption was enough to stop Beth in her stride. She released her grip on the table and carefully moved her tea to the right of her books.

"I'm so sorry, you must forgive me. I tend to get rather carried away by my subject. I'm sure you must be getting bored."

"Actually, not in the least" said Tom, "I like people who are passionate about what they do and there aren't so many of them around these days. I'm afraid, as I've already said, I'm not very familiar with this period of history, other than through bits of Tennyson and Mallory and the odd epic movie, and I dare say they all employed a good deal of artistic licence in telling their tales."

"Indeed they did. Most of the great chroniclers of the Arthurian legend drew much of their material from Geoffrey of Monmouth. He wrote his *History of the Kings of Britain* more than five hundred years after the death of Arthur. Geoffrey was responsible for a fair bit of embroidery when it came to writing about Arthur too. People need their heroes. To medieval Norman Britain, Geoffrey's Arthur was the ideal hero. He won great victories over the invading Saxons and was a wise and noble ruler."

"Yes, I can see that," said Tom. "But you haven't told me what all this has to do with this remote corner of Wales? I don't imagine you're just looking for a nice quiet spot to pursue your studies. Something tells me that there must be a local angle to the story, or am I wrong?"

Tom could see that Beth looked a little uncomfortable when he posed this question. Her response confirmed that she was concerned about how he would view her answer.

"I'm afraid that many of my fellow historians are convinced that I'm following a completely false trail. I've even been described as a lunatic by one senior Oxford professor. But, the thing is… " she paused for a moment as though she feared that what she was about to say might be too much for Tom to swallow. "The thing is that I'm pursuing the unpopular theory that Arthur's last great battle, the battle of Camlan, was fought in the fields somewhere above these cliff-tops, that it was there that he was struck down by his nephew Mordred and then carried in a boat across to Bardsey where he was healed and restored to health by the Lady Morgan." These last sentences were delivered with so much passion that she had to stop to take a breath before continuing. Then, with an air of triumph, she clenched her fist and brought it down firmly on the table. "You see, I believe that Bardsey Island may well be Arthur's Avalon!"

Tom looked at her with a degree of astonishment. This was as much because of the glow of excitement on her face as it was as a result of her historical assertion. He wanted to respond but didn't know quite what to say. As it happened, the matter was taken out of his hands. For at precisely that moment, a loud cheer went up from the direction of the bar, followed by a raucous rendering of 'Happy Birthday'. This intervention seemed to stop Beth in her tracks. Tom was amazed at how instantly her feverish excitement evaporated. She looked down with a worried frown and began to gather up her books.

"I'm so sorry, but I think I got a little carried away," she said, standing up and pushing her chair aside. "I really didn't mean to bore you. Please excuse me but I'm terribly tired. It's been a long day and I absolutely must get some sleep." She managed a half smile before turning and heading for the door without once looking back in Tom's direction.

Tom, who had half risen to say goodnight as she left the table, sat back down. He took a last sip of coffee and picked up his newspaper. A wry smile crossed his face as he focused on the clue for nineteen down. 'Unfinished business' it read.

# CHAPTER SIX

Upstairs in her room Beth sat on the edge of the bed and listened to the rain lashing down outside. The wind had got up so much that she could hear the window rattling in its frame. She got up to close the curtains and shut out the night and the worst of the storm. She had heard that the weather could be unpredictable here, at the tip of the peninsula. However, she had not bargained for such a violent bout of wind and rain so soon after her arrival. She was concerned that her plan to spend the next two days mapping out the supposed scene of Arthur's last battle might be in jeopardy. It was all the time she had before she was due to cross over to the island.

She undressed, folding her jeans neatly and hanging them with her jacket in the large wardrobe opposite the bed. Her remaining clothes she carefully separated into two neat piles. She put her jumper in the bottom drawer of the chest of drawers next to the wardrobe and her dirty linen into a plastic bag she had brought with her. Although it was quite warm in the bedroom she still experienced an involuntary shiver as she briefly stood naked in the middle of the room. She slipped quickly into her nightdress and headed for the bathroom. When she had brushed her teeth she returned to the bedroom selecting Nennius' *Annales Cambria* from the small pile of books she had earlier stacked on top of the chest of drawers. Armed with her bedtime reading she climbed into bed and switched on the bedside light.

Lying back in the comfort and warmth of her bed, with the storm raging outside she found it difficult to concentrate on her reading. Her mind kept wandering back to her encounter with Tom, that tall, gaunt figure with the engaging smile. He had listened with such apparent interest to her explanation of the quest that had brought her to the village. In contrast to her academic colleagues who had ridiculed her latest venture, he had seemed sympathetic to her cause, even enthusiastic. But then, he was no Arthurian authority and had readily pleaded his ignorance of the subject. Nevertheless, she had been touched by his obvious interest and encouragement. At the same time, she wondered what had persuaded her to open up so willingly to a total stranger, warm and friendly though he might be. By nature she was a private person, generally happy to keep to her own company. She knew her fellow academics found her cold and unreceptive, even reclusive. She found it just as difficult to engage with her students, most of whom she considered to be immature and insufficiently committed to their studies.

Beth herself had been an outstanding student. She had been diligent, intellectually outshining most of her contemporaries. From the moment she had first entered the local primary school, it had been clear to all those who taught her, that they had an exceptional talent on their hands. But, as is so often the case with a gifted child, while she had stood out academically, she had been less adept at developing her social skills.

She was the only child of working class parents who had done little to encourage her to mix with children of her own age. Her father, who ran a small grocery shop on the outskirts of Manchester, came from a long tradition of non-conformist chapel-goers with Victorian views about how to bring up his child. He had allowed her little licence to stray beyond the narrow world of helping her mother carry out her domestic duties, studying for the next round of school exams and attending chapel twice every Sunday. This was the world he felt comfortable in. It had never crossed his mind that by bringing up his daughter in this way she might be out of step with her contemporaries. Her mother was a kind and caring woman, but her natural timidity held her back from challenging her husband's authority.

Like many respectable middle-class people, both her parents were ambitious for Beth to go up in the world. However, their sights were limited to her becoming a schoolteacher, local government employee or perhaps marrying a church minister. Their expectation was that she would marry, have children and live locally so that they could fulfil their cherished role as dutiful grandparents. It had never crossed their minds that she might find a career outside these narrow confines, let alone move away from her home town.

Given the narrow and rigid nature of her background it was perhaps surprising that Beth didn't rebel earlier. But somehow, throughout her school years, she remained compliant to the will of her parents. She was generally considered to be an unusually pretty child and as the years passed she grew into a beautiful young woman. But because her parents never drew her attention to them, she remained largely unaware of the effect that her good looks had on other people. The strict and regimented discipline of her home and winning a scholarship to the local Girls' High School meant that, while she was growing up, she was mostly protected from the advances of young admirers. At school she was naturally timid and shy with few close friends. Her superior intelligence guaranteed her the admiration of all those who taught her but, at the same time, contributed to her isolation. She found the youthful rowdiness of the other girls in her class intensely annoying, but suffered it without protest. She chose to maintain as low a profile as possible to avoid drawing attention to herself after seeing how easily the slightest provocation from one of her classmates could lead to a bout of bullying from the rest of the class.

It was in this way that Beth managed to pass through her school years largely unnoticed until she reached the sixth form. She felt considerably more comfortable in the more select company of the brighter pupils who had stayed on to do their A-levels. By then she had also begun to excel as a hockey player and at athletics. This finally won her the admiration of her fellow sixth formers and while never particularly popular, she was no longer treated like a complete outsider.

While nobody would have described Beth as rebellious, for this was outside her nature, by the time she left school she knew her own mind. Her favourite subject had always been history. And so it was, on the advice of her history teacher, that she determined to apply for a place at the University of London. Initially this decision was bitterly opposed by her father who had his heart set on her studying nearer home. However, although she had remained close to her parents, she recognised that she needed to break away from their over-zealous protection. With a little helpful support from her mother, she finally managed to convince her father that she was sufficiently strong-willed to be able to resist the evils and temptations of the metropolis, and he somewhat reluctantly agreed to give her his blessing.

The three years of her degree course laid the foundation for the academic life of which Beth had always dreamed. They also represented a rite of passage during which she ceased to be the timid and acquiescent child of puritanical parents and turned into a determined young woman with a clear set of values and a mind of her own. But her new found self-confidence did not endear her to her fellow students who regarded her as arrogant and opinionated and avoided her company whenever they could. But Beth was so intensely absorbed by her studies that she hardly noticed and certainly didn't appear to care very much.

Her good looks and athletic body initially drew the attention of a number of the more adventurous male students on her course. However, it was not long before their enthusiasm gave way to disappointment, even anger, at the way in which their approaches were consistently rejected. After a while, it was generally assumed the Beth was simply not interested in forming any kind of meaningful relationships and she was largely left to her own devices.

As a result, it came as something of a surprise when rumours began to spread that Beth was engaged in a relationship with one of the senior history lecturers, although there seemed to be some doubt as to who it might be. The news had been greeted with scepticism at first, until one of the more courageous of her fellow students had raised the matter with her. Then, she had looked her inquisitor straight in the eye and said "It really isn't any of your business, but if you really want to know, yes, Bill and I are lovers."

Once the identity of her suitor had been revealed, Beth's status had immediately been enhanced. The only possible 'Bill' in the department was none other than the much-admired Dr William Matthews, specialist in the early Celtic settlements across Europe. Tall and handsome and with a bucket-load of charm, the affections of Dr Matthews had been much sought after by several of Beth's contemporaries. However, physical relationships between staff and their students were heavily frowned upon by the university authorities and Matthews had, until then, managed to resist their approaches. It remained something of a mystery to the student community as to why he should have finally succumbed to the attractions of one of the starchiest and least communicative of their number. But, over the ensuing months, Beth and Bill Matthews continued in their relationship. They shared each other's company whenever they could discreetly find the opportunity. Indeed, it had only come to an end, at the conclusion of her second year at university, when Matthews moved north to accept a more senior position at the University of Durham.

At the time of his departure, Beth was overwhelmed with self-pity. Not only had Matthews been her first and only lover and helped her discover some of her hidden passion, but he had also been her only truly intimate friend and confidant. She was particularly distraught by the abrupt way in which their relationship had ended, for he only told her about his new position a few days before the end of term, leaving her with little opportunity to discuss their future. Inevitably, she began to question how much their relationship had actually meant to him. Feeling betrayed, she retreated further into herself, pursuing her studies with manic intensity and living a hermit-like existence between the lecture halls and her study bedroom. Needless to say, at the conclusion of her third year she had gained a first-class honours degree. Encouraged by her tutors, she opted to stay on to study for her Master's, supplementing her student grant and the modest allowance reluctantly provided by her father with some part-time teaching work in the department.

Beth had never doubted her own academic ability and had taken the doctorate that followed her Master's in her stride. Her thesis on 'The Civil and Military Administration of Britain under Roman Occupation' won her the university's award for 'outstanding original scholarship' and the praise and admiration of fellow academics. It was from then that her academic career had really taken off.

And now, lying in bed, with the wind maintaining a constant howl outside, she felt considerable satisfaction at how far she had progressed over the few years since completing her doctorate. Her research into the Roman and post-Roman Occupation had produced three publications and established her reputation as a leading authority on the subject. In addition to her salaried lectures in the university's history department, she now received regular invitations to speak at specialist conferences both at home and abroad. In the previous year she had even been called upon to provide her expert advice to a series of documentaries for the BBC on Roman Britain.

But while her rapid climb up the ladder of academic recognition was the envy of other aspiring historians, there had been a heavy price to pay. Her life outside academia was almost entirely without meaning. She rarely returned home to visit her aging parents any more, finding the atmosphere in their well-ordered and clinically clean home stifling. She also knew that, given the first opportunity, she would be subjected to a barrage of criticism from her father. She deeply resented the fact that, not once, had he congratulated her on her success. Indeed, he seemed to remain unconvinced that her work was of any value. He constantly chided her for not settling down to a solid marriage and motherhood. While her mother was more sympathetic, she was too much in awe of her husband to speak out in her daughter's support.

Beth closed her eyes and imagined she was looking down on herself from above. She saw herself shrouded under the cover of the soft white duvet, cloistered within the four walls of her hotel bedroom with the elements battling away outside, in the same way that she tried to shield herself from the blows and challenges of the outside world.

So, what was it, earlier that evening that encouraged her to open up to a total stranger? It was something she would never consider doing with her university colleagues? Perhaps that was it, the very fact that he was a stranger? But then, of course, it was not as if they had talked about anything at all intimate. But even the way she had talked with such enthusiasm about her Arthurian quest was out of character. The only times she normally displayed such enthusiasm for her subject were when she was holding forth in the lecture hall. But this evening had been different. She had gone down to dinner hoping to find a quiet corner to bury herself in with her books. Circumstances had led to her sharing a table with a stranger and, before she knew it, she had been engaging with him as if it was the most natural thing in the world.

She opened her eyes again, reached out to turn off the bedside lamp, turned over onto her side and tucked her arm under the pillow. Her breathing became shallower and soon she drifted off into a more contented sleep than she had experienced for a very long time.

# CHAPTER SEVEN

In his bedroom at the far end of the corridor, Tom also lay awake. His room was on the opposite side of the inn to Beth's and looked out over the backyard. Here the storm was less evident. What a contrast between this first night back in Aberdaron and his first visit all those years ago, when he arrived in the coach with the other pilgrims.

He remembered the warm welcome they had received as they joined together for Evensong in the ancient parish church, before sharing in a generous spread of sandwiches and cakes the villagers had kindly provided for them in the quaint old village hall. Then how, later that night, after they had all climbed into their sleeping bags on the village hall's hard concrete floor that the only sound had been the contented breathing of his sleeping companions. The near-silence had occasionally been broken by an involuntary snort coming from Father Beuno in the far corner of the hall. Although they had only met that afternoon, he had already felt a growing affection for their warm-hearted and jovial pilgrimage leader.

At the age of eighteen, Tom was fairly clear about most things. He was confident about his faith and was used to defending it from the challenges of sceptical fellow students. He was pleased to have chosen London over the less cosmopolitan and more cloistered environment of an Oxbridge college. For a former public school boy, Oxbridge would have represented more of the same, rather than a challenging and exciting new scene. He had even become more certain about his politics. He questioned his Tory parents' political beliefs, such as they were, and had rebelled. Like so many young people of his generation, he wanted to change the world for the better and naively believed that it was possible. There is a certain arrogance in youth, but Tom was not intolerant of the views of others.

He was, by nature, a good listener and always tried to understand both sides of any argument.

Looking back on his first year at college, he had been pleased with the way it had all gone. King's was widely recognised as one of the best places to engage with exciting and progressive theological ideas. He had found the way in which Old and New Testament were examined against their historical background especially enlightening. He had particularly relished the opportunity to take courses in Philosophy and Comparative Religion, at that time the college was not afraid to expose its students to concepts that might challenge the fundamentals of their faith. Yes, he had thoroughly enjoyed his first year's studies. He made many new friends, several of whom came from overseas, opening up his view of the world.

The solid concrete floor had hardly been conducive to his falling into an easy sleep. But Tom had been content to lie awake, surrounded by those with whom he would be sharing a new adventure. He thought of the saints and religious fanatics who had chosen to wear hair-shirts and lie on wooden boards, and had wondered what creature comforts, if any, Franciscan Friars gave up in their pursuit of greater sanctity. Not all that many, he guessed, judging by the corpulent figure of Father Beuno and the way he had tucked into the sandwiches that evening.

And now, all these years later, memories of that first visit were as vivid as if it had been yesterday. He could almost sense the musty smell of damp that had pervaded the village hall and hear the rustle of the welcome breeze that blew in through the open window on that unusually humid midsummer night.

An unexpected and violent rattling of the bedroom window by the wind woke him from his reverie. Looking back over the day, he could only marvel at how returning to this wild and wonderful place had exceeded his expectations. The leisurely walk along the empty beach, the pounding of the waves on the rocks and the excitement of the oncoming storm had done much to raise his spirits.

And then there had been that odd, but beguiling first meeting with the Beth. At first she seemed so awkward and shy that it had been difficult to draw her into conversation. He had been so surprised when she unexpectedly launched into a passionate description of her quest and her reasons for coming to the Llŷn Peninsula. What an enigma she presented, so suddenly withdrawing into her protective shell as if she had regretted her fervent outpouring. Goodness knows, he had met some odd people over the twenty-five years of his ministry. But here was someone full of blatant contradictions, someone who managed, somehow, to appear to be shy, offhand, engaging, passionate and dismissive, all within the space of a single hour.

Tom couldn't help comparing these characteristics with those of the woman with whom he had so happily shared his life, until she had suddenly been taken from him. The one thing everybody had always said about Martha was that she was unstinting in her warmth, generosity and good humour. Over the entire twenty years of their marriage, hardly a cross word had passed between them. She had been a loving and caring wife, a devoted mother to their two children and a trusted friend to so many of his parishioners. Despite the demands and unsocial hours of his job, he had hardly ever heard her complain. He had loved Martha with such an intensity that her sudden and tragic death had left him a physical and emotional wreck. So much so, that he had found it increasingly difficult to deal with other people's emotions. He continued to minister to his parishioners and tried his best to provide the range of support and advice expected. However, he had soon found that he could no longer share the burden of their suffering. His own loss had damaged him so severely that he had erected a protective barrier around himself, leaving him in a state of permanent emotional numbness. Over the five years since Martha's death, there had not been a single day when he had not continued to mourn her. If anything, his sense of loss had grown even more intense as had his sense of loneliness and isolation.

With both his children now away at university, Tom had found the large Victorian vicarage a lonely place that no longer felt like home. His son Ted, who was now in his third year at Durham reading law, had, to all intents and purposes, left home when he had first gone off to university.

Of necessity, he had filled his vacations with various temporary jobs to help to supplement his modest student grant. His daughter Annie had only left home the previous October after winning a scholarship to read English at Oxford. Tom and Annie had always been especially close. She, more than anyone, had been a source of great comfort to him as he struggled to deal with Martha's death. Annie was only in her early teens when her mother had been killed. But the enormity of her grief combined with supporting her father had thrust her towards an early adulthood. Now that she too was no longer there to tease him out of his darker moods, he had no-one to lighten his days. How he missed her cheerful and loving presence and those witty impersonations of the more eccentric members of his congregation. Although she dutifully telephoned home regularly, Tom was reluctant to allow his self-pity to remain the focus of their conversations. Annie had her own life to lead and he was determined not to hold her back.

In dealing with the bereavements and other personal crises of his parishioners, Tom had always stressed that 'time is a great healer'. But, sadly, such a trite phrase didn't seem to bring him much comfort. The more he floundered in his own grief, the more he yearned to run away from his responsibilities and cut himself off from other people. Such longing for a more solitary existence was, of course, in direct conflict with his parish duties. Whatever the depth of his grief, he was still required to conduct services, participate in a continual round of social activities care for his flock. As he became further withdrawn, he spent many tormented hours each day in turmoil and doubt and increasingly confined himself to carrying out only the essential duties of his calling.

At first, the parishioners who were closest to him had been generous with their sympathy and support. They had loved Martha and considered her a great asset to the parish and, of course, to Tom and his ministry. She had been tireless in her involvement with parish activities and had a particular gift with young people. She was known and admired for the warmth of her welcomes, her remarkable energy and her sense of fun. Her other outstanding gift had been her beautiful soprano voice. Whenever she was called upon to sing a solo, people flocked to hear her pure and angelic voice rising to the rafters. It was spine tingling experience.

Because they had felt such affection for Martha, Tom's parishioners had found it easy to understand the scale of his sense of loss. However, as the weeks since her death passed into months and then years, they reluctantly reached the conclusion that their rector was heading for a breakdown. They feared that, while he remained officially in charge, nothing would ever return to normal either for the parish or for Tom himself. And so a number of leading parishioners had met privately to discuss the best way forward. From this informal gathering had come the decision that they would take the matter up with the Bishop and suggest that Tom needed professional counselling, followed by a period of rest and recovery. They felt confident that, given Tom's natural resilience, he would soon be able to resume his parish duties. As it happened, their meeting with the Bishop never took place. For, having picked up a whisper of the rumours flying around the parish, Tom decided to take the bull by the horns and see the Bishop himself.

As he had so often done in his childhood, Tom stared up at the ceiling trying to make sense of the patterns created by cracks in the plaster. He remembered his meeting with Bishop George, and the anxiety he felt as he hesitated outside the Bishop's Palace just ten days ago. It had been an unseasonably mild and sunny morning, and he had wandered up and down the cathedral cloisters for a while first thinking about what he was going to say. He had a great deal of affection for Bishop George Alexander. His sound judgement and inspiring leadership had earned him the respect of clergy throughout the Diocese. He knew that his Bishop held him in high regard. He had hinted, on more than one occasion, that he had him in mind for preferment to a higher office. But knowing that he was one of the Bishop's favourites had, if anything, made the task that lay ahead more difficult. He knew his parishioners believed his problems were solely related to the death of his wife. What none of them knew was that Tom was facing an even more serious personal crisis. Since Martha's death, he had found it increasingly difficult to reconcile his loss with a continuing belief in the God who he had served so faithfully for the better part of his life. He found it hard enough to face up to this harsh reality himself. The thought of sharing it with Bishop George filled him with apprehension.

As it happened, the Bishop had swiftly and unexpectedly put him at his ease. On arrival, he had been shown to the Bishop's study, been warmly greeted and invited to sit down in the familiar leather armchair in which he had so often sat before. Bishop George had listened throughout with evident concern as Tom had poured out his heart to him. When it became apparent that he had nothing left to say, Bishop George had reached across and placed his hand gently, but firmly, on Tom's arm. At the time his head had been such a confusion of emotions that he was unable to remember his exact words of reassurance and encouragement, just how much comfort and hope the Bishop's response had brought him. He particularly remembered the warmth with which the Bishop had embraced him when the time came for him to leave, promising to write within the next few days when he had had sufficient time to think matters over.

Tom had read and re-read that letter from Bishop George many times. It had been a great source of comfort to him and he was moved by the generosity of spirit in which it had been written. At a time when he could see no way forward, it had, at least, provided him with a possible way of putting his doubts to the test. Reaching for his briefcase, Tom unzipped the front pocket and took out the neatly folded letter to read it once more before settling down for the night.

# CHAPTER EIGHT

The Bishop's Palace
Chester

My dear Tom

I am so glad that you came to see me yesterday and felt able to open up your heart to me. I understand how difficult this must have been for you and how much courage it must have taken, but then courage has never been something that you have lacked.

I know how devoted you and Martha were to each other. She was a remarkable woman, full of love and compassion with that most wonderful sense of humour. She had such a zest for life and brought out the very best in others. As many learned to their cost, she also knew just how to make sure that you never took yourself too seriously, a common fault in our calling! I admired and loved her greatly, as did so many others.

It is almost impossible for anyone who has not experienced such a loss to really understand the level of pain and suffering that you are now experiencing. As a priest, of course, you will know that it is at such times that we are most likely to begin to question all those things that we have previously taken for granted. However solid our faith, not one of us is wholly immune to doubt. For did not Our Lord Jesus in his moment of despair cry out from the cross "My God, my God, why hast thou forsaken me?"

I am sure that you know that I will do all that I can to try to help you at this difficult time. It is clear to me that you need both time and space to come to terms with your present grief and to consider where your future may lie. For this reason, we must, for the time being, relieve you of your current responsibilities as a parish priest. I believe you need to go away somewhere to think things through, preferably somewhere special to you where you have experienced God's presence in the past and where you feel that he may speak to you again.

As I write to you, I think of those confident words of St Paul "For I am persuaded that neither death, nor life, nor angels, nor principalities, nor powers, nor things present, nor things to come, nor height, nor depth, nor any other creature, shall be able to separate us from the love of God, which is in Christ Jesus Our Lord."

I would ask that you come to see me again next week so that we can discuss how best to proceed. You are in my prayers.

Your friend in Christ

George Cestr

# CHAPTER NINE

MONDAY LATE AT NIGHT

O ut on the island, where the ravages of the storm were even more intense, old Mrs Davies coughed and wheezed and retched under a thick layer of blankets, which failed to bring much warmth to her elderly bones. So intense was the howling of the wind and the driving rain that nobody heard her feeble gasps.

A sudden flash of lightening momentarily lit up the old woman's wizened features as she spat another globule of yellowed phlegm into the china bowl she clutched tightly to her chest.

Staring out of her attic bedroom window she wondered on how many more nights she would lie there awake watching the steadily revolving light beaming from the glass prism of the lighthouse.

§

GEOFFREY OF MONMOUTH

*'The battle on a sudden began with great fury; wherein it would be both grievous and tedious to relate the slaughter, the cruel havoc, and the excess of fury that was to be seen on both sides. In this manner they spent a good part of the day, till Arthur at last made a push with his company, consisting of six thousand six hundred and sixty-six men, against that in which he knew Mordred was; and having opened a way with their swords, they pierced quite through it, and made a grievous slaughter. For in this assault fell the wicked traitor himself, and many thousands with him. But notwithstanding the loss of him, the rest did not flee, but running together from all parts of the field maintained their ground with undaunted courage. The fight now grew more furious than ever, and proved fatal to almost all their commanders and their*

*forces. For on Mordred's side fell Cheldric, Elasius, Egbrict, and Bunignus, Saxons; Gillapatric, Gillamor, Gistafel, and Gallarius, Irish; also the Scots and Picts, with almost all their leaders: on Arthur's side, Olbrict, King of Norway; Aschillius, king of Dacia; Cador Limenic Cassibellaun, with many thousands of others, as well Britons as foreigners, that he had brought with him. And even the renowned king Arthur himself was mortally wounded; and being carried thence to the Isle of Avalon to be cured of his wounds, he gave up the crown of Britain to his kinsman Constantine, the son of Cador, duke of Cornwall, in the five hundred and forty-second year of our Lord's in carnation.*

*Geoffrey of Monmouth,*
*writing in the 12th century*

# CHAPTER TEN

The following morning, Beth was up early after sleeping well, despite her excitement at the prospect of spending the day in search of the site of Camlan, Arthur's last great battle. She soon found herself revisiting her encounter with Tom the previous evening. She could see that it had been a rather one-sided conversation and, on reflection, was disturbed by the thought that she had conversed so enthusiastically with someone she had never previously met.

Confused by the events of the previous evening, she decided to take an early breakfast in the hope of avoiding a further encounter with Tom. When she drew back her bedroom curtains she was relieved to see that the previous evening's storm had passed and there were now occasional breaks in the clouds. On arriving downstairs she found she had the dining room to herself and was able to eat her breakfast without being disturbed. After breakfast, she returned to her bedroom with the packed lunch she had ordered earlier and collected together the few items she needed for her excursion in search of the Camlin battle site. She took a final look at her map of Llŷn Peninsula West before packing it away in her rucksack. She went back downstairs and out into the little square opposite the old pilgrim's rest house, now a café. Taking a sharp left, she set off along the narrow country lane that follows the coastline, heading almost due east towards Rhiw and Llanfaelrhys. She passed a row of terraced cottages and, a little further on, the ancient church of St Hywyn. She was impressed by the size of the graveyard which seemed far too extensive for such a small community.

At first, the lane ran almost parallel to the sea but at some height above it. The tide was in and she could just hear the waves breaking on the shore below. Although the wind had dropped overnight, out at sea there was still a considerable swell. White horses glistened in the sunlight, creating a magic halo for the two tiny islands that lay just beyond the headland. She stopped to look at her map and noted that the larger of the two islands was named Ynys Gwylan-fawr and the smaller one Ynys Gwylan-bach. A quick look at her English-Welsh dictionary revealed that these translated into 'large' and 'small' 'gull island'. She continued on up the lane passing the occasional cottage and farmstead. It was a steady uphill climb. Now exposed to the wind she began to feel it bite into her face and numb her fingers. Although the sun was now higher in the sky it felt considerably colder than it had lower down. Crouching down below the still leafless hedgerow, she loosened the cords on her rucksack and took out a warm woollen jumper. She put it on under her anorak and set off again up the lane.

For the next half mile, the lane was straight and level. In the hedgerows there was an occasional scattering of wild primroses as well as numerous yellow and white spring flowers that she would have liked to be able to identify. Carrying on a little further, she came to a track off to the right with a 'no through road' sign. Her excitement grew as she noted that the next track was the one that she would take. Although she could no longer see the sea, she could hear the waves breaking on the rocks below. She drew near to a traditional whitewashed Welsh long house and a cluster of stone cottages on her left and spotted the public pathway on the opposite side of the road.

After clambering over the stile she began a steady descent down towards the sea, towards the two areas marked on her map as Cadlan Uchaf and Cadlan Isaf, 'upper' and 'lower' 'battlefield'. The path was sodden and thick with mud from the previous night's rainfall. It finally came to an end and she found herself on the edge of an open field where, judging by the number of fresh molehills, a mole had recently been very busy. A sudden movement in the hedgerow startled her but then she relaxed and smiled as a small rabbit shot out and darted down the hill. She remembered her father telling her about the scores of emaciated bodies of dead rabbits he had seen along the roadside, when he and his parents had motored down to Anglesey on a childhood holiday. They had been the victims of the terrible Myxomatosis epidemic that had swept across North Wales.

According to her map, three separate sets of farm buildings marked the northern boundaries of the upper battlefield. She remembered passing the westernmost of these a little earlier and, as she made her way across the field, the other two became clearly visible. She continued her descent towards the sea and Cadlan Isaf, the lower battlefield. There was little sign of life, apart from a flock of sheep grazing in the corner of one of the fields. An occasional gull glided and swooped down and out of sight below the cliffs at the foot of a second field which she had now entered. Feeling thirsty after the stiff walk up from the village, Beth found a small wind-protected hollow just above the cliffs where she could sit down for a cup of coffee. From here she could look back at the lower battlefield she just crossed and down to the sea and a detached rock her map told her was named Maen Gwenonwy, 'Gwenonwy's Rock'.

A brief survey of the battlefield sites had already convinced Beth there was unlikely to be much, if anything, in the way of physical proof that Cadlan Uchaf and Cadlan Isaf were where Arthur had fought his last great battle. As far as she knew, this was a site where there had never been any archaeological digs. The most convincing arguments she had come across in support of this claim had come from the author Chris Barber and Dark Age historian David Pykitt in their recently published book *'Journey to Avalon, The Final Discovery of King Arthur'*. After expertly dismissing most of the other sites with a similar claim, Barber and Pykitt had been drawn to the Llŷn Peninsula because of its associations with the family of Mordred, or Medraut as he is sometimes known. After a tireless scouring of maps in search of the name Camlan, they had finally come across Porth Cadlan or battlefield harbour, just east of Aberdaron, above the small inlet where Maen Gwenonwy now lay in front of her. They had argued that Gwenonwy was Arthur's sister, being the daughter of Meurig ap Tewdrig who was Arthur's father. They then argued that the rock had probably been named after Arthur's sister through folk memory of the battle that had taken place there in the sixth century.

Beth tried to imagine what it would have been like for a sixth century fighting force to land there successfully, for this was precisely where Barber and Pykitt had suggested Arthur and his army had landed, after sailing across from Ireland. They were returning from a battle with the Irish King Llwch to settle a dispute over the payment of tribute. The story went that while they had been away, Arthur's nephew Mordred had seized the reins of power and Arthur returned to quash the rebellion. Beth could see that to land an entire army in such a place would have presented considerable challenges. The success of such a venture would have been heavily dependent on a far kinder sea than the one she was looking down on today.

She tried to imagine the state of Arthur's seriously depleted army, following heavy losses in Ireland. By the time they had gained the grassy slopes of the lower battlefield they would have been exhausted from clambering up the cliffs. Watching them from above, with the twofold advantage of having taken up their position on higher ground and of being well rested, Mordred's army would have been lying in wait. Geoffrey of Monmouth's description of the battle suggests that after they had fought for much of the day, Arthur had led a single division of his army, comprising the magic number of six thousand, six hundred and sixty six soldiers, into that part of the battlefield where he knew that he would find Mordred. Beth realised that such numbers would have been greatly exaggerated by Geoffrey to add a sense of drama. Indeed, in his telling of Arthur's supposed battle against the Romans, Geoffrey had recorded that 'The total number of the entire army, not including the foot soldiers, who were not at all easy to count, was therefore one hundred and eighty-three thousand, three hundred.'

Beth shared the view of most historians that the numbers of those actually involved in battles were more likely to have been in the upper hundreds or low thousands. Far from being the mighty king described in the later chronicles, setting forth with a vast army of knights in armour and thousands of foot soldiers, Arthur had almost certainly been more of a tribal warlord. He and his small but highly disciplined force of fighting men would have travelled swiftly on horseback across those parts of Britain threatened by the Saxon invaders. The images of Arthur and his knights mounted on horseback, with both rider and horse in full battle armour, had been conjured up by later writers such as Mallory, Chretien de Troyes and, much later, Alfred Lord Tennyson. They had spun their romantic tales wrapped in the chivalric splendour of the later Middle Ages.

As far as this possible battle site was concerned, if Arthur's approach had been from the sea, then it was unlikely that his forces would have brought many horses with them and so most of the fighting would have been on foot. Soldiers on both sides would have been similarly armed with swords, shields and lances. Some of the privileged amongst them would perhaps have worn rudimentary chain mail or leather armour and metal helmets. Looking at the slope towards the upper battlefield, Beth could see that Arthur's forces would have needed to be exceptionally fit and have fought fiercely to gain the upper ground.

She closed her eyes. The fresh sea breeze gusted around her ears and the loud screeches of gulls overhead helped to conjure up the hue and cry of Arthur and Mordred's forces as they pitched into each other on that fateful day. According to the tenth century *Annales Cambria* the battle had taken place in 537 AD. Beth shivered as she visualised the violent hacking of limbs, piercing of bodies and spilling of blood that would have occurred in this most hostile of battle sites.

As she stooped down to pack away her flask, she was startled by a violent flapping of wings just above her head. A large gull swooped down from behind and flew so low that she felt the full draught of its passage as it passed overhead. A little shaken, she headed up the grassy slope away from the treacherous cliff edge. She tried to visualise what the battle ground would have looked like to a contemporary observer watching Arthur's forces advance towards the upper battlefield. The historical records of the battle, such as they were, indicated that there were heavy losses on both sides, with several of the foreign mercenary kings and Celtic princes and nobles on both sides being killed. There would have been dead and wounded bodies strewn all the way up the hillside. The groans and cries of the injured would have only been partially drowned out by the battle cries and sound of clashing swords from above, where the battle still raged but by now was reaching its fatal conclusion.

Making her way to the upper level, Beth spent the rest of the morning exploring every corner of the site. She wondered where first Mordred and then Arthur might have fallen in the final stages of the battle. She felt a tingle of excitement as she imagined the mighty rush and clamour of arms as Arthur and his supporters forced their way to where Mordred was slain, but not before striking down the King himself. Geoffrey of Monmouth's account suggests that Arthur was mortally wounded in this final attack. But then Geoffrey had gone on to write that Arthur had been carried off to the Isle of Avalon so that his wounds might be attended to. Beth felt that Geoffrey's account certainly left room for conjecture that, although seriously wounded, Arthur had not actually been killed in the battle.

Standing at the highest point of the upper battlefield, she looked down to where the land fell away to the sea. As the day had progressed, the wind had finally blown away the few remaining clouds and the sun shone out of a pure blue sky. Beth realised that, despite her vivid imaginings, there was no solid proof that this was the Camlan of history. However, the map references to Cadlan Isaf and Cadlan Uchaf certainly indicated that some kind of significant historical battle must have taken place here, which added to the possibility that this was where Arthur and Mordred had joined in battle.

Feeling tired after her morning's exertions, Beth looked for somewhere to sit and eat her lunch. She settled on a flat piece of ground beneath a broken stone wall and unpacked a neatly wrapped parcel of sandwiches and a large slice of fruit cake that had been provided by the kitchen at the inn.

She sat for a while looking out towards the distant horizon. But her thoughts were no longer of Arthur and Mordred, nor of the violent conflict that may have taken place on this hillside. Instead her thoughts returned to the events of the previous evening and her chance meeting with Tom. She lay back and closed her eyes. Yes, she really needed to keep out of his way from now on. This ought not to be too difficult as she would be taking the ferry over to the island the next morning. To avoid a repeat of the previous evening's encounter, she would drive over to an inn in a neighbouring village for her dinner that evening.

# CHAPTER ELEVEN

That same morning, Tom woke from an untroubled night's sleep. When he looked at his watch, he was surprised to see that it was already well after eight. He shaved and washed, taking a little more trouble than usual to comb his hair, standing in front of the oak-framed mirror over the washbasin. If challenged, he would doubtless have denied his efforts were in any way connected with his chance encounter the previous evening. A strong impulse appeared to be guiding his actions. He hurriedly finished his ablutions, hoping he might be in time to catch Beth before she set off on her planned excursion to the battlefield sites.

However, on entering the dining room, he was disappointed to discover that the only other remaining guests were an elderly couple sitting by the window, lingering over their toast and coffee. He headed for the table where he had sat the previous evening, proffering a cheerful 'good morning' in their direction to which they responded warmly with enthusiastic references to how the weather had changed for the better. And then, as if they couldn't wait to be out enjoying the delights of such a fine morning, they pushed back their chairs and rose to leave the room, wishing him a pleasant day as they passed by his table.

Tom helped himself to cereal and a glass of fruit juice and a waitress soon appeared, a different girl to the previous evening, from whom he ordered bacon, scrambled eggs and coffee. He was on the point of asking her whether Beth had already been down for breakfast, but thought better of it. His plate soon arrived, covered with a generous portion of smoked bacon, rich yellow scrambled eggs and two large tomatoes. He poured out a cup of coffee from the steaming cafetiere and buttered himself a slice of wholemeal toast.

Tom had never much enjoyed eating on his own. But on this occasion he was grateful for the opportunity to gather his thoughts without being disturbed. He was surprised at how the passing of just a one day could have had such an impact on his emotions. Just the morning before, he had set out from his parish on the outskirts of Manchester, weighed down by a perpetual sense of gloom and deeply apprehensive about the future. He had paid a further visit to Bishop George a few days after he had first opened up his heart to him. The Bishop had remained insistent that Tom must embark on a period of quiet and undisturbed contemplation as a matter of urgency. He told Tom that he had already made arrangements for a visiting priest from Australia to take over for an indefinite period. He had also informed the parochial church council that Tom was taking a break for personal reasons with immediate effect. He had then asked whether Tom had decided where he intended to go to find the peace and inspiration to come to terms with his loss and, hopefully, rekindle his faith. Tom had told the Bishop about the three pilgrimages he had made in North Wales in his student days. He had explained that Bardsey Island stood out in his memory as a place of extraordinary spirituality. Bishop George had commended his choice. Although he had never visited the island, he had no doubt that it could provide Tom with the peace and tranquillity he required. He had then informed Tom that, in the short term, the Diocese was prepared to continue to pay his salary for an initial three-month period, after which they must meet again to discuss the next steps to be taken.

As Tom contemplated the weeks that lay ahead, he felt a deep sense of gratitude for Bishop George's generosity in offering him this lifeline. He felt a very real responsibility to use the time he had been granted to carry out a diligent process of self-examination. In the first place, he had to find a way of reconciling himself to Martha's death. Only then might he be able to consider whether he had any future within the church. For as long as he continued to blame God for her loss, there could be no such reconciliation. One thing he did accept was that Martha would have expected him to make a much braver effort at coping with her death.

Although a genuinely sympathetic woman who cared deeply about others, she had never been one to tolerate too much in self-pity.

Tom's thoughts were interrupted by the sound of the kitchen door crashing open as the young girl who had served him breakfast barged her way through and noisily began to clear the neighbouring table. Taking this as a clear hint that he had dallied too long over his breakfast, he drank the remains of his coffee and stood up to leave the dining room. Out of the window he saw that the sun was trying to break through. He had the whole of this day and the next to fill before crossing over to the island. Just up the lane, perched above the cliffs, was the ancient church of St Hywyn which he remembered so well from those pilgrimages of his youth, and that was where he intended to spend the better part of the morning.

# CHAPTER TWELVE

The Reverend Huw Pritchard strode purposefully out of the vicarage garden, closing the black iron gate behind him and heading up the lane to his church. He had been installed as vicar of Aberdaron just two years ago and went about his parish work with the enthusiasm of one truly dedicated to his calling. He was short and rotund with ruddy cheeks and plenty of flesh about the jowls. While not yet completely bald, he had lost most of the hair from the top of his head, which was something he tried to conceal by brushing over the few remaining strands which still grew above his left ear. To all intents and purposes, dressed in a heavy black cassock, he had the appearance of a medieval monk, save for the gold-framed spectacles on a chain round his neck.

On this particular morning, Huw Pritchard was in an especially cheerful mood as he strolled the short distance between the vicarage and the church. He offered a beaming smile to everyone he passed on the way, whether they were known to him or were amongst the increasing number of visitors who had begun to arrive in advance of the Easter holiday. The reason for the vicar's ebullient mood was that his wife had just told him that she was pregnant and was expecting their first child sometime during Advent. For someone who had waited so long to become a father, there could have been no more welcome news. Indeed, it was little less than a miracle after all their years of failed attempts to produce a child, the years of consultations with their GP and endless hospital visits and tests. And finally, when they were least expecting it, when they had almost given up hope, finally, Rose Pritchard was pregnant. As he entered the churchyard, verses from Psalm 127 came to his mind, "Lo, children are an heritage of the Lord, and the fruit of the womb is his reward. As arrows are in the hand of a mighty man, so are children of the youth. Happy is the man who hath his quiver full of them." "Happy indeed" thought Huw to himself, as he unlocked and pushed open the heavy door of the church under the Norman arch directly beneath the tiny tower with its single bell.

It was only two years since his induction, and yet every time he entered St Hywyn's church, Huw Pritchard felt a great sense of privilege. It was such an honour that he had been chosen to continue to minister to this small and scattered village community, and the many hundreds of pilgrims and other visitors who called by each year from all over the world. As he entered the church, he marvelled at the thought of all those who had gone before him. The first of these had been the humble St Hywyn himself, who had established a tiny cell here in the fifth century. Hywyn had chosen the warrior Saint Cadfan as his companion, who had gone on to establish the first religious settlement on Bardsey Island. It was his joy to serve the island community too, or what was left of it. 20,000 saints were reputed to be buried there. To the people of medieval England and Wales, right up until the time of Henry VIII's Reformation, the monastery on Bardsey and the great church at St David's had been holy places of special significance. Three pilgrimages to either had been regarded as equivalent to a pilgrimage to Rome.

As the portly vicar crossed the larger of the two aisles which constituted the principal nave of the church, he looked up at the magnificent East window above the altar. The mid-morning sun was shining through, casting rays of dappled light onto the stone floor and rough wooden pews. He loved St Hawn's in the morning, especially on a morning as fine as this before the day visitors had arrived.

He sat down at the end of the old oak pew from where generations of incumbents before him had led their congregations in worship and prayer. He reached down to pick up the black prayer book on the shelf in front of him and opened it for his daily offering of Morning Prayer. As he was alone, he chose the Welsh version rather than the English, which he only tended to use at the height of the summer when the majority of the congregation was made up of holidaymakers from across the border. He looked up into the lofty roof above and began to recite in a soft but determined voice "Gann yr Arglwydd ein Duw y mae Trugareddau a maddeuant." 'Oh yes', he thought to himself 'on this joyful morning, it is undoubtedly true that to the Lord our God belong mercies and forgiveness'.

He was well into the service before he became aware that he was no longer alone. His back was to the main church entrance and he was unable to see anyone entering the building. The old church door hung heavily on its hinges and usually squeaked noisily when opened, so he was surprised that anyone could have entered without being heard. However, from the sound of light footsteps, followed by the scraping of a chair on the stone floor, it was evident that someone had come in and was sitting quietly in the shadows, towards the back of the side nave. Resisting the temptation to turn and look to see who it might be, he raised his voice and continued to recite the Te Deum.

"Ti, Crist: yw Brenhin y Gogoniant", his voice rose to a higher pitch as he lauded the 'King of Glory', savouring every word as it passed his lips. He stared up into the dark shadows of the vaulted roof as though he might see a whole host of angels and archangels waiting there to herald the sudden appearance of his Lord and Saviour. In common with those powerful non-conformist preachers of the of South Wales valleys, he had always given it his all when reading from the scriptures or preaching the Sunday sermon. He had a fine and clear tenor voice that easily filled the two naves of St Hawn's. He delighted in reciting Morning Prayer aloud, even when he was completely alone. When a parishioner once asked him why he chose to do this, he said it was because the good Lord deserved nothing less than to be praised and honoured with all the voice he could muster. But, to get a little nearer to the truth, Huw Pritchard was very fond of the sound of his own voice as it reverberated around the ancient building, bouncing off the stone walls and pillars and echoing back to him from the rafters.

From the far corner of the church, where he believed that his unseen observer was sitting, there was not a sound as he continued his way through the Office. And then, as if to challenge his silent companion to bear witness to his faith, he raised his voice even higher and launched into the

Apostle's Creed "Credof yn Nuw Dad Hollgyfoethog, Creawdwr nef a daear." It was only after he had completed the Creed, had made his way through the Responses and had begun to recite The Lord's Prayer that he first heard the voice of the stranger also quietly reciting The Lord's Prayer, but in English not Welsh. In a sudden burst of generosity towards his hitherto silent companion, Huw Pritchard determined to conclude the Office in the English language:

"O Lord, shew thy mercy upon us", to which came the response "And grant us thy salvation." Thus they continued through to the final Collect "O Lord our heavenly Father, Almighty and everlasting God, who has safely brought us to the beginning of this day: Defend us in the same with thy mighty power; and grant that this day we fall into no sin, neither run into any kind of danger; but that all our doings may be ordered by thy governance, to do always that is righteous in thy sight; through Jesus Christ our Lord. Amen".

At the conclusion of the Office, Huw briefly remained on his knees in silent prayer. And then, no longer able to contain his curiosity, he stood up and gathered together his prayer book then he made his way towards the rear of the church in search of the stranger. He found him standing in front of the small display that had recently been assembled in tribute to the Reverend R S Thomas, the distinguished poet and late incumbent of St Hywyn's .

"Good morning and welcome to St Hywyn's", said the vicar with a warm smile, holding out his hand which the tall stranger accepted. "Allow me introduce myself, I'm Huw Pritchard and, as you will no doubt have gathered, I am the vicar of this parish."

"Good morning," responded the stranger "I'm Tom Gregory".

"It's rather unusual for me to have company for the Daily Office, other than on Sundays. It makes such a pleasant change to have someone to share it with. Forgive me for saying so, but I don't think I've seen you around here before. Am I to assume that you are on holiday down here? I do hope you didn't find the Welsh too confusing. You see, for many of us, in this corner of Wales, it is our first language. Is this your first visit to Llŷn?"

"Actually no, but it's many years since I was last here," said Tom "in fact it must be the best part of a quarter of a century."

"Well I never. As it happens I don't suppose that you'll find much has changed around here over all those years" said Huw, smiling. "We are not a people given to embracing change for change's sake and, let's face it, we're pretty much off the beaten track and less subject to what may be occurring in the rest of world. Indeed, most of you folk who come to visit us do so because you like things the way they are here."

"That's certainly true" Tom said

"I see you've discovered our modest tribute to my predecessor" said Huw, pointing at the display of poems and photographs on the wall behind Tom. "He's a fine man and a remarkable poet, you know. We're very proud that he was vicar here for eleven years until he retired back in 1978. He lives over near Criccieth now and must be approaching eighty."

"Well, as it happens, I actually met him when I was last down here" said Tom, "I was on a pilgrimage with a lot of other young people, mostly from North Wales. It was led by the Franciscans from Cerne Abbas in Dorset. We spent a night here camping out on the floor of the village hall and he took Evensong for us here in the church. I can see it all as clearly as if it were yesterday. I don't think many of us had heard much about him before we arrived. I remember that we were rather impressed to be told that he was a famous poet. When he welcomed us here, outside in the churchyard, he made a most striking figure, dressed in his rather faded black cassock and with his long white hair blowing in the breeze. To be honest, I thought he looked rather like one of those images of Merlin you see in so many paintings and illustrations." Tom paused as he summoned up more memories from the past and then continued, "The majority of our party being Welsh-speaking, he chose to conduct Evensong in Welsh. It was the first time I had ever sat through an entire service in which the only words I recognised were 'Dduw' and 'Amen'. But what I remember most clearly was the majesty of his voice. I can still picture his gaunt profile, eyes lifted to heaven, hair cascading down to his shoulders like the waves breaking on the rocks below, hands clasped firmly in front of him as he led us in worship."

"It sounds like he made quite an impression" Huw said. He took a quick look at his watch and continued "do you know, I would so much like to be able to continue this conversation but look now, I'm afraid I'm in a bit of a hurry, parish business, I have a sick pensioner to call on. I don't suppose you'd be free to join my wife and me for a coffee in an hour or so?"

"That's very kind of you" said Tom, "but I have another commitment this morning." He was looking forward to a long, solitary walk along the coastal path around the headland. He needed time and space to think and was determined that nothing should get in his way."

"Well, perhaps we could meet up again while you're down here. Will you be staying for long?"

"Yes, I'd like that" said Tom, "I'm hoping to cross over to Bardsey the day after tomorrow, if the weather holds. I'm booked into one of the cottages there for a while. I may well need to come back over to pick up more provisions at some stage. Perhaps we could get together again then?"

"Well, that's a deal then!" said Huw, beaming and extending his arm to shake Tom vigorously by the hand. "Everyone knows where the vicarage is, you'll have no trouble finding us. So, if you are happy to take us as we are, just pop by, anytime, and we'll have the kettle on right away". So saying, he swept out of the church to make his way down to the village and his waiting parishioner.

Left on his own, Tom returned to where he had been sitting during Huw Pritchard's theatrical rendering of the Morning Service. He couldn't help contrasting the short and Friar Tuck-like figure of the current incumbent with the tall, thin and rugged R S Thomas of his memory. In the years since his youthful pilgrimage, he had regularly delved into Thomas's poetry. He admired his wonderful simplicity of expression, especially when dealing with complex ideas and emotions. There was a profoundly stark beauty in his work, perhaps a reflection of the unforgiving landscape and the hard lives of the people who lived there. He had been particularly moved by Thomas's continuing dialogue with God, seemingly on a constant search for an elusive God. He had been especially impressed by some telling lines in the poem 'Revision' and had written them down in the notebook he always carried which he now took out of his coat pocket. They came so close to expressing his own struggle to overcome his doubts about the presence and reality of God.

*'Life's simpleton,*
*know this gulf that you have created*
*can be crossed by prayer. Let me hear*
*if you can walk it*
*I have walked it.*
*It is called silence, and is a rope*
*over an unfathomable*
*abyss, which goes on and on*
*never arriving.'*

"An unfathomable abyss, which goes on and on never arriving", he repeated to himself. How perfectly this poet priest has described the journey he must take across his own unfathomable abyss. The poet's words brought him a little comfort. It was reassuring to know he was not alone in his search for the God who he felt had abandoned him.

He closed his eyes to take in the silence that enveloped him. Other than the sound of his own breathing, all he could hear was the occasional creaking of a rafter as the ancient timbers began to expand in the warmth of the April sun. His mind wandered back to the first time he had been in this church. In those days of youthful certainty he had few doubts about his faith or about the path which he had been called to follow. Then he had been sure of the presence of God, not only in the long-hallowed places of worship like St Hywyn's, but all around him and often in the most unexpected of places.

He found himself remembering the first of a number of visits he had made to the derelict remains of bombed out buildings in the East End of London, which still remained in the early Sixties. He had gone there with a priest friend who saw it as part of his ministry to bring comfort and hope to the 'meths' drinkers who sought sanctuary in what remained of the basements of houses devastated by Hitler's bombs. On a cold winter's evening, they had crawled through holes in the ground where they had come across small groups of those twentieth-century 'lepers' huddled together around their pitifully inadequate bonfires. His friend had told him that these so-called 'derelicts' of society survived mainly by begging, rummaging through dustbins, or theft. With what little money they managed to acquire, they bought cheap cider or, in desperation, bottles of methylated spirits and even tins of boot polish out of which they boiled the alcohol over a fire, straining it through a filthy cloth. They smoked homemade cigarettes made from the butt ends that they found in the streets. They fed their fires by ransacking the bombsites for old broken doors, abandoned furniture and fallen roof timbers.

Before setting out on that first visit, Tom had been understandably apprehensive. He had heard that knifings and muggings were not uncommon in the wastelands of Stepney and beyond. However, he had been assured that such acts of violence normally only occurred between members of the same group. To his surprise, Tom had found that all the groups they visited to be courteous and welcoming. Despite their dire circumstances, they had been happy to share in a cheery conversation and a laugh or two. He had been astonished by some of the stories they were willing to tell about their earlier lives and how they had ended up where they were. Amongst them were former bankers and lawyers, teachers and doctors, and even an unfrocked priest. But most striking of all was the comradeship they shared. However low they had sunk, they knew that they were not alone in their suffering. In this, the most degrading of all environments, there was something deeply touching about the way in which they had managed to retain an element of dignity in their lives.

These experiences had formed a vital part of his spiritual rite of passage. The extent to which these unfortunates were shunned by society was all too reminiscent of the way in which Jesus had been scorned for eating with publicans and sinners and for forgiving the woman who had been taken in adultery. At the time, he had felt that if his God was anywhere, it was here in the very midst of this despised and rejected remnant of humanity.

Looking back now, he still felt the same unyielding compassion for such social outcasts, who were mostly victims of one form of human tragedy or another. If anything, his own personal loss had increased his empathy for those who, under similar circumstances, had simply been unable to cope. He trusted that he would never descend to the same depths, but couldn't do so with absolute certainty. Martha's death had certainly driven a sizeable wedge between him and his God. His sadness was so overwhelming that it had left little space for hope. At times, he felt so overwhelmed by the cruelty of life that he found it impossible to engage with the concept of a loving God. If he was ever to find his faith again, he knew he would have to find a way of coming to terms with life without and beyond Martha.

When he had set out that morning for St Hywyn's church, he had hoped to rediscover the power of prayer in a place where, for many centuries, so many had prayed before. But instead he had stumbled upon the theatrical performance of a well-meaning but over-exuberant cleric. The atmosphere had become oppressive and he was overwhelmed by a heavy bout of claustrophobia. In equal measures of despair and panic, he hurried to the door in search of fresh air and light. He only began to recover after taking in several deep breaths of cool sea air and looking out across the bay which was bathed in glorious mid-morning sunshine.

# CHAPTER THIRTEEN

Without looking back at the church, Tom walked down towards the centre of the village, past the Gwesty ty Newydd hotel, turning right in front of 'The Ship'. He was so deep in thought that he hardly noticed the fine old post office designed by the illustrious Clough Williams-Ellis and the old pilgrim's hostel. He took the lane climbing out of the village before heading west towards Llwchmynydd and the head of the peninsula. A short way up the lane, he turned off onto the coastal footpath towards Porth Meudwy, the small sheltered cove from where he would soon be catching the ferry to Bardsey. This was the same route that thousands of pilgrims had taken before him on their final journey to the island.

As he made his way along the cliff path, he hoped to banish the melancholy that had descended on him earlier. It was a mood which he knew from experience would take some shifting. Indeed, in a strange and ironic way, it may well have been the warmth of the vicar's welcome and evident and unquestioning passion and certainty he had in his faith and role as parish priest that had weighed Tom down. It offered such a stark contrast to his own doubts and fears.

He soon reached the vantage point from where it was possible to get the first glimpse of Porth Meudwy. Looking down, he could clearly see the slipway from which the ferry boat was launched. The small sheltered beach was quite deserted. He was glad that there was no-one else around. The last thing he wanted was to engage in pleasantries with the hikers or holiday-makers who walked the coastal paths in the summer months. He turned to look back at what was known locally as the 'Gallows Field', towards Pwll Diwael, the bottomless pool. Many centuries ago, it was said that the abbot would come over from Bardsey and stand on the large red rock that stood over the pool. From there he would pronounce judgement on those charged with various criminal offences. Those convicted of the most serious crimes would be strung up on the gallows, after which their bodies would be taken down and flung into the pool, where it was said that they sank from sight never to be seen again. He shivered involuntarily before moving on at a brisker pace.

From Port Meudwy, Tom carried on along the coastal path past the tiny coves at Porth Cloch, Porth y Pistyll and Hen Borth, to Pen y Cil at the south end of the headland. Here, looking out over the sound, he caught his first sight of the island in more than twenty-five years. It was the side of the island facing due east past the Llŷn Peninsula towards Harlech and the Cambrian Hills beyond.

It was such a clear morning, with hardly a hint of sea mist that he could quite clearly make out the features of the mountain which lay there like a giant whale basking in the spring sunshine. He could see where the relentless winter storms had eaten into the side of the mountain, causing large hunks of rock to break away and slide down towards the sea where they lay scattered like tombstones in an abandoned graveyard. The sea was calmer than the previous evening but there was still a considerable swell around the island. The waves that met its rocky shoreline sent great sheets of spray high up towards the cliff-tops where, at this time of year, tens of thousands of birds would be nesting. Tom sat down on a patch of coarse grass under an outcrop of rock. He stared into the distance, mesmerised by the relentless rise and fall of the ocean around the island. He remembered the words of the medieval Welsh bard Bleddyn Fardd 'White waves make loud the holy hill of Enlli'.

In the warmth of the sun, soothed by the sound of the surging ocean breaking on the rocks below, he lay back and fell into a deep sleep. But this was no contented sleep, for he dreamed that he was trying to swim to the island, rising and falling in the heavy swell. At times, the island seemed to be getting closer but then, when he next looked, it appeared much further away again. He could hear the roar of the waves as they broke on the island's rocks not far beyond where he was floundering. He fought for his life against the power of the ocean. He felt himself being dragged under by the currents that sucked and pulled beneath him. He thrashed out with what little energy he had left in one final struggle against the relentless tugging from the deep. And then, from somewhere in the far distance, he heard a woman's voice, calling out to him "Wake up, wake up, please wake up, it's all right, it's only a dream, please wake up!" and then a second, deeper male voice saying "For goodness sake help me to hold him down before he goes over the edge!" A strong pair of hands gripped him by the shoulders and began to drag him none too gently up over the rough ground. And then someone else was holding onto his legs as he continued to struggle, still only half awake in that mysterious space between the two worlds of sleep and consciousness.

The strong hands that had been pulling him now relaxed their firm grip. He opened his eyes and found himself looking up into the young man's concerned face

"Thank goodness you've woken up", the young man said "You must have been having a terrible dream. We spotted you when we were coming down the rise. We seriously thought you were about to fall over the edge. Are you all right now?"

The perspiration was dripping down the back of Tom's neck. He was finding it difficult to breathe and it took him a few moments to recover enough to be able to reply.

"I... I'm so sorry, I really don't know what to say" he stammered. "I must have nodded off... I was having a most horrible nightmare. . . what can I say? I am so very grateful. I'm sorry to have caused you so much trouble."

A second face then came into his view, the face of a young woman wearing an equally worried expression.

"The main thing is that you're all right now" she said. "Look, I know it's none of our business but, if you don't mind me saying, you really ought to be more careful. That was a damned stupid place to choose to have a nap. Goodness knows what might have happened if we hadn't come along when we did. Do you realise how close you were to the edge? Much more of that thrashing around and you'd have been over and impaled on those nasty rocks down below. You were jolly lucky we were passing by."

"Of course, you're absolutely right" Tom replied sheepishly. "The truth is I didn't mean to fall asleep. I only lay down for a short rest. The walk along the coastal path must have taken more out of me than I realised. I suppose that I must have simply dozed off. I feel such an idiot now."

The young man put his rucksack down on a rock next to where he was crouching and took out a bottle of water. "Here", he said, offering it to Tom "Take a drink of this, it looks like you could do with it."

"Thanks" said Tom, "My throat is incredibly dry. In my nightmare I think I was drowning and I still feel like I've swallowed half the ocean."

Tom saw the girl smile. She was sitting on a rock a little further away from the young man. She had taken off one of her sandals and was massaging her foot. She turned towards him and smiled again and he smiled back. They were smiles of genuine affection. They were a good-looking young couple. The young man had thick wavy dark hair and the sort of rosy cheeks that only a fresh wind will bring to the face of someone with such pale skin. The young woman, by contrast, had long, flowing, blonde hair and naturally golden skin.

"Do you think you'll be all right now? The thing is, Kate and I have to be back in Aberdaron by twelve thirty to meet some friends for lunch."

"Of course" said Tom "I'm fine now. You must get on your way. It's a fair stretch back to Aberdaron. I want to go a little further along the headland to take a look at St Mary's Well. Look... I... I can't thank you enough. You've probably saved my life and we haven't even properly introduced ourselves. I'm Tom and I gather you're Kate," he said smiling at the girl.

"Yes, and I'm Max", said the young man, holding out his hand which Tom warmly shook. "We've rented a cottage down here for a couple of weeks. Perhaps we'll see you around?"

"Only if you are planning on a visit to Ynys Enlli out there" said Tom, pointing to the island. I'm hoping to cross over tomorrow morning and don't expect to make it back to the mainland for a while."

"So that's what the Welsh call Bardsey. Ynys Enlli, that's got a really nice ring to it. I wonder what it means in English?" Kate asked.

"Well, I suppose the nearest translation is the 'Isle in the Currents'. It's barely three miles to the landing place on the far side of the island. But it's reckoned to be one of the most treacherous crossings around the British coast. The island has a very long and fascinating history you know. St Cadfan founded a monastery there in the sixth century and it was an important place of pilgrimage for hundreds of years. It's sometimes known as the island of 20,000 saints because of all the Christian believers who came to die and be buried on the island over the centuries." And then, recalling his conversation with Beth the previous evening, Tom added "There's also some evidence to suggest that Ynys Enlli could be the Isle of Avalon, where King Arthur was taken after being wounded at the battle of Camlan and where Merlin is supposed to be buried."

"Wow, that really is quite a story" said Kate. She turned to look at Max and asked "Do you think we might manage to fit in a visit to the island while we're down here, it sounds fascinating?"

"Oh do let's see if we can fit it in" said Kate "I'd really like that"

"Let's see how things go over the next few days" Max said cautiously, as though he didn't entirely share his girlfriend's enthusiasm. "Anyway, we must be on our way. I hope we bump into each other again and please be more careful about where you choose to take a nap in future! We all love to tell stories of our adventures on holiday but this is a cliff-hanger I'd have preferred to have avoided!!"

They all laughed, shook hands again and set off on their separate ways.

# CHAPTER FOURTEEN

The inn in the neighbouring village that had been recommended to Beth turned out to be disappointing. The season was not yet in full swing, the landlord was only running a limited bar menu and the service was offhand, to say the least. Beth imagined that everything would probably be rather different in the summer tourist season.

The only other customers that evening were evidently all locals, mostly dressed in their work clothes and talking to each other in Welsh. When Beth arrived she received the usual lingering stares offered to any stranger entering the pub at that time of year. Conversation was temporarily suspended for just long enough to allow the locals to give her the once over before resuming their exchanges. Feeling far from comfortable, Beth ordered a farmhouse cheese platter and a half pint of bitter from the bar. She sat at a small table in an alcove at the opposite end of the room to where the locals were gathered. Here, at least, she hoped she would be able to find some privacy. She was fairly sure that one or two of the younger men were continuing to give her the odd glance but, by and large, life in the pub appeared to have returned to normal.

Tired after her visit to the battlefield site, she was content to sit back and take in her surroundings. She was pleased to see that the room had avoided the seemingly inevitable makeover that was being inflicted on most of the pubs with which she was more familiar in London. However, the beams supporting the ceiling and the wall timbers had been painted black, which Beth thoroughly disapproved of. She preferred exposed timber to retain its natural colour. But, overall, the room was pleasant enough. Logs were blazing away in a large open fireplace. The floor was paved in what were, presumably, its original stone flags. The wooden tables and chairs had the bright sheen of old and well cared for furniture. Hanging on the walls were a number of prints, mostly of local scenes — the parish church, a view out to sea from the beach, a panoramic view of Bardsey set against a setting sun and a large painting of highland cattle which seemed a little out of place. The only concession to the twentieth-century was the inevitable fruit machine in a corner near the bar. It was currently being fed a seemingly endless supply of ten and fifty pence coins by a gaggle of noisy young women who let out high-pitched squeals of delight on the rare occasions that the machine paid out.

Beth's cheese platter was delivered to the table by a sullen young girl. She was hungry and grateful for the generous hunks of nutty Pembrokeshire cheddar, crumbly Caerphilly and, a new cheese to add to her repertoire, Red Devil from Rhyl. When she had eaten her fill she pushed her plate to one side. She reached down for her shoulder bag to take out the notebook where she had recorded details of the battlefield. It seemed like a good opportunity to scribble down the thoughts and theories that had been running through her head on the long walk back to the village. She soon became so deeply absorbed that the general chatter around the bar, the clinking of glasses and even the hubbub around the fruit machine all slowly faded into the background. After years of studying in college libraries, heaving with students, Beth was used to shutting out other people's conversations.

Suddenly she was distracted by the sound of the pub door slamming shut as a new arrival entered. When she first looked up she thought that it was Tom, for he bore a striking resemblance to the man she had shared a table with the previous evening, the very Tom she was trying to avoid. For a moment her heart rate shot up, but she soon regained her composure when she saw that she had been mistaken. A closer examination revealed the new arrival to be both shorter and more heavily built than Tom. She watched him make his way over to the bar where he was warmly greeted by the landlord and a small group of the locals. It was evident he had been expected. Soon they were all engaged in conversation, from time to time bursting into raucous laughter as one of them shared a joke. As they were speaking Welsh, Beth had no idea what they were talking about. But, she was mildly disconcerted as the new arrival kept looking in her direction. He did his best to conceal his interest by quickly looking away, but she felt that level of discomfort that most women feel when they suspect they are being mentally undressed by a stranger.

She was used to the roving eyes of men and normally able to cope with their attentions. However, there was something about the way in which this particular stranger was looking at her that made her uneasy. Before long she decided she had had enough of his lustful stares and that the time had come to head back to her hotel. It was just after nine o'clock but she would have to be up early in the morning to catch the ferry from Porth Meudwy. She stood up and crossed the room to the door. When she lifted the latch, the room went silent and she could feel several pairs of eyes following her as she made a swift exit. Once outside, she hurried across the car park to reach her car, sandwiched between a rusty old Landrover and an equally battered pickup. She unlocked the car door, threw her bag inside and jumped in after, slamming the door shut and pressing the button to lock the doors from inside. She had come out in a cold sweat and her heart was pounding. Fumbling for the ignition, she dropped her keys on the floor. Cursing under her breath, she groped around until she found them and quickly inserted the key into the ignition. She looked over her shoulder to see if she had been followed. Much to her relief, the car park was deserted and she was fairly sure that the pub door had not opened again after she had left. She took in a few deep breaths, started the engine and reversed out into the middle of the car park. She swung the steering wheel over to the left and put her foot down hard on the accelerator, speeding away from the inn as fast as the narrow and twisting lane would allow.

It was some minutes before her sense of panic began to ease. The car headlights lit up the road ahead with a reassuring brightness in the clear night. As she rounded a corner she had to brake suddenly to avoid a large rabbit whose night wanderings she had disturbed. The rabbit ran ahead of her, zigzagging along the lane, mesmerised by the bright beam of her headlights before finally diving through a gap in the hedge. She drove the rest of the way back at a much reduced speed and, as she drove, began to question why she had gone to such extreme lengths to avoid Tom.

The more she thought about it, the more she recognised that it was much more to do with her own fear of relationships than it was to do with Tom himself. The abrupt and painful manner in which her only serious previous relationship had ended had damaged her. Bill Matthews had, in so many ways, been the man of her dreams. But the callous way he had abandoned her had left deep and permanent scars. Her love had turned into anger. The only way in which she had survived her anguish had been by immersing herself in her studies. She had vowed never to leave herself open to such rejection again. She had gone out of her way to avoid any possible advances from her fellow students and, later, her academic colleagues. She knew that her anti-social behaviour meant she had established a mistaken reputation for arrogance, but she would rather that than expose her vulnerabilities to the masses.

And then, one night, nearly a year after Bill Matthews had gone out of her life, she reluctantly, agreed to accompany one of her colleagues to the University Summer Ball. The evening started out pleasantly enough with the usual end of term camaraderie between her fellow academics. She had always enjoyed dancing and had managed to make her way around the dance-floor with several of her colleagues without needing to engage in anything but the most trivial conversation. When the evening came to an end, having consumed rather more wine than she was used to, she had accepted her host's offer to accompany her back to her flat. Exactly what had happened next, after they had consumed another bottle of wine and she had been persuaded to share a couple of joints with him, remained a complete blur. But it turned into a terrifying nightmare over the following days. She became convinced that she had been taken advantage of in her semi-conscious state, before passing out completely. She regained consciousness in the early hours of the next morning with a dry throat, sore eyes, a crashing headache and a searing pain between her legs. She was alone in her flat. It was only when she staggered into the bathroom that she saw the black and blue bruises on her arms and legs in the mirror.

Beth challenged her assailant in the deserted Common Room the next day. But his response had been to laugh in her face and deny everything. He told her that he considered her to be 'a cold fish' and that nothing could have been further from his mind than having sex with her. He claimed that she had been so drunk when they had arrived back at her flat that she had fallen over on the way up the stairs, and that this was, no doubt, the cause of her bruising. At this point they had been joined by other members of staff and she had decided to let the matter drop. However, from the knowing glances between her assailant and his male colleagues, she couldn't help wondering whether she had been the victim of some kind of challenge or dare. However, she recognised that this was not the time to pursue the matter further. But over the days and weeks that followed, her nightly dreams were full of terrifying memories of that evening.

It was these disturbing memories that were doubtless the cause of her fears earlier that evening. Her mind was still in turmoil when she reached Aberdaron and parked her car around the corner from the hotel. She turned the engine off and sat there for a while, not feeling ready to return to her room yet. When her eyes grew accustomed to the dark, she could just make out the shapes of the cottages dotted about the hillside. She was surprised to see how few still had their lights on and assumed that they must either be occupied by early risers, fishermen and farmers, or were holiday cottages, empty at this early time of year. Hoping to dispel some of the dark thoughts racing around her head, she decided to take a short walk down to the promenade that ran along the top of the sea wall from where she had taken her first look at the bay the previous afternoon. When she reached the promenade, she leaned against the railing and fumbled in her coat pocket for her pack of cigarettes. She had always preferred to smoke alone, rarely joining the dwindling number of her colleagues who still smoked back at college.

Looking out over the bay, she was just able to make out the tip of the headland running out to the right. An almost full moon shone through a thin layer of cloud but she had difficulty making out individual features of the coastline. A sea fret had begun to drift in towards the shoreline casting a veil of mist over the landscape. The tide was well out and apart from the distant sound of the waves breaking on the shore, there was hardly a sound.

# CHAPTER FIFTEEN

When he returned from his long walk along the headland, Tom was still quite shaken by his near accident. Back at the inn he showered, changed and made his way down to the bar for supper. Having failed to encounter Beth at breakfast he was hoping to meet up with her again this time and to pick up where they had left off the previous evening.

The bar was less crowded today and Tom's meal arrived much more quickly. The village shop had sold out of newspapers when he went in that morning so he had to content himself with observing the few other customers. He had long since mastered the skill of watching other people without appearing intrusive, and it was something he rather enjoyed doing.

His attention was especially drawn towards an elderly couple sitting at a table by the window. Hardly a word passed between them as they tackled the generous plates of food in front of them. They appeared to have acquired that particular level of mute understanding that only comes after many decades of contented partnership. On the rare occasions when one or other of them spoke, it seemed to be simply to echo the thoughts of the other. In their twenty years of marriage, he and Martha had often found themselves articulating each other's thoughts. He remembered the warm glow of mutual contentment that comes with such intimacy. It was something that they had both grown to celebrate and represented what others saw as the remarkable bond that existed between the two of them.

Tom found himself thinking about Beth again. She was so very different to Martha. He couldn't help comparing her all-too-evident awkwardness and reserve with Martha's easy- going and relaxed openness. Martha's overriding concern had always been to ensure that others felt comfortable in her company. She had possessed a natural gift for breaking through the protective barrier of other people's innate shyness. He remembered how awkward his conversation with Beth had been to begin with and the abrupt way in which she had left him the previous evening. He began to suspect that her non-appearance today was deliberate.

Casting his mind back to the previous evening's conversation, it struck him that it had been remarkably one-sided. It had focused almost entirely on Beth's Arthurian project. She hadn't shown any interest in him or in what might have brought him to Aberdaron. In many ways this had suited him. After all he certainly didn't wish to discuss his current difficulties with a stranger.

He looked at his watch and saw that it was approaching ten thirty. He was tired after his long walk with its attendant drama. But, before going up to bed, he felt the need for some fresh air to clear his head. He paused for a moment outside the door of the inn. Should he walk up the lane towards the church or head for the sea front? It wasn't so much the exercise he needed as a good dose of fresh sea air, so he opted for the sea wall. He crossed the square and made his way down between the cottages, towards the promenade above the beach. Although there were no street lights and most of the cottage lights were also out by now, the moon was shining brightly enough for him to make his way without too much difficulty.

When he reached the front he was surprised to see that a sea fret was sweeping in fast swallowing up the bay. It had already enveloped the two headlands, most of the beach and the far end of the walkway to his right, and the moon was gradually disappearing into the misty gloom. He leaned against the railings and stared out into the night. Soon the foreshore was swallowed up by the swirling mist. Somewhere out there, shrouded in the same mists, was the island, his destination for the coming weeks. He imagined himself standing beside the old ruined tower of St Cadfan's monastery, looking out across the island. It wasn't difficult to understand how readily myths might grow into legends in such magical places.

Until now he had thought that he was alone. It had never crossed his mind that anyone else might have chosen to make their way down to the sea wall so late in the evening, especially now that the sea fret was advancing inland, threatening to envelop the whole village. But he was sure that he had heard a faint sound from further along the walkway. He listened intently and heard it again, a clicking sound. A few moments later he realised what it was when he picked up the smell of tobacco smoke. Someone must have just lit a cigarette. The mist was too thick for him to see who it was, but he was pleased not to be totally alone.

He continued to stare out into the void, surprised by the stillness. Even the sound of the waves breaking in the far distance seemed to have been dulled. It was as if the world beyond had ceased to exist. But such moments rarely last for long as all it takes is the faintest trick of light or sound to reawaken the senses. Tom was drawn back to the present by a muffled sob, followed by another and then by the sound of someone blowing their nose. He was embarrassed at the thought of being an unseen witness to another person's private grief and was reluctant to make his presence known. And yet he was persuaded by his natural curiosity to remain where he was. He heard the sound of a nose being blown again and then of light footsteps coming slowly towards him. He backed away from the railings intending to hide in the shadows, but the walkway was narrow and any kind of retreat was impossible. A dark and indistinct shape slowly emerged through the swirling mist. The light footsteps made him think it was a woman, but he was unable to make out any of her features as her head was concealed under a hood. She groped her way a few steps further towards him and raised her head to see more clearly. As she looked up she saw him and froze in her tracks, stepping back and raising her arms as if to defend herself against an unexpected attack.

"I'm so sorry, did I startle you?" Tom said, peering into the near impenetrable darkness, trying to make out the woman's features. "Please, there's no need to be frightened. I don't mean you any harm."

"Oh, it's you!" said the woman, pushing back her hood. "You gave me quite a shock. I had no idea that there was anyone else out here." Tom found himself looking into the anxious face of the very woman he had hoped to meet again in the bar earlier that evening. Her saw that her hair, which had been neatly tied back the previous evening, now hung down, well below her shoulders in long untidy strands. Her features stood out chalk white in what little moonlight was filtering through the mist. To Tom she bore all the appearances of a ghostly spirit wandering through the night on some long-forgotten quest.

She raised her hand to brush aside the loose strands of hair that had fallen over her eyes. Tom thought he saw a slight movement of her lips as though she was about to say something but thought better of it. She turned away to look out over the railings towards the sound of the sea.

"You must have watched this sea fret drifting in too" said Tom, "I can't believe how quickly it has swallowed everything up. When I first came down here I could just make out the two headlands on either side of the bay and then, a few minutes later, they'd completely disappeared. Then the beach vanished too and just about the only thing I could still see was the white railings on top of the sea wall. I wouldn't want to be out there in a fishing boat on a night like this."

"No" said Beth, staring out into the invisible distance.

"I imagine that fishermen must have a well-developed instinct for knowing when the weather is going to turn" Tom continued. But this time he didn't receive even a monosyllabic response, nor did Beth turn to look at him, and he wondered whether she had even heard what he said.

He stepped forward to stand next to her at the railings. He wanted to say something to penetrate the wall of silence that separated them but was at a loss for the right words. He half wondered whether he should simply turn and quietly walk away. He hardly knew this young woman, so what right had he to invade her privacy. At the same time, he couldn't quite bring himself to leave her alone in her present state of mind. He was certain that he had overheard her crying. He wasn't quite sure why, but he wanted to help her if he could and he felt responsible for making sure that she returned safely to the inn.

For a while, they stood next to each other, lost in their separate thoughts. Tom felt the night breeze strengthen and before long the sea fret began to clear. In the growing moonlight it was now just possible to make out the outline of the beach down below. He wanted to turn to look at Beth but felt that even that might be an unwelcome intrusion. He found himself thinking ahead to the crossing he had booked over to the island, frustrated by the thought that it might be postponed on account of the weather. While a day or two's delay really wouldn't matter, he was impatient to make the crossing as soon as possible. If he was ever to rekindle his faith, it would be there on the island that he would have to do battle with his doubts.

Beth hardly moved. She seemed to be lost in her thoughts. There was a chill in the night air and Tom was grateful for the warmth provided by his old parka. He was about to suggest that they should return to the inn when he sensed her moving closer to him. He could hear the sound of her breathing quite distinctly and was surprised to feel a cold hand take hold of his. He turned to look at her. She stood quite motionless, looking up into his face. Her eyes were glistening in the moonlight, tears ran down her cheeks and her lower lip was quivering uncontrollably. Once again he was struck by her exceptional beauty.

They stood there for a while, locked in silence. Then Tom felt Beth tightening her grip on his hand. He could see that she was struggling to say something but wasn't sure what was expected of him. He wanted to hold her close, to embrace her, to bring her comfort and yet, she looked so vulnerable that he was afraid of how she might react. She was gripping his hand so firmly now that it was beginning to hurt. He gently placed his other hand on her shoulder. This appeared to reassure her. Her lips moved again and this time, in a voice that was little more than a whisper, she finally managed to speak.

"Please, please stay here with me, I feel so very alone!" And then, a little louder, she continued in short staccato sentences interspersed with renewed sobs "It really isn't easy, I'm so sorry. . . I don't know how to explain... I... I can't expect you to understand... I had to come out here... . You see I thought it would be safe".

"Safe?" said Tom, "safe from what? What or who on earth has upset you?"

Beth let go of his hand and took a step back. He was now able to see her face more clearly. She was terrified of somebody or something, but goodness knows who or what it was. He took a firmer grip of her shoulder, leaning towards her so that their faces were closer together, smiled and said "You don't need to be afraid any more. What is it? Please tell me, I only want to help."

At first he thought that he felt her body stiffen as if she was unsettled by his physical contact. But then, finding reassurance in the softness of his tone and his evident concern, she allowed herself to be drawn closer to him. She turned her head to rest the side of her face against his chest. He lowered his head until the top of her head was nestling under his chin. He gently stroked the top of her head and then she began to weep again, clinging to him more tightly, and burying her face into his chest.

"My poor dear girl" Tom said, "Whatever is the matter? It's all right, you're safe now, I promise". He held her in his arms, rocking gently from side to side. She clasped him around the waist. After a while she stopped crying and her breathing became less strained. He pulled away just far enough to look down at her face. Her hair had fallen down over her eyes and was sticking to her tear-stained cheeks. He wanted to brush it aside but feared she might consider this to be too intimate. His head was full of confused thoughts. Above all, he had an overwhelming sense of the strangeness of the situation in which he found himself. Was it just by chance that he had come down to the seafront on a night such as this, when he would normally have happily retired to the warmth of his bed? What accident of fate had brought them together again? If truth be told, other thoughts were also beginning to enter his head. Thoughts that were both pleasing and disconcerting.

He was brought back down to earth again when Beth released her grip on his waist. He felt her hand move over his chest and saw that she was attempting to pull away the knotted strands of hair that hung over her face. Her eyes were still glistening with tears. A ripple of emotion ran through his body. He sensed that she too felt that something unexpected and inexplicable had passed between them.

He didn't know what to say and it was she who broke the silence. "Thank you Tom, thank you" she said in a hesitant voice "You have no idea how... how very grateful I am... you really have been so very kind and understanding". She clasped his hands and squeezed them together. "I shall be all right now" she said "I think that I'd like to go back, it must be very late." Turning away, she began to walk back along the sea wall, leaving Tom staring after her in bewilderment. The sound of her receding footsteps trailed away, and was soon lost in the sound of the relentless breaking of the waves on the stony seashore, for the tide had turned and he sensed that nothing would ever be quite the same again.

# CHAPTER SIXTEEN

The sea fret that had begun to drift in steadily during the afternoon now lay like a thick blanket over the entire island. What little moonlight had at first managed to filter through the thickening clouds had now been blanked out. It was pitch black outside and Rhiannon had to grope her way around the back of the farmhouse to find her way to the chicken shed door which she had forgotten to lock up earlier. She was only wearing a thin cotton dress under her coat and shivered in the cold night air.

She looked up when she saw the light being turned on upstairs in her Nan's bedroom. She heard the old woman coughing and wheezing as she always did at this time of night. Rhiannon was devoted to her grandmother, despite the old woman's regular bouts of ill humour and her constant grumbling. For beneath the old woman's severe exterior there lay a generous heart. Rhiannon had always known how much her grandmother loved her, more so indeed than she loved either her older brother Gareth or her sister Gwen. Rhiannon hadn't quite understood what it all meant at the time, but she had been diagnosed as having learning difficulties when she first attended primary school on the mainland. From that moment, she had sensed her grandmother's added affection. Rhiannon's father was a man of few words and her mother was far too busy with her many chores as a farmer's wife. So the old woman had taken it upon herself to provide the additional support that she felt that Rhiannon needed, establishing a strong bond between the young girl and the old lady.

When it came to understanding such a difficult subject as death, even at seventeen Rhiannon had difficulty grasping what it really meant. However, from the hushed conversations that regularly took place between her mother and father, she knew her grandmother was very ill and that she might never recover from her current bout of pneumonia. In her short life, the only loss that Rhiannon had experienced so far was a pet rabbit that she had been allowed to keep in a hutch in the farmyard. She remembered how she had cried and cried until her eyes were red, her nose was running and her throat was sore when he died. Faced with the possibility that her grandmother might die too, Rhiannon couldn't imagine she would be able to find enough tears.

She looked up at her Nan's bedroom window. Eventually the coughing stopped and the light was turned out. Rhiannon imagined her grandmother lying there, propped up in bed on a large pile of cushions and feather pillows. A tear ran down her cheek. "I'll pray for you tonight Nan" she said. In the distance, the regular rotating beam from the lighthouse swept across the deserted landscape. To Rhiannon it had always brought comfort and reassurance.

# CHAPTER SEVENTEEN

It was just before six o'clock the following morning. The sun had not yet risen above the horizon and hardly any light filtered through the bedroom window. Beth sat in front of the dressing table, staring into the large mirror which she had tilted so that she could examine her face more closely. She had slept badly. There were far too many thoughts flying around in her head. The previous evening's tears had left her looking deathly pale. The only colour in her face was a rim of red around her eyes.

She got up and crossed the room to where a grey plastic kettle sat on a wooden tea tray. She rifled through the bowl swore under her breath when she discovered that she had already used up the last of the coffee when she had come to bed the previous evening. Oh well, she would just have to make do with a cup of good old builders' tea. As she filled the kettle in the bathroom she caught a further glimpse of her pallid face in the mirror. She let out a deep sigh, returned to the bedroom and plugged in the kettle.

While she was waiting for it to boil, she heard the sound of a door being closed in the next room and wondered who else might be up so early. When the kettle had come to the boil she poured the water into a mug and squeezed the tea bag firmly against the side of the mug. There was nothing she enjoyed less than a cup of weak tea. Her preference for a good strong cup of tea was something that she had picked up from her northern parents who held very definite views about what constituted a proper brew. Her mother had always said that the leaves should be left to stand in the pot for a good five minutes. Her mother had equally definite views about the sort of people who resorted to using tea bags.

Beth was cheered by these happy memories from her late childhood at a time when she still lived with her parents, even although they had not always been the easiest of times. But it wasn't long before her thoughts returned to her less happy experience of the previous evening. She had been terrified by the thought that she was being pursued into the pub car park. Her fears had stayed with her all the way back to the village and down to the sea wall. As soon as the sea fret had begun to drift in she had begun to feel even more uneasy. She had been overcome by sorrowful memories of her failed relationship with Bill Matthews. She hadn't cried at first. This came later when the memories of her lost love had been replaced by a frightening recollection of the night she feared she had been raped, a kaleidoscope of startling images of leering eyes and grappling hands.

It was hardly surprising that she had been so terrified when she heard a voice calling out to her. It was as if her worst fears had been realised and someone had pursued her down to the deserted seafront where she was so vulnerable to attack. It was only when the call had been repeated that she realised it was Tom. The feeling of relief had been immense. Instinctively she felt that Tom was someone she could trust.

It had been a long time since Beth had found herself in the warm and comforting arms of any man. And yet to seek sanctuary in Tom's embrace had seemed so utterly natural. He had followed her back to the inn after she had left him alone on the seafront. She could see that he had wanted to be sure that she had recovered sufficiently to be on her own. While naturally reticent, she recognised that she owed Tom some kind of explanation. But she hadn't felt ready for that. There had been an undeniable look of disappointment on Tom's face when he had turned to head off to his room. She had been tempted to call him back but then it was too late; he had already rounded the corner at the end of the corridor.

Her thoughts were interrupted by the loud cry of a gull passing close by her bedroom window. She had intended to return to bed to read for a while, but thought better of it. She had a great deal to do this morning as she needed to reach Porth Meudwy by ten thirty for the crossing to Bardsey. She went over to the window and pulled back the curtains to see whether the mist had cleared. It was still dark outside, although it would not be long before the sun rose behind the village. She could just make out the rooftops of the houses between the inn and the bay. The sea fret had been completely blown away by the night breeze and it looked as though she would be able to make the crossing. It was with a considerably less heavy heart that she began to pack her belongings. She would take an early breakfast and then stock up on provisions for her stay on the island from the local shop. She was so busily occupied with her preparations that all thoughts of Tom passed from her mind. It was only when she was on her way down to breakfast that she wondered whether she might see him there. As it turned out, it being so early, she found herself taking breakfast alone. She wasn't quite sure whether she felt relieved or disappointed.

But, by the time she returned to her room to pick up her rucksack, her mood had changed. Despite her natural reservations, she was saddened by the thought that she might never see Tom again. She also felt guilty that their encounter had been so one-sided. He had been so genuinely sympathetic when she had needed his support and she had offered him nothing in return. On a sudden whim, she tore a sheet of paper out of her notebook, sat down on the end of the bed and wrote him a note. She wasn't sure what to say, finally settling on "Sorry to have missed you this morning. Am up early to catch the boat to Bardsey. Thank you for being so kind. Perhaps we shall meet again one day, Beth". She folded the note neatly, opened her bedroom door and walked along the corridor to the Tom's room. She listened outside his door but there wasn't a sound from within. She thought of knocking but was overcome by shyness, so she bent down and pushed the note under the door as quietly as she could. She tiptoed back along the corridor, gathered together her belongings, made her way downstairs and paid her bill. As she stepped out through the front door, the sun was shining and her spirits rose as she set out on the next stage of her Arthurian quest.

# CHAPTER EIGHTEEN

As it happened, Tom never saw the note that Beth had slipped under his door. Bleary eyed from a sleepless night following the previous evening's unusual turn of events, he stepped right over it on his way to breakfast. Later on, an unsuspecting chamber maid assumed that the scrap of paper had been discarded and disposed of it in her rubbish bag.

There was no sign of Beth when Tom arrived in the dining room. He could only imagine that she had taken an early breakfast and set off in search of some other local site with an Arthurian connection. However, when he went back upstairs, he knocked on her bedroom door on the off-chance that she might still be there. Having caught sight of him from down the corridor, the chambermaid informed him the young lady had left earlier that morning. He felt a mixture of disappointment and relief. Disappointment because he was intrigued by this troubled young woman; relief because he was determined that nothing should distract him from his own mission.

He determined therefore to put all thought of Beth aside. He wasn't due to sail to Bardsey until the following morning so decided to spend his last day on the mainland at the ancient church of St Beuno at Pistyll, a short distance back along the Peninsula. He remembered this tiny church with particular affection. It had been one of the high points of their Franciscan pilgrimage all those years ago. Nowhere had made a greater impression on him than this ancient and isolated stone sanctuary where pilgrims on their way to Bardsey had gathered to rest over so many hundreds of years

As he set off from the village, he was pleased to see that the previous evening's sea fret had been dispelled by the welcome warmth of the April sun. By the time he arrived at Pistyll it had become a fine, clear morning. He parked the car and stood for a while looking down at the spot where the revered St Beuno had sought solitude in his later years. The church nestled high up on the hillside. Far down below, the deep blue sea was topped with flecks of white where the wind ruffled the tips of the waves. There were many legends related to Beuno, whose life straddled the late sixth and early seventh centuries. Perhaps the most notable of the miracles it was claimed he had performed was the restoration of the head of St Winifred after she had been beheaded by the Romans. Beuno was a gifted preacher and evangelist who travelled through North Wales under the patronage of Cadfan, King of Gwynedd. He had established the impressive abbey church further back up the Peninsula at Clynnog Fawr. He thought affectionately of the saint's namesake who had led the pilgrimages he had joined as a young man.

Looking down at the little church, Tom experienced the magic of the place all over again. He was pleased that he had chosen to return here, to do so was to be reminded of the engaging simplicity of the faith of those early evangelists. He had been brought up in the Anglican high church tradition. But there were times when he longed to escape all the ritual that went with it, to express his faith in a simpler manner, uncluttered by distracting liturgical ceremonial. The tranquillity of Pistyll was just what his present mood demanded.

He walked slowly down the path and through the churchyard, breathing in the fresh air which, even at this height, still retained a hint of saltiness. The graveyard was covered in long meadow grass which had almost swallowed up many of the graves. There was the delicate scent of wild spring flowers and the air was full of the humming of bees. He wondered by what miracle of nature they found their way from flower to flower without once revisiting a plant from which they had already removed the pollen.

Dotted around the graveyard there was the occasional more substantial tomb covered in soft yellow lichen. Tom was struck by different it was to the graveyards of more prosperous communities. There were no stone crosses towering above their massive plinths, no angels blowing trumpets and no weeping Madonnas. He reached the entrance to the church. For more than fourteen hundred years a building had stood on this site. Over the centuries, thousands of pilgrims had worshipped here and rested overnight in the nearby farmhouse.

The entrance was through a large wooden door beneath a small bell-tower. The neatly carved stones encasing the doorway formed a semi-circular arch. The inside of Beuno's church was simplicity itself. There was nothing in the way of intricate carving or ornate woodwork and it was altogether rather smaller than Tom remembered. A few rows of pews ran down either side of the narrow aisle. The altar was decked in spring flowers, placed there in celebration of St Beuno's day which fell on 21st April, Tom supposed. The sweet floral fragrance had replaced all traces of the mustiness so often to be found in old church buildings. Although large parts of the church had been rebuilt in the twelfth and fifteenth centuries, it retained the feeling of a much older building. Tom thought about all the men and women of unquestioning faith who had worshipped there over the centuries. It was difficult not to be overwhelmed by the holiness of the place.

There was no-one else about and Tom was grateful to have the place to himself. He sat down in the back row of the pews and allowed his eyes to grow accustomed to the dark interior. He had forgotten how much the side walls of the church leaned outwards, weighed down by its heavy timbers and stone roof. It was almost as if the building was opening its arms to embrace the Almighty. A small window above the altar let in a narrow shaft of sunlight. The steady breeze outside stirred the branches of the trees so that the light filtering through shimmered on the stone floor. Tom ran his hand over the wall and felt how rough and unyielding the stone was. He sat back and closed his eyes to absorb the silence. After a period of quiet contemplation, he unfastened his rucksack and took out his black, leather-bound prayer book, its hundreds of paper-thin pages edged in gold and red. It had been a present from his godfather on the day of his ordination and he took it with him wherever he went. He had fallen out of the regular practice of saying the Daily Offices of Morning and Evening Prayer since being relieved of his parish duties. However, he knew that if he was to have any hope of rekindling his faith it would call for a considerable degree of self-discipline. Where better to start than by saying the Daily Offices again? He also determined that, from now on, he would begin and end each day with the Offices of Prime and Compline.

He opened the prayer book and turned to the Order for Morning Prayer. In a subdued voice, not much more than a whisper, he began with his favourite Sentence from St Luke's Gospel: "I will arise and go to my father, and will say unto him, Father, I have sinned against heaven, and before thee, and am no more worthy to be called thy son". He continued through the General Confession and Absolution and then knelt to say The Lord's Prayer. He remained on his knees through the Venite and Te Deum and the two lessons of the day. Most of the words were so familiar that he was able to recite them from memory. But the brain plays funny tricks, and after a while he realised that the very familiarity of the words had led his mind to wander. He paused to regain his focus. The Apostles' Creed came next and he knew that this was where his real challenge would lie. For here, in little more than a hundred words, lay all the tenets of the Christian faith. He stared at the words but they seemed to dance about on the page as if they were daring him to contradict the absolute truths which they encapsulated. Since Martha's death, he had even struggled to subscribe to the very first tenet of the Creed, belief in "God the Father Almighty, Maker of heaven and earth". How could a loving God allow such a thing to happen? Martha's faith had been unwavering and her commitment to his ministry selfless. So, who was this God who did so little to safeguard the lives of those who served him with such generosity? Throughout his ministry he had unfailingly acquiesced to a deeply spiritual acceptance of the God-based mystery that lay behind the meaning of life and death. But since Martha's death he had seen man's ability to survive as the ultimate human gamble, a gamble in which God played little or no part at all.

Tom's head was so full of such disturbing thoughts that he could only feel the full force of his growing disbelief. He could no longer bow down to the full import of the words of the Creed. He put his prayer book down on the narrow shelf on the back of the pew in front of him.

84

With a mournful sigh, he closed his eyes and sat motionless. Perhaps he would be able to rediscover some kind of peace in the stillness of the morning. But his head was full of images of his beloved Martha. He saw the wonderful smile which had brought so much warmth into the world; the look of motherly concern whenever one of the children was ill. He would never forget her exceptional elegance and her intoxicating beauty. Each passing image brought more tears to his eyes. Over the months and years since her death he had found it impossible to give full vent to his grief. He had been too afraid of entering that world of perpetual darkness from which he might never be able to return. His only answer had been to bury himself in his ministerial duties. He had so completely shut out his own emotions that the celibate life that had been forced upon him had hardly troubled him at all. For someone so naturally loving and affectionate, this had been a remarkable transformation and had not gone unnoticed by those who knew him well. He had continued to offer sound advice to the parishioners who came to him with their problems, even to those who irritated him because of the pettiness of their concerns. But he closed his own ears to the advice he received from those who cared about him the most.

He had set out that morning planning to spend the day in quiet spiritual contemplation. He had believed that this profoundly holy site would be a good place to begin the long journey back to rediscovering the essence of his religious belief. But, on this particular morning, his powers of self-discipline had deserted him. The ancient church which had seemed so welcoming when he had first arrived was now dark and oppressive. The sun no longer shone through the window and where its bright beams had danced on the stone floor there was nothing but murky shadows now. He shivered, picked up his few belongings and hurried out into the open air. He felt faint and breathless and leaned back for support against the wall of the church. The rough stone dug into his back. It took some time for his head to clear and for him to feel steady enough to walk back up the path to where he had parked his car. When he reached the road, he turned to take a final, tentative, look back down at St Beuno's church. The sun suddenly re-emerged from behind the clouds and the whole hillside was bathed in golden light. But even such a magnificent sight could do little to lighten Tom's mood. Where he had hoped to find the beginning of a way forward he had only found greater despair. The journey ahead looked even more impossible. However, although he may not have recognised it at the time, he had taken one crucial step in the right direction. He had finally been able to give way to tears.

# CHAPTER NINETEEN

Beth would have preferred to walk the old pilgrim's route along the cliff path to Porth Meudwy. However, a two-week stay on the island required her to stock up with provisions, ruling out making the journey on foot. She had made arrangements to leave her car at Cwrt Farm, directly opposite the track down to the little harbour. Her luggage would be carried down from the farm in the ferryman's Land Rover. She had been given strict instructions to travel as lightly as possible as there was limited space on the boat. With this in mind, she purchased vegetables rice and pasta, tea, coffee, washing up liquid, toilet rolls and, her only luxuries, a fruit cake and large tin of shortbread biscuits. She had been told that fresh milk and eggs would be available on the island.

She drove the short journey out of Aberdaron and round the curve of the bay in a cheerful mood, turning left towards Uwchmynydd then left again for the final short stretch to Cwrt Farm. It was a fine morning; the final traces of the previous night's sea fret having given way to a clear blue sky. It would have been pleasantly warm were it not for the light breeze blowing in from across the Irish Sea.

She turned into the farmyard and parked alongside a couple of other vehicles, receiving an over-exuberant welcome from a friendly border collie when she opened her car door. The dog danced round in rapid circles furiously wagging its tale and leaping up at her. She was saved from these attacks by a tall, rosy-cheeked young man who emerged from one of the barns and shouted sternly "Down girl, down!" The dog froze and then slunk off with her tail between her legs.

"Sorry about that" the young man said, strolling towards her across the yard. "She's not much more than a pup and still has a lot to learn."

"Oh, it's quite all right" Beth said, "I'm used to dogs. I grew up with two Jack Russells and they were bouncy enough. I hope I've parked in the right place."

"Yes, you'll be fine there" the young man replied, pulling out a large, and not altogether clean, handkerchief from the pocket of his navy-blue overalls. He turned his head to one side, blew hard into the handkerchief and then vigorously wiped his nose. He grinned a little sheepishly and, by way of apology, said "I've had this wretched cold for the best part of two weeks, just can't shift it. I'd blame it on the weather but, apart from last night, it's been unusually mild for the time of year." He gave her such a winning smile that Beth felt her natural reserve melt away. She smiled back and asked "Where will I find Mr Price? He's kindly offered to help me get my stuff down to the ferry."

"That'll be my Dad" the young man replied. "I'm Will, by the way. Dad's on his way back from the first crossing of the day. He said to look out for you as you'd need a lift down. There's another couple who should be turning up any minute and I've a load of provisions for the island farm over there." He pointed to a large stack of boxes and bags just inside the barn door. "The Land Rover's out the back, I'll just go and bring her round, I'll be back in a tick." He set off towards the barn walking with that rolling gait which is the particular preserve of the farming community.

Beth went round to the back of her car and opened the boot, taking out her luggage and the modest supply of provisions and putting them in a neat pile on the ground. She opened the back door of the car and took out a thick knitted woollen jumper and her anorak. She had been warned that the crossing was likely to be cold and wet as well as rough and so wasn't taking any chances. She was putting on her anorak when she heard the sound of Will starting up the Land Rover from somewhere behind the barn. He came around the corner and headed straight towards the open barn door. It was evident that he intended to load up the islanders' provisions first. She walked over to him.

"Let me give you a hand" she said.

"Kind of you to offer" he replied, as he struggled with a large cardboard box "but, as you can see, some of this stuff's pretty heavy and there isn't that much room in the back so it won't all go in unless it's loaded in the right order."

"Well, if you're sure" said Beth. "Is there anything else I can do to help?"

"No thanks, I'll have this lot sorted in a jiffy and then I'll drive over to your car for your bits and pieces. I only hope the other couple are travelling light. We tell everyone there's very limited space on board, but you'd be surprised how much stuff some people try to take across."

"I hope I haven't overdone it" said Beth "I really have tried to bring along as little as possible."

"Oh no, you're absolutely fine. If only everyone was as thoughtful it would make life a good deal easier."

Beth left Will loading up and made her way back to her car to carry out a final check, discovering her ordnance survey map tucked away in a pocket on the back of the driver's seat. When she was satisfied that she had everything she needed, she locked the car and put the keys in her pocket. By now Will had finished loading up and gave her a wave to indicate that he was ready to drive over to collect her things. Soon they were tidily stacked inside the Land Rover and she saw Will was looking anxiously at his watch.

"I can't give those other folk much more than another fifteen minutes as the boat is due to leave in less than an hour. I'm sorry you're having to hang around but I'm afraid there isn't enough time to take you down then come back up for them."

"Actually, if you don't mind, it's such a nice morning thought I might walk down, if there's time. I'm not sure how long it will take?"

"Okey dokey. If you set off now you'll have stacks of time, it only takes about fifteen minutes. If you turn right outside the gate and cross over the lane you'll see an opening on your left just a little further along. The track down to the beach is at the far end. It's an easy enough walk, downhill all the way. Don't worry about your things; I'll bring them down when the others get here."

Beth thanked Will profusely, took a bottle of water out of her rucksack and headed off. There were half a dozen or so vehicles parked on the grass, where the day visitors left their cars, but there was no-one around. She was grateful to be on her own. She wanted to take everything in without being distracted. There had been little rain so the track was dry and easy to negotiate. It led steadily downhill with a steep bank rising up on the left. To her right, the land fell away down to a narrow cleft in the hillside, filled with bracken and scrubby bushes. Everywhere she looked there were white and yellow wild-flowers. Not for the first time in her life, she regretted being able to name so few of them. Apart from the occasional distant cry of a seabird, there was hardly a sound.

She made her way further down the track and felt a strengthening in the breeze as she rounded a corner. Although it made her eyes water, she enjoyed the feel of the cool salty air blowing in her face. She could feel all the tension and fears of the previous evening being steadily blown away. She had so much to look forward to when she reached the island. After all, she had two whole weeks in which to focus on her project and to distance herself from her fears

When she rounded the final bend in the track, Beth caught her first view of the small sheltered bay of Porth Meudwy. She quickened her pace and was soon standing on the stony beach. There were a couple of fishing boats pulled up on the shore and a small group of well- clad adventurers were waiting in a huddle near to an iron trolley which lay half out of the water. She imagined that this was some sort of cradle for the ferry boat.

Beth was in no mood to exchange pleasantries with her fellow travellers, so she made her way towards an unusual looking rock formation at the foot of the cliffs. Even from a distance it stood out from all the other rocks scattered around on the beach. It was surprisingly rounded and smooth and reminded her of the work of Henry Moore. It was part of an unusual formation that could only have been washed so smooth by the relentless sucking and swirling of the sea over countless millennia. It was so perfectly formed that it might have been hand-crafted.

Just beyond her, two young children were running full-pelt along the beach with their arms out-stretched making aeroplane engine noises as they scattered the gulls in their path. They disappeared briefly round a large outcrop of rock before the smaller of the two children reappeared, excitedly calling out "Dad, Dad, come and look, we've found a cave, look Dad, look." A tall, lanky, ginger-haired man, wearing sunglasses with enormous lenses, stepped out from the melee of waiting boat passengers and strolled cross the beach towards the two young children. "All right boys, I'm coming" he called out "Don't you go exploring inside until I get there, it could be dangerous."

At the same moment Beth heard the sound of a high-pitched engine. It grew steadily louder and then she caught her first sight of the island ferry. It was a small, bright yellow craft which was now making its way round the headland with its bow high out of the water as it was powered along by two outboard motors. She was surprised at how fast it was approaching. But just when she began to think it might not be able to slow down in time, there was a loud roar as the engines were slammed into reverse and the boat was skilfully steered into its waiting cradle.

She made her way across the beach to join the other passengers. In no time at all the cradle had been towed out of the water by a large dumper truck and turned sideways to allow easier access for the passengers up a short metal ladder. The skipper, Will's father Alun Price, emerged from a covered wheelhouse towards the bow of the boat. He immediately took charge of the unloading of a stock of large crates, assisted by a couple of young lads who had been waiting on the beach. While this was going on, a middle-aged, weather-beaten man, wearing a chunky seaman's jersey, climbed down from the stern of the boat and went over to supervise the unloading of a stack of large, flat, rectangular objects heavily wrapped in paint-stained cloth. From the careful way in which each of these items was being handled, Beth wondered if the man was an artist and that the objects were completed canvasses. Perhaps his works were on their way to a studio on the mainland in readiness for the influx of summer visitors.

Once the boat had been unloaded, Alan Price climbed down the ladder carrying a clipboard and began to tick off the names of the passengers for the next crossing, calling out their names one by one. He did so with such a jolly smile that it was impossible not to feel welcome. Beth watched as he made a particular fuss of the two young aeronauts and she took an immediate liking to this warm-hearted sailor. The boys' mother fished in her bag for a bar of chocolate which she broke into small pieces and fed to the boys as though they were young chicks. Beth noticed that none of her fellow passengers had any luggage with them. She assumed that they must be day-trippers, spending just a few hours on the island before being ferried back to the mainland later that afternoon.

Once they had all been signed in, they waited patiently to climb aboard. Alan Price kept looking anxiously at his watch, clearly concerned that his son had not yet arrived with the remaining passengers. At last the sound of Will's Land Rover could be heard making its way round the last bend in the track. There was a squeal of well-worn brakes and the heavily laden vehicle came to an abrupt stop on the shingle a little further up the beach. Will and the young lad who had helped with the unloading of the boat hurriedly began to carry down the boxes and luggage, politely declining any help from Beth and the two latest arrivals. As their offer of help had been rejected, Beth and the newly arrived, middle-aged couple introduced themselves.

"It looks like you're planning to take up residence on the island for a while too." Beth said. "Is this your first visit or are you regulars?"

"Oh, we're old hands love" said the chubby, rather plain-looking woman. She was wearing a home-knitted, multi-coloured, jumper over a long, pleated skirt. Her greying hair hung down to her shoulders, which Beth imagined it had probably done since she had been a child. It was a style which she thought didn't altogether suit her. Beth noted the poorly applied makeup on her face and neck which tended to draw attention to rather than disguise the heavy acne she clearly suffered from. "Bert and I've been comin' up here for the best part of ten years." She said in a strong London accent. "We're keen bird watchers you see and we always try to get here for nestin' time. I'm Joan by the way. There's no point in standin' on ceremony, specially as it looks like we're goin' to be neighbours. This your first time is it?" Beth nodded "Then you'll love it. There's plenty to see and do on the island if you're into wildlife and lookin' for a bit of peace and quiet. Mind you, it ain't all that quiet when the birds is gatherin', quite a racket they make, I can tell you. Of course, there's folk what don't find the island's quite their cup o' tea. But we find somethin' new every time we come, don't we Bert? Why I was only sayin' the other day that, believe it or not, we still haven't explored every corner of the island."

Out of the corner of her eye, Beth saw that Joan's husband was trying, with considerable difficulty, to catch his wife's attention. In contrast to his plump wife, Bert was tall and skinny. It seemed that he had difficulty getting a word in when his garrulous wife was in full throttle. He was balding on top and judging by the way he kept running his fingers through his few remaining straggly wisps of hair; this was something he was keen to conceal. Finally, when Joan paused to take a breath, Bert managed to interrupt.

"Forgive me for askin' my dear" he said "but I can't find the binocs. Can you remember which bag we packed them in?"

"'He never knows where anythin' is" Joan said dismissively. "Most of the time the silly chump doesn't have a clue what time of day it is, never mind simple things like where we've put the binoculars! Oh Bert, you really are a twerp, what do you think those things are hangin' round your neck, a bunch of bleedin' bananas?"

Bert fumbled under his dark blue anorak and uncovered an impressive looking pair of binoculars. "Sorry dear, it ain't my day is it!"he said with an embarrassed grin.

Not one for small talk, Beth was pleased when she saw the boxes and luggage had been successfully stowed away in the boat and they were being invited to climb aboard. She stood back while the mother of the two boys helped them up the short ladder and climbed up herself. There was comparatively little room on board. The dozen or so other passengers were busy finding seats for themselves, either on the benches running either side of the cockpit, or on a wooden bench that ran down the middle. Alun Price was busy handing out life jackets and showing the young boys how to put them on. When he came to Beth, he pointed to the only space left, on one of the benches next to the wheelhouse. "You'll be safe enough there and you'll get a good view" he said, "but I should warn you, you may get a bit of a soaking when we head out beyond the bay, so I'd wrap up well if I were you."

One of the young men who had helped to load up the boat climbed into the dumper truck and started up the engine. There was a loud cough, a puff of blue smoke from the exhaust and the acrid smell of diesel fumes. He carefully manoeuvred the boat-laden cradle back into the water. Beth felt the slight rise and fall of the vessel as it began to float. What she wasn't prepared for was the deafening roar from the boat's motors when Alun Price put the boat into reverse and applied full throttle. She put her hands over her ears as they backed out of the harbour. As soon as the water was deep enough, their skipper turned the wheel hard over until the bows were pointing out to sea. She was impressed by how quickly they picked up speed as they headed out of the bay.

At first the sea remained relatively calm. However, once they rounded the headland, the small craft began to pitch and toss in the rougher waters. It felt as though they were suspended in the air as they flew from the crest of one of the larger waves to the next. Endless sheets of spray flew up into Beth's face and she was grateful for Alun Price's suggestion that she should zip up her anorak. However, she was enjoying the stiff breeze blowing through her hair so she didn't pull up her hood. Although she was soon drenched, it was an exhilarating experience. The two young boys, who had persuaded their parents to allow them to sit in a similar position on the opposite side of the boat, were yelling with excitement every time the boat crashed through a wave.

There was a shout from the wheelhouse and Beth saw the skipper was pointing ahead, to where the island had come into sight for the first time. It lay some way off like a large whale, floundering in the sea with its back standing high out of the water. From an earlier study of her map, she knew that all they could see from this side was the mountain that ran the full length of the island, from north to south. The narrow creek where they would land, the lighthouse, the abbey ruins, the farmsteads and cottages were all out of sight behind the mountain.

To Beth's surprise, rather than turning to head straight for the island, Alun Price was maintaining a course which would take them well to its right. They had been proceeding at a considerable speed, but then he eased back on the throttle, turned the wheel hard over to the left and brought their small craft sideways onto the waves. They rose and fell awkwardly in the swell and Beth became more aware of the height of some of the larger waves. She experienced a slight twinge of fear. She saw that most of her fellow passengers were equally alarmed by the sudden and dramatic change in the motion of the boat. Even the two small boys who had been chattering away excitedly since they left Port Meudwy were reduced to silence. The boat continued to wallow for a while as they made slow but steady progress towards the island. And then, to their relief, they turned again and began to run with rather than against the waves.

They were close enough to the island now to both see and hear the waves breaking on the perilous rocks along the foot of the mountain and hear the piercing cries of thousands of seabirds dipping and diving along the cliff-face. The boat picked up speed again. As they edged their way along the length of the island, Beth felt her first real tingle of excitement. She crouched down, reached into her rucksack and pulled out her copy of Geoffrey of Monmouth's twelfth-century *History of the Kings of Britain*. She leaned forward to gain the shelter of the wheelhouse and opened the book at the page describing how Arthur was conveyed to Avalon.

*"After the battle of Camlan we took the wounded Arthur to their island, led by Barinthus who was familiar with the sea and stars. With our ship under his direction, we arrived there with our leader and Morgan received us with due honour. She placed the king on golden coverlets in her bedchamber and herself exposed his wound with her noble hand. After examining it for a long while, she said that he might eventually recover his health, if he remained with her for a long time and was willing to submit to her care. So we joyfully entrusted the king to her and returned with a following wind to our sails."*

Looking up, she saw they were making good progress and would soon reach the point where they would turn and head for the island's flatter coastline. As soon as they cleared the headland and changed direction to head for the small inlet where they were to land, they entered more placid waters. On a low promontory to her left, Beth could see the squat red and white striped lighthouse tower surrounded by a cluster of low white buildings. This side of the island was even flatter than she had imagined and the large bay they were entering was more sheltered than she had expected. The island lay stretched out before her, golden in the sun, and Beth couldn't wait to clamber ashore.

# CHAPTER TWENTY

As Alun Price skilfully steered the boat up a narrow creek towards the landing jetty, Beth saw a small group of people had gathered to await their arrival. As soon as the boat had been tied up to the rusty iron rings on top of the jetty, Beth and the other passengers climbed ashore. After the exhilarating crossing, the two young boys were beside themselves with excitement. It took their mother's attention to keep them under control while their father rooted through the contents of his rucksack in search of a map of the island.

While the boat was being unloaded, the day visitors quickly dispersed, wanting to take full advantage of the four hours they had to explore the island. This left Beth alone with Bert and Joan who were busy supervising the loading of their luggage onto a trailer attached to an old green and yellow tractor, which from the state of the its paintwork and the large patches of rust on its bonnet looked like it had been exposed to the extremes of the island's weather over many years. A sturdy, rather handsome, weather-beaten man stepped forward and shook hands with Bert and Joan. "Lovely to see you both back again. You know the drill of course, so please just go ahead and load your stuff onto the trailer and I'll drop it off for you at the observatory." He turned to Beth and greeted her with a smile, puckering the leathery creases around his mouth.

"Dr Davenport, I presume, a very warm welcome indeed to Ynys Enlli. You may already know that my family and I are the only permanent residents left on the island. There are, of course, the people who service the lighthouse and the folk up at the observatory, but they come and go with the tides and the seasons. We are all that is left of what was once a thriving community. But please be assured that, although there may not be many of us, we shall do everything we can to make sure that your stay on the island is a happy one. My wife and I pride ourselves on making our visitors feel at home."

Throughout this well-rehearsed but genuine speech of welcome, Beth noticed that her island host never quite looked her in the eyes. The warmth of his welcome was tempered by an obvious bashfulness, so often found in people who exist outside the normal hustle and bustle of everyday life.

"I'm Harry, by the way, Harry Evans. There are a fair few of us Evans's around this end of Llŷn. You won't be surprised to hear that we are mostly related one way or another and people are always getting us mixed up... but I'm the only Harry so there's no need for any confusion there!" He chuckled as if he'd cracked a huge joke before turning to point towards where the tractor was standing by the jetty and continued "If you'd like to pop your bags on the trailer, I'll run them up to Llofft Plas for you. There's no sign of any bad weather about, so I'll just leave them outside the front door."

He shuffled from one foot to the other staring down at the ground. And then, for the first time, he seemed to pluck up enough courage to look Beth full in the face.

"I hope you'll find your accommodation comfortable. We don't provide many luxuries I'm afraid, just the basics."

"That's exactly what I'm looking for. I haven't come here expecting five-star treatment. Anyway, I shall be working most of the time."

Beth saw that Harry still wore an embarrassed grin on his face, suggesting that he was a little unsure of himself in the company of attractive young women. She wasn't surprised when he politely made his excuses and rejoined Alun Price, who, with the help of Bert and Joan, was still loading up the trailer. She felt that it would be difficult not to take a liking to this shy islander and couldn't help feeling rather amused and flattered by the effect she seemed to have had on him.

Once they had finished loading the trailer, Harry made his way back to Beth.

"Am I right in thinking that this is your first visit to the island? I certainly don't recollect seeing you here before."

"Yes, this is my first visit" Beth confirmed. "I've been wanting to come to Bardsey for ages but have had difficulty escaping the rigours of academia. I'm a junior lecturer at a busy university college in London, you see, and the demands are pretty exacting. This is the first vacation over the past three years where I've been able to steal some time to pursue my own studies."

Once again, avoiding looking her in the eyes, Harry said "Well, I suppose it depends what you're looking for. But I don't think you'll be disappointed in our little island. Most of our visitors are looking for a little peace and quiet away from the stresses and strains of life on the mainland. Even the day-trippers don't normally turn out to be your ordinary holiday-makers. They are looking for a brief encounter with nature in the raw too, so to speak. Ynys Enlli is a wild and wonderful place. I've lived and farmed here since I took over from my Dad and you'd have to drag me away. Of course, we have our difficult times. The weather can be a pig. There are long periods when we can't be reached by boat, but somehow, it's not that lonely an existence. Apart from the visitors and the folk up at the observatory, there are often people carrying out maintenance at the lighthouse. And then, how can you be lonely when you share the company of scores of seals and thousands of seabirds. Oh, for sure, as you'll find out, we have to do things a little differently here, but that's something you'll soon get used to. One thing I've learned over the years is that you can't take anything for granted when you live on an island, and that must be a good thing, mustn't it?"

This was said with such passion that Beth was quite moved. There's more to this man than meets the eye, she reflected.

"Anyway, that's enough of me ranting on. You're booked in for a couple of weeks I believe. You'll soon find out what it's like to wake up every morning to a world in which we humans are in the minority and where we have to work our arses off to stay even with the forces of nature. Mattie, that's my wife, she'll show you the ropes. What I suggest you do now is to follow that track there, carry on through the gate until you come to the stone farmhouse just off to the right. That's Ty Pellaf, where we live. You'll find Mattie there, she's expecting you and she has the key to Llofft Plas. I expect she'll want to walk over with you to explain how everything works."

While Harry had been introducing her to the ways of the island, Beth had watched Joan and Bert busily loading their belongings onto the trailer. As soon as they had finished, Bert pointed excitedly at something on the rocks on the far side of the creek. After a short, animated exchange, the couple offered her a parting wave and hurried off in that direction. Whatever it was that had attracted their attention, she was pleased to be left alone. The last thing she wanted was to have to listen to any more of the couples' prattling. She wanted a little peace and quiet to take in her new surroundings.

She thanked Harry for making her feel so welcome and set off along the track at a leisurely pace. The sun was high in the sky and it was pleasantly warm. Directly ahead, the mountain provided a dramatic backdrop to the flatter terrain stretching out beneath it. Its rocky outcrops were interspersed with soft green carpets of sward where the new grasses and wild flora of spring were breaking through. In the fields on either side of the track, sheep were grazing peacefully. She reached the gateway mid-way between the harbour and the Evans' farmhouse. From here she could see where the track veered off to the left beyond the farmhouse and ran along the foot of the mountain. Further along the track there was another sizeable whitewashed farmhouse with a large stone barn, and, further on, a number of other buildings, including what looked like a traditional Welsh chapel. The island was once home to a sizeable community, but she was surprised at the abundance of buildings and at how substantial so many of them were.

She stopped by the gateway to familiarise herself with the island's layout. Looking back, she had a much clearer view of the narrow peninsula beyond the jetty, broadening out onto the higher ground where the lighthouse stood with its cluster of outbuildings. The lighthouse itself was a solid-looking structure, rising up a hundred feet or more. It was painted with alternate bands of white and red. She wondered why the plinth was square rather than the more usual circular. An unexpectedly ornate railed balcony ran around the glass chamber housing the lantern. Beyond the jetty she could just make out two diminutive figures, crouching down, staring at something in the sea beyond the rocks. One of the figures raised a pair of binoculars to their eyes and Beth realised it must be Bert and Joan.

She turned to look again at the stretch of land between the mountain and where she was standing. It was a comparatively barren landscape with a noticeable absence of trees. But it was a landscape that appealed to Beth with her northern background and brought back happy memories of childhood excursions onto the Lancashire moors. While the proximity of the sea and the many varieties of seabirds flying overhead were a dramatic contrast to that more familiar environment, she felt very much at home. She was no recluse but there was something of the solitary in her nature. She was happy with her own company. She looked forward, with intense pleasure, to searching the island for any clues to help justify its claim to be Arthur's final resting place.

She set off again on the short walk up to Ty Pellaf, the Evans' farmhouse. The day visitors had long disappeared off on their various adventures and, apart from Joan and Bert, there was no sign of anyone else. As she approached the farmhouse she saw it was an impressively solid, well-proportioned, two-storey, twin-gabled stone house with three tall chimneys rising above an elegant sloping slate roof. Access to the house was along a path leading off the main track to the rear of the property. The house's main entrance was sensibly positioned to provide maximum shelter from whatever weather the gods might throw at the island. Jutting out from the main house was an archway leading through to a sizeable walled enclosure where there were a number of outbuildings.

As she drew nearer, a stout, middle-aged, woman stepped out of the back door. Her thick shoulder-length hair showed a few hints of grey near the roots. She was wearing a woollen jumper and mid-length brown tweed skirt. The white ankle socks which she wore inside her flat-heeled brown leather shoes reminded Beth of a long-standing spinster friend of her mother.

"You must be Dr Davenport." The woman's strong Welsh accent had a delightful lilt to it. "I hope Harry is bringing your luggage up on the tractor?"

"Yes, indeed he is, thank you Mrs Evans" Beth replied, "I wouldn't have fancied struggling with it myself. I hadn't realised it was quite so far from the harbour. Your husband said you'd kindly show me where I'm staying."

"I'll be more than happy to. But I thought you might like a nice hot cup of tea before we go over to Llofft Plas. The kettle's boiling and I expect you'll be ready for one after the crossing. By the way, do call me Mattie, everybody does and Mrs Evans sounds so very formal, don't you think? Now then, come along in and let's have that cuppa."

Beth was happy to succumb to Mattie Evans' hospitality. She followed her into a large, cosy farmhouse kitchen. A big copper pan bubbled away on the stove. From the appetising aroma Beth deduced it must be a casserole or stew. She looked around. Next to the stove was a range of rather crude, waist-high, homemade looking wooden cupboards. The work surface above was completely covered with pots and pans, an enormous kettle and two precariously stacked piles of crockery. There were more cupboards under the window which housed an unusually large Belfast sink. On the opposite side of the room, two well-worn leather armchairs with brightly coloured hand-knitted covers stood on either side of a large stone fireplace. The fireplace itself was mostly hidden behind a rickety-looking clothes horse heavily laden with clothing.

"I hope you'll forgive the mess" Mattie said, removing a pile of folded clothes from one of the chairs by the kitchen table. "Please, do take a seat and rest your legs."

It was evident that Beth had entered the heart of the Evans' family home and, as she sat down at the table, she felt very much at ease. Much of her own childhood had been spent in similar surroundings. She was no stranger to the distinctive and not unpleasant smell of clothes drying in front of an open fire. She thought of the many times she had sat at their own kitchen table, doing her homework, while her mother did the ironing or prepared their evening meal.

"So, what brings you to Ynys Enlli?" Mattie enquired, removing a small kettle from the stove where it had been steaming away ever since they had entered the kitchen.

Beth hesitated before answering. She wasn't sure how much she wanted to reveal of her reasons for visiting the island. She had no way of knowing what the islanders might make of it all. She didn't even know if they were interested in their island's history. But then she would need to find out if they knew anything that would help with her research.

"Well, I'm a historian specialising in early Celtic history. There are so many interesting legends associated with the island that I thought I'd come to take a look. You know, links with the Arthurian legend, that kind of thing."

"Ah, so that's it, is it? I wondered what kind of doctor you were. It's Harry you'll want to talk to. He knows a good deal more about the island's history than I do. I know some of the stories are good for tourism but, to be honest, we tend to take much of it with a pinch of salt. They call this the island of 20,000 saints and all those good souls are supposed to be buried here somewhere. Mind, all we've ever dug up have been the bones of dead cattle and sheep!" Mattie chuckled and presented Beth with a large mug of tea. "Do you take milk and sugar?"

"Just a little milk please."

"You know, you won't find much here that's older than the farmhouses and cottages. Of course there are a few remains from much earlier times and there's what's left of the old abbey, just part of the tower you know, and that's seen better days. Pity the rest of it was knocked about in good King Henry's time when he was busy dissolving the monasteries and kicking out the monks. I've always thought what a funny word dissolving is, sounds like he was melting everything down, if you know what I mean. Anyway, as you can imagine, as soon as the abbey was closed down and the monks had gone, the islanders set about nicking the stone for their cottages and other buildings. You've only to look around to see where it's been put to good use."

Beth nodded. It certainly explained why so many of the island's buildings had such a solid look about them. Reluctant to say anymore about the true purpose of her visit, she changed the subject.

"I see you have children" she said, looking in the direction of the washing.

"Yes, a boy and two girls, but only our little Rhiannon is still living at home. Our eldest, Gareth, he's a carpenter in Pwllelli and our older girl, Gwen, is married to a schoolteacher in Bangor. She's got two small children of her own you know. Rhiannon, that's our youngest, she just finished school last summer and now she helps us here on the farm. She's a lovely girl, as you'll discover for yourself, but… well you see, poor thing, she's not been blessed with the greatest of brains. At school they told us that she had serious learning difficulties, ESN they said she was. Don't you hate labels! Anyway, they wanted us to send her to a special school. Can you imagine how impossible that would have been, living on the island? Anyway, as it turned out her head teacher was on our side, 'it's good for the other children to have her around', she said. So she stayed on at the secondary until her sixteenth. Well, I can tell you, she may not have quite all her chairs at home, but she's certainly far from stupid. She's such a cheery little thing and a wonderful help here on the farm. Harry isn't getting any younger and he was saying only the other day that he didn't know how we'd manage without her. She looks after the chickens, helps him with the cattle and milking the cows, and she's a joy to watch with the new-born lambs. She knows every nook and cranny of the island and in the winter, when the weather's bad, she knows all the places where an animal might get into trouble. She's rescued many a ewe that's wandered off with her lambs."

"She sounds lovely" Beth said "I look forward to meeting her."

"Oh, I'm sure she'll pop down to see you at the Llofft. She loves meeting new people and taking round the eggs and milk for our visitors. I can't tell you what a help she is with my mother. She's in her eighties, you know. She hasn't enjoyed good health for quite a while now. She suffers from very bad bronchitis, keeps her awake at night and the rest of us too often enough. Well, my little Rhiannon has a way with her. They get on like a house on fire. The old lady can be very demanding and has a nasty temper on her. But she thinks the sun shines out of our Rhiannon, and that she can do no wrong."

They chatted on for a while, with Mattie doing most of the talking and Beth finding herself lulled into a rare moment of relaxed contentment. So much so that she lost all sense of time. It wasn't until she caught sight of the kitchen clock that she realised that it was well after four o'clock and she still hadn't made it to her lodgings. Fortunately Mattie spotted Beth glancing at the clock.

"Oh my goodness" she said apologetically, "here I am, prattling on about all manner of nonsense and you'll be wanting to settle in. Just give me a moment and I'll take you over."

Beth was pleased to have received such a warm welcome. She had been prepared for an altogether different first encounter with the islanders, expecting that they would be as remote and forbidding as the island they lived on.

# CHAPTER TWENTY-ONE

"Hello Annie, is that you?"

"Dad, where on earth are you? I've been calling and calling you ever since last Sunday but all I've got is that wretched answer phone. I've left endless messages. Why on earth haven't you called back? I was worried something awful has happened."

Tom felt an immediate surge of guilt. Ever since she had left home for university, he had telephoned his daughter unfailingly every Sunday evening. The long weekly telephone conversations were something they both looked forward to and had become an important part of Tom's emotional survival.

"I'm so very sorry darling... I really did mean to call you before now to explain... but everything's been rather difficult these past few days."

"But you always call me on Sundays!" Annie exclaimed. Tom could hear her nervously fingering the mouthpiece on her telephone. "Where have you been? I've been so worried I nearly called Mrs Murdock to see if she knew anything. But then you know what a busybody she is so I thought better of it." Mrs Murdock was the parish secretary and not known for her discretion.

"I'm not quite sure how to explain it all to you Annie" Tom said. He sat down on the bed at the inn. He knew how much Annie cared for him. He needed to find a way of explaining everything which would cause her the least possible worry. He continued "I haven't been at home since last Friday... you see I'm actually in Aberdaron."

"Aber where?" his daughter exclaimed, unable to disguise her growing unease.

"Aberdaron, it's a small village at the tip of the Llŷn Peninsula in Wales."

"What on earth are you doing there?"

"It's a long story and I don't want you to get too anxious about what I'm about to tell you. You see, I thought it would be easier to come to terms with your mother's death as time passed. But over the past few months I've been finding it more and more difficult to cope."

"But Daddy, I thought you were doing really well. Ted and I were discussing it only the other day. We both thought that you seemed to be coping so much better."

"Well, Annie, you know what it is. Sometimes we try to put on a brave face. The last thing I want is to worry you or Ted any more. I've done enough of that already. You've both been such a tower of strength to me, especially you Annie. But I want you to be able to get on with your own lives without worrying about me all the time."

"For goodness sake, I'm your daughter and that's what I'm here for and I'm sure that Ted feels the same way! But you still haven't explained what you're doing at Aber... Aberwherever it is and why you aren't at home."

"Well, you see the long and short of it is that I went to see Bishop George last week. I've been feeling very low for quite some time. I needed to talk to someone who would understand and who could offer spiritual guidance as well as general advice. After all, Bishop George is my father in God as well as my employer if you know what I mean, and you, you of all people, know what a sympathetic man he is and how wonderfully kind and considerate he's been ever since... ever since your mother was killed. Well, I think I told him rather more than I originally intended. He's just got that gift for getting you to tell him the whole story and not just the bits you feel safe in sharing. Anyway, it all came pouring out and before I knew it I was telling him that I was finding it more and more difficult to serve the parish while still struggling to come to terms with your mother's death." He paused for a moment, not sure how much more he should tell his daughter. However, he had little doubt that she would eventually tease the truth out of him one way or another, so he continued.

"You, more than anyone, know how hard I've found things since your mother died. Of course, I thought it would gradually get easier as time passed and that, eventually, I'd be able to accept her death and to move on.

But, the truth is... the truth is that the opposite has happened. I've found myself missing her more and more." Tom paused again. He had reached that part he knew would be the most difficult for her to understand.

"I know that what I'm about to say will sound very stupid" he continued. "In fact, the more I dwell on it the more difficult I find it to make sense of what's going on in my head. You see, and I hate having to admit this, but over the past few months, my self-pity has slowly been turning to anger. I'm angry that your mother was taken from us so needlessly. I'm angry with myself for not being able to accept her death. But, most of all, I'm angry with God for letting it all happen, so much so that I've seriously begun to question my faith."

There was a stunned silence at the other end of the telephone while Annie grappled with the enormity of what her father had just told her. The one thing she had never doubted was the strength and solidity of his faith.

"Of course, I know this feeling of unrelenting despair is something many people go through in times of crisis. Over the years, I've done my best to offer comfort to scores of parishioners who've been bereaved, or faced some other crisis in their lives. I've told them that the certainty of a loving God is the one constant they can depend on. And now... and now, having spent so much of my life offering such consolation to others, I find myself quite unable to cope with my own loss. I know I must try to move on and yet, somehow, I can't, Annie, I can't... I just don't seem to be able to." His last few words were almost lost as his voice faded away.

"Daddy, oh Daddy, why haven't you been more honest about all this before?" Annie said. From the snuffling at the other end of the line, Tom could tell she was crying. "You know that Ted and I will do anything we can to help. We're here for you, do you hear that? Both of us, we're here for you. We know how very lonely you have been since Mummy died. But you've put on such a brave face. I had no idea that you were finding it this difficult."

"It's the pointlessness of it all that I can't cope with. That final morning when your mother drove off, she was so cheerful, so full of life. When the police called round to break the news of the accident it just didn't seem possible, she was always such a careful driver too. At first, I simply couldn't believe she was dead. I'd be sitting in my study, working on a sermon or something, and every time I heard a noise I'd look up, expecting to see her pop her head round the door to ask if I wanted a cup of coffee. Then, after a while, everything just went numb and I couldn't feel anything anymore. I guess that's how I coped, by stifling my emotions. And then, one morning, I woke up. It must have been a couple of months ago. The reality of it all came flooding back. I remember, it was my day off. I shut myself in my study and wept like a child. It all seemed so incredibly unfair. Your mother wasn't just the light of our lives, everybody loved her. 'Why?' I kept asking myself, 'why Martha?', 'Why not someone else, someone who had nothing useful to offer this world, somebody no-one would miss?" I tried to pray, but I couldn't concentrate. I hated myself for some of the selfish thoughts that were flying through my head but I couldn't hold them back. I was on my knees, looking up at the crucifix that hangs above my desk, when the most awful thought entered my mind and I found myself saying over and over again 'If you exist, do you know something? I don't think that I like you very much!'"

There was a gasp at the other end of the telephone. Annie had never heard her father talk in this way. She cursed the physical distance that separated them. All she wanted to do was to reach out and put her arms around him. She could hear his uneven breathing, interrupted by the occasional snuffle at the other end of the line. She visualised him, slumped over a desk or table, his hands clasped tightly together, rubbing his thumbs up and down as he always did when trying to concentrate on anything difficult.

"I can't believe I heard you say that!" she said, still shocked by her father's last remark. "You say you've been to see Bishop George. What on earth did he make of all this, or perhaps you didn't tell him what you've just told me?"

"Oh yes I did, I told him everything, and if I hadn't done so willingly he'd have dragged it out of me anyway! He wrote to me the very next morning. He told me I needed time away from the parish, time to learn to live with the reality of your mother's death. He said I needed a complete break from the parish and from my duties and that he wanted me to go away immediately to somewhere especially significant to me, to somewhere where I might be able to rediscover God again."

"But what about the parish?"

"Oh, you know Bishop George, he'd got that all sorted out already. He asked me to see him again and told me not to worry about any of my parish responsibilities because they would be well taken care of until I was ready to return. All I had to do was to decide where I wanted to go, pack my bags and set off without letting anything get in the way. He didn't even want me to tell anyone in the parish. He said he'd take care of all that."

There was a long pause while Annie took it all in and then said "So what's so special about Aberdaron? I don't remember you ever mentioning it before. I can't even picture quite where it is."

"You remember when we used to go on holiday to Anglesey, when you were kids, and we stayed on that caravan site down by the Lion Rocks at Rhosneigr? I don't think we ever explored much further down the coast, but just below Caernarvon there's another peninsula. It's due south of Anglesey and sticks out even further into the Irish Sea. Well, that's the Llŷn Peninsula. At the very tip there's a tiny village called Aberdaron. That's where I am.'

"But you still haven't told me what's so special about the place!"

"Did I never tell you about the pilgrimages I went on with the Franciscans, when I was a student?"

"I think you may have done." She paused for a moment while she delved into her memory. "Yes, I do seem to have a vague memory of it. Didn't you spend time on a remote island, somewhere off the coast?"

"Ah, so you do remember, and you're right about the remote island. That's where I'm going tomorrow. It's called Bardsey, or Ynys Enlli to give it its proper Welsh name."

"I see" said Annie, although Tom wasn't altogether convinced that she did. "And how long, exactly, are you planning to stay there?"

"Well, that's difficult to say at the moment. Bishop George has been quite firm in insisting that I stay there for as long as I need to. The Diocese is being very generous. They're continuing to pay my stipend during this period. Otherwise I simply wouldn't have been able to consider taking so much time out. It's being treated as a sabbatical. Of course, I won't be able to stay there indefinitely and there's bound to come a time when Bishop George will be looking to me for some answers. However, the way I feel right now, I think that it may be quite a long time before I feel able to give him any."

"What do you mean by 'quite a long time?" Annie asked, sounding even more concerned.

"The truth is that I honestly don't know, but I fear it may be weeks, even months. I feel so incredibly confused about everything."

"Are you sure you've chosen the right place to go? Surely, a remote island like Bardsey's going to be a bit grim at this time of year. Couldn't you come up with somewhere a bit more comfortable? I don't like the idea of you being there all alone, facing up to the elements."

"But, don't you see? That's the whole point. I need to be on my own and I really want to avoid too many distractions. As for being up against the elements, well, I've always rather enjoyed battling against the worst that nature can throw at us. There's something wonderfully stimulating about it."

"But I've never seen you as a recluse. Don't you think you may find it all a bit too much after a few weeks, living the simple life in semi-isolation? We all know you thrive on good company. Don't you think you need other people around you right now to give you support? Wouldn't that be better that wallowing alone in self-pity?"

Tom was surprised by the vehemence of his daughter's entreaties. She had always been so good at understanding how he felt, so much so that she had often been able to read his mind better than he could himself.

"Listen Annie, it's not going to be like that at all. First of all, I'll be living in a solidly built little stone cottage with an open fire to keep me warm and adequate supplies of food. And then I can always call on the Evans family who farm the island if I'm feeling lonely. There are the regular visitors to the bird observatory too and I expect there'll be others renting properties on the island, not to mention the day visitors."

"Well, that's something I suppose" Annie said, sounding a little relieved. "But I guess you aren't exactly going there for the company."

"No, of course I'm not. I chose Bardsey because I believe it's somewhere where I should be able to think more clearly and resolve the issues that are troubling me so much. I can't continue with my normal life until I've found a way of accepting your mother's death and until I'm able to do that, I don't feel that there's much room for God in my life. Annie, you know me better than anyone. I'm sure you'll understand that I can't cope with all of this while trying to run the parish. The worst part has been having to pretend that everything's all right when it most certainly isn't. I can't go on living a lie." At this point, from the break in his voice, Annie knew that her father was fighting to hold back tears.

"Oh please don't cry. If only I could be with you now... look, I'm sure I could get on a train this afternoon and be with you by tonight. Please let me come to look after you!"

"Annie, you are the dearest, sweetest most adorable child and I love you so much. But please, try to understand. This is something I have to do on my own. Anyway, I'm not exactly good company at the moment. Trust me; if there's anywhere where I shall be able to overcome these wretched depressions, it's on Bardsey. There's such a magical quality about the place. It feels like somewhere where you can be healed. The island has a bleak but indescribable beauty and there's an all-pervading sense of peace and calm. I've never been anywhere else that possesses quite the same qualities. When I first visited there, all those years ago, I was a young man with my whole life in front of me. Then I had absolutely no doubts about my faith or what God wanted me to do with my life. I can only hope that my return visit will help to rekindle some of that faith and certainty."

"I feel utterly helpless so many miles away. But, I'll try to understand. Will you call me again, before too long, to let me know how you're getting on? I can't bear the thought of you disappearing off and not being able to get in touch with you. I'll worry myself silly."

"Well, I doubt whether there's a telephone on the island but I expect I'll be coming ashore now and again to stock up on provisions and, of course, I'll call you. What I can't do is to give you a precise day or time. So, if you don't hear from me for a while you simply mustn't worry, I'll be fine."

"All right, but you will promise to let me know if there's anything I can do, won't you?"

"The most important thing you can do for me is to promise that you'll try not to worry. Also, will you let Ted know? I don't think that I'm quite up to taking on the inevitable inquisition from him!"

"OK Daddy."

"Thank you dear, sweet, Annie. Now, listen, I have to go now because I've got a lot to sort out before crossing over to the island tomorrow. Thank you for listening so patiently to your silly old father's troubles. I love you to bits, you know that. Look after yourself and I promise to call you again when I can."

"Goodbye Daddy. You'll come through this, I know you will. Take good care of yourself. We'll all be thinking of you, you know that don't you? Goodbye."

"Goodbye Annie."

Tom put the telephone down and stared out of the window. He wiped the tears from his eyes. It had taken him all his strength to turn down his daughter's offer to come and look after him. But this was something he had to do alone.

# CHAPTER TWENTY-TWO

She is running as fast as she has ever run and her long golden hair streams out behind her in tangled clusters, buffeted by the wind. She knows he is close behind and, if she slackens her pace, he will catch up and overtake her, as he always does. If this happens, it will be on the last long run down to the fold in the side of the mountain to where the big black rock stands. But this time will be different. This time she is determined to be the first to get to the black rock and climb until she is standing on the ledge, halfway up. From there she will just be able to stretch up and squeeze her hand into the small round hole on the very top of the rock. For it is only by touching the magic white pebble at the bottom of the hole that she can claim to have won the race.

She is nearing the place where the path begins to slope down towards the black rock. She can see it shimmering in the bright spring sunlight. It is on this final stretch that the race will be decided. There are only one or two places where the path is wide enough for him to overtake her. She will have to put in an extra effort to make sure she stays ahead. Her heart is racing and she is breathing so fast that it feels as though her lungs will burst. She is sure that she can hear his light footsteps somewhere close behind. "I mustn't let him catch me, I mustn't let him catch me" she says to herself as she puts in one last final effort to stay ahead. She comes to a narrow ditch and launches herself forward into an enormous leap which carries her flying across. But she lands awkwardly, loses her balance and falls to the ground. She rolls over and over in a scatter of flailing arms and legs until at last she comes to rest in a patch of soft, muddy peat. She is fortunate not to have hurt herself more seriously. As it is she has only scraped her knee. There is a trickle of bright red blood running down her leg. She dabs a finger into the wound, raises her hand and takes a closer look at the smeared drops of blood. She is surprised that it is such a deep shade of red. She raises her finger to her nose but the blood doesn't really smell of anything. She opens her mouth and cautiously licks her finger. It tastes bitter and reminds her of the taste of the plastic skin on the cod liver oil tablets her mother used to make her take. She feels a little dizzy but otherwise she is all right.

She looks around for her brother but he is nowhere to be seen. Surely, he must have seen her fall, why hasn't he come to help her? She calls out for him, "Dafydd, Dafydd, please help me, can't you see, I've fallen and hurt myself? Where are you Dafydd?" But there is no reply. And then she remembers. There will be no reply, for Dafydd isn't there anymore. He only exists in her memory. But sometimes she is quite sure that he is still alive. For although they put up a gravestone for him in the cemetery, they never found his body. She and Dafydd were twins. They always knew how the other felt. Sometimes they even shared each other's dreams.

Rhiannon looks down at her knee again. It has stopped bleeding now. She tugs at a tuft of soft green grass until it comes away in her hand. She uses it to wipe away the blood that had been running down her leg. She doesn't feel dizzy any longer. She walks slowly down the steep slope to where the black rock stands. She climbs up onto the ledge as she has done so many times before. She reaches up until her hand finds the small round hole. She wants to be sure that the magic stone is still there. At first, she can't find it. She begins to panic, fearing that someone has taken it. And then, reaching right down to the bottom of the hole, there it is, just as she last left it. She doesn't need to take it out to look at it for she knows the feel of the magic stone. It is perfectly round and cold and smooth to the touch.

# CHAPTER TWENTY-THREE

Wednesday evening

Beth enjoyed the short walk with Mattie over to Llofft Plas. They talked mostly about life on the island and the interesting mix of people who made up the regular visitors. She was delighted when Llofft Plas turned out to be part of the sizeable stone barn next to Plas Bach, the whitewashed farmhouse she had admired on her walk up to Ty Pellaf.

"We could have put you up in the main house but we thought you'd be much cosier in here" Mattie said, leading the way across the yard and unlocking a door in the side of the barn. "I think you'll find that you have everything you need.

The ground floor room they entered was modestly furnished with a good-sized table and two chairs and a comfortable looking armchair. At the far end of the room were kitchen units housing a shiny metal sink and gas cooker, with a small Welsh dresser to their left. Next to the table there was a wooden staircase letup to the bedroom. True to her word, Mattie soon had Beth 'sorted out', showing her how the gas cooker worked, how to light the lamps and how to operate the chemical toilet outside in the yard. She also helped Beth to carry in her luggage and provisions which Harry had neatly stacked outside the front door. Even for someone as reticent as Beth, it was impossible not to take an immediate liking to the farmer's wife and to appreciate her kindness and generosity.

"I don't think there's anything else" Mattie said as she headed for the door. "You should be all right for gas; Harry checked the canisters the other day. Rhiannon will be round in the morning with fresh milk and eggs, if you need any. I do hope you'll be comfortable. Please feel free to pop round any time if need anything or fancy some company."

"You've been very kind and make me feel really welcome. Thank you so much. I look forward to meeting Rhiannon in the morning. Good night then."

When Mattie had gone, and she was on her own for the first time since arriving on the island, Beth realised how tired she was. It seemed a long time since she set out from the inn that morning. The excitement of the crossing, her arrival on the island and the challenge of meeting new people had been more than enough for one day. She decided to leave any exploration of the island until the following morning. From the small window above the kitchen sink she could see the lighthouse in the far distance. It stood out majestically against a darkening sky, tinged with flecks of gold and orange, as the sun sank below the horizon.

She decided to unpack before the light went completely. Picking up her rucksack, she climbed up the wooden staircase. The tiny bedroom had been built into the original loft space. With its exposed beams and its walls and ceiling freshly painted in white, Beth found it very much to her liking. The room was sparsely furnished, with two single beds, a small chest of drawers, a low bedside table and a colourful woven rug on the floor. She unpacked her rucksack, putting her clothes neatly away in the chest of drawers, then carried it back downstairs to find a home for its remaining contents. She placed her map of the island, books for her research, two notebooks, an assortment of pens and pencils, a large box of matches and several packets of cigarettes on the table where she would be writing up her notes.

It was quite dark by now so Beth lit the oil lamp sitting on the work surface next to the cooker and placed it on the kitchen table. She was pleased to see how much light it gave off as she would need it when she was working late into the evenings. She was thirsty after the effort of unpacking, so she filled the kettle, lit one of the cooker rings and put it down on top. She took out a packet of loose-leaf Earl Grey tea, her favourite, from the cupboard. She had already spotted a small, bright red teapot sitting on a shelf, very similar to one her mother had had when she was little. She remembered how her mother had treasured that little red teapot. It was as if it had been one of the few genuinely bright and cheery things in her life. Before long the kettle came to the boil. Mattie had explained that, although there was no fridge, she would find a cold food storage box outside the back door in which she had left her a jug of fresh milk. When she opened the box's wire mesh door she saw that, Mattie had also, thoughtfully, left her a tray of large brown eggs.

She went back inside, poured the boiling water into the teapot and left it to stand for a few minutes before filling a mug. She had been introduced to the delights of Earl Grey by a college friend who had come from a much wealthier and more sophisticated background. Her friend insisted that it should only be drunk with a slice of lemon. However, Beth had never taken to the idea, much preferring to add a little milk. This had not altogether endeared her to her friend who seemed to regard it as an act of idolatry.

'It is strange how one thing reminds you of another' Beth thought, as she stared at the red teapot. She had an image of her mother, standing at the kitchen table, teapot in hand, offering to refill her father's cup. She had been amused by this daily ritual because her father had always refused. But this hadn't stopped her mother from asking the same question every day. Like most northern lower middle-class families, they had taken their evening meal, or 'tea' as they called it, at six o'clock, soon after her father had returned home from work. It was only after she had gone off to university and started to mix with people from a wider social background that she had discovered that, to most of them, 'tea' meant a mid-afternoon snack. What had seemed even odder was that they took their evening meal later and referred to it as 'dinner'. 'Dinner', in Beth's parlance, had always been eaten at midday.

She reflected on how different her life was now to that of her childhood. Her ambitions had carried her far away from the narrow, repressive and ordered environment in which she had been brought up. She had never been close to her father, who had remained strict and aloof and generally disapproving of the life she had chosen. It was as if he thought that the whole of his daughter's generation was conspiring to devalue everything he had been brought up to believe. At times his anger was unabating. He was angry with local politicians for failing to maintain proper services; he was angry with the local newspaper for only reporting the inconsequential; he despised all those who came into his shop wanting something for nothing; but most of all he was angry with himself for failing to convince others of their stupidity.

Beth's mother, on the other hand, had been unconditional in the love, kindness and generosity she had showered upon her daughter. Although rarely able to stand up for herself against the railings of her husband, she always defended her daughter when he turned his anger in her direction. Although he would never admit it, Beth was certain that the main cause of her father's disapproval was nothing other than jealousy. He couldn't accept that she had the right to choose her own destiny. As a result, he refused to acknowledge her achievements. She knew that he considered her particular area of study to be a luxury in a world where, as he saw it, more basic human needs were crying out for attention. He was not a cruel man in the physical sense, or even particularly mean or inconsiderate. But his own background had been so philistine that he was simply not equipped to adjust to the changing times and rejected the 'new morality' out of hand. He had regarded it as his right and responsibility to determine how, where and with whom his daughter should live her life.

When she finally rebelled and chose to go off to university without his approval, he had been so dismayed that he hardly spoke to her for five long years. He had been equally disappointed that she had rejected a number of potential suitors he had lined up for her. These were, in his opinion, young men of good character, unswerving in their commitment to the local Methodist cause and with a proper regard for their civic responsibilities. It had only been over recent months, and after a great deal of pleading by his wife, that he had finally agreed to make peace with his daughter. Since then, Beth had made just one short visit home. To her relief, the atmosphere had been markedly more welcoming than she had expected. It was clear that her mother had worked wonders behind the scenes, because her father had managed to suppress his misgivings about his daughter's way of life. For her part, Beth had gone out of her way to appease him. She had even agreed to attend Sunday service at the local non-conformist church. It was the same church she had been obliged to attend as a child every Sunday morning with dreary Sunday School sessions in the grim, unwelcoming Victorian church hall.

Throughout the weekend of her visit Beth, recognised the effort her father was making to keep his narrow views under control. Much to his credit, he genuinely appeared to want to avoid any unpleasantness and ensure the weekend passed without incident. The reconciliation so fervently sought after by her mother had been just as difficult for Beth. Her father had never shown her any real affection. As a child, she had never sat on his knee and she couldn't remember him ever putting his arms around her or kissing her. The most she had come to expect from him was a reluctant pat on the back of the head. It was as if he was afraid of closer contact.

Her thoughts were interrupted by a sudden gust of wind rattling the kitchen window, which she had left open to get rid of the slightly musty smell that had taken hold over the winter months. She decided to go outside for a cigarette before preparing her supper.

She couldn't remember when she had last looked up into such a clear night sky. She walked down the path to where it met the track that led up from Ty Pellaf, then turned and looked back. The moon lay low in the sky behind the barn and cast giant shadows reaching out towards her across the rough field grass. There was a chill in the night air. She perched on the low stone wall marking the boundary between the barn and the open fields beyond. She felt in her pocket for the packet of cigarettes, took one out and lit it. She inhaled deeply, enjoying the first few moments of pleasure as the nicotine hit home. She knew that she was dicing with death but had found it impossible to kick the habit. In her stressful college life, it was one of the few things that helped her to maintain an element of calm. Her father always strongly disapproved of her smoking. But then that was only to be expected for he disapproved of almost everything that she did. She was cross with herself for allowing her thoughts to wander back to him. She stood up and looked out across the fields. The lighthouse itself was hidden behind the farm buildings but she could see its rotating light beam sweeping across the island. The wind had dropped and there was hardly a sound.

On a night such as this, it was possible to believe almost any of the myths and tales she had read about the island. She could see why St Cadfan had chosen to establish his monastic community here. The land was fertile enough to offer the monks a life of simple self-sufficiency and all the solitude they might seek.

She shivered. It was getting colder now and there was dampness in the air. The flickering light from the oil lamp inside the barn looked warm and welcoming. She was hungry and so she headed back inside. It was almost as cold indoors as it had been outside. She lit the gas stove which soon gave off a surprising amount of heat. She was almost as tired as she was hungry and settled for scrambled eggs on toast.

When she had finished eating, she reached for her map of the island. She needed to decide where to begin her explorations. It was only a mile and a half from one end of the island to the other. However, as well as the abbey ruins, there appeared to be a number of other sites which looked as though they might be worth visiting. These included some ancient structures which it could prove difficult to date. But, if truth be told, she already knew that she was unlikely to uncover much in the way of physical evidence to support claims that Bardsey was the true Isle of Avalon.

What Beth wanted most was to absorb the island's atmosphere and to find out as much as she could about its history. She was keen to learn what life was like for those living on the island many hundreds of years ago. Of course, Bardsey was best known for its inherent wild beauty and as a nesting place for thousands of wild seabirds. She wanted to see and enjoy all that too. She decided that she would set out the following morning to look at the remains of the abbey. It was only half past nine but she opted for an early night. She left her dishes to soak in the sink, turned off the gas heater, picked up the oil lamp and made her way up to the bedroom.

She undressed and was about to climb into bed when her eyes fell upon a row of books, neatly lined up on a small shelf beneath the window. She hadn't noticed them earlier on when she had taken her belongings upstairs. She assumed they were probably the usual assortment of detective stories, romances and other light reading you find in holiday accommodation. She knew she would find it easier to sleep if she read for a while and there might just be something there that would catch her interest. She crouched down in front of the bookshelf. As she had expected, at first sight, there didn't appear to be much of interest. There were a couple of P D James detective stories, several novels by Hammond Innes, Alistair Maclean and Dennis Wheatley, and a well-worn, hard-back copy of John Buchan's *Thirty-Nine Steps*. There were also a number of North Wales tourist guides and a handsome early edition of George Borrow's *Wild Wales*, published in the early 1870s. Finally, there was a small and insignificant-looking cloth bound volume with the intriguing title *I know an island* by R M Lockley, an author she had never previously come across. At first glance, she had taken it to be another novel. However, when she began to turn the pages she discovered it was one of the *Country-Lovers Library* series, published by George G Harrap & Co Ltd.

She took the book to bed with her and read on with growing interest. The author had made a study of the changing life on the main islands that lie off the west of the Welsh and Scottish coasts. Lockley was himself an islander. He had lived on Skokholm for some time and had written a detailed account of his first years on that island. Like the other islands Grassholm and Ramsey, Skokholm lies off the Pembrokeshire coast and is renowned for its bird life. He had clearly been an inveterate note-keeper. As a result, he had been encouraged by the editor of *The Countryman* to visit other islands and to write up accounts of them. This had resulted in the publication of the book that she now held in her hands. The list of contents revealed that Bardsey was one of the many islands he had visited. She quickly turned the pages until she came to the relevant chapter.

Beth was particularly drawn to Lockley's description of his crossing over to the island from Porth Meudwy. It very much mirrored her own experience, save for the fact that he had braved it in an open motor boat in the middle of winter. 'I looked up at the almost sheer hill above us' he had written 'only a strayed sheep, a raven, and a falcon could be seen along the height. Bardsey has turned its back on the world. To go there is to lose all sight and sound of the mainland — unless you are willing to climb 548 feet to the top of the wild hill to look back at Wales. Suddenly we swung round the southern shoulder of the cliff... and then we brought up in a low, sandy harbour. There was something very satisfying and grateful in that unexpected transition from high precipice to low fields. Bardsey is like that. There is no halfway scene. A mountain has been crudely cemented to a lowland valley and the whole thrown into the middle of a violent tide-race.'

'Bardsey has turned its back on the world'. Yes, she thought, what a perfect way to describe the island. She was surprised to read that on his arrival he had 'swelled the population of twelve men, including the pastor and three light-keepers, eight women, ten boys, and five girls to a round three dozen'. Over the past fifty years nearly every one of these people and their children had either died or left in search of a more comfortable and prosperous life on the mainland. It was such a sad tale. In the few hours since her arrival, the island had presented itself as a paradise on earth. But she could see that while visitors, like her, would be enchanted by the island's strong romantic appeal, those who had chosen to make the island their home might share a very different perspective. Normally she would have read on, but she was so tired that she put the book down, turned off the oil lamp and almost instantly fell asleep.

# CHAPTER TWENTY-FOUR

Tom was emotionally drained after his visit to the ancient church at Pistyll. So much so that he had spent the afternoon walking the cliff top paths in the hope of easing his mind. He had finally returned to the village and a lonely supper at the inn. Afterwards he settled for an early night with a P G Wodehouse novel in the hope of clearing his head of some of its darker thoughts. When he finally turned out his bedside light he almost immediately fell into a deep and undisturbed sleep.

He woke up soon after dawn feeling surprisingly refreshed. A light breeze blew in through the window, allowing the early morning sunlight to filter through. Later that morning he would be sailing across to Bardsey and his black mood of the previous day had given way to one of more optimistic, if not eager, anticipation. Whatever challenges might lie ahead, he was looking forward to reacquainting himself with the island where he had once found such peace and contentment. He relished the thought of having all the time in the world to explore every nook and cranny of the island. All that it remained for him to do after breakfast was to call at the village shop to order provisions to be sent over to the island for him each week.

As it was a good hour before breakfast, he had time to take a stroll down to the beach. He decided to head for the western shore rather than the more extensive eastern shore where he had been caught in the rain on his first evening. It was a near perfect morning with just a few wispy clouds scudding across an otherwise clear, pale blue, sky. He strolled down the stony beach to where the light waves of the outgoing tide washed the shore. His spirits were lifted by the sheer beauty of the scene and he began to feel more confident about the future. Life back home was far too complex with its many demands. But out there, on the island, he hoped he might be able to rebuild his faith around the simple things in life. Halfway down the beach he stopped to gaze into the far distance where the dark sea met a sky so pale it was almost pure white. There was something truly remarkable about the quality of light along this particular stretch of coast.

He leapt over a tangled pile of freshly washed up sea weed and stopped to take off his shoes and socks. Rolling up his trouser legs, he took a few tentative steps into the ice-cold shallows. He stood motionless for a while, watching the waves eddy and swirl around his feet. He enjoyed the tickling sensation as the retreating water sucked the sand away from under his feet.

Turning to look back at the village, his eyes were drawn to the seawall where he had chanced upon the distraught Beth. It looked so different now, bathed in the brilliant morning sunlight. It made the events of that mysterious evening seem even more surreal. His encounter with Beth had been deeply unsettling. On reflection, he was as disturbed by his own reaction as he had been by Beth's all-too-evident distress. For the first time since Martha's death, the incident had reawakened some of those emotions that had lain dormant for so long.

From the moment they first met, Tom had found that he wanted to know more about this uncomfortable young woman. He had worked hard to overcome her natural reserve. But when he had finally broken through it was as though she had been released from some unseen restraint. He had been captivated by her infectious enthusiasm and intoxicated by the gleam of excitement in her beautiful eyes. But then, how disappointing it had been when she suddenly withdrew as though she was conscious of having passed beyond some forbidden boundary. At first he had wondered whether he was responsible for the sudden change in her mood. But, on reflection, he could see that it was something else that was troubling her.

Their unexpected encounter on the seawall the following evening was an altogether different matter. He had been genuinely shocked when he heard her sobbing her heart out. He couldn't imagine what could be causing her so much grief.

It was what had taken place next that had most unsettled him. At first, he had convinced himself that his own reactions were entirely natural and honourable. But now he was not quite so sure. He couldn't put the delightful softness of her body when she had sought refuge in his arms out of his mind; she had clung to him as if her life depended on it. Nor could he forget the way in which she looked up at him. Her tear-stained eyes were so enormous that he felt he might be swallowed up in the intensity of their blackness. But what he remembered most vividly was the delicious scent of her hair when she buried her head against his chest, the steady rise and fall of her breasts and the compulsive shivers that ran through her body as she cried and cried until there were no tears left to dampen the collar of his jacket.

He had responded by willingly offering his protection. He had spoken to her as if she were a child. His soothing words had come easily. It had seemed the most natural thing in the world to hold her tight and run his reassuring hand up and down her spine. But now, in broad daylight, with the icy waters washing around his feet, he began to see everything rather more clearly. His response to the young woman's torment may have been generous, even compassionate, but it certainly wasn't simply the reaction of a disinterested bystander. Whether he liked it or not, he had to admit, he had fallen under Beth's spell.

Later, that night, when he had walked her back to the inn, he had wanted to ask her to share what had been troubling her. But, standing outside her bedroom door, his courage had failed him. And now he feared that that moment would never come for he would probably never meet Beth again.

He looked out to sea and watched a small fishing boat edging its way across the bay. He could just hear the sound of its engine as it pulled hard against the outgoing tide. He stooped down to pick up an almost perfectly round stone, lying where the sea had recently washed over it. It was jet black and glistening in the sunlight and he thought again of the colour of Beth's eyes.

# CHAPTER TWENTY-FIVE

On looking out of the window on her first morning on the island, Beth saw the clear skies of the previous day were giving way to a blanket of heavy grey cloud steadily blowing in from the west. The temperature had dropped sharply and she shivered as she stood by her bed, in her blue and white striped pyjamas. She reached for her dressing gown and made her way downstairs to put on the kettle. For Beth, no day truly got under way without a cup of coffee to awaken her senses. She had always been a deep sleeper. When she was a child, it had taken a considerable effort on her mother's part to wake her for school. She had continued to be a heavy sleeper into adulthood. So much so, that during her undergraduate years she had often turned up late to her morning lectures, white-faced and dishevelled. As she was known to be correct and punctilious on other occasions, this had greatly amused her fellow students who had nicknamed her 'the late-runner'.

She was spooning the coffee into a pot when there was a loud rap on the door. Surprised that anyone should call so early, she made her way to the door. Standing outside, enveloped in a dark brown coat, several sizes too large for her, and clutching a large brown jug, was a very pretty young woman. Her long golden hair hung well below her waist and her ruddy cheeks had a healthy glow about them. Beth noticed that she was swaying slightly, from one foot to the other, as if a little apprehensive. When she opened her mouth to speak, the girl stared down at the ground, self-consciously scraping the boot on her right foot into the gravel.

"Mummy thought you might like some fresh milk." She held the jug out in front of her and looked up tentatively. When she saw the friendly smile on Beth's face she was immediately reassured. "I'm afraid I tripped and spilled a bit on the way" she said.

"Never mind, I can see there's still plenty left in there. You must be Rhiannon. Your mother was telling me all about you yesterday. It's really kind of you to carry it all the way up here for me. I could easily have called down at the farm myself a little later on."

"Oh, it's one of my little jobs. Daddy says that I'm the island's official milk delivery girl and Mummy says it gets me out from under her feet. Anyway, I like meeting everyone."

Beth took an instant liking to this innocent, childlike young woman. She had never found it easy to relate to her own generation, but children and young people were a different matter. As an only child, brought up in a puritanical home, her own upbringing had been exceptionally lonely at times, and she had longed for a little brother or sister. However, her parents had not been able to oblige. To her great joy, their next-door neighbours had adopted a baby girl, when Beth was approaching her sixth birthday. Despite the age gap, as the two little girls grew up, they become inseparable and shared each other's secrets. Their paths only separated when Beth had gone off to study in London. They had stayed in touch for a while. But, sadly, as the years passed, Beth found she had less and less in common with her childhood friend, who had settled for a clerical job in a local bank. They drifted even further apart when her friend had married an insurance salesman.

She gave Rhiannon a reassuring smile, "I wonder, would you like to come in? I've just boiled the kettle if you'd care to join me for a cup of coffee."

The young girl's face lit up and Beth was pleased she had made the offer. She imagined life on the island would be lonely for someone of Rhiannon's age, especially now that she had left school. Rhiannon followed Beth into the kitchen where she sat down at the table and took a good look around while Beth was busy making the coffee.

"Do you take milk in your coffee?"

"Yes, please, and can I have three spoons of sugar?"

"Oh dear!" said Beth "I don't think I've got any sugar. I didn't bring any with me. I don't use it myself, you see."

"There used to be some in that pot over there", Rhiannon said, pointing to a large brown earthenware container on a shelf at one end of the dresser. "Mr Pollock left it behind when he was staying here last summer. I liked him. He used to tell me stories about the people who lived on the island in the olden days. He was very funny and he made me laugh. Mummy said he was far too kind to me and that I shouldn't call on him so often. But I told her that he really didn't mind. He said it was like having his own little girl all over again 'cos his daughter was grown up and had gone away to Africa. He used to give me ginger biscuits out of a big blue tin with a picture of a sailing boat on the lid. Do you like ginger biscuits? I like to dip them in my tea and they go all soft."

"Yes, I do. I like them very much, but I'm afraid that I haven't got any. But I tell you what; I've got a rather nice fruit cake I bought in the village, yesterday. I think it's homemade. Shall I cut you a slice?"

"Oh yes please. Has it got sultans in it, I love sultans?"

Beth laughed "I think you must mean sultanas. Sultan is the name for a prince in the Arab world. I haven't eaten any of the cake yet, so why don't I cut you a slice and we can see whether there are any sultanas." She took the cake out of the greaseproof paper in which it had been neatly wrapped and cut Rhiannon a generous slice.

"I haven't had my breakfast yet so I won't join you, but do tuck in" she said, putting the slice of cake onto a plate and passing it to Rhiannon.

While Beth poured the coffee, Rhiannon set about breaking her cake up into little pieces. When she had completed this delicate operation she looked rather disappointed. "I can't find any sultans!" she said.

Beth peered across the table to take a closer look.

"I think that's one there isn't it" she said "and look, isn't that another?"

"Oh yes" Rhiannon replied, with a broad grin. "That must mean it's a very special cake mustn't it? Whoever made it must know I like sultans."

Beth smiled but chose not to correct Rhiannon on this occasion. She was enjoying the company of the cheery youngster who appeared to have taken a liking to her. She remembered what Mrs Evans had told her about her daughter's learning difficulties. She thought it sad that this attractive young woman was unlikely ever to grow beyond childhood.

She watched Rhiannon munch her way steadily through the cake. The two pieces in which she had discovered the sultanas she had left on one side. She remembered how, as a child, she too had always left the best to the last, whether it was the pork crackling or the custard on top of the trifle.

"It looks like the cake was all right then." said Beth when Rhiannon was mopping up the few remaining crumbs.

"Yummy" Rhiannon replied, licking her fingers.

Beth was about to ask her about her life on the farm but Rhiannon got in first with a question she had been dying to ask ever since she had arrived.

"Mummy says you're looking for Arthur. I don't remember meeting him here on the island. Who is he and where did you lose him?"

Beth laughed. "Oh, I didn't lose him! You see, Rhiannon, Arthur is someone who lived hundreds and hundreds of years ago. He was a kind of prince or king who was very brave and fought lots of battles against the Saxons who'd come across the sea and invaded England. I teach history and this is the period I know best. Some people believe that Arthur's final battle, which was called the battle of Camlan, took place just along the coast from Aberdaron. They think Bardsey may be where he was brought after the battle when he was very seriously wounded."

"How did he get wounded?" Rhiannon asked eagerly

"Well you see, Arthur's last battle wasn't actually against the Saxons but against an army commanded by his nephew Mordred. Mordred had tried to seize power while Arthur was away defending the country, and so Arthur had to fight him to win back his kingdom. There was a very fierce battle in which lots of people were killed on both sides, including many of the leaders. At the very end of the battle Arthur and Mordred came face to face. They fought each other very bravely. Eventually, Arthur managed to kill Mordred but only after he had been very badly wounded himself. When the battle was over and his side had won, Arthur was carried from the battlefield by his supporters. He was taken in a boat, across the water, to an island which they called Avalon. It was all so long ago that nobody's quite sure exactly where the battle took place and so it's difficult to be sure where to find Avalon."

From the sparkle in her eyes Beth, could see that she already had Rhiannon's full attention and that, to her, Bardsey had already become the magical Isle of Avalon.

"What happened to Arthur when they brought him to the island? Did they mend his wounds and did he get better?"

Beth was about to answer when she heard approaching footsteps. There was a knock on the door. She found Mattie standing outside, looking concerned.

"I'm so sorry to disturb you Beth, but you haven't seen Rhiannon have you?"

"Hello Mattie, don't worry, she's in here with me."

Still puffing from her brisk walk up from the farm, Mattie put her head around the door. "Ah, there you are dear. I do hope you haven't been bothering Dr Davenport. She's very busy with her research you know and I'm sure she hasn't got all day to spend talking to you, young lady. And, in any case, I need you to feed the chickens. They were making a dreadful racket when I came to look for you and it's well past their feeding time."

"I'm sorry Mummy" Rhiannon replied, looking at her mother imploringly "but she invited me to stay for a cup of coffee. I've had a lovely slice of fruitcake with sultans in it and she was telling me all about King Arthur and the battle and did you know…"

"Rhiannon!" said her Mother sternly "I've told you before. It's very rude to refer to people as 'she' or 'he'. Dr Davenport has a name and I am sure she would prefer you to use it and to show a little more respect."

From the crestfallen look on Rhiannon's face Beth felt compelled to leap swiftly to her defence.

"It's alright Mattie. Rhiannon and I have been having an interesting little chat and she's been no trouble at all. It's rather nice to find someone who's so interested in my studies."

Rhiannon's face lit up and she pleaded excitedly "I want to hear what happened to Arthur after they brought him here, please tell me, oh please do."

"Perhaps another time Rhiannon. I think we should leave Dr Davenport to get on this morning. She's only just arrived and I'm sure that she needs time to settle in."

Beth saw the disappointed look on Rhiannon's face and said "I tell you what Rhiannon. Your mother tells me you know every inch of the island. I wonder if you might like to show me around."

"Oh, please Mummy, please I'd really like to do that. Can we go now?"

"Actually, I was thinking of a little later on today perhaps. You've those chickens to feed and I need to have my breakfast and to sort out my books and things. How about you come over again after lunch, if it's all right with your mother? Perhaps we could start off by you showing me the best way up the mountain. I'd very much like to get a really good view of the whole island?"

"Yes, of course, it's all right with me" Mattie said "but only if you're absolutely sure that she won't get in your way. As you've probably already observed, Rhiannon has an enquiring mind. I dare say that you will be tired of answering all her questions before you're halfway up the mountain."

They both laughed and Rhiannon did a little dance of joy, and then began to tug at her mother's sleeve

"Come on Mummy, let's go back home. I can feed the chickens and tidy up those tools that Dad asked me to put away in the barn. Then we can have some lunch and I can come back here. I want to show Dr Davenport my secret way up the mountain and she can tell me what happened to King Arthur."

"By the way, thanks for the milk, it's lovely to have it so fresh." Beth said.

"It's one of the joys of living a life of self-sufficiency" Mattie said. "Thank you for being so kind to Rhiannon. It's good for her to meet new people."

"I shall enjoy her company" said Beth "and I'm sure that she will be a splendid guide."

Mattie took Rhiannon's hand and they set off back down to the farm. When they were a short way down the track, Rhiannon let go of her mother's hand and began to skip lightly up and down, singing as she went. It was a bright and cheerful song that she sang in her own language and one that Beth had certainly never heard before. Soon mother and daughter were out of sight, although it was a while before the sound of Rhiannon's happy voice trailed away. When Beth turned to go back inside she had tears in her eyes, tears of regret at her own lost childhood.

# CHAPTER TWENTY-SIX

When Tom and his fellow pilgrims had visited Bardsey back in his student days, they had taken the coastal path from the village hall, where they had slept the previous night. They had carried their belongings and enough food to last them the three days of their visit. It was the same route that pilgrims had taken over fourteen hundred centuries. Many of them would have travelled great distances across England and Wales before reaching Aberdaron. More often than not, they would have spent several days recovering from their long journeys in the pilgrims' hostel, now a tea house opposite the Ship Inn. The pilgrims would have waited anxiously for suitable weather to make the dangerous crossing to the island. They would have taken this last short journey together to Porth Meudwy with mixed feelings of excitement and awe. The monks and priests amongst them would have led them in prayer as they made their way along the rugged coastal path. Medieval pilgrimages had, for the most part, been highly social events conducted in a festive spirit. There was no shortage of communal bonhomie. But this would have been a time to set aside secular thoughts to meditate on spiritual matters.

However, on this occasion, Tom travelled to Porth Meudwy in much the same way as Beth had done the previous day. If anything, the morning sun was even hotter, with hardly a cloud in the sky to be seen when he set off to drive the short distance to the Price's farm. He was by no means a man of modest taste when it came to food. But he had already determined to eat simply while on the island to suit the life of solitude and contemplation he intended to live there.

The short walk down from the farm to the beach brought back more memories from the past, not least of his former companions. He wondered what had happened to them over the intervening years. He assumed Father Beuno might well be dead by now and the other brothers Ninnian, Andrew and Mark would be well beyond middle age. He had a vivid memory of Father Beuno, clambering ahead over the rough terrain, his brown habit flapping in the breeze. He remembered the fine tenor voice of Brother Andrew, leading them in the joyful singing of hymns as they walked along the headland path. He was so distracted by these memories that at first he didn't register someone calling out from behind. And then the call came again:

"Tom, Tom, hi there, it's me, Max. Great to see you again. I guess you're on your way to catch the ferry to Bardsey?"

Tom turned. He smiled when he saw the cheerful faces of the young couple who had come to his rescue above the cliffs.

"Hello you two. I'm sorry, I was miles away. I was thinking about when I last came down here all those years ago. Lots of happy memories, and yes, you are absolutely right, this is the day I sail for the island."

"We thought we might come across to Bardsey ourselves sometime next week" said Kate, "Max is keen to look for the colony of Manx Sheerwaters and we'd both like to see the grey seals."

"Yes, and we might just be lucky enough to see some choughs and oystercatchers at this time of year" said Max. "Are you a bird man, Tom?"

"Well no, not really. Don't get me wrong, I love to see them and there are literally tens of thousands of sea birds on the island. But I'm no expert and can't really tell one species from another, I'm afraid." Tom looked at his watch. "Do you mind if I get a bit of a move on. I don't want to miss the boat, so to speak!"

"Of course not "Kate said "We're heading down there anyway. Max has booked himself a morning out with one of the local fishermen. Meanwhile, I shall look for a nice quiet corner, somewhere out of the wind, where I can settle down for an uninterrupted read."

"Well, that shouldn't be too difficult on a nice day like this."

"Do you know, by any chance, how long you get on the island if you take one of the day trips?" Kate asked.

"Oh, four or five hours, or something like that I believe. I suppose that to some extent it depends on the weather and the tides and time of year. At least you should get enough time to do some exploring and to look out for those birds and the seals."

"That sounds OK for a start. We might even be able to stay over for a night or two." Max paused and then turned to look at Tom. "If you don't mind me asking, seeing as you're not into birds but are planning a lengthy stay on the island... well, I can't help wondering what else there is to do there. Are you a writer or something?"

"Max, really, don't you think you're being a little nosy!"

Tom was amused to see how instantly Max's face turned red with embarrassment at Kate's admonition. He was far from ready to share the real reason for his extended stay on the island with his new friends, but he decided to come to Max's rescue.

"I don't mind you asking at all. Put it like this, my life's been pretty demanding of late, well, you know, things have been crowding in rather, as they can from time to time. For a while now I've felt the need to get away, to escape from the pressures that have been building up. Frankly, I need a good long rest and time to recharge my batteries. I shall do a lot of reading, a great deal of thinking and, possibly, a little writing. At first, if it doesn't sound too Zen-like, I shall try to allow the natural rhythms of the island to determine what I do from day-to-day."

"That sounds pretty wonderful to me" Kate said, giving him a warm smile.

"Wow, I doubt whether I'm cut out for that sort of thing!" Max exclaimed. "Don't you need to be a committed recluse?" And then seeing Kate glaring at him he quickly added "I guess what I'm really trying to say is that it doesn't sound like a very easy thing to do and I don't think I'd be any good at it. You must have to be amazingly self-sufficient."

"Yes" said Kate chuckling "and let's face it, you're too needy to be able to rise to such a challenge. You're just not that sort of person. I can't see you giving up your football or those evenings in the pub with your mates. You're far too fond of your home comforts. I doubt whether you've ever spent more than half an hour on your own without longing for the company of others. No, the one thing you weren't cut out to be is a hermit, that's for sure!"

From Max's crestfallen face Tom feared Kate had gone too far. But almost immediately he abandoned the exaggerated pout he had clearly put on for effect, and exchanged it for a broad grin. It was clear that Max and Kate thoroughly enjoyed winding each other up.

They continued their light-hearted conversation until they rounded the final corner just above the cove.

"That looks like your fisherman" Tom said, pointing to a swarthy middle-aged man with a bushy ginger beard. They watched him busily fold up a large piece of tattered tarpaulin and stow it away in the bows of a small clinker built open boat. It looked as though it was many years since the boat had last received a coat of paint.

"Yes, that's Jim all right. We got chatting to him in the pub last night and he kindly offered to take me out lobster-potting this morning. He's good fun and I'm looking forward to it. Well I suppose I'd better go and see if there's anything I can do to help. Have a fantastic time on Bardsey, Tom!"

They warmly shook hands. Max gave Kate a quick hug before hurrying off down the beach towards the fisherman.

Kate, meanwhile, had been looking round for a suitable place to set up camp.

"I reckon your best bet will be just round that corner" Tom said. "You can't see it from here, but there's a second little bay beyond that cliff. You should be able to find a sheltered spot there."

"Thank you, that's sounds like good advice. Gosh, it's quite chilly in the breeze down here isn't it? I think I'll put my sweater back on."

Tom watched Kate untie the sweater from around her waist and stretch her arms up to pull it over her head. With her long brown legs, and golden hair glowing radiant in the breeze, she reminded him, momentarily, of his beloved Martha. But he had little time to dwell on such thoughts for, at that very moment, he caught first sight of the ferry speeding round the headland, leaving a trail of bubbling white foam in its wake.

"Looks like your boat's coming in." Kate said. From their earlier conversation she sensed there was something deeply significant about Tom's extended visit to Bardsey. "I do hope everything works out for you. Who knows, but we may bump into you again, if we come over to the island. Obviously, we don't want to intrude, but it would be lovely to see you again."

"Yes, I'd like that" Tom said. He gave her a quick hug, turned and made his way down to where the ferry was about to dock. Looking out across the bay he saw that heavy grey clouds were blowing in from the west. There was also an unmistakable shift in the direction of the wind which now seemed to be blowing in directly from the open sea. For now, the sea itself appeared to be unusually calm. But he knew how quickly things would change if the wind really got up.

# CHAPTER TWENTY-SEVEN

Tom was relieved to finally reach Carreg Bach. One of the smallest and most modest dwellings on the island, it was full of character. Inside the solid stone walls, there was a living room and tiny separate galley area downstairs. The upper floor was reached by a wooden ladder, which had a single bedroom under a steeply sloping slate roof. It was so small that it could only just accommodate a modest double bed. 'I shall certainly be comfortable enough here over the coming weeks.' he thought to himself, noting the pile of driftwood and old fencing beside the open fireplace in the living room.

Despite the brisk breeze, it had been a relatively calm crossing and his earlier fears had been unfounded. He had been the only passenger and Alun Price had been happy to engage him in conversation, telling him about some of the dangerous crossings and near escapes the ferryman had experienced over the years. In return, Tom shared his memories of previous visits to the island. He recollected making the crossings in a much smaller craft, a large open boat with an outboard motor.

By the time they reached the island it had been early in the afternoon. The sky had brightened a little, although the sun remained hidden behind a thin layer of white cloud. Tom had wasted no time in calling at the farm to pick up a key. He had turned down Mattie's offer of a cup of tea and had immediately made his way up the track to Carreg Bach. He had wanted time to unpack so as to leave himself time to revisit the remains of the old abbey before darkness set in. On the way up to Carreg Bach he had passed by Llofft Plas, noting that considerable work had been carried out to convert part of the old barn into a holiday let. There had been no sign of life and so he had assumed that it was probably empty.

He was just settling in when he heard the hoot of a tractor horn from outside. Looking out of the window he saw his luggage and supplies being unloaded from the trailer by a well-built, middle-aged man. He opened the front door and hurried down the path. The aged tractor's engine was still running when he reached the gate and there was a strong smell of diesel fumes.

"Sorry about the stink. I daren't turn the engine off as it's a devil to get started again. Nice to meet you Mr Gregory. I'm Harry by the way, Harry Evans, Mattie's husband. I understand you're booked in for a lengthy stay. I hope you'll be comfortable here at Carreg Bach. It's small but very snug and you should have everything you need. I don't think you'll be disappointed, providing that you weren't expecting the Ritz that is!"

"I'm sure I shan't" said Tom "it's the simple life I'm after. The cottage is going to suit me just fine."

"Mattie and I have been wondering if you're a writer. We get quite a few of those out here. It's an ideal place for putting pen to paper. You'll find plenty of peace and quiet, that's for sure."

"Well, that's the main reason I've chosen the island" Tom replied. "I came here over 20years ago, three summers in succession. I was a student then and came on pilgrimages organised by the Franciscans. I fell in love with the place and have been meaning to come back for years. I intend to do plenty of reading while I'm here although I'm not actually planning to write very much."

Tom felt he had said enough. He hoped Harry would be satisfied with his answer. But he needn't have worried because the friendly farmer had been distracted by an unhealthy choking sound from the tractor's engine. He climbed back onto the driver's seat and opened up the throttle. There were puffs of thick black smoke before the engine returned to its more normal rhythm.

"I'd best be on my way before this old girl gets choked up again." Harry shouted over the noise of the engine. He waved, put the ailing machine into gear and drove off up the lane.

Tom stood watching until the tractor disappeared round a bend. Soon the only sound was of the breeze whispering in his ears and the occasional cry of a gull passing overhead. The clouds had thickened and the island lay spread out in front of him, a dark, almost colourless, expanse of flat land. In the distance, the lighthouse stood out, a solid bastion against the black sky, its rotating beam now clearly visible as it sent its warning of danger to passing ships. He looked at his watch. It was five o'clock. If he set off straight away there would just be enough time to visit the abbey ruins before night set in. It had become much colder than when he had arrived, so he hurried back inside to put a thick sweater on under his parka.

On the short walk up the track he was surprised by how much he could remember from his former visits. The cluster of buildings on his left as he neared the ruined abbey tower hardly seemed to have changed. It was in one of these that he and his companions had lodged on their last visit. He remembered how they had foraged around the farmyard for wood for their fire. Even in summer the nights had been chilly. Their party of 30 had occupied a number of the island's houses. Although they had eaten their main meals together they had taken it in turns to prepare breakfast in their separate lodgings. They had always started the day with a substantial cooked breakfast. They were young and the strenuous life they led together, rehearsing the play and exploring the island, had added to their already considerable appetites.

As he approached the entrance to the abbey tower, he felt a lump in his throat. It was here they had worshipped together, turning the interior of the ruined tower into a makeshift chapel. They had placed tall white candles and glass jars filled with wild-flowers on the stone altar. He remembered how, during the late evening Office of Compline, the light from the candles lit up the faces of the assembled company and how their shadows had danced around the stone walls. He also remembered the strength of the bond they shared in their common belief, knowing that they were gathered in the same place that Christians, unshakeable in their faith, had worshipped for 1400 years.

And where was he now in his struggle to understand the true nature of human existence and God's purpose behind it all? It was so dark inside the tower that he could only just see. He stared at the last glimmer of light coming through the tiny window above the stone altar. Any moment now the final curtain of night would fall. His surroundings were as dark as his inner emotions and his faith as insubstantial as that last glimmer of light.

# CHAPTER TWENTY-EIGHT

After feeding the chickens and completing her other tasks back at the farm, Rhiannon arrived on Beth's doorstep, breathless and impatient for them to set off on their adventure. When Beth opened the door to her, she looked out on a leaden grey sky. The bushes by the gate were shivering in the cool breeze. She saw that Rhiannon was wearing jeans and a bright red pullover. A green anorak was draped around her shoulders.

"Are you ready, can we go?" the young girl asked, hopping from one foot to the other with excitement. "Mummy says it looks like it'll rain later and that we shouldn't hang around if we want to avoid a soaking."

"Just give me a moment", Beth replied "I need to put my boots on and I think I'd better find a thicker jumper. I imagine it'll be quite chilly up the mountain."

A few minutes later they set off up the track, in the opposite direction to the farm. Rhiannon proudly led the way and Beth could see that she was thoroughly enjoying her new role as expedition guide. Soon they came to a fork where a path led off from the main track towards a small solid-looking stone structure.

"What's that building?" Beth asked.

"That's our little island chapel" Rhiannon informed her.

"Oh, do you still have services there?"

"Not very often. Sometimes, in the summer, Mr Pritchard comes over from the village and takes a service there for the visitors. Mummy usually comes over to give it a good clean and I pick some wild-flowers and put them in a vase on the step in front of the pulpit. Mummy says that if she came to give it a good clean every day it would still smell of damp. I don't like that smell. It reminds me of the school changing room. When it's hot and sunny we sometimes have the service outside on the grass by the abbey. I like that much more."

When they reached the chapel Beth couldn't resist trying the door and was surprised to find it was unlocked. The inside of the chapel was dominated by an enormous wooden pulpit. Otherwise there was nothing much worth noting. It certainly had a dank smell about it and there were some impressive looking cobwebs hanging from the rafters. She stood in the doorway trying to imagine what it would have been like when the island was more heavily populated. In those days the entire island community would doubtless have turned out for Sunday worship. She felt a tug on her sleeve and turned to see Rhiannon looking up at her impatiently.

"Can we go now please? I want to show you the way up the mountain."

Beth smiled. "Yes, of course we can. Which way do we go?"

Rhiannon pointed to a place where the path appeared to divide into two separate tracks.

"There are two ways up from here." She pointed to a narrow path that went round the back of the chapel. "That's the easy way, but it takes ages to get to the top. It's the way most of the day-trippers take. Daddy says it's because they live in towns and don't have proper boots and things" she said dismissively, and then added rather proudly "We islanders always go up the short way. It's quite steep but much quicker."

"You're the boss" Beth replied, flattered that Rhiannon hadn't placed her in the day-tripper category.

The young girl grinned, clearly pleased that Beth was game for taking the tougher route.

"It's OK, really it is. Just watch out for the loose stones" she said, setting off at such a pace that Beth feared she would soon lose sight of her. But Rhiannon had the good sense to stop now and again to wait for her to catch up. The first part of the climb was relatively straightforward. On either side of the path were a wide variety of wild-flowers, most of which she didn't recognise. They grew in clumps, almost hidden by the long coarse grass. However, as they climbed further up, Beth found herself having to clamber over jagged pieces of fallen rock partly concealed under the rotting remains of the previous year's bracken. On this last part of the climb, Rhiannon had raced ahead, leaping from rock to rock, with her golden hair streaming out behind her. Beth struggled on, grateful for her regular winter sorties onto the hockey field that meant that she was relatively fit. Even so, she was out of breath and her legs were aching by the time they finally reached the top.

She found it difficult to hold her balance now they were exposed to the full force of the wind. She saw Rhiannon had taken refuge behind a large outcrop of rock and was sitting on a flat shelf, staring out across the wind-tossed sea towards the mainland. Beth's hands were frozen and she dug them deep into her pockets. She watched Rhiannon run her fingers through her hair in a vain attempt to untangle the knots. She couldn't help thinking that she resembled a child from another era, sweet and innocent and wholly untouched by the contemporary world.

Even with her hood tightly fastened around her head, the wind was blowing with such force that Beth's ears were ice-cold. But thankfully the wind had blown away some of the clouds and there were occasional patches of the faintest blue through which shafts of sunlight illuminated first one and then another part of the distant coastline. The sea pounded relentlessly on the rocks far below and the air was full of minute droplets of salty water. Further out, in the channel between the island and the mainland, towering white-crested waves tossed their spume of foam high into the air. It was a daunting sight.

She made her way cautiously over to where Rhiannon was sheltering and sat down next to her. The girl turned to speak, but it was impossible to hear what she said against the howling of the wind and the cries of hundreds of swooping and swirling sea birds. Rhiannon grinned and pointed excitedly into the distance.

"Look" Beth just managed to hear her shout, "look, there's the ferry going back."

Beth scanned the channel between the island and the tip of the mainland peninsula and spotted the ferry, halfway across, rolling violently in the heavy swell. Apart from the skipper there only appeared to be one other person on board. Whoever it was had their hood up and was crouching low in the centre of the boat. At this distance it was difficult to tell whether it was a man or a woman.

Seeing the look of alarm on Beth's face, Rhiannon shouted "That's nothing. You should see what it's like in winter!"

Beth nodded. The two of them sat side by side, following the slow but steady progress of the small craft as it battled its way through the heavy seas. Neither of them attempted to speak again until the boat finally disappeared round the headland.

"They'll be all right now. It's the last bit that's so dangerous. Daddy says that lots of boats have got washed up on the rocks passing round the headland into the bay." Rhiannon shouted above the wind.

"I wouldn't want to cross over on a day like this!" Beth shouted back, "I'd be absolutely terrified."

Rhiannon smiled. "If you lived here all the time you'd soon get used to it."

Beth shuddered at the thought. She looked out again across the now deserted channel. She sensed that, if anything, the wind had increased in strength. It was far colder on the top of the mountain than she had expected and she regretted not having put on another layer of warm clothing under her jumper. Meanwhile, Rhiannon, who appeared to be oblivious to the cold, was pointing to where two gulls were struggling to keep their balance, perched on a rock far down below.

"You'd think they'd have more sense than to try to perch there!" Beth shouted.

"They're only playing. It's like a kind of dare to see who can hang on the longest."

"Rather them than me" Beth said, and they both laughed. She leaned forward to speak into Rhiannon's ear.

"I can see why you enjoy sitting up here, it's such a wonderful view." She paused for a moment. "But look, I don't want to sound pathetic but could we find somewhere a little more sheltered? I'm absolutely freezing!"

At first, Beth thought she detected a look of disappointment on Rhiannon's face. But then a new thought appeared to have entered her head, and she grinned back at Beth. There was an unmistakable gleam of excitement in her eyes.

"I know" she said "I could take you to our secret hiding place. Nobody knows about it but me and Dafydd. We often go there when it's wet and windy. When you're inside nobody knows you're there. But you have to promise not to tell anyone 'bout it 'cos it's our secret place."

As they had only met that morning, Beth was surprised and flattered that the girl seemed so willing to share this secret with her. She wondered who Dafydd might be. From her earlier conversation with the girl's mother, she had gathered that Rhiannon was the youngest child and that her siblings were grown up and living on the mainland. As far as she knew, there were no other children on the island. Perhaps Dafydd was an imaginary friend. After all it was not that unusual for lonely children to invent a playmate. She decided not to pursue the matter further at this stage. In any case, Rhiannon had already stood up and was impatiently tugging at her sleeve.

"Come on, it isn't far, but you'll have to be careful' cos the path is very slippery." She looked Beth full in the face. "And there's another thing. Our secret place is where magic things happen. You can only enter if you believe in magic, otherwise it won't let you in. If you promise to tell me a magic story when we're inside, I can whisper to the invisible gatekeeper that you're a believer."

"I promise" Beth said, fascinated by the girl's vivid imagination. "You lead the way, but please, don't go too fast. These shoes I'm wearing aren't really suitable for clambering over all these rocks."

Soon they were making their way down a narrow path along the top of the mountain towards the southern end of the island. In places the path was barely visible. After a short distance, it dropped down steeply away from the sea. Beth was glad to be leaving the dangerous cliff-tops behind. Rhiannon hurried on, jumping over the rocks that were strewn along their path. It took Beth all her energy to keep up with her. Eventually, she was relieved to see that Rhiannon had stopped a little way ahead and was waiting for her. When she caught up with her she saw they were standing outside what appeared to be the entrance to a small cave. Rhiannon crouched down and Beth heard her whisper what sounded like a string of magic words into the dark opening. Then she turned, beckoned Beth to follow, and scrambled through the narrow entrance on her hands and knees

Beth stooped down and stared into the cave. It was pitch black inside and it took a while for her eyes to adjust. Had she been alone, she doubted whether she would have had the courage to venture further. She had a natural fear of confined spaces. However, when she heard Rhiannon calling out to her from inside, she cast her fears aside and edged her way slowly forward into the black hole. Somewhere ahead of her she heard the sound of a match being struck and the narrow passageway was immediately filled with welcome light. Rhiannon looked back at her holding a small metal container in which she had lit a candle.

"So, this is your secret hideout" Beth said, taking a good look around. Although they were surrounded by dark shadows there was something quite enchanting about the inside of the cave. The candlelight was reflected in numerous flecks of a black mica-like substance in the ceiling of the cave, which glittered like minute shards of broken glass.

Rhiannon pointed to a dark crevice to the left of where Beth was crouching. "That's the way to the inner chamber" she said "nobody's 'lowed in there 'cept me and Dafydd. You have to squeeze through on your tummy."

Beth was relieved that she had not been invited to explore the inner sanctum. "I can see why this is your secret place." She said. "Nobody could possibly know it was here unless they came across it by accident. How did you find it?"

"Oh, it was Nell found it, not me. She's one of our collies. She went missing and Dafydd went to look for her. Mummy was worried 'cos she was 'bout to have puppies. Dafydd thought she might have gone up the mountain. You see, we often used to take her with us when we went on our 'ventures, 'splorin' and things. Anyway, when he got to the top of the mountain, you know, near where we sat down to watch the ferryboat, he said he could hear her barking but he couldn't see where she was, not anywhere. He spent ages trying to find her. He looked all over but she just kept on barking and 'though he called and called she wouldn't come. He knew he must be getting closer 'cos her barking got louder and louder. He was scared she might have fallen over the edge and got stuck on a ledge or something. He peered over but he couldn't see her and it was too scary to climb down. He'd almost given up when he found the path down here and then he saw her, standing there, with her nose sticking out of the cave. She'd 'scovered our secret place."

Beth listened with growing fascination. It wasn't so much the story itself that interested her as Rhiannon's vivid description. Whatever labels the Education Authorities might have hung around her neck, she was bright and enthusiastic and a natural communicator. Clearly there was much more to the girl than the label 'learning difficulties' might suggest. She could imagine how exciting it must have been for the two children to have discovered the cave and then made it their secret hiding place. It was certainly some way off the mountain's well-trodden paths. She remembered reading somewhere about there being a cave on the mountain that was commonly known as 'Merlin's Cave'. She wondered if this could possibly be it.

From what Rhiannon had told her it was clear that Dafydd was no mere figure of her imagination. However, some instinct held Beth back from questioning her further. She would ask Mattie about Dafydd when a suitable opportunity arose. Her thoughts were disturbed when she felt Rhiannon lightly prodding her arm.

"Come on then, you have to tell me your magic story, you promised."

"Yes, I did, didn't I?"

"Yes, you did and you can't break a promise."

"All right then" Beth said, leaning back against the wall of the cave and stretching her legs out as best she could in the cramped space. "Did you know that there's a cave on this mountain where Merlin was buried with the 13 treasures of Wales. Wouldn't it be amazing if it is this cave?"

"Who's Merlin?" Rhiannon asked with a puzzled look on her face.

To any serious historian this would have been a challenging question. After all Beth knew only too well that much of the mythology surrounding the Merlin of history had been fabricated in the Middle Ages. Historians of that era had been anxious to build up the romance and chivalry of the Arthurian Court to provide an exotic backdrop for their own times. But this was not a moment to dispel myths or to spoil the story so eloquently recorded by the monk Nennius in the ninth century.

"You remember me telling you about King Arthur this morning, back at Llofft Plas? Well, Merlin was a sort of wise man, a prophet and a bit of a magician. According to some of the stories, he lived at the same time as Arthur and became his closest adviser. But the story I'm going to tell you is about when Merlin was a young boy. At that time, there was a warlord called Vortigern who ruled over the Britons. He was like a kind of king. In those days, what we now call England was constantly being attacked from the far north by people called the Picts and the Scots. They loved fighting and they lived in what we now call Scotland. Vortigern found it impossible to defeat them in battle on his own. Well, about this time, two Saxon Princes called Hengist and Horsa arrived from across the North Sea and landed on the south coast of Britain. Vortigern welcomed them as friends and agreed they could settle and make their homes on the island of Thanet."

"Where's that, I've never heard of it before?" Rhiannon asked, stretching out her legs and snuggling up to Beth.

"It's to the south-east of London in the Thames Estuary off the coast of Kent. In Vortigern's time it was a proper island. But the channel between the island and the mainland has been silted up over the years and it's now attached to the mainland. Anyway, to continue my story, after Hengist and Horsa and their followers had been there for a while, Vortigern promised to give them clothes, food and other things they needed if they would agree to help him to fight his enemies in the north. But Vortigern had difficulty keeping his promise because the number of Saxons had grown so much. He suggested they should go back home as he no longer needed their support. But Hengist was very cunning. He could see that Vortigern only had a very small army and that he was weak. And so he offered to send a message back to his own country to ask for more some soldiers to be sent across so that he could help the king fight his enemies. But, secretly, he had a different plan. He wanted to rule these islands himself. Once he had a large army to support him, he planned to ask for more and more land where his people could settle."

Rhiannon frowned. "That's a dirty trick! Couldn't Vortigern see what Hengist was up to?"

"No, he couldn't. He wasn't very wise and so he willingly agreed that Hengist should send for reinforcements straight away. Before long, sixteen warships arrived. Over the following years more and more Saxons came over and took possession of the Scottish islands and of Scotland itself. They also settled in many parts of England on land which they forced Vortigern to give to them."

"We don't quite know what happened next. Some say that Vortigern took up arms against the Saxons but was defeated in battle, captured and only allowed to go free again when he promised the Saxons that they could keep all the lands and cities that they had captured. Others say that he disgraced himself by marrying his own daughter and having a child by her and that he was forced to flee in shame."

"He doesn't sound very nice to me" Rhiannon said, wrinkling up her nose.

"No, whatever the truth behind the different stories, Vortigern doesn't come out of it at all well. Anyway, you wanted to know about Merlin and this next bit of the story is where he comes in."

"Is this the magic bit?" Rhiannon asked excitedly.

"Yes, we're coming to that." Beth paused for a moment, hoping her story wasn't too long or boring for the eager-eyed young girl. "Well, whatever actually happened, Vortigern didn't know what to do next. He sent for his council of 12 wise men to ask for their advice. As you can imagine, they must all have been pretty fed up with seeing their leader lose battle after battle against the Saxons and their villages laid waste and their people slaughtered. They all knew that it was largely Vortigern's fault because who else had invited the Saxon leader Hengist to come over in the first place? They decided that the best thing he could do would be to get as far away as possible from the Saxons. They advised him to choose a remote part of his kingdom where he could build a strong fortified city. Here, he and his people would be able to defend themselves. Vortigern could see that this was good advice and he and his followers travelled through many parts of his kingdom in search of such a place. Finally, they came to the foothills of the mountains of Snowdonia and here, at last, they found just the right place to build their citadel."

"What's a city doll?" Rhiannon asked.

"A citadel" Beth corrected her "Well it's like a small city built inside a castle and surrounded by high walls so that everyone inside is kept safe."

"We went to Snowdonia last summer" Rhiannon said excitedly, "we went all the way to the top on the train. When we got there we had tea and Welsh cakes in the little café. And then Daddy made us walk all the way down again so that we could stop to look at the views and take lots of photos. I want to go again sometime. It was such fun, 'specially the train."

"Well I'm afraid that there was no mountain railway in Vortgern's time and I am pretty sure that there wasn't a café selling tea and Welsh cakes either." They both laughed. Rhiannon scratched her knee and then wriggled back to tuck herself up even closer to Beth.

"So, what happened next? You know, after they'd found this place to build the city doll."

"Citadel" Beth corrected her again but not unkindly. She found herself taking to this enthusiastic and affectionate girl with her many questions and all the innocence of a child half her age. She was flattered by Rhiannon's openness with her and was touched by the way she snuggled up to her without any apparent inhibition.

"Vortigern was pleased with the place they had found to build the citadel. It was high up on the top of a hill and easy to defend. There were clear views in every direction so they would be able to see if any of their enemies were approaching. He sent for the workmen whose job it would be to build the citadel — his architect, carpenters, stone-masons and labourers — and they collected all the materials they would need for the building work. But then, one night soon after, all the building materials mysteriously disappeared. There was nothing left at all."

"Whatever happened to them, where did they go?" Rhiannon asked looking very puzzled.

"I'm coming to that, but you'll have to wait and see. Anyway, the king ordered them to go out again and collect together all the materials that they needed. But the following night the same thing happened again. Everything disappeared. And the same thing happened a third time. As you can imagine, Vortigern could hardly believe what was happening and so he sent for his wise men and asked them what he should do, and you'll never guess what they said."

Rhiannon shook her head.

"Well, they told Vortigern that he must look for a child who had been born without a father. When he found him he should put him to death and sprinkle his blood all over the ground where they were trying to build the citadel."

"Oooh that's horrible. Why would they want to do that? And, anyway, where could they find a child without a father? There's no such thing!" Rhiannon exclaimed.

"That's why it's all such a mystery. You see in those days they really believed that such a thing was possible. They believed that there were evil spirits around that could enter into people and that these spirits could sometimes give a woman a child."

"That's horrid!" Rhiannon said looking quite shocked "Do you believe that they really existed?"

"I don't know for sure, but I very much doubt it" Beth said, seeing the worried look on Rhiannon's face. "This is only a story, but many, many years ago people really did believe in all sorts of strange things."

"Did they find the poor boy they were looking for?"

"Yes, they did. They sent messengers to search everywhere and eventually they came to a place where a group of boys were playing with a ball. They overheard one of these boys shouting at another, telling him that he would come to no good because he didn't have a father. So they went straight to this boy's mother to ask if it was true and she told them that she didn't know how he'd been born because she hadn't slept with any man."

"Isn't that a bit like the story of Jesus?"

"Yes, in a way, I suppose it is. But, of course, Jesus' mother Mary was given her child by God which is a different thing altogether. In this case, the wise men believed that the boy's father was an evil spirit."

"What happened next, did they kill the boy?"

"First of all, the boy, who was called Merlin, was taken back to where they had tried to build the citadel and locked up for the night. The next day he was brought before the king as they prepared to put him to death. Merlin asked why the king's servants had brought him there. Vortigern told him that his wise men had prophesied that the citadel could not stand firm unless his blood was sprinkled all over the ground on which it was to be built."

"Poor Merlin, he must have been very scared."

"I'm sure that he was, but then he knew something that none of them knew." Beth paused and put her arm around Rhiannon, who she could sense had stiffened with anxiety. "Merlin stood and faced the king. He asked him to call for his wise men to be brought before them. The king was surprised by this request but agreed to do so. When the wise men had assembled, Merlin asked them from where they had learned their prophecy. Then he turned to the king and asked him to ask his wise men what was hidden under the stone floor on which they were all standing. But the wise men were unable to say. So Merlin told them that if they dug a hole they would find a pool of water. And it was just as he had said; they dug the hole and came upon a pool of water. Then he asked the wise men to say what was in the pool of water. They couldn't answer this question either and by now they were beginning to feel rather ashamed. But, of course, Merlin knew and told them they would find two large vases in the pool. Once again, he was proven right. When they had pulled out the two vases he asked the wise men if they knew what was inside them. And yet again, they didn't know the answer."

"What was it, do tell me? I think it must have been gold or jewels or some kind of treasure."

"You'll never guess. You see, Merlin told them they would find a small tent inside each of the vases and when they looked inside, what should they find but two folded tents just as he had prophesied."

"We've got a tent for when we go camping, but it's far too big to fit into a vase" Rhiannon said, looking even more puzzled.

"Well, you see these were very small tents, more like canvas bags for storing things in. Now then Rhiannon, I' m sure you can guess Merlin's next question, can't you?" said Beth smiling.

"I 'spect he wanted to know if they knew what was inside the tents didn't he? That's what I want to know." The young girl called out excitedly.

"Well, how right you are. And as you'll have already guessed, of course the wise men had no idea at all what it might be. You can imagine how surprised they were when Merlin told them that in one of the tents they'd find a white serpent and in the other a red serpent. They unwrapped the tents and the wise men soon came across a white serpent and a red serpent just as Merlin had said. The serpents were lying quite still as if they were asleep. Merlin told everyone to watch them very carefully. Soon they began to fight each other and, before long, the white serpent, which looked as though it was the stronger of the two, threw the poor red serpent down three times. But, after a while, the red serpent regained its strength and managed to drive the white serpent away, chasing it through the pool until it crawled off and disappeared. Merlin turned to the wise men and asked them if they understood the meaning of what they had just seen, but not one of them was able to give him an answer. So Merlin turned to the king to explain. He said that the pool of water was the world and that the tent in which the serpents had fought each other was Vortigern's kingdom. He said the two serpents were really dragons. The red serpent was Vortigern's dragon and the white serpent was the dragon that belonged to the Saxons who had invaded their lands. The meaning behind what they had all seen was that before long Vortigern's armies would drive the Saxons back across the sea from where they had originally come. Merlin warned the king that he must not try to build his citadel where he had chosen as it was a place in which only Merlin himself would be able to settle down and live. The king must go to find another place in which to build his fortress."

For much of the time that Beth had been telling her story, Rhiannon had sat quietly, sucking her thumb like a small child, taking in every word. But now she was so excited that she could hold back no longer.

"What did the king do?" she asked, gripping Beth's hand.

"You'll be pleased to hear that Vortigern believed everything that Merlin had told him. He gave him all the lands around where they were. And it all turned out just as Merlin had prophesied. After a number of battles, in one of which Hengist's brother Horsa was killed, the Saxons were driven out of the kingdom by the king's son Vortimer."

"Is that the end of the story?" Rhiannon asked.

"Well no, not quite. Because Hengist did return later with a large army and many of the Saxons managed to settle in various parts of Britain, and there are many people today who are descended from them. But here in Wales, most people like Vortigern and Arthur are descended from the Celts who invaded Britain long before the Saxons and who fought so bravely to try to keep them out. The Celts were forced to retreat into Wales and Cornwall and parts of Scotland and Ireland, and that's why you still speak a different language."

"What happened to Merlin?"

"There are many different stories. However, the one that many people like to tell is that, when he was much older, he became an adviser to King Arthur. But I think that's a story for another day, don't you?"

Rhiannon squeezed Beth's hand affectionately and then closed her eyes tight shut. Beth saw that the girl's lips were moving and she could just hear her whispering very quietly but was unable to make out what she was saying. Then Rhiannon opened her eyes again and smiled up at Beth.

"That was a lovely story. I've spoken to the gatekeeper and he has given permission for you to come here whenever you want."

"Beth gave Rhiannon a hug. "Thank you. It's a very great honour to be allowed to visit your secret place and I'm sure I'll come here again." Then, looking at her watch, she said "do you know, it's nearly six o'clock? It'll soon be getting dark. I think that we should go back now, don't you?"

# CHAPTER TWENTY-NINE

After walking back from the abbey the previous evening, Tom had taken a light supper and sat back in one of the comfortable armchairs to read for a while. It wasn't long before the exertions of the day had caught up with him and he had made his way up to bed where, despite the troubled thoughts running through his mind, he had fallen into a deep sleep.

When he woke up the following morning, a shaft of bright sunlight was already playing on the wall at the foot of his bed. He sat up, stretched his arms above his head and took in a number of deep breaths, allowing the air to escape slowly. Once he felt life returning to his body he looked at his watch. He was surprised to see that it was already approaching half past eight. This was unusually late for someone who customarily rose at six in preparation for the seven o'clock daily Eucharist. 'What the hell' he thought to himself, 'I've all the time in the world.'

He lay back in bed for a while, enjoying the silence. He felt considerably more cheerful than when he had gone to bed the previous evening. It was remarkable what a good night's sleep could achieve. He wasn't conscious of having dreamed but felt that something must have taken place somewhere in the inner recesses of his mind to have brought about this change of mood. He stared at the shimmering pool of golden light on the bedroom wall and hoped it might be a portent of happier times ahead.

It was the sound of voices from the track in front of the cottage that finally persuaded him to get out of bed. He put his dressing gown on and made his way downstairs, half expecting that whoever was passing by was intending to call on him. However, the voices slowly receded into the distance and he saw that he had been mistaken. Now that he was up, he realised that he was hungry. He cut himself a thick slice of bread and filled the kettle.

While he was waiting for it to boil, he went over to the window. Looking out across the fields, he could see that last night's stormy winds had blown away much of the heavy cloud over the island. The piercing whistle of the kettle drew him back to the kitchen. Soon he was sitting at the rough-hewn table enjoying his first breakfast on the island.

When he had finished eating he poured himself a second mug of tea and sat down in an armchair. It felt strange to have so much time on his hands. There were no mundane duties to perform, no church services to officiate, no parish meetings, no hospital or home visits, no young couples to take through their wedding rehearsals or young boys and girls to prepare for confirmation. And yet he knew that the time he had been granted was not to be squandered. He fully understood the importance of taking a disciplined approach to the examination of his faith. He knew that it wasn't going to be easy. The overwhelming sense of emotional suffocation that he had experienced in the little church at Pistyll had left its mark. He was deeply apprehensive. He wasn't even sure that he would be able to reopen his prayer book without experiencing that same feeling of panic and desolation. So how was he to set about the seemingly impossible task that lay ahead? He felt that his main hope lay in finding inspiration in what others had written about their faith. He had brought a number of books with him which he intended to read over the coming weeks. He trusted that from somewhere within the writings of Knox, de Chardin, Bonhoeffer and others, he would be drawn back towards to an irresistible revelation of God's being. But before this could happen he needed time to consider the nature of his existence. That was why he had chosen to escape to such a remote and isolated island. He needed to be far removed from the pressures and distractions of a world in which he no longer felt able to function.

He was lost so deeply in his thoughts that he didn't respond to the first light tap on the cottage door. It was only when the knocking was repeated more loudly that he woke from his reverie. He stood up and was halfway across the room when there was an even louder rap on the door and he heard someone calling out "Hello, Mr Gregory, hello, are you there?"

When he opened the door, he saw a young woman standing on the step, clutching a wicker basket. In her other hand she was holding the swivel handle of a large white enamel milk can.

"Hello" the girl said with a cheerful smile "sorry to 'sturb you. I'm Rhiannon. I live at the farm. Mummy thought you might like some milk and I've got some eggs too, they were laid fresh this morning."

"That's very kind of you" Tom said, smiling back "I'm fine for eggs just now, thank you, but I would certainly like some fresh milk. Why don't you come inside I'll see if I can find a jug."

"There's a big blue one in the cupboard" Rhiannon said "that's what people normally use."

Tom crouched down in front of the cupboard and soon found the blue jug. He rinsed it under the tap, dried it with a clean tea towel and put it down on the kitchen table.

Rhiannon filled the jug to the brim.

"How much do I owe you?" Tom asked.

"Oh you can sort that out with Mummy later; I'm not very good with money."

"So you're called Rhiannon, that's a lovely name."

"Yes, I'm named after the goddess Rhiannon who married Pwyll. He was a prince you know" she said proudly.

"I'm not very good on Celtic folklore I'm afraid" Tom said "but it must be rather nice to be named after a goddess. Did she have golden hair like you?"

"I 'spect so", the girl replied looking down at the floor.

Tom could see that she was shy and decided to change the subject. "You've got lots of milk left in your can. Are there a lot of other visitors on the island at present?"

"No, not really. There's a couple staying at the bird 'servatory and a family with three young kids up near the abbey but they're leaving tomorrow. I've got a special friend too. I met her yesterday. She wanted to climb the mountain, so Mummy said it was all right if I showed her the way up to the top. We went the steep way, it's much shorter and we watched the ferry going back and I showed her my secret hiding place. You can only go there if you can tell a magic story, otherwise the gatekeeper won't let you in. And she told me all about Merlin and the king, I can't 'member his name, and about how they wanted to kill him and to sprinkle his blood on the ground so that they could build their city doll. But Merlin told them about the two dragons and the red dragon fought the white dragon and the white dragon ran away and the red dragon is the dragon of Wales."

This all came out in such a rush that Rhiannon was quite breathless by the time she had finished. Meanwhile, Tom was staring at the girl with his mouth open, firmly gripping the top of the table. When she saw the startled expression on his face Rhiannon asked anxiously "Are you alright Mr Gregory?"

Tom quickly checked himself and replied "Yes, oh yes, I'm fine thank you. It's just that I think I may know your new friend. I may have met her a few days ago in Aberdaron. I had no idea that she was planning to visit the island, she never told me. Can you remember her name? Is she called Beth by any chance?"

"Yes, she's a doctor and she's ever so clever and she's a really nice lady. She's staying at Llofft Plas."

"Llofft Plas" Tom repeated "Is that one of the houses up by the abbey?"

"No, it's really close to here. It's the farmhouse on the right when you go back down to Ty Pellaf. She's staying in the old stable. That's where I'm going next. Shall I tell her you're here?"

Tom paused for a moment. He hadn't expected this at all. Of course, he should have realised that Beth would be coming to the island. After all, she was bound to want to examine the evidence supporting Bardsey's Arthurian claims. How could he have been so stupid not to have foreseen this?

"If you don't mind, I think I'd rather you didn't say anything to her for the time being. I'm sure we'll meet up in due course but I need a little time to myself." He saw the puzzled expression on Rhiannon's face. He was sorry that he couldn't explain things to her in a way she would understand. But soon her frown turned into a grin.

"I know what it is. You want to give her a s'prise don't you? She'll like that, I know she will."

Tom nodded, relieved that there was no need to explain matters further. "You're a clever girl. That's just it. I want to surprise her. So, it's very important that you promise to keep this a secret."

"I promise. I love secrets and this can be our secret." The young girl said, picking up the basket and milk can from the kitchen table. "Shall I call again tomorrow?" she asked, as she headed for the door.

Tom smiled. "Well I should be all right for eggs for a day or two, but it would be lovely to have some fresh milk every day if it isn't too much trouble."

"Bye then" she said, opening the door and setting off down the garden path, singing cheerfully as she went.

Tom stood in the open doorway, watching until she had passed out of sight before turning and going back inside. The news that Beth was on the island had taken him very much by surprise. How strange it was that he hadn't foreseen this possibility. The real question now was what was he going to do about it? Didn't he face enough challenges already? But, perhaps he was assuming too much. After all, she had left Aberdaron without even saying goodbye, hardly what you might expect from someone who had taken a liking to you. The more he thought about it, the more he became convinced that his feelings for Beth were probably not reciprocated. And, under the circumstances, it would surely be better if this were the case. He decided that he would make no effort to contact her. He would bury himself in his books or walking the remoter parts of the island, where it was less likely they would bump into each other. He would stay his course and commit himself to a period of contemplative solitude.

# CHAPTER THIRTY

When Rhiannon called on Beth that same morning she kept her promise and made no mention of her conversation with Tom. Beth, for her part, showed little interest in the other visitors to the island. Her earlier encounter with Bert and Joan had hardly warmed her to the kind of companionship that might be on offer. Her only real interest was in pursuing her research.

Although it was probably a long shot, she was particularly keen to talk to Harry and Mattie. They were the last remaining permanent residents on the island. She wanted to know if they could throw any light on the Bardsey claims. And so, when Rhiannon called round with eggs and milk, Beth asked if she would mind if she accompanied her back to Ty Pellaf. She explained that she wanted to find out if there was a convenient time when she could call round to chat to her parents. Rhiannon's face lit up when she said this, after all Beth was her new special friend.

"Course you can come back with me. Will you ask Mummy if we can go 'sploring again? You haven't seen the seals yet and there's the lighthouse and lots of other places I want to take you."

"I'd love to see all those places, but not today, I'm afraid. I've got loads of work to do and you'd get bored if you came with me. But, tomorrow perhaps?"

When they reached Ty Pellaf, Rhiannon said goodbye and went off to feed the chickens. Mattie had seen them arrive and gave Beth a warm welcome. Beth explained that she needed to find out everything she could about the island and its history and wondered whether she might call round sometime to talk to Mattie and her husband.

"Of course you can" Mattie said "What about tomorrow evening, can you manage that? If you came round at six, you could join us for supper.

Harry and I are off to the mainland the following morning, one of our regular monthly trips to do some shopping in Pwellhi. We always call on our son Gareth while we're there. He runs a carpentry business in the town you know, he's doing very well. I'm sure Harry'll be more than happy to talk to you about the island. He knows so much more than me about the history and all that kind of thing. After all, he was born here. He's full of stories about the old abbey and the pilgrims who used to come here in their thousands. And he's sure to want to tell you about the kings of Bardsey and what it used to be like to live here."

"That really is most kind of you, if it isn't too much trouble."

"No trouble at all. We enjoy a bit of company. It can get pretty lonely out here you know, especially during the winter months. And Rhiannon's taken a real shine to you. She's talked about little else other than King Arthur and Merlin since you arrived! You've really got her hooked!"

"She's a sweet girl. She seems to want answers to everything. She clearly knows the island inside out and I'm sure she'll be a great help, if you don't mind her spending time showing me around."

"As long as she doesn't get in your way. I'm afraid she doesn't always understand when she's not wanted."

"I'm sure we'll get along fine" Beth replied, putting her hand reassuringly on Mattie's arm. "She's so bright and cheerful, it's lovely to have her around and, as I've said, I think she may well prove to be very helpful to me in my research."

"Well, you must say if she becomes a nuisance."

"Don't worry, I shall. Anyway, I'd better be off. See you tomorrow evening then and thanks so much for the invitation."

"We shall look forward to it."

Beth called back at Llofft Plas to pick up her rucksack before making her way up the track towards the abbey ruins. As she approached Carreg Bach she saw a pair of wellington boots and a stout walking stick outside the front door. She also noticed that one of the small downstairs windows was wide open. She couldn't remember seeing any sign of life there when she and Rhiannon had passed by the cottage the previous day. She assumed a new visitor must have just moved in. When she drew level with the cottage, she heard the sound of a man's voice from inside. Something about it struck her as being odd. It didn't sound in the least bit conversational. It was more as if someone was reciting something from memory.

She walked on past the cottage, not wishing to appear inquisitive. She had only taken a few more steps when the recitation came to an end. There was a short pause and then she heard the voice again, this time singing. She stopped to listen. Although she didn't recognise the tune, she was familiar with the words. They came from one of the psalms she had been made to memorise as a child. A soft, mellow baritone voice floated out into the crisp morning air. The words were quite distinct and there was an edge to the voice, almost as if it was pleading to be heard.

*"Like as the hart desireth the waterbrooks,*
*so longeth my soul after thee, O God.*
*My soul is athirst for God,*
*yea, even for the living God.*
*When shall I come to appear before the presence of God?*
*My tears have been my meat day and night,*
*while they daily say unto me,*
*"Where is now thy God?"*

This was followed by a long silence. Beth shivered. There had been something forlorn, even desperate, about the way in which the voice had trailed away. And then the silence, what was that all about? She walked on slowly, looking back over her shoulder from time to time. But there was no further sign of life from the cottage.

She continued up the track. The sun was now shining, there was hardly a cloud in the sky and the wind had dropped. It was pleasantly warm but as she approached the ruined abbey the grass under her feet was still damp from the early morning dew.

Apart from the crumbling remains of the tower, which was leaning at a precarious angle, there was little else left of the old abbey. Beth had read somewhere that the Breton monk St Cadfan had been invited to found the abbey by Einion Frenin, the 'golden-handed Prince of Lleyn'. Cadfan was said to have arrived on the island with 25 kinsmen. The original buildings would almost certainly have been of timber. The monk's life would have been a simple one devoted mainly to prayer, offering hospitality to pilgrim guests, growing their own vegetables and wheat for bread and gathering fish from the sea. Later on the abbey had been taken over by the Augustinians. It was soon after that the Pope had declared that three pilgrimages to Bardsey were equal to a visit to Rome. From then the abbey had begun to flourish as a major centre of pilgrimage. Despite the paucity of the remains, she had little difficulty imagining what a hive of activity St Mary's abbey must have once been. There had been a fine bell tower with six bells and a scriptorum where the monks had produced fine manuscripts. It had been torn down during Henry V111's Dissolution of the Monasteries. No doubt most of the stone had been recycled over the years by grateful generations of the island's inhabitants.

If there was any truth in the legend that the wounded Arthur had been brought to Bardsey after the battle of Camlan, it would, almost certainly, have been in the days when Cadfan had presided over the island's newly founded monastery. This may also have been during the time that the elderly St Dubricius, or Dyfrig as he was known to the Celts, was living on the island, in retirement from his former role as Archbishop of Wales. Beth leaned against the tower wall. She closed her eyes and tried to visualise how it would have looked after the monks had erected the first wooden buildings of their modest religious settlement. What a haven of peace and tranquillity it must have been. The monks would have lived an ordered life, with regular prayer and worship. But this was long before the highly disciplined rules of the Augustinians and other religious orders had been established, and there would have been a much more relaxed atmosphere as the monks went about their daily lives. Above all, there would have been a powerful bond of camaraderie between the brothers. She felt sure that there would have been much laughter and joy within the community.

Beth was so wrapped up in her imaginings that she failed to hear the soft tread of approaching footsteps. It was only when she felt the light touch of a hand on her shoulder that she turned and saw Rhiannon standing beside her.

"Hello. I know Mummy says I mustn't 'sturb you when you're working. But I've been watching and you don't really seem to be very busy. I can go away again if you want...'

Beth put her hand on Rhiannon's arm "It's all right, really it's fine." She smiled to reassure the girl who immediately smiled back. "Actually, I was just trying to imagine what life was like here when they built the first abbey."

"It must have been very quiet then, with just a few old monks saying their prayers and things."

"Actually, I'm not so sure that it was all that quiet. You see, I expect the monks would have been very happy with their lives, always laughing and teasing each other as people so often do when they live together in a community. And then, of course, there were all those hundreds of pilgrims who used to come to the island. They'd have been a noisy lot. They'd have been so pleased to have got to the end of their journey and had lots of stories to share about their adventures on the way. Travelling any long distance in those days could be a dangerous business. The richer pilgrims would have ridden on horseback but everyone else would have made the journey on foot, with their few essential belongings stacked on a horse-drawn cart. They'd have had to watch out for robbers and thieves as they made their way through the dense forests on their journey. You see, much more of the countryside was covered in trees in those days. There were no proper doctors to go to if someone fell ill. If they made their journey in winter they would often have to struggle through rain and snow. Sometimes, they would travel many miles without passing a single inn or farm. They must have often felt very hungry. And, to crown it all, at the end of their journey they had to face the dangerous crossing from Porth Meudwy. They would have been rowed across in open boats, nothing like Mr Price's fine boat with its powerful outboard motors. Most pilgrims would have never seen the sea before and so it would have been very frightening.

Rhiannon was sitting cross-legged on the grass at Beth's feet, listening intently to every word. Until now, the crumbling remains of the abbey tower had been nothing much more to her than a pile of old stone. But now it was all beginning to come alive and she was bursting with questions.

"If it was such a dangerous place to get to, why did the monks come here?" she asked.

"That's a very sensible question. From the very earliest days of Christianity there were always some people who wanted to escape from the hustle and bustle of daily life. There are still people who choose to do that today because they think it's the best way to get close to God. Years and years ago there were quite a lot of people who chose to do this all on their own and we call them hermits. They'd go off into the desert or the mountains or to an island like this and live the simplest of lives making their home in a cave or simple wooden shack and spending all their time in prayer."

"Is that why they're called hermit crabs? They burrow into the sand and into tiny cracks in the rock, I've seen them."

"Yes, I'm sure you're right" Beth said with a smile. "But while a few people chose to go off on their own, more people preferred to live together in communities. Some of those communities cut themselves off almost completely from the outside world. Others would spend part of the day in worship but would welcome visitors, as they used to do here at St Mary's Abbey. There were even communities where the monks or nuns saw it as their duty to go out into the world to tell people about Jesus and to give support to the poor."

Rhiannon continued to ply Beth with questions until she was finally satisfied. Then, looking up and seeing how far the sun had travelled across the sky, she frowned and said "It must be nearly lunchtime. I promised Daddy I'd help him move the cows into another field so I'm 'fraid I'll have to go now."

"Of course, off you go then. But just before you do I've got a question for you. On my way up here I passed that little cottage that stands back off the track. It looks like someone's moved in since yesterday morning. I was wondering, do you know who it is?"

Rhiannon pursed her lips and Beth noticed that she was rubbing her fingers together and looking slightly anxious. "I'm sorry but it's a secret. I promised I wouldn't tell anyone!"

Beth was surprised by her answer. However, she took the girl at her word and didn't pursue the matter. Unless her new neighbour was a total recluse, she felt sure that she would find out for herself in due course.

"Never mind, it's no matter. You'd better be off then Rhiannon. I'll see you tomorrow at supper time. Your Mum has very kindly asked me over so that I can chat to your Dad about the island."

"Yes, Mummy said. I can't wait. Don't be late will you."

"I'll try not to be." Beth waved as the young girl ran off down the lane. She was beginning to appreciate how much she enjoyed her company.

She took one more look round. If the Arthurian legends associated with the island were to be believed, the monks were not the only inhabitants in the time of Cadfan. For it was here that the Lady Morgan was reputed to have received the wounded Arthur after the battle of Camlan. She reached inside her rucksack and took out the slender volume of Geoffrey of Monmouth's 'Vita Merlini' and sat down on a low stone wall. She wanted to read again the passage in which the poet Taliesin described this dramatic episode.

*"There nine sisters rule by a pleasing set of laws those who come to them from our country. She who is first of them is more skilled in the healing art, and excels her sisters in the beauty of her person. Morgan is her name, and she has learned what useful properties all the herbs contain, so that she can cure sick bodies. She also knows an art by which to change her shape, and to cleave the air on new wings like Daedalus; when she wishes she is at Brest, Chartres or Pavia, and when she will she slips down from the air onto your shores. And men say that she has taught mathematics to her sisters, Moronoe, Mazoe, Gliten, Glitonea, Gliton, Tyronoe, Thitis; Thitis best known for her cithern. Thither after the battle of Camlan we took the wounded Arthur,*

*guided by Barinthus to whom the waters and the stars of heaven are well known. With him steering the ship we arrived there with the prince, and Morgan received us with fitting honour, and in her chamber she placed the king on a golden bed and with her own hand she uncovered his honourable wound and gazed at it for a long time. At length she said that health could be restored to him if he stayed with her for a long time and made use of her healing art. Rejoicing therefore, we entrusted the king to her and returning spread our sails to the favouring winds."*

She closed the book and sat for a while. 'Such a fantastical story' she mused, 'but most such stories are founded on at least some elements of truth. If Morgan and her sisters really did live on the island at the same time as Cadfan and his community, I wonder how they got on?' She chuckled when she considered what a challenging diversion nine beautiful young women would have presented to Cadfan's religious community.

# CHAPTER THIRTY-ONE

Not long after the unsuspecting Beth passed by his cottage, Tom prepared to go in search of a remote corner of the island where he could be sure to be alone. He put on a thick pullover, packed sandwiches and a thermos of coffee and set off down the track towards Ty Pellaf. The sun was at its zenith and the island was flooded in a silvery light that left the fields looking bleached and colourless. Once he passed the farm, he continued on down the track towards the harbour. There were a couple of skiffs pulled up on the shore but not a soul to be seen. As he headed for the narrow strip of land that led to the promontory where the lighthouse stood, he remembered that somewhere near the track to the lighthouse he would find a small bay, with a good stretch of soft white sand and a scattering of large rocks.

It was much as he had remembered. As soon as he clambered down onto the narrow strip of beach he was protected from the worst of the stiff breeze that had followed him all the way from the harbour. A few feet away the waves washed lightly over the jagged outcrops of rock that ran out into a relatively calm sea. He found a suitable place to settle between two large rocks with a clear view of the sea. He took out a rug from his rucksack which he laid out on the sand and sat down.

Tom leaned against a rock and reached inside the rucksack for the leather-bound notebook he always carried with him. This contained a lifetime's collection of his favourite poems, prayers and extracts from his extensive theology library. There were also literary quotations and personally written accounts of interesting occurrences he had considered worth recording.

He clasped the notebook to his chest where it remained unopened while he surveyed the scene in front of him. He took in a deep breath, savouring the smell of the sea. Earlier that morning he had struggled to remain focused while saying Mattins. He had not experienced the depth of melancholy that had overcome him at Pystyll. But he had felt uneasy. The words had seemed almost too familiar. He had felt as though his faith was on hold but his instinct told him that it was essential to maintain the discipline of saying the Daily Offices.

He turned his head slowly, taking in every detail of the wild seascape. He watched the sea birds nestling on the black rocks that ran out into the sea. They seemed to know instinctively when one of the approaching waves was about to wash over the rock on which they were so precariously perched, frantically flapping their wings and taking off like miniature jump jets. Other birds were flying low over the water, swooping down in search of their prey. Further along the beach, long strands of green and yellow seaweed lay abandonned above the tide line. From where he was sitting, the sea was a deep blue-black as dark as the colour of the ink he had used as a schoolboy. The scattering of clouds rarely seemed to change shape as they slowly passed over. Tom leant back onto the hard rock and closed his eyes. He waited for his other senses to fully savour the sound of the birds and the sea and the pleasant salty taste of the air.

He sighed. It wasn't so much a sigh of contentment, more an expression of relief at escaping the demands of everyday life. His home town felt a million miles away, as did his parish and its people and the many demands they made on him. One day, hopefully, they would become his responsibility again. But not before he had found a way of renewing his faith and reconciling himself to the loss of the one person who had sustained him throughout the challenging years of his ministry. At times, the burden of his two-fold loss had seemed too heavy to bear and the road to recovery impassable. But this morning he felt that there was a faint glimmer of hope. How wise Bishop George had been to insist on sending him away.

He opened his eyes and stretched out his legs. He put his notebook down on the rug and reached inside his rucksack for his thermos flask. When he had satisfied his thirst, he leaned back against the rock again and opened his notebook. The notebook was well-ordered and neatly written. The contents were grouped together under key headings. Here and there, selected passages were heavily underlined in red ink to emphasise their particular significance. He had kept the notebook assiduously since his college days and it had regularly provided him with useful material for his sermons. It had also provided a source of continuing inspiration.

When Tom had visited Bardsey as a student pilgrim, he and his companions had spent three days on the island where they had rehearsed the play that they would subsequently put on in several parish churches on their way to Bangor Cathedral. Often they had walked in silent contemplation as they progressed from one parish to the next. Father Beuno would choose a subject on which they were expected to meditate. More often than not he would come up with a single word for them to contemplate, like 'love', 'community', 'sunshine' or 'faith'. This had proved to be such an effective way of focusing the mind that it had stayed with Tom throughout his ministry and he had regularly continued the practice.

He turned the pages of the notebook until he came to the subject heading 'Faith'. 'Not a bad place to begin my journey he thought'. The first entry was a quotation from St Augustine of Hippo "Faith is to believe what you do not yet see: the reward for this faith is to see what you believe."

'That's all very well, I've been there before' Tom mused 'but I'm not yet ready to take that path again.' The next entry was a short quotation from Samuel Butler, "You can do very little with faith, but you can do nothing without it". Tom thought that a little too clever to jostle with in his present state of mind.

The entry that followed was heavily underlined in red ink. It was a quotation from *The Comedians* by Graham Greene. "If you have abandoned one faith, do not abandon all faith. There is always an alternative to the faith we lose. Or is it the same faith under another mask?" 'Hmm, I can see why I liked that one so much' Tom thought "and I suspect I'll be returning to it again."

There were then a number of biblical quotations, including one he often shared with others. It was from Hebrews: "Faith is the substance of things hoped for, the evidence of things not seen". He felt that for the time being, that degree of faith was well beyond his grasp. As he continued to read through the many entries he began to regret opening the notebook in the first place. He was disturbed that others were able to find such fine words to explain something which he found to be so frustratingly intangible.

He turned to the next page where he came across a short poem by Emily Dickinson that he had completely forgotten.

> 'I never saw a Moor -
> I never saw the Sea -
> Yet know I how the Heather looks
> And what a Billow be.
>
> I never spoke with God
> Nor visited in Heaven -
> Yet certain am I of the spot
> As if the Checks were given.'

It was such a simple poem and yet it contained sublime elements of the metaphysical. He had often wondered where Dickinson's remarkable gift of imagination had come from. She had lived such a sheltered life in a comfortable home in nineteenth-century Massachusetts. He remembered that he had written down another of her poems somewhere in the notebook, something to do with the soul and the sea. He thumbed through the pages until he found it. The poem was called 'Joy':

> Exultation is the going
> Of an inland soul to sea,
> Past the houses, past the headlands,
> Into deep eternity!
> Bred as we, among the mountains,
> Can the sailor understand

*The divine intoxication*
*Of the first league out from land.*

He re-read the poem, this time out loud. Whatever the extent of his current confusion, it was hard not feel some sense of hope as he pondered these lines, looking out at the deserted beach, drenched in the pure white sunlight of early spring.

But beneath this feeling of hope there lurked a growing sense of anger. He was now close to acknowledging a dreadful truth. It was a truth he had been trying to avoid for months but it had been creeping up on him. Wasn't it obvious? All he had to do was to look around to know that God existed. The order and beauty of this world could not possibly be here by accident. It may have taken millions of years to evolve and, doubtless, would go on evolving into the infinite future. But surely, somewhere, behind everything that existed, there must be the hand of a creator God. The truth that he had been trying to avoid wasn't that God didn't exist. It was a more dreadful truth. The God he had strived to serve so faithfully throughout his ministry had abandoned him. Why else would he have allowed Martha to die so needlessly?

He shivered. The sun had disappeared behind an ominous looking blanket of black cloud and it was getting colder. The beach no longer seemed so welcoming. A tear trickled down his cheek. He had never felt quite so alone.

# CHAPTER THIRTY-TWO

Late in the afternoon, soon after returning from her visit to the abbey, Beth looked out of the window at Llofft Plas and saw someone making their way up the track. The approaching figure was tall and thin. It was too late in the day for it to be one of the day- trippers. She wondered whether it could be the new occupant of the nearby cottage. As the figure approached there was something familiar about the way in which he stooped forward as he walked. Her natural sense of curiosity got the better of her. Opening the door she hurried down the path, reaching the gate, just as the stranger drew level.

"Hello" she called out "I see the weather has taken a turn for the worse."

The man stopped dead in his tracks. He had been so busy shielding himself from the wind that he had not seen Beth emerge from the house. He had hoped to pass by without being observed. As he didn't answer her immediately, Beth feared that she had in some way offended him. She hesitated before continuing:

"I'm so sorry, I can see that your thoughts must have been elsewhere. I do hope that I haven't taken you too much by surprise. You see, I was just wondering whether, by any chance, you might be my new neighbour from the little cottage just up the lane?" She pointed towards Carreg Bach.

"Ah, yes, indeed I am" he replied and then, feigning surprise as if he had only just recognised her, he pushed back his hood and said "Goodness me, it's Beth isn't it, what are you doing here?... I had no idea..."

Beth stood with her mouth open, staring at the dishevelled figure standing in front of her with an embarrassed grin on his face.

"Well, I'll be... this is a surprise! I didn't expect to see you here Tom!"

They stood looking at each other, neither knowing quite what to say next. And then Beth smiled and said:

"Look, it's quite nippy out here, the kettle's on and you look as if you could do with a hot drink, why don't you come in?"

When he saw how her face lit up when she smiled, Tom felt his earlier resolve weakening. In any case, he could hardly turn down her invitation, that would be altogether too discourteous. They were on a tiny island, scarcely a mile and a half long. However hard he might have tried to avoid her, they were bound to have bumped into each other at some stage.

"Well, if it isn't too much trouble? It is damnably cold out here and that offer of a cup of tea is altogether far too tempting."

They made their way inside. Tom put his rucksack down near the front door and hung his coat up. Looking around, he saw that the modest downstairs room was not unlike his own, simply furnished but warm and comfortable with all the basic needs provided for.

Beth pulled out a chair. "Why don't you sit down at the table while I make the tea and you can tell me what you've been up to over the last couple of days?" She pushed aside a small pile of books to make room for him.

"You must forgive me, I'm hopelessly untidy, I always have been."

She walked over to the cooker where the kettle had come to the boil and poured the steaming hot water into a large red teapot.

"I think we'll let that stand for a minute or two if you don't mind. I can't bear tea that hasn't brewed properly."

"I couldn't agree more" Tom said "My mother liked her tea so weak that father used to describe it as gnat's piss!" They both laughed. Beth leant back against one of the kitchen units. He sensed there was something she wanted to say but wasn't sure whether she should. He smiled and this seemed to reassure her. He watched her take a deep breath.

"I've so much been hoping that you would come over to the island. Please don't misunderstand me. I realised, of course, that there wasn't really any reason why you should, at least, not to see me. After all we hardly know each other and, besides, you probably think I'm a complete fruit and nut-case who ought to be locked up. It's just that... well that last time we met, I've thought about it so many times. The thing is, if nothing else, I... I feel I owe you some kind of an explanation for my odd behaviour that night. But then I thought you probably had other plans and, even if you didn't, you'd want to run a hundred miles rather than put up with me and my obvious paranoia."

Tom smiled, but didn't reply immediately. She turned to take two mugs from the shelf. Unlike the last time he had seen her when her thick dark brown hair had hung down below her shoulders, it was now neatly tied up in a ponytail, exposing her long and slender neck. What a strange enigma this young woman was. If she had been so keen to see him again, why had she had left the inn so abruptly without telling him where she was going. He had suspected that she was not entirely without feelings for him. Had her initial instinct been to flee to avoid the risk of further involvement? After all, had he not felt rather the same way, even if it was for an entirely different reason? It would hardly be surprising if she had nursed similar doubts to his own. Their last encounter had been exceptionally strange. It would not be in the least bit surprising if she was embarrassed at having exposed her vulnerability to a virtual stranger.

While these thoughts were running through his head, Beth had poured out the tea. She came over to join him and sat down on the opposite side of the table. She looked at him expectantly, clearly hoping for some kind of response. He leaned back in his chair and looked straight at her.

"You don't have to explain anything you know, not if you don't want to. Of course, I could see that something was very wrong when I came across you the other night. At first, I thought that someone or something must have frightened you. But when I looked around I was fairly sure we were alone. And then I thought that, maybe, you had imagined some invisible threat. It was so dark and forbidding out there. It was just the kind of night in which one's imagination could run wild. But thinking about it all later on, I began to suppose that something else must have been troubling you, something from the past perhaps. I may be completely wrong Beth, but there was a moment, when we were back at the inn, upstairs in the corridor outside your bedroom... there was a brief moment when I felt there was something you wanted to tell me. But something else, whatever it was, seemed to be holding you back. Perhaps it was because we had only just met and hardly knew each other. So when I came down to breakfast the next morning to find that you had left without even saying goodbye, I assumed that you were deliberately avoiding me. I understood but was genuinely disappointed."

"But I left you a note!" Beth exclaimed "You must have got it; I pushed it under your door before I left. I wanted you to know that I was on my way to Bardsey."

"Oh no! I never saw it I'm afraid. I'm not at my best first thing in the morning. Martha used to say that it was a wonder I ever managed to find my way downstairs for breakfast. Goodness, I must have walked straight over it and I don't think it could have still been there when I went back upstairs after breakfast. I'm so sorry, but I feel much happier now that I know that you tried to leave me a message."

"Not to worry, it's just one of those things."

"When I think about it, I must have been pretty dumb not to realise that you were bound to come over here at some point. You could hardly complete your research without doing so. How long are you planning to stay on the island?"

"I've booked in for a couple of weeks. To be honest, that should be more than enough time to do what I need to do. I thought I'd spend the rest of my time exploring the island and enjoying a bit of a break. I very much want to see the seals and those seabirds I've heard so much about. As for my project, well, to be frank, I'm not really expecting to find much in the way of hard physical evidence. If I discover anything at all, I reckon it's more likely to come from talking to folk who know the island well. It will be interesting to see what tales have been passed down the generations. My best hope is Mattie's husband Harry. He was born on the island. Even if he can't throw much light on the subject himself, he may know others who can. I expect he'll have kept in touch with some of the island's former residents. Mattie's kindly invited me over for supper tomorrow evening. I intend to give her husband a gentle but thorough grilling!"

"Well, I wish you luck. He seems like a nice man. I am sure that he'll help you if he can"

Tom watched Beth tilt her head back and run her fingers lightly through her hair. He had seen her do this before and assumed that it was a nervous habit. After a few moments she turned her attention back to him. "That's enough about me, how long are you here for?"

"A very good question. To be honest, I'm not absolutely sure. I'm officially booked in for four weeks but I may well stay a little longer. It all depends." Although Tom had anticipated the inevitability of this question he couldn't help feeling uncomfortable. His response could only lead to further questions, questions that he wasn't sure he was ready to answer.

"Depends on what, if you don't mind me asking?"

"Shall we say that I have to grapple with some rather difficult personal issues. I've come here hoping to find the time and space to think things through."

Beth was surprised. In the short time she had known him, he had seemed so self-assured and confident. He had certainly not appeared to be nursing problems of his own. But looking at him now, she saw that he was nervously biting his lower lip. She was dismayed by her own inadvertent insensitivity.

"Look, I'm so sorry; this is none of my business. It's just that when you said you were planning to be here for such a long time, I assumed you must be working on a special project or something. But listen, I really don't want to stick my nose in where I shouldn't. The thing is, it's just come home to me. When we first met, I was so busy telling you all about my project that I didn't think to ask you anything about what you do or why you're down here. You seem so confident and dependable. It never crossed my mind that you might be trying to cope with some kind of personal difficulty. I fear that I may have just put my foot in it."

"Don't worry about it, you weren't to know."

"But I shall completely understand if you would prefer to be left alone while you're here on the island."

"As it happens, I'm not at all sure that I'm altogether suited to the life of a hermit. Oh yes, I shall definitely need time alone to try to sort my life out. However, if you don't mind me saying so, right now I am very much enjoying your company."

Tom thought that he detected a slight colouring of Beth's cheeks when he said this. She was looking down at the table, fiddling abstractedly with her teaspoon. He wondered whether he might have gone too far. She decided to change the subject.

"You know we were talking about Harry and Mattie just now. Well I was wondering whether you've met their daughter Rhiannon yet."

"You bet I have!" Tom replied "and what a delightful young thing she is. She called round this morning with milk and a basket of eggs. She spoke at such a gallop she quite took my breath away. I can't help feeling she's rather young for her age."

"Yes, isn't she lovely? Mattie told me she has learning difficulties. But I've found her to be as bright as a button. She must get pretty lonely out here on the island with no other young people around. She did tell me about a friend, Dafydd I think she said he was called. I don't think he can be a brother because Mattie never mentioned him when she was telling me about her other children. They're both grown up now, married and living somewhere on the mainland."

"Perhaps Dafydd is an imaginary friend" Tom suggested. "After all, it's not all that unusual for lonely children to invent a friend. I remember my brother used to have a friend called Hasteby who went everywhere with him. He even used to set a place for him at table, come tea time."

"You're probably right. I know that children can be remarkably inventive. It wouldn't be all that surprising if Rhiannon has invented a little world all of her own. She has a vivid imagination and appears to find little bits of magic everywhere she goes. She took me up the mountain yesterday. Every rock and every stone seemed to mean something special to her. When I told her what I am studying, she wanted to know all about Merlin and Arthur. She has an unquenchable thirst for knowledge of such things. I'm sure she will be pressing me for more stories. The other thing is that she knows the island like the back of her hand and genuinely enjoyed showing me around."

"Well, I've only had one brief conversation with her so far, but I found her thoroughly engaging."

"You know, when I passed your place earlier this morning, I heard you singing one of my favourite psalms, the one about the hart desiring the waterbrook. We often used to sing that in chapel when I was a child."

"Oh, yes, it's one of my favourites too; the words and images are so beautiful, especially in the King James translation."

"Is that where they're from? I'm afraid that I don't know much about that sort of thing. To be honest, when I was a kid I was dragged along to chapel rather unwillingly by my father. He was one of the elders. He had an unquestioning belief in his God and was determined that I should be brought up in the faith. I was a member of the choir and enjoyed all the singing, but I can't say I ever shared his level of commitment. To be honest, much to his disappointment, I soon dropped out of the habit of attending chapel after I left home to go to university."

"How easily that can happen, especially when you've been press-ganged into compulsory worship. But tell me, do you retain any kind of faith."

"I'm not sure. To be honest, I suppose that I don't think about it much. Church-going seems to be pretty much out of fashion these days. I find all that meek kow-towing to God and the long list of things that you aren't supposed to do just doesn't do it for me. Even when I was a child, I couldn't help feeling that, if there is a God, he'd much prefer us to be out there doing positive things and showing a little love to our neighbours. Instead of that, all I seem to see is a load of hypocritical nonsense. The people who are down on their bended knees one moment, doing all that grovelling and confessing of their sins, are the very same people who are quick to pass judgement on everybody else."

"I know just what you mean" said Tom laughing, "I'm afraid the world is full of hypocrites."

He noticed a small picture hanging on the wall over Beth's head. It was a picture of three fishermen landing their boat on the beach. He wondered if it was Porth Meudwy. He turned his attention back to Beth.

"I think this may be the right moment for me to own up to something."

Beth was listening intently.

"Before we get too caught up in our theological discussion, I think it only fair that I should come clean. You see, I have a vested interest in the subject...." He hesitated. He now had Beth's full attention. "The thing is, you see, I'm a priest."

Beth laid her palms flat on the table.

"Well you do surprise me. But it explains what I overheard when I passed by your place earlier this morning. It wasn't so much the singing but all that intoning. I couldn't actually hear what you were saying. I rather thought that you might be reciting poetry or something, that's what it sounded like. Do you know, I don't think that I've ever had a serious conversation with a priest before. Forgive me, but you must find my ill-considered ideas about religion rather naïve."

"On the contrary, you've only been expressing views that are shared by the vast majority of the population."

"Yes, but you see, I'm not really certain about anything, least of all when it comes to determining whether or not there's a God. It must be very reassuring to be so confident in your beliefs. Have you always been a Catholic?"

"Ah, but I'm not a Catholic or, to be more specific, I am not a Roman Catholic. I'm an Anglican."

"I thought it was only the Catholic and Orthodox churches that have 'priests.'"

"Oh no, there's a large part of the Anglican Communion where we call our clergy 'priests'. The C of E is extremely broad-ranging in its different types of churchmanship. From evangelical tub-thumpers through to high church Anglo-Catholics, we've got 'em all. I appreciate that this can be very confusing to those outside our communion."

"So where do you fit in?"

"Well, I suppose somewhere just to the right of centre. I certainly don't think of myself as an evangelical. But I feel equally uncomfortable in the precious environment of the High Anglicans. When all's said and done, I suppose that the way we choose to express our religious beliefs is largely based on the way in which we are brought up and what makes us feel comfortable."

"In the north, where I come from, it was drummed into me that Catholics were the instruments of the devil and that the Church of England was 'The Tory Party at prayer'. My Dad was an old-fashioned Socialist as well as an evangelical and it has to be said that he didn't go short on prejudice. I used to think that if that's what religion does for you, I can get on very well without it!"

"I understand what you're saying more than you might appreciate." Tom ran his fingers through his hair until it fell untidily over his ears. "I suppose you're wondering what on earth an ordained clergyman is doing taking such a long break away from his duties."

"Well, I assume that clergy get holidays like everyone else. But, four or more weeks, that's quite a long break by anyone's standards. I imagine you must be on some kind of retreat or sabbatical or something unless, of course, you've just been appointed vicar of Bardsey. If that's the case you won't have many folk to preach to here other than the Evans', a few cows and sheep, thousands of birds, the odd seal and, of course, Rhiannon's chickens!"

"I'm afraid the days of Bardsey having its own resident minister are long gone. And much as I might fancy preaching to the island's many creatures, I'm not at all sure that they're particularly keen to listen to me." They both laughed.

"To be serious for a moment," Beth said "yes, of course, I am rather intrigued to know what's brought you here. But, then, it's none of my business is it, unless, of course, you choose to tell me."

"I think I probably shall, and I want to know more about you too. I'm sure there's more to you than the world of academia and your search for Arthur's true Avalon." Tom glanced at his watch. "Look it's nearly five and I need to get back to my place and out of these damp clothes. I wonder, perhaps, if you don't have any other plans... well would you like to come over a little later for a bite of supper? It won't be anything very sophisticated I'm afraid, I'm not much of a cook and the facilities are a little limited. But I could manage fried mackerel and scrambled eggs, they go rather well together."

"Yes, I'd like that" Beth said with a smile.

"Well then, how about seven o'clock?"

"Perfect" said Beth.

Tom stood up, crossed over to the door and picked up his coat and rucksack. "See you later then. There'll just be the two of us so no need to dress for dinner!" he grinned, opened the door and walked out into the failing light of the early evening.

# CHAPTER THIRTY-THREE

As Tom was making his way back to Carreg Bach, Rhiannon was shooing the chickens back into the walled yard at Ty Pellaf. The early evening forecast was predicting heavy rain for the whole of West Wales, due to hit Bardsey later that evening. Mattie had told her daughter to make sure that the chickens were safely confined within the protective stone walls of the yard.

Rhiannon had a special song for rounding up the chickens. It was 'David of the White Rock'. There was a considerable tenderness in her singing. Her voice rose pure and clear above the sound of the clucking hens. The chickens knew this voice well for, rather than flapping their wings in startled disarray and running madly in every direction, they cocked their heads to one side and listened, as if captivated by the magic of the song, before strutting obediently back through the gate into the yard.

Sitting up in bed, old Mrs Davies heard her granddaughter's voice through her bedroom window. She had a wooden tray on her knee and was dipping her spoon into a bowl of steaming hot broth. Like the chickens down below, the old woman had her head cocked to one side as she listened to the song. With two hair combs fastened on the top of her head, she bore a remarkable resemblance to the chickens.

"Of course that's really a song for a young man, not a girl" she croaked at her daughter, who sat sewing by the side of her bed. But this was an observation rather than a criticism. She loved her granddaughter dearly, much more indeed than either of her other grandchildren. The sweetness of the girl's voice brought tears to her eyes.

When the child's voice finally died away, Mattie looked up from her sewing and smiled at her mother. "How she loves 'Dafydd y Garreg Wen'. You know she first heard it at that local Eisteddfod over in Nefyn, a couple of years ago. She learned it by heart and sang it at the end of term school concert. It was the first time she'd done anything like that in public and she rather stole the show. The teachers and parents were so impressed that they all stood up to clap. I don't think I've ever been so proud of her as I was that evening."

"I wish I'd been there" the old lady said. "If it hadn't been for my wretched arthritis."

"I know. But, if you remember, she was so sorry you weren't able to be there that she gave you a special performance back here at Ty Pellaf the following afternoon. I'll never forget how she stood there in the living room, with the sunlight pouring in through the window lighting up her face, and announced the song, formally, as if she was about to perform in St David's Hall. I think we were all crying by the time she finished. Even Harry had to fetch out his hanky!"

"I felt very honoured Mattie, very honoured indeed. It is one of those moments that I've always treasured." her mother said, putting her spoon down and picking up a napkin to wipe her mouth. She was about to speak again. But this had not been one of her better days and the effort of talking brought on a severe coughing fit which had Mattie reaching for the oxygen mask that always stood beside the bed. By now the old lady's face had turned purple as she gasped for air. Her mother's health had been steadily deteriorating over the past couple of years and Mattie was used to dealing with the not-infrequent moments of crisis such as this. She knew that her mother would soon drift off into sleep. She removed the supper tray, leaned across the bed and pulled her gently forward so that she could pile extra pillows behind her.

"That's better then" she said "is there anything else I can get you?" But there was no reply. Her mother was already asleep. Mattie kissed her tenderly on her forehead. She quietly withdrew, leaving the door slightly ajar so that she would be able to hear if he mother called out.

# CHAPTER THIRTY-FOUR

The stiff breeze that had blown across the island all day had risen to gale force by the time Tom had washed and changed out of his wet clothes. He could hear the rain splattering on the cottage roof as the storm passed over. It was pitch black outside. He began to wonder whether the worsening weather conditions would dissuade Beth from venturing out. It was only a short distance between their two dwellings but far enough to guarantee a serious soaking if she happened to get caught in one of the increasingly frequent showers. He was glad that he only had to prepare a simple meal. This could wait until she arrived. He sat in one of the armchairs in front of the open fireplace feeling an increasing sense of disappointment at the thought that she might not be able to make it. He looked at his watch and saw that she was already nearly three quarters of an hour late. There was a part of him that thought that it might be for the best if the storm prevented her from coming. His life was already in turmoil. He had come to Bardsey to escape from external distractions.

Before sitting down, he had picked up a copy of Paul Tillich's *Shaking of the Foundations*. But he soon found that his mind was elsewhere and he was unable to concentrate. He sat there, continually checking the time and indulging in an old habit of massaging his right ear lobe between his thumb and forefinger. His anxiety was growing by the minute. "This is ridiculous" he told himself "Why, on earth, am I in such a lather?" But try as he might, he couldn't help feeling that strange mixture of excitement and apprehension.

He hadn't felt this way about anybody apart from his beloved Martha.

A sudden blast of wind rattled the window frames and the rain was now pounding on the roof. He closed his eyes and sighed deeply. Everything seemed to be so much out of his control. He was aroused by a loud hammering on the front door. His heart missed a beat as he rose quickly and hurried to the door. When he raised the latch, the door was almost snatched out of his hands by a violent gust of wind. He took a firm grip of the handle and eased the door carefully open. She was standing on the doorstep. The wind had torn the hood from her head and her long dark hair was trailing out behind her, twisted and knotted. Her plastic raincoat had been severely savaged by the wind and there was tear down the front. She was still trying to hold the torn fragments together, but it was a futile battle and she was soaked from head to foot. Tom thought that she resembled the survivor of a shipwreck who had just managed to make it to the shore.

"For goodness sake, look at the state of you; come on in before you're blown away."

"Phew, I don't think I've ever been out in anything quite like that before." Beth said as she staggered across the threshold.

Tom stared at her as if he couldn't quite believe what he was seeing. "Here, let me help you take off what's left of your waterproof, although I have to say, it's hardly lived up to its name."

When he had thrown the dripping remnants of torn plastic over the back of a chair, he turned to look at her again. It seemed that not a single item of her clothing had escaped the violence of the storm. Her hair was limply plastered to her cheeks and the back of her neck. Her jeans and sweatshirt were soaked through. She was so cold that she had begun to shiver.

"Look, before we do anything, we'd better get you out of those wet clothes." Tom said. He unhooked a large towel from a row of pegs next to the cooker. "Why don't you rub your hair down while I go upstairs to see if I can find something you can put on while we try to get your clothes dry?"

He handed the towel to Beth, lit a small oil lamp and hurried up the ladder to the bedroom. He realised she would be embarrassed and determined to do everything he could to put her at her ease. The only suitable items of clothing he could come up with were a thick woollen navy-blue jumper and a pair of striped blue and white pyjama trousers.

They were far too big but it was the best he could do. He stood at the top of the stairs and called down to her:

"How are you getting on down there? Look, I've had a quick forage through my things. I'm afraid I can't find anything that's likely to set the Paris fashion houses on fire. However, if you don't mind disappearing into these, at least they should keep you warm and respectable – that's unless you've got a thing about women dressing up in men's clothes." He took careful aim and threw the clothes down onto a chair at the foot of the stairs. "Let me know when you're decent and I'll come down and put the kettle on. You must be in need of a hot drink."

"Actually, I'd rather have a drop of whisky." Beth called back up. She had taken off her sodden clothes and was standing in the middle of the room with the towel wrapped tightly around her. She picked up the bundle Tom had thrown down "Wow, thanks for the knitted jumper and convict's trousers. Just give me a mo' and then you can come down and admire this 'haute couture' mam'selle." She could hear Tom chuckling from somewhere in the rafters above. She finished drying herself and put on Tom's pyjama trousers. She pulled the cord as tight as she could around her slender waist and rolled up the trouser legs until they were just above her ankles. She decided to put the woolly jumper to one side for the time being, preferring the warmth of the towel which she wrapped carefully round her chest.

"OK, you can come down now" she called out, "I think that I'm about as respectable as I'm ever likely to be, given the fact that your pyjama bottoms weren't exactly made to measure!"

Tom descended the ladder. He was unable to suppress a chuckle when he looked at Beth. "Well, that's different. I've seen some becoming images of women in my time but I think you must steal the show, what I can see of you anyway. I've heard men say that there's something exceptionally appealing about a woman dressed in men's pyjamas."

"A rather sexist image, if you don't mind me saying so!"

"Oh, no doubt. But less of this nonsense. We need to get you warmed up. I'm afraid I'm not much of a whisky drinker, but I can lay my hands on a drop of brandy if that'll do? Now where did I put it?" He opened several cupboards until he eventually found what he was looking for and set two glass tumblers and an unopened bottle of cognac down on the kitchen table. "I had a feeling that this might come in handy, although not perhaps for quite this sort of situation." The both laughed. Tom poured out two generous portions of the pale golden liquid and handed one to Beth.

"A life-saver!" she said, holding the tumbler in both hands and raising it to her lips. She stood with her eyes closed and let out a deep sigh of pleasure as the warming liquid trickled down her throat. Then, she grinned. "It's amazing how quickly it works, but I feel better already." She gestured towards the dining table where her rain-soaked garments were hanging over the backs of the chairs. "Look, I hope you don't mind but I've put my wet things over there. I've wrung them out in the sink as best I can. To be honest I don't know how I shall ever get them dry again."

"Ah" said Tom "I've been thinking about that and I'm going to light a fire. We can pull up the armchairs on either side of the fireplace and put the chairs with the clothes on in front of the fire."

Within a few minutes Tom had a fine fire roaring away. They moved the chairs in and he gestured to Beth to sit down. He fed a large piece of driftwood onto the fire.

"So, how are you feeling?" he asked.

"Oh I'm beginning to thaw out nicely thank you."

Tom picked up the brandy bottle and topped up her glass. She clutched it in a tight grip just below her chin.

"Wonderful stuff, I'm feeling so much better" she said, "and you can now tell everyone, truthfully, that you've been keeping the brandy strictly for medicinal purposes. If you don't mind I think I'll try to dry my hair out a bit more. I can still feel the water dripping down the back of my neck." She knelt down on the rug in front of the fire and lowered her head. Her hair hung down reaching almost to the floor. "You couldn't pass my bag over could you? I'm pretty sure I've got a comb in there."

Tom reached for the canvas bag which Beth had dumped on the table when she first arrived. It, too, was soaking wet. He passed it over to her and she rummaged inside, eventually pulling out a large brown comb with unusually long teeth. She tossed her head back and ran her fingers carefully through her hair to separate the tangled strands. Tom watched, fascinated. He noted the practised way in which she set about her task. When she had successfully untangled the worst of the knots, she bent her head forward again. This time, comb in hand, she set about separating the few remaining knots. She knew Tom was watching but felt surprisingly relaxed. There was something reassuring about this tall and gaunt man of God who she had met so serendipitously. Serendipitous, yes, that was the right word to describe their chance first meeting. She hadn't felt so drawn to anyone since her hapless affair with Bill Matthews. Tom had exceptional qualities, she felt sure of that. She had already experienced his kindness and understanding, and he had proved to be such a good listener. But she was sure there was a great deal more to him than that. She wanted to know more about why he had come to the island. She sensed that somewhere beneath his warmth and good humour there lay a more troubled soul.

Tom, meanwhile, was content to sit back in his chair and watch. When he had first married Martha, she too had had exceptionally long hair which had hung down to well below her waist. It had been one of the first things that had attracted him to her. It was back in the 60s when hippies were handing out flowers in London's streets, students were rebelling against authority all over Europe and thousands of young people were marching for peace. At the time, most of the young women in his university circle wore their hair long. By now, Beth had managed to comb through most of the tangles but was battling with a particularly resistant knot.

"I don't think this one's ever going to come out" she said "there's always one!" She glanced up a Tom. "I'm sorry, you must be bored stiff sitting there watching me fighting these Medusa-like snakes. You know, there are times when I really think I should have it all cut off. It would make life a lot easier."

"Oh, you mustn't do that, you have such lovely hair."

"It's all right for you, you're a bloke!" She pulled a few loose hairs out of her comb and tossed them onto the fire. She ran her fingers through her hair again in a vain attempt to free the one remaining tangle. She looked across at Tom in desperation. "I give up. At the risk of appearing forward, you don't think you could give me a hand do you?"

"Don't be silly, of course I can" He made to stand up but Beth gestured to him to stay where he was.

"Actually, I think it might be easier for you if I come and sit on the floor in front of you."

She stood up with her back to him and adjusted the towel to make sure it would stay securely in place. She passed Tom the comb and sat down in front of him, tossing her head back so that her hair hung down behind. He experienced a tingle of pleasure as he ran his fingers through the shining dark strands. Her hair was softer to the touch than he had imagined. When he found the offending knot he gently separated the matted hairs. Soon he was able to run the comb down the full length of her hair. As he did so, tiny droplets of water fell onto her bare shoulders. He wanted to wipe them away with his hand but resisted the temptation. By now she had relaxed her head down and he was aware of the pleasure it was giving her. Neither of them spoke as they shared this unexpected moment of intimacy.

It was Beth who finally broke the silence. She turned to look up at him, smiled and gently took hold of the hand which was holding the comb.

"Thank you so much Tom, but you must be getting tired and I think we'd better stop now don't you?"

He returned her smile and, for an answer, leaned forward until his lips came into contact with the cold damp flesh just a above her collarbone. "I'm sorry, but I just couldn't resist that!" He said, intoxicated by the musky scent of her skin. The tender kiss he planted there sent a shudder through her body. His eyes were closed but he felt her move and, thought she was about to pull away. But then he felt her cool fingers running lightly through his hair and realised that she must have turned and was kneeling in front of him. She clasped him behind his neck and slowly but firmly pulled his head down towards her. She kissed his lips and sensing the warmth of his response, she pressed her tongue more forcibly against his lips until they parted and their tongues met.

When she finally withdrew her tongue, she kissed him lightly on the lips and then pulled away. She reached forward to part his knees and pulled herself up so that she could slide her body between his legs. She lay against him with her head resting beneath his chin. Tom wrapped his arms around her. He could feel the soft cushion of her breasts through the towel which was still wrapped firmly around her.

He kissed the top of her head, relishing the fresh scent of her hair. He ran his fingers gently up and down her back and over her bare shoulders and she emitted little groans of pleasure. She was breathing more quickly now. She leant back and pulled him towards her and soon they were lying side by side on the rug in front of the fire. She turned to lie on her side with one arm hooked around his head. He stroked the side of her face, tracing his fingers lightly over her cheeks, down over the her lips and her chin and down still further to her neck and shoulders while she gave herself over to the pleasure of his touch.

Beth was surprised at how safe and secure she felt. Somehow, enough had already passed between them for her to know that Tom was different from the other men she had known.

He wrapped his arms around her again, pulling her towards him. He could feel her warm breath on his neck. He too was surprised. Surprised that he should feel so comfortable and relaxed with this young woman. When Martha had died, he had been certain that no-one would ever be able to replace her. Indeed, the very thought of engaging in a relationship with anyone else had felt like a betrayal of the love they had shared together. After Martha's death, there had been no shortage of hints that he should start looking for a new partner. After all, didn't every clergyman need a loyal wife by his side? That they should think he could contemplate such a possibility had made him feel physically sick.

He felt Beth stir. She raised her head and he looked down at her upturned face. He felt a pang of emotion when he saw that her eyes were moist with tears. He reached down to caress the nape of her neck. She buried her nose into his chest and he sensed that she didn't want him to know that she was crying. He sensed she retained an element of uncertainty, perhaps, even of fear. He remembered that night on the seawall. If only he knew what it was that continued to haunt her.

"Hush" he whispered "It's alright, you're quite safe here, I promise." He ran his fingers tenderly through her hair. After a while he sensed that she had stopped crying. He parted the hair that had fallen over her eyes and kissed her on the forehead.

"My dear sweet girl" he said "do you have any idea how utterly seductive you are. It's a long time, a very long time since I last felt so content, so utterly relaxed, so... "

"So happy and yet so surprised? Oh yes Tom, I feel it too."

Tom put his hand under her chin and raised her head until they were looking directly into each other's eyes.

"But, my dear, do you know something? Much though I don't want to, I think this is where we have to stop for now. I could happily lie here with you all night. But don't you think we need a little more time to get to know one another? I sense that I may not be alone in needing to come to terms with some shadows from the past. And look, the fire is almost out and all this activity has landed me with a cruel appetite."

Beth chuckled. "Yes, I've got a cruel appetite too, but I suspect that you're thinking of your stomach, which is not exactly what I had in mind."

"Well, here's hoping that mackerel isn't an aphrodisiac, I wouldn't want you to get the wrong impression about me!"

"And just what might that wrong impression be, may I ask? Are you worried that I may be thinking you invited me over with the express intention of feeding me a fishy love potion so that you could drag me into bed? And you a clergyman too!"

They both laughed.

"Come on then, let me get up so that I can put some more wood on the fire and then you can sit here and dream, while I attend to our supper."

Tom caressed Beth's cheek affectionately and stood up. He rearranged the glowing embers of the dying fire and placed some smaller pieces of wood on top. He knelt down, took a deep breath and blew determinedly until they began to smoke and finally burst into flames. He placed two larger logs on top and stood back with a satisfied look on his face.

"I always knew I should have been a boy scout" he said "and now for supper. There's nothing like fresh mackerel straight from the sea. I picked these up from a fellow down at the harbour when I was out walking this morning. He'd just landed with his catch."

Beth watched Tom walk over to the small kitchen, open the fridge and take out butter, eggs and a brown greaseproof paper package of fish. "Five minutes on each side and they'll be done" he said as he broke the first of the eggs into a bowl. Beth was impressed by his dexterity as he cracked open each of the remaining eggs using just his right hand.

""It looks like you've been on one of those 'Cordon Bleu' courses" she said."You're full of surprises."

He grinned. "Actually, I learned that trick when I was a kid. My younger brother was jealous as hell. He couldn't do it without dropping most of the shell into the bowl. I can still see him cursing as he picked out all the broken pieces."

Beth continued to watch Tom with growing fascination. From the relaxed ease with which he went about his business, it was clear that he was used to cooking for himself. Soon he was standing over the kitchen table transferring the mackerel onto two dinner plates and spooning the scrambled egg onto thick slices of buttered bread.

Out of the corner of his eye, Tom saw Beth getting up from her armchair.

"Don't get up, stay where you are, I'll bring it over and we can have it on our knees. It's warmer by the fire and you're still drying out."

"You make me sound like an alcoholic" she said with a broad grin "but thanks, that's very thoughtful."

He handed one of the plates to Beth. Before sitting down he ran his hands over Beth's clothes. There was a pool of water on the floor beneath them.

"These are still soaking, I'm afraid. I can't see you putting them back on tonight. Besides, it's still lashing down outside."

"If I didn't know you were a man of God, I'd suspect you were planning to seduce me" Beth said with a chuckle. Seeing the anxious expression on

Tom's face, she wondered whether she had gone too far. But he allowed her remark to pass without comment, picked up his plate and sat down.

They were both hungry and ate in silence until they had emptied their plates.

"That was delicious" Beth said, wiping the corners of her mouth with her fingers. "I'd forgotten how tasty fresh mackerel can be."

"How about a cup of tea?" Tom asked.

"I'm fine for now thank you. I haven't finished that generous brandy you gave me. Do you know, I think I may be beginning to get a bit of a taste for it." She picked up the glass, took a sip and then sat back in her chair. "Tom, can I ask you something?"

"I don't see why not".

"I do hope you won't think I'm being too nosy but you mentioned your wife earlier this afternoon and... well... clearly, she isn't here with you. I was wondering... Tom, you aren't in some kind of difficulty with your marriage are you?"

She saw a shadow pass over his face but then he smiled and said:

"No, no, nothing like that. Martha and I were always the very best of friends. In fact, I don't think we ever really fell out over anything, not anything that really mattered." He stared into the fire, and said, almost in a whisper "I'm afraid she's no longer with me. She died in a car crash five years ago."

"Oh! I'm so, so very sorry!" Beth said, reaching forward and taking hold of his hands "I'd no idea... I... I shouldn't have asked... How very tactless of me. Oh, do please forgive me!"

"There's nothing to forgive. How could you possibly have known? But I'm glad you asked because it may help to explain my rather unpredictable lapses into depression."

"Actually, I haven't noticed them at all. You must have loved her very much."

"More than I can ever describe. If it doesn't sound too much of a cliché, Martha was the light of my life."

"How did you meet?"

"We were both students at Kings. I was reading theology and she was reading English. I was a year ahead of her. We first met when I was helping to man an Oxfam stall at her first-year Freshers' reception. I noticed her as soon as she entered the hall, everyone did. She was stunningly attractive, tall and slim, and she had incredibly long golden hair. Everyone watched her as she made her way round the hall. She gave the impression that she was genuinely enthusiastic about everything and seemed so comfortable and relaxed meeting new people. Because she showed so much interest in their various activities and causes, everyone instantly warmed to her. And yet there was nothing to suggest that she was aware of the affect that she was having. I remember how I willed her to come over to my stall. And then, of course, when finally she did, I could hardly put two words together. She found this very amusing, she told me so later. And do you know what the first thing she said to me was? 'Oxfam, well I never, I didn't know that there was a famine in Oxford!' She kept such a straight face that it took me a moment to realise she was teasing me. And then her face broke into a broad grin and she started to laugh and so did I, and I was hooked from that moment on."

"So was that it then? Did you two get together right away?"

"Well that's the strange thing. As I've already said, she made such an impression when she first entered the room. I could feel most of the guys watching us as I was stammering out something about the Oxfam group's plans for the coming term. I felt sure that she would soon lose interest and politely move on to the next stall. But to my utter astonishment, she asked question after question and signed up as one of our volunteers then and there."

"It sounds like she took a fancy to you right from the start."

"Well, I'm afraid I was rather short of self-confidence in those days. She seemed so committed to campaigning for the starving masses of the Developing World that it never crossed my mind that she might actually be interested in me. And even when Richard, one of my fellow stallholders, made some unflattering comment about my well-concealed sex appeal, I remained totally unconvinced that she was in the least bit interested in me."

"So, what happened?"

"Absolutely nothing for quite a long time. When we held our first Oxfam fund-raising event, you can imagine how disappointed I was when she didn't show up. I kicked myself when I realised I hadn't even asked her what she was studying and so had no idea where I might find her. King's is a big college with so many different academic departments. It hasn't been described as the only college in the university to have all its faculties for nothing! As a result, we didn't bump into each other either in college or the Union. As a shy and inexperienced 19-year-old, I was far too unsure of myself to go and search her out."

"Poor you. But you said she'd been really keen to sign up as one of your Oxfam volunteers, surely she was bound to show up some time?"

"Well, that's the thing. I kept hoping she would, but she didn't. Several weeks passed by and, to be frank, I'd given up on her. But then, one day she came looking for me. I could hardly believe it. She appeared out of nowhere in the theology faculty corridor, just as I was coming out of a lecture. She said she'd been meaning to get in touch for ages and, if I had time for a coffee, she'd explain why she hadn't. Well, of course I agreed. It was a beautiful, sunny, late autumn morning when we walked out into the Strand. Martha was a very demonstrative kind of person, in the nicest possible way. I can't tell you how thrilled I was when she took hold of my arm as we crossed over the road leading to Waterloo Bridge. She didn't let go until we arrived at the Lyons Corner House in Trafalgar Square. Over several cups of coffee, she explained that she, and a couple of girls she was sharing with, had fallen out with their landlord. They'd been out almost every night trying to find alternative accommodation and had only just succeeded. She told me that it had all been a bit of a nightmare, and that everything else had been put on hold during their search. She was full of apologies but, of course, there was nothing to forgive. All that I was thinking about was how incredibly lucky I was to be sitting across the table from her."

"It sounds like it was love at first sight for both of you."

"Yes, it really was. Within six months we were engaged. We finished our studies at the same time as I had to do a fourth year's training for the ministry. We got married as soon as I'd been made a deacon and had taken up a curacy in a parish in South London."

"How did she feel about marrying a clergyman? I imagine that she must have shared your faith, otherwise it'd be quite a thing to take on?"

"To be honest, that was the only thing she was a little uncertain of at first. She hadn't been brought up in a particularly religious household. In fact, her father was a lapsed Catholic and pretty cynical about the church generally. Fortunately, as a curate's wife she wasn't expected to become all that involved with church life. She took up a position as an English teacher at the local comprehensive. It was a tough school. Many of the kids came from very deprived homes, were difficult to handle and, in some cases, semi-illiterate. But she had the gift of never talking down to anyone, and they respected her for that. I don't think that I met anyone who... who. . . "

Beth saw Tom's eyes had begun to water and she hastily intervened:

"I'm so sorry Tom; I can see that this is really difficult for you. I shouldn't be asking all these questions, it isn't fair."

Tom wiped his eyes.

"It's stupid of me, I know, but I just can't talk about Martha without experiencing a massive flood of emotion. There hasn't been a single day since she died, when I haven't thought about her and missed her and felt angry that she was taken from me so unnecessarily."

"I wish I could help, I really do. But then it's incredibly presumptuous of me to even think that I could. Let's face it, we're only just beginning to get to know each other."

Tom took hold of her hands.

"You say that, but that's the strange thing. You see, I'm pretty sure that the time will come when I shall be able to share it all with you more fully. I don't think I'm quite ready for that just yet. I'm battling with too many conflicting emotions. But I sense that you and I may not have met entirely by accident. And if that sounds ridiculous, well, at the very least, let's accept that it's a matter of the greatest good fortune that we have met. Do you know, in the five years since I lost Martha. I haven't felt able to talk to anyone about how I really feel? My daughter Annie has been wonderfully loving and caring, but I can't expect her to fully understand. In any case, she has had to deal with her own grief. The last thing I've wanted to do is to add to her burden. The nearest I've come to sharing my true feelings with anyone is with my Bishop. He's a remarkably perceptive, kind and understanding man. It's he who encouraged me to come here to try to sort myself out. But even when I talked to him, there were things left unsaid, thoughts that I'm not yet able to articulate."

"I'm so glad you've felt able to trust me." She gazed up into his watery eyes, which were glistening in the light of the fire.

"Of course, trust is an essential part of it. But then, there are quite a few people I trust in the accepted sense of the word, but I haven't felt it appropriate to confide in them. There's more to it than trust but I don't know what it is yet."

"I think I do, and I think that probably you do too, but perhaps it's too soon to put it into words."

She felt Tom tighten his grip on her hands, he smiled and took in a deep breath.

"Yes, it is too soon and we must allow time to be sure that we know and understand each other better." He turned away to look back at the fire and closed his eyes. His lips were moving and she wondered if he was praying. And then he turned to face her again and said "I think perhaps it's time to be practical. I don't know about you, but I'm whacked. It would be insane for you to try to make your way back to your place tonight. Please stay over. There's a comfortable bed waiting for you upstairs. I'll bring a blanket down here, put these two armchairs together and sleep in front of the fire."

"That's kind of you Tom, but don't be silly, you really don't need to abandon your bed. I'm sure that I can trust you. All I ask is that you give me a few minutes to have a wash and put on that sexy pullover of yours."

"Look, I'm sure you'd welcome a little privacy. Why don't you pop through into the kitchen and have a wash while I make up the fire. We must try to get your clothes dry by morning."

Beth picked up Tom's pullover and disappeared into the kitchen. Tom fed more driftwood onto the fire and moved Beth's damp clothes closer to the heat.

When she re-emerged from the kitchen she was wearing Tom's woolly pullover. It was far too big for her and hung down almost as far as her knees.

"Not exactly made to measure, but it should keep you warm."

She had rolled up the sleeves to free her hands. The neck of the pullover was so wide on her that he was able to see her collar bones and the soft folds of skin at the base of her neck. He thought that she looked exceptionally beautiful but just a little vulnerable.

As if reading his thoughts, she looked away shyly, placing a hand over her collar bones.

He smiled. "Look, I'll just pop upstairs to get my pyjamas and then I'll come back down and you can head off to bed while I wash."

He lit a small oil lamp and climbed up into the loft. Leaving the lamp upstairs he was soon back down again. He took Beth's hand and led her over to the bottom of the stairs. "Give me a call when you're safely tucked up."

"Thank you Tom, thank you for everything. I'm sorry to be such a nuisance" She kissed him on the cheek, turned and climbed up the steps. Tom could hear her moving about upstairs and soon there was a creaking sound s she climbed into the bed.

"All clear on the Western Front" she called down.

"I hope you'll be warm enough. There's a spare blanket in the bottom of the chest of drawers if you need it."

"I'm quite snug up here thank you."

"Well you know where it is if you change your mind."

He spent a few minutes tidying up, turned off the lamp and made his way upstairs. Beth had turned down the lamp and in its dim light he could only just make out the shape of her body, buried under the bedclothes. She was lying on the far side of the bed with her back towards him. He wondered whether this was how she normally slept or if, perhaps, it was out of respect for his privacy. He climbed into the bed next to her and turned off the lamp.

The only sound was the soft but steady rhythm of Beth's breathing. He whispered "goodnight", but there was no response.

In the early hours of the following morning, long before the first glimmer of daylight, Tom was disturbed in his sleep. He was lying on his side facing away from Beth when he felt a slight movement behind him. He lay still as he felt a hand wander up his back until it rested lightly on his shoulder. In his confusion, he nearly called out Martha's name. But as the mists of sleep evaporated, he knew it wasn't Martha. The hand resting on his shoulder tightened its grip and he felt Beth's warm body pressing into him from behind.

"I'm so sorry, I didn't mean to wake you."

Tom turned onto his back and put his arm around her and she snuggled up closer resting her head on his chest.

"I just want to lie here with you, I don't want anything else" she whispered.

Tom traced his fingers lightly down her spine.

"It's all right" he said, it's all right."

Soon he sensed a change in the rhythm of her breathing and he knew she must have fallen back to sleep. He lay awake for a while, his head teaming with thoughts of the unexpected events of the evening. And then, just as the first light of dawn was invading the night sky, he too fell into a deep and untroubled sleep.

# CHAPTER THIRTY-FIVE

Tom woke up to a room full of cheerful early morning sunlight. At first, when he opened his eyes and looked up at the sloping ceiling, he couldn't recall where he was. He had been dreaming, a dream that had taken him far away from the storm-battered island. But, as the confused images of his dream slowly faded, the events of the previous evening came flooding back. He reached out to where Beth had lain beside him but all he found was an empty space. He sat up and rubbed his eyes, but when he looked around the room she wasn't there either. He climbed out of bed, put on his dressing gown and hurried downstairs but, once again, there was no sign of Beth. He saw that the chairs where her clothes had been laid to dry had been put back around the table. The supper dishes had been washed and put away and the bottle of brandy had been returned to the dresser. If it hadn't been for the neatly folded towel and his pyjama trousers and pullover over the back of an armchair, she might never have been there at all. He picked up the pullover and held it to his nose, savouring the faint remaining traces of her sweet scent. He went over to the sink to fill the kettle.

As he watched the blue flames of the gas ring dancing around the base of the kettle, his thoughts were far away.

He looked out of the window at the large puddles on the path. The leaves on the scrubby bushes in the garden were shimmering in the early morning sunlight. A thin layer of mist hung over the rest of the island. Only the very top of the lighthouse was clearly visible.

He heard the kettle whistling, turned away from the window, made himself a cup of tea and sat down at the table. From the moment Beth had arrived, half drowned, on his doorstep, everything had taken a totally unexpected path. Since Martha's death, nobody had been able to pull on his heart strings. And then, out of the blue, this exceptional young woman had reawakened feelings that he had forgotten he possessed. Sitting alone at the kitchen table, he felt a deep sense of disappointment that Beth had left without waking him. Was she regretting what had passed between them? He had spent much of the previous day telling her about his undying love for Martha. It would hardly be surprising if she didn't feel able to compete with this.

He was relieved they had managed to control their yearnings. How easily they might have ended up making love. But he wasn't yet ready for that and sensed that she too had been holding back.

Amongst his confused emotions there also lurked considerable doubts. What if Beth's show of affection had been little more than a generous expression of sympathy? Perhaps she had simply taken pity on a pathetic cleric who, even after five long years, couldn't get over his wife's death? Why would she be interested in him anyway? He was a good deal older and somewhat the worse for wear. She might have issues of her own, but she was young, highly intelligent and beautiful. He stared blankly at the wall. How could he be sure about anything? If only he knew why she had disappeared.

# CHAPTER THIRTY-SIX

Tom's worst fears about Beth's reason for leaving him that morning couldn't have been further from the truth. When she first woke up she had felt exhilarated. She turned to look at Tom, lying beside her. She wanted to put her arms around him but saw that he was in a deep sleep. So she had lingered downstairs, tidying up the room, hoping he might wake up and call out for her. But it was not to be. Her clothes had dried overnight, so she had dressed, gathered together her belongings and quietly stepped out into a new day.

It was a cool morning with a fresh northerly breeze. And the sun was only just beginning to penetrate the mist. When she arrived back at Llofft Plas, she lit the gas heater before going upstairs to change. When she had put on a fresh pair of jeans and a thick woollen jumper she prepared a simple breakfast of coffee and toast. She pulled the gas heater closer and sat down to consider how she was going to spend the rest of the day.

As far as Tom was concerned, she had already decided to leave the next move to him. While she would have liked to take the initiative, they could only move forward if and when Tom felt ready to do so. She could see how deeply he mourned his wife's death. She began to regret their intimacy of the previous evening, which she felt that she had instigated. She knew she would have to be patient. There was no doubt he was attracted to her. But she would have to give him time to see off the ghosts of his past.

In the meantime, she would concentrate on her project. She was due to have supper with the Evans' that evening. This would provide her with an opportunity to find out if Harry might know anything of the island's Arthurian connections. She would spend the day exploring other parts of the island that might help with her research.

She decided to begin by investigating some of the island's oldest signs of habitation. Her studies had revealed differing accounts of when the island had first been settled. But, there was clear evidence that some of the hut circles which had been discovered dated back at least two or three thousand years. There were even claims that there may have been human activity on the island several thousand years before. According to her map, some of the hut circles were located on a small terrace on the lower slopes of the mountain. There were other rectangular structures too, at a place called Penrhyn Gogor. These were thought to be much later structures, most probably agricultural buildings from the Middle Ages. She opted to go there first. The site lay right on the coast, at the extreme north end of the island, and she was keen to catch a closer glimpse of the sea on such a fine morning.

She picked up her rucksack and set off towards the abbey ruins. As she passed Carreg Bach there was no sign of life. She wondered whether Tom was still in bed. She was sorely tempted to knock on his front door but held back. If he was still asleep, she didn't want to disturb him. In any case, she had already determined to leave the next move to him.

She continued up the track, passing by the chapel and the path she had taken with Rhiannon the previous day. When she reached the abbey ruins she took out her map. There wasn't enough detail to show whether there was a path down towards Penrhyn Gogor. She decided to head straight across the fields. Although this meant she might have to scramble over a wall or two, there didn't appear to be an obvious alternative. In many places the ground was still sodden from the previous night's heavy rain, but she made good progress, grateful for her stout pair of walking boots.

She came across the remains of the rectangular stone structures without difficulty, although, in most cases, there wasn't much to see. She sat on one of the large flat stones that formed part of a remaining wall and looked down to where the sea was pounding on the rocks below. A cold wind was blowing in from the north. She wondered whether the buildings had originally been constructed to protect the island's livestock from the island's winter storms. On the other hand, she supposed, they might have simply been used for storage. She knew that archaeologists generally believed the buildings had been constructed in the medieval period. However, she wasn't sure how they could be quite so certain. What if they dated back even earlier to the time of Arthur and Merlin? What if some of the structures formed part of the settlement where Morgan le Fay had held court with her nine sisters? But, of course, this could only be the wildest of conjectures.

By now, the wind had strengthened and it was bitterly cold. Beth sought out a sheltered corner, in a hollow to the side of one of the better preserved buildings. She took out a small plastic mat from her rucksack and laid it down on a relatively dry piece of flat ground. It was approaching mid-morning and there was just enough heat in the sun to cause the moisture from last night's rain to evaporate into a thin layer of swirling white mist.

It was a magical scene and she was content to sit there for a while, absorbing the atmosphere. The mountain stretched along the full length of the east side of the island and looked dark and uninviting. It was just as well that Rhiannon had been her guide the previous day, otherwise who knows what difficulties she might have faced. Above the upper reaches of the mountain there was an endless stirring of birds. She could recognise the gulls but wished that she had a greater knowledge of sea birds. She would have liked to be able to identify the many other species perched on the rock face or floating effortlessly in the sky above. The island was renowned for its large colony of Manx shearwaters and there were also choughs, oystercatchers and many other species. But she couldn't tell one from the other. She thought of Bert and Joan, the odd, bird-loving couple, who had travelled with her over to the island. She chuckled at the thought of the long and tedious lecture Bert would have delivered on the subject.

And then she found herself thinking about Tom again. He had seemed so kind and self-assured when they first met. It had never occurred to her that he too might be a troubled soul. But, in all honesty, it had come as something of a relief when he had told her about his own emotional struggles. It had put their relationship on more of an equal footing.

Life was full of surprises. When she had set out on this trip, the last thing she had been looking for was any kind of relationship. She had kept men at a distance ever since the night she had been sexually assaulted. Indeed, she had shunned the approaches of her male colleagues so completely that she was laughingly referred to as the 'ice-maiden'. But she knew of no other way to protect herself, even at the cost of being considered cold and arrogant. Her female colleagues showed her little more respect, despite accepting her academic gifts. By contrast, her students were full of admiration. She was an inspiring lecturer who knew her subject inside out and she selflessly gave time to any of her students who needed her advice or support.

What she found most endearing about Tom was his willingness to take her for what she was. Most of the men she knew had either been over-judgemental or run a mile as soon as they had sensed she had issues. Tom had offered a sympathetic ear. He had not sought to delve into areas that she was not yet ready to share. If there was anyone she could ever talk to about the night she had been raped, it would be Tom. But she wasn't yet quite ready for that yet. The natural consequence of her work colleagues 'rejection of her rape claim was for her to doubt whether anyone would ever believe her. She would never forget the way they had looked at her, trying to laugh it all off as if it had been some kind of drunken misdemeanour on her part. How typical of men to assume that she must have led her assailant on.

She sighed and muttered under her breath, "enough of all this. There's work to be done. Let me see if I can find those hut circles."

As it turned out it was to be a morning of disappointments. Her search for the hut circles turned out to be extremely frustrating. What few paths there were, along the lower levels of the mountain, proved to be virtually impassable. If that wasn't enough, she had considerable difficulty trying to establish exactly where she was in relation to the map. It was impossible to distinguish between one pile of stones and another. She wished she had Rhiannon with her as she felt sure that she would know where the hut circles were. Finally, scratched and bruised from scrambling over rocks and through thistles and bracken she gave up. It was well past lunchtime. A bank of heavy grey cloud was blowing in. Anxious to avoid a further soaking, she headed disconsolately back to Llofft Plas. She would have to spend the afternoon studying before heading off for supper with Harry and Mattie. It was just as well that she decided to hurry, almost as soon as she had returned the heavens opened and more heavy showers swept across the island.

She spent the afternoon re-reading Geoffrey of Monmouth's references to Avalon in his *Life of Merlin*. Geoffrey had been writing several centuries after the time of Arthur and Merlin and his account was generally considered to be heavily romanticised. However she was intrigued by his detailed description of the island and its supposed inhabitants. She wondered about his sources. There were very few reliable written texts still in existence but she had never underestimated the power of the oral tradition. Who could possibly know what stories of Arthur and his quests might still have abounded in Geoffrey's time? Sometimes it was just too tempting to dismiss everything as myth or fantasy. However much stories may be embroidered over the years, they often point back to real incidents. There was one particular reference which she found especially interesting:

*'The isle of Apples, which is called the blessed, has gained this name for its nature, since it produces all things spontaneously.'*

'The isle of apples'. Beth was fairly sure she had read somewhere that Bardsey was famous for its apples. This was odd. She had seen precious few trees of any description growing on the island, let alone fruit trees. It was something else she would ask Harry about.

# CHAPTER THIRTY-SEVEN

"Rhiannon, would you mind taking this tray up to Grandma, and be careful how you go, I've filled her bowl rather full and you know how she hates it when it slops over the side."

"Shall I take Grandma a slice of bread so she can mop up her gravy?"

"Thank you, my angel, that's very thoughtful. Oh, and while you're up there, perhaps you might check to see if she needs any more water. Her cough seems to have got much worse and she's been drinking buckets."

"I took her a jug up when I came in from feeding the chickens, but I'll check."

"That's a good girl. Perhaps you'll stay up there with her for a while. You know how much she likes to have someone to talk to while she's eating her supper. You can tell her what you've been up to. I'll give you a call when your Daddy comes in and we are ready to sit down for our tea."

"All right Mummy."

Beth watched Rhiannon pick up the tray and carry it carefully through the door at the bottom of the stairs. Meanwhile Mattie had sat down at the table opposite Beth.

"You have a lovely girl there Mattie, you must be very proud of her."

"Oh I am, she's a gem. She never gives us any trouble and she's so helpful around the farm. I don't know what we'd do without her." She looked up at the kitchen clock. "I hope you don't mind waiting a little while for your tea. Harry should be back before too long. He's feeding the cattle. Perhaps you'd like a cuppa while we're waiting?"

"I'm fine, thank you. Actually, there's something I've been meaning to ask you. When I first arrived on the island, you told me you had two grown up children apart from Rhiannon."

"That's right dear. There's Gareth, he's our eldest. He's a carpenter and lives in Pwllheli. And then there's our Gwen. She's married to a schoolteacher in Bangor. As it happens, Harry and I are hoping to take the ferry over to the mainland tomorrow morning and to catch the bus over to Pwllheli. You see, Gareth's moving into a new house there. He's asked for a bit of a hand to move his bits and pieces of furniture in and Gwen's coming over as well, with her two little ones."

"That will be nice for you all. I don't expect that you get all that many opportunities to leave the island, what with the visitors, the animals to look after and all the other work to be done on the farm."

"No, I'm afraid we don't, so we try to make the most of it whenever the opportunity arises. To be perfectly honest, if it wasn't for Rhiannon, I'm not sure we'd be able to get away at all. But as long as we leave her a list of all the things she has to do while we're away, she's wonderfully dependable. She may be a bit slow, but she's got a good deal more about her than many a young girl without her limitations. To be honest, the only thing I'm a little bit worried about this time is that my mother isn't at all well. She has this dreadful hacking cough you know and she hasn't left her bed for over a week. She's aged a great deal these last few months. She was such an active woman, right up to her late seventies, but now she's turned eighty she seems to be going downhill rather fast. Rhiannon will be here to look after her and everything should be fine. She loves her grandmother very much and I'm sure that she'll take good care of her. But you know what it's like, you can't help worrying that something will go wrong and she'll take a sudden turn for the worse."

"Rhiannon strikes me as being a very capable young woman" Beth said "and she's wonderful company, such a delight to talk to and so interested in everything. We had a lovely time together when she took me up the mountain."

"I only hope she isn't bothering you too much. She tends to latch on to new people when they arrive on the island. It can get quite lonely out here at times and I suppose she relishes the opportunity of finding a new friend. But you must tell her if she's getting in your way. What with your researches and everything I'm sure you'll need time to yourself."

"Honestly Mattie, she's been very helpful and I enjoy having her around."

"Well that's all right then, but you will tell her, won't you, if she's becoming a nuisance. But forgive me, I've been babbling on about all manner of things, wasn't there something you wanted to ask me?"

"Well, it's nothing really. It's just that when we were up on the mountain Rhiannon mentioned someone who seemed to be a rather special friend. Someone called Dafydd. I was a little intrigued. I didn't think there were any other permanent residents on the island. From the way she talked about him I wondered if, perhaps, he was an imaginary friend?"

Beth saw the smile on Mattie's face give way to a look of intense sadness. She turned her head away as if attempting to hide her discomfort. When she looked back at Beth, there were tears in her eyes.

"I'm so sorry" she said, taking a handkerchief out from the sleeve of her jumper "I'm afraid sometimes it still hits me hard even after all these years." She wiped her eyes and blew her nose.

"It was all a very long time ago you see, the day Dafydd died. He and Rhiannon were twins and as close as twins can be. From the moment he could first understand such things, Dafydd took special care of Rhiannon. He knew she needed help. When they were old enough to go out on their own, they went everywhere together. They explored every nook and cranny of the island. They knew the mating seasons of all the birds and when to look out for the spring and autumn migrations. They would sit for hours above the little beach next to Carn Enlli, where the boats come in, to listen out for the howling of the grey seals on the rocks below. But the mountain was their special place, their kingdom if you like. They would disappear up there for hours at a time, only coming home when they were hungry or when one of them had grazed themselves on one of the rocks."

She paused for a moment. Beth could see she was struggling to retain her self-control as the memories of her lost child came flooding back. "So what happened?" She hardly dared to ask, but sensed that she must and that Mattie seemed to want to talk about it.

"Well, it was the day before their ninth birthday. Harry had promised to take them out fishing as a special treat, but the weather turned nasty and so he had to call it off. I can still see the look of disappointment on their faces. It rained cats and dogs all morning and we had to stay indoors and try to make the best of it. My other two were still at home in those days so they played cards with Dafydd and their Dad, while Rhiannon helped me to bake a birthday cake for the next day. After lunch the rain passed away and the sun came out. It must have been somewhere round about three o'clock when Dafydd and Rhiannon asked Harry if they could go out to play. I was out in the backyard feeding the chickens at the time. Well, he told them that he couldn't see why not as long as they were back for their tea at six, and so off they went. When tea time came round there was no sign of them and I began to get worried. It was so unusual for them not have come back on time. Harry was out in the fields, so I couldn't call on him to help. But thank God, I had Gareth and Gwen who immediately volunteered to go out and look for them. An hour or so later they came back but neither of them had had sight or sound of the twins. Harry was also back by now. The one place Gareth and Gwen hadn't searched yet was the very top of the mountain. Gwen had cut herself rather badly on some barbed wire, scrambling over a fence, and so we left her behind, thinking that, in any case, somebody should stay at home in case the twins returned. The rest of us set off up the mountain. Gareth took the path behind the farm here that takes you up this end of the mountain. Harry and I headed off towards the schoolhouse and took the path that leads up to the far end. It was getting dark by now and I was beside myself with worry. Harry did his best to keep me calm but all I could think of was of our two poor little kiddies in trouble somewhere out there, all on their own."

"When we finally got to the top it was almost dark and the mountain was covered in thick cloud. You couldn't see more than a few feet in front of you. Harry went ahead with the torch and I did my best to keep up with him. We stopped every few yards to call out their names, but there was no reply. It was just after we'd reached the highest point of the mountain that we heard a faint cry from somewhere down below. We shouted back and the cry came again, but there was such a devil of a wind that it was impossible to tell where it was coming from. This part of the mountain is very dangerous if you are not familiar with it, especially in the dark. Harry told me to stay where I was while he tried to make his way down towards where we thought the cry had come from. Left alone in the dark, I was absolutely petrified. All I could think of was of my two little darlings, all alone out there in goodness knows what kind of trouble. The cry came again. You could only just hear it through the howling wind. This time, it seemed to me that it had come from a different direction, from somewhere down below for sure, but further back along the track and not where Harry had gone at all. I called out to him but realised he probably wouldn't be able to hear me. And then I heard the cry again, and this time my maternal instincts took over. I knew I had no choice. I had to go to look myself. Harry had gone off with the big farm torch and all I had was a small one we only use around the house. I scrambled down on my hands and knees. And then, when I heard the cry again, I began to edge my way carefully down the far side of the mountain. I had to shut out of my mind all thought of the 400 foot drop just below me. As I struggled down the slope, the cries became clearer and I shouted back to say that I was coming, that I would find them and that they mustn't try to move until I got to them."

"I found Rhiannon clinging onto a large boulder right down at the cliff edge. I could hear the waves smashing into the rocks down below. At first, I could hardly see anything. But when I got closer, I saw she was nursing one of her legs and I thought she must be badly hurt. There was no sign of Dafydd and my heart sank. My one hope was that he might have managed to clamber up the slope and was somewhere up there above us. I inched my way towards Rhiannon. The slope was very steep and the ground kept giving way under my feet. I could hear the loose stones falling away below me. When I finally reached her, I could see the poor thing was drenched from head to toe. She was shivering uncontrollably, so much so she could hardly speak. I don't know how, but eventually I managed to pull her just a few feet away from the edge of the cliff. I couldn't pull her any further because I was worried about hurting her injured leg. I took my jacket off and wrapped it round her as best I could. Then I got her to lie back, wedged between two rocks. I asked her 'Where's Dafydd?', but she just stared back at me with a puzzled look on her face. I kept asking but she carried on staring at me as though she didn't understand what I was saying. I didn't know what to do. I couldn't leave her to go to look for Dafydd and I couldn't possibly move her on my own. We lay there, side by side, for what seemed an eternity. My head was in turmoil about what might have happened to Dafydd and what we were going to do. All I could hope was that, before long, Harry would come looking for me. I shouted out for him, time after time, but there was no answer. And then I heard a voice calling from the other direction and realised it was Gareth. He must have given up his search at the other end of the mountain and come to find us. I shouted to tell him where we were and warn him how dangerous it was. And then I heard another voice and knew that Harry was somewhere there too and my hopes began to rise."

Mattie rested her elbows on the table and buried her head in her hands. Beth could see how much pain it was causing her to retell the dreadful events of that night. She wished there was something she could say that would help. She sensed that Mattie needed to share this tragedy with her and so she waited patiently without saying anything. Mattie dabbed her eyes with her handkerchief and continued.

"Well, Harry and Gareth soon made it down to us. Rhiannon was in a terrible state and I was really worried about her. She could hardly speak and was almost completely incoherent. When we asked her about Dafydd all she kept saying was, "Dafydd's gone, he's gone". Harry and Gareth searched every corner, but there was no sign of our little boy. By the time they came back Rhiannon was much worse and nearly unconscious. We knew if we didn't find a way of getting her back home immediately, she might not survive. Although she was cut and bruised and had sprained one of her ankles, we didn't think she'd broken any bones. There was nothing for it; the two men had to carry her back down the mountain between them. We had no choice but to abandon the search for Dafydd until we had got her home. After that the men could return to the mountain with whatever additional help they could muster."

"I can't put into words how painful a decision it was to leave the mountain, not knowing what had happened to Dafydd or whether he was even still alive. But we didn't have a choice. We did what we had to do, otherwise we risked losing Rhiannon. If I'm really honest, I suppose that, in my heart of hearts, I already knew we weren't going to find Dafydd alive. He and Rhiannon were inseparable. If he had still been alive he would have been with her. The only ray of hope we had to cling onto was the possibility that he he'd set off back home to get help after seeing her so badly injured.But that hope was immediately dashed the moment we finally got back home and Dafydd wasn't there. At this point we were close to giving up hope. Anyway, I stayed to look after Rhiannon while Harry and Gareth went back out to search again, with the help of two young lads who were staying at the observatory.

"They searched all night but there was no sign of him anywhere. We had to accept he must have fallen off the cliff edge. Gareth ran over to the lighthouse to get a message to the mainland and as soon as it was light the lifeboat went out and an air sea rescue helicopter joined the search. They scoured the cliffs in case Dafydd had fallen and was trapped on a ledge somewhere. Later the coastguard vessel ran up and down the length of the island, searching for his body on the rocks or in the sea, but there was still no trace of our little boy. By lunchtime we had to accept there was no way he could still be alive. They put out a general call to all the fishing boats that use the waters around the island. They expected to find his body floating somewhere in the channel. They searched the coastline from Nefyn all the way down to Mynydd Cilan. But they found nothing, absolutely nothing."

"It's so difficult to come to terms with death if there is no body to bury. It was almost as if Dafydd had never existed. You need to be able to lay your loved ones to rest." Listening to Mattie, Beth felt her own eyes well up. How could any mother survive such an ordeal? She took hold of Mattie's hand. The only words that came to her lips were "I'm sorry, I'm so very sorry". And then she looked away, embarrassed at the inadequacy of her response.

Finally, after a long silence, Mattie drew back her chair and stood up. She looked at Beth and said "It was all a very long time ago now. Although the pain will never go away, at least I've learned to live with it. Harry and I thought it would be even worse for Rhiannon, what with his being her twin. But, do you know, the amazing thing is that, somehow, she's coped with it all far better than the rest of us. It's as if he's still here for her. Do you know, just now and again I come across her talking aloud and I'm sure she's talking to Dafydd." She smiled and folded her arms across her chest. "Well, praise the Lord that he kept our little Rhiannon safe that night. I really don't know what I'd have done if I'd lost them both."

There was the sound of a tractor approaching from the direction of the harbour.

"Beth, do me a favour dear. Please don't say anything about our little chat to Harry when he comes in. He still blames himself you know. So much so that I avoid bringing the subject up, he gets so upset."

"Of course. But, surely, no-one was to blame. I mean, wasn't it just one of those quite dreadful things that happen sometimes?"

"Well, the truth is, that afternoon, after I came back in, I asked Harry where the twins were. When he told me he'd let them go out, I threw a bit of a wobbly. I said that although the weather might have brightened up, it was still very wet and muddy outside and goodness knows what state they'd come back in. You see, Rhiannon was wearing a new white frock I'd bought for her birthday. Oh, I was ever so cross. So, you can imagine how much he blamed himself for what happened, even although I've told him time and time again that it wasn't his fault."

"Poor Harry, what a burden to carry. Mattie, it may seem an odd thing to say, but I feel incredibly privileged that you've told me about all of this. It must hurt a great deal to relive it all over again."

"Actually, dear, it kind of helps in a way. As I've said, it's not something I can talk about to Harry and I don't want to bring all those sad memories back to Gareth and Gwen. My mother's been a great support, but she's an old and sick lady now with other things on her mind. And Rhiannon?

218

Well I think that she's the lucky one, for in her own little world, she believes Dafydd's still there for her."

Mattie paused, smiled and grasped hold of Beth's hands.

"We don't see all that many people out here, apart from the day-trippers that is, certainly not many that I would choose to confide in. It's a funny thing, but from the moment you and I first met I felt sure that we were going to get on."

Beth returned her smile. "As I said, I really do feel that it's a privilege. I only wish there was something more that I could do..."

"But you mustn't feel that way" Mattie said, interrupting her, "I've so wanted to talk about it to somebody and, bless you; you've come along at just the right moment. It's been very hard not being able to talk to Harry about it. I sometimes think he's trying to eradicate Dafydd from his memory because he simply can't bear the pain. But I know you can't do that. You can sit on your emotions for a while and hide the truth from yourself, but you can't do it for ever. No, you have to face up to life as it is however cruel it may seem to be. If only Harry could do that and talk about what happened and accept that it was just an accident and not anyone's fault. He would find it so much easier to live with himself."

The sound of the tractor engine suddenly ceased with a final cough and a splutter.

"Goodness me, all this talking and I've quite forgotten to put the veggies on. I'd better get a move on or else I'll be in no end of trouble with the boss! He's always starving when he comes in for his tea."

# CHAPTER THIRTY-EIGHT

*T*hey *sat in a tight circle, some of them sitting on the large stones that had fallen on the inside of the tower, others seated cross-legged on the ground. Father Beuno had chosen to conduct the service from a folding wooden chair from the nearby farmhouse. The fact that his ample frame only just fitted into it was causing some amusement amongst the brothers. Tom had been surprised by their seemingly unembarrassed fits of giggling during services. When he had challenged Brother Ninnian about this he had been assured that it was nothing especially unusual or to be concerned about. Apparently such light-hearted ribaldry was a common feature of life back at their mother house in Dorset. It was a sign of the genuine affection that the brothers held for each other and, surely, God would understand.*

*It had been a glorious, hot, summer's day, the very best that August could bring. The rehearsals for the play had gone well. Most of the cast were now sufficiently familiar with their lines to have abandoned their scripts. Tom had been able to turn his attention to directing their positions and movements around the rehearsal space on the grass beside the abbey ruins.*

*Earlier on, they had shared a simple communal supper of sausages, baked beans and boiled potatoes in the yard of the farmhouse next to the Abbey. They were all tired after a morning exploring the island, followed by the rehearsals which had taken place under the blazing sun throughout the afternoon. They were gathered now for their day's final act of worship. Of all the Church's Offices, the Order for Compline was Tom's favourite. He considered the words to be the most beautiful in the prayer book.*

*Father Beuno began by thanking them all for working so hard at learning their parts in the play. He reminded them they only had a few days together on the island. He urged them to work even harder to ensure the play would be ready for them to share with the parish communities on the road to Bangor.*

They would be travelling the old pilgrim's route in reverse because it was important to end their journey in a live centre, where they could bear witness to their faith.

The elderly friar took off his glasses and rubbed them vigorously up and down the front of his habit. This action was a regularly repeated little ritual which, as the material was extremely coarse, doubtless accounted for the many scratches on the lenses. His prayer book lay unopened on his knee, for he knew the Office by heart and Tom couldn't help wondering why he carried it with him at all. He closed his eyes in deep concentration.

"The Lord Almighty grant us a quiet night and a perfect end" to which they all responded with the communal "Amen".

There then followed the first of the many exhortations that Tom loved so much.

"Brethren, be sober, be vigilant; because your adversary the devil, as a roaring lion, walketh about, seeking whom he may devour: whom resist, steadfast in the faith." They were words Tom was very familiar with for they were recited every evening in his college chapel. But, somehow, here, on his third pilgrimage to the island within the ruins of the ancient abbey, they were charged with special meaning. They were the same words that had been uttered countless times, over many centuries, by the monks who used to maintain the abbey, and by the thousands of pilgrims who had braved the currents. He wasn't sure that he could come to terms with the very real 'devil' in whom they had, no doubt, believed. But that didn't really matter. The message was clear. It was about resisting temptation and, in that sense, its meaning was as relevant and powerful today as it had ever been.

After they had joined together in reciting the opening verses of Psalm 31 and the ensuing Responses, they sang together the hymn 'Before the ending of the day'. Father Beuno had opened his eyes and was smiling benignly at the gathered company. Tom noticed how his younger Welsh-speaking companions struggled with some of the English words. The two languages were so different. It was their Celtic ancestors who had settled this island and the mainland beyond and he could understand the pride they felt in their own language and the fears they had of domination by the English. He found himself thinking *about the Reverend Ronald Thomas, the austere, white-haired priest, who had welcomed them to his church in Aberdaron. It was said he had taught himself Welsh so he could more fully identify with the people he served and with the Celtic cause. They reached the end of the hymn and Father Beuno intoned "Keep me as the apple of an eye" to which they responded "Hide me under the shadow of thy wings". They sang the Nunc Dimittis and as they drew towards the conclusion of the short Office, Tom was especially pleased that Father Beuno had chosen his favourite collect:*

*"Visit, we beseech the, O Lord, this place, and drive from it all the snares of the enemy; let thy holy angels dwell herein to preserve us in peace; and may thy blessing be upon us evermore; through Jesus Chris our Lord."*

*When they had first assembled, Brother Paul had lit a white candle and placed it on the makeshift altar. Throughout the short Office it had flickered in the light evening breeze that blew in through the tiny window over the altar. Now, as they remained seated together in silence, the wind had dropped and the candle burned tall and bright. On the distant horizon a deep red sun was setting in a scarlet sky.*

# CHAPTER THIRTY-NINE

After a brisk walk up to the abbey ruins and back, Tom had finally managed to put thoughts of Beth out of his mind. He had come to the island to rekindle his faith. He was determined not to allow the events of the past few days to steer him away from this course. He resolved to spend the rest of the day at Carreg Bach in study and contemplation.

He pulled one of the armchairs away from the fireplace and placed it directly beneath one of the front windows. It was dark inside and he needed all the daylight he could get.

He opened his copy of Tillich's *Shaking of the Foundations*, the same volume on which he had found it impossible to concentrate the previous evening. He turned the pages until he came to the section he was looking for. It was the chapter where Tillich tells of how, as a young man about to receive confirmation and full membership of the church, he had been instructed to choose a passage from the Bible to express the nature of his faith. He had chosen a passage from St Matthew's Gospel 'Come unto me all ye that are heavy laden and I will give you rest. Take my yoke upon you, and learn of me; for I am meek and lowly in heart; and ye shall find rest unto your souls. For my yoke is easy, and my burden is light.' Tillich argued that 'these words of Jesus are universal and fit every human being and every human situation. They are simple; they grasp the heart of the primitive as well as that of the profound.'

Tillich had then gone on to ask 'What is the labour and burden from which we can find rest through Him? What is the easy yoke and the light burden that He will put upon us? Why is He and He alone able to give such rest to our souls?' These were the very questions that Tom had so much difficulty in answering. He felt that far from lightening his burden, God had allowed Martha, his main support, to be taken away from him.

Of course, trial through tribulation was a constant theme of the Jewish and Christian faith. How often had he himself retold the story of Job to his congregations? But until Martha's death he had never been fully tested. After that nothing had been the same. How was he to reconcile Martha's meaningless death with the concept of a loving God?

He read on. Tillich's next argument was that 'The burdens and labours of which Jesus speaks are not the burdens and labours of daily life. In any case how could he possibly ease such burdens and labours even if he wanted to?'

In the next passage, Tillich challenged the traditional view that through prayer, God can be called upon to intervene in the human situation. 'Whether or not we come to Him' he submitted 'The threats of illness or unemployment are not lessened, the weight of our work does not become easier, the fate of a refugee driven, from one country to another, is not changed; the horror of ruins, wounds, and death falling from heaven is not stopped; and the sorrow over the passing of friends or parents or children is not overcome. Jesus cannot and does not promise more pleasure and less pain to those whom He asks to come to him. On the contrary, sometimes He promises them more pain, more persecution, more threat of death — 'the cross', as He calls it. All this is not the burden to which He points.'

Tom closed his eyes and sat back, deep in thought. If only he could truly believe that what had happened to Martha was no fault of his God. He found it difficult to grapple with the full import of what Tillich was saying. What was the burden that Jesus wanted to take from us? He read on, hoping for further enlightenment. He was struck by Tillich's next proposition which was that the burden Jesus was speaking of was 'the burden of religion' which demands that the believer 'accept ideas and dogmas, that he believes in doctrines and traditions, the acceptance of which is the condition of his salvation from anxiety, despair and death. So, he tries to accept them, although they may have become strange or doubtful to him. He labours and toils under the religious demand to believe things he cannot believe. Finally, he tries to escape the law of religion. He tries to cast away the heavy yoke of the doctrinal law imposed on him by Church authorities, orthodox teachers, pious parents, and fixed traditions. He becomes critical and sceptical. He casts away the yoke.'

Tom stared at the page. He had read this chapter before, but that was back in his student days when it hadn't had the same resonance. So, was that it? Was that the journey he had taken into the darkness of non-belief? But no, he hadn't stopped believing in God. How else could he lay the blame for Martha's death on his doorstep? What Tillich seemed to be saying was that he had misunderstood the nature of his relationship with God, that he had been wrong to believe that God would or even could intervene in human events. He thought of the endless intercessions in which he and his fellow clergy sought God's intervention on a daily basis. Had the Christian Church, within which his own beliefs had been moulded, become too dependent on the concept of divine intervention? As Tom contemplated the profound import of what Tillich was saying, he saw the first glimmer of an essential truth. Could it be that it was outside the nature of God to interfere directly in the affairs of man? Had the true purpose of the life and death of Jesus been to show us how we could take control of our own lives, for the good of humankind, and to offer spiritual strength in times of adversity?

He looked out through the window. A lone gull swooped low over the track letting out an ear-piercing screech as it passed by. He was reminded of 'the voice of one calling in the wilderness'. He had been waiting to hear that voice for a very long time. And now, at last, a new understanding was emerging from the darkness. How could he have been so wrong? How could he have blamed God for something that was not of his making? Perhaps it was no more than the natural human need to find somebody to blame for everything that goes wrong? How could he have been so stupid? Yes, he could see the truth now. He had been wrong to blame God for Martha's death. It had just been one of those terrible accidents and that was something with which he would just have to learn to live.

# CHAPTER FORTY

"Hello Dr Davenport. Excuse me if I don't shake hands, I'm covered in oil. Mattie, that wretched tractor's been playing up again and I've had to clean out the air filter. I'm going to have to get someone over from the mainland to take a look at it, before it packs up completely."

From the expression on Mattie's face, Beth gathered that this was almost certainly not the first time Harry had had problems with his tractor. She smiled.

"Please call me Beth. Dr Davenport sounds so formal."

"Of course, if you really don't mind. Everyone is so casual these days and I don't like to take things for granted."

Harry took off his heavy oilskin jacket and hung it up at the foot of the staircase. He went over to Mattie who was standing next to the cooker. Stretching his arms out in front of him he clenched his fists while Mattie pulled off his voluminous woollen jersey which was full of holes and looked much the worse for wear. Mattie rolled his shirtsleeves up to his elbows while Harry stood there with a broad and slightly embarrassed grin on his face.

"You must forgive our little evening ritual, but I have to do the washing oil stains are a devil to get out" Mattie said, looking at Beth over her shoulder. She gave Harry a tap on the bottom and said "Off you go then, there's a fresh bar of soap in the plastic container by the sink. I'll have tea on the table in five minutes so you'd better get a move on." She opened the door at the foot of the stairs and called up "Rhiannon, your Daddy's home. Can you come down please and help me to put the tea on the table."

"I'm coming" Rhiannon called back.

"How's your Nan, dear?" her mother asked, looking at the half eaten bowl of stew Rhiannon had carried downstairs. "It doesn't look as though she's eaten very much again." She turned to Beth "She seems to have lost her appetite since she got this ghastly cough. She normally eats rather well for an old lady."

"I think we'll have to get Dr Richards over to take a look at her Mattie" Harry said from over by the sink where he was vigorously rubbing his soapy hands together.

"We'll call in at the surgery when we're over on the mainland tomorrow. If he can't come over right away, he may be able to prescribe something to ease the congestion. She's had that cough for far too long now and it's really got onto her chest."

"I propped her up on her pillows like you said. She was fast asleep when I left her" Rhiannon said. "You know how she normally likes to know about everything I've been doing. Well, she hardly asked me a thing and she was wheezing like an old goat."

"Rhiannon dear, I'm not at all sure that your Grandma would like to be described as an old goat, but thank you for looking after her. You're ever such a good little helper." Mattie smiled at her daughter. Beth couldn't help thinking how strange it was to see this young woman being spoken to as if she were still a child. And yet, of course, that was exactly what fate had decided that Rhiannon would always be, a child who would never grow up. She glanced at Harry and saw that he was drying his hands on a kitchen towel. "I do hope I haven't come over at a difficult time." she said.

"Don't you worry about that" Harry replied "It'll do us good to talk about something other than my clapped out old tractor!"

Mattie lifted the lid off a large copper saucepan bubbling away on the cooker and poked a fork inside. "Ah, good, the potatoes are ready so we can sit down and eat. Beth, why don't you sit there between Harry and Rhiannon" she said pointing to the far side of the dining table "and I'll sit opposite you so that I can get up when I need to. Rhiannon, be a good girl and pass the plates round will you?"

Soon they had all been served and Rhiannon and Mattie joined the others at the table. Harry cut four thick slices of homemade bread. "You'll need something to mop up the gravy" he said, offering them round.

"This stew smells delicious" Beth said "My father always used to say that mopping up the gravy was the best part."

Harry ate in silence, tired and hungry after a hard day's toil on the farm. It was left to Mattie to keep their guest entertained, telling Beth about some of the more eccentric visitors to the island.

"Do many people come back year after year?" Beth asked "I got the impression that the couple I travelled over with are regulars. They seem to be very into ornithology."

"You mean the Cartwrights. Yes, they've been coming here years. They usually stay up at the observatory. An odd couple, if you know what I mean. They always seem to be arguing about something or other, but I reckon that's what keeps them going."

"I thought Bert looked a little hen-pecked but he seemed to take most of what Joan said with a pinch of salt."

"Oh, for all her nit-picking and bickering, she's a good soul underneath it all. The truth is, I reckon they get on like a house on fire. They certainly look forward to coming over here every year."

"A rum couple if you ask me" said Harry, mopping up the last of the gravy with a large chunk of bread. Rhiannon hadn't spoken since she had sat down but Beth saw that she was listening intently to everything that was said.

"Yes, but harmless enough" Mattie said. "Anyway, enough of the Cartwrights, I invited Beth over for supper so that you could tell her what you know about the island's history, Harry. It's the early times she's most interested in, if I remember right."

"Well, yes" Beth said "I am particularly keen to hear anything you may know about the island's association with King Arthur and Merlin."

"Beth's told me all 'bout when Merlin was a boy and 'bout how he told the king where to build his city doll and 'bout the red and white dragons" Rhiannon interjected excitedly.

"Has she now" said Mattie with a smile. "But hush now, Rhiannon, you must let Beth talk to your Daddy. I'm sure she's got lots of questions she wants to ask him."

"It's fine, really it is" Beth said smiling. "Your daughter's the most enthusiastic student I've had for a long time."

"I'm not quite sure how much I can help," Harry said, "You see Mattie always tells everyone that I know all about the island but I doubt whether I'll be able to live up to your expectations. Of course, I've picked up a bit, as you might expect, what with all the archaeologists who've been here over the years, and those bods from the history department at the university. But, to be honest, they've mostly been looking into the island's very early history, you know the prehistoric stuff. Otherwise they've wanted to find out more about the foundation of the abbey and that kind of thing."

"I took a look at the remains of those rectangular stone buildings down at Penrhyn Gogor this morning. I gather it's generally believed that they're the remains of farm buildings. Have you heard any other theories about them?"

"Well no, I haven't. From the way the stones have been laid, they say they're typical of late medieval farm structures. I can't think of any other use for them."

"I suppose I was just wondering whether they might have been contemporary with the abbey and have had some kind of religious significance."

"I suppose that's possible. But, of course, the ruined tower and the few other remains of the abbey buildings only date back to the thirteenth century. The original abbey, founded by St Cadfan, was probably built largely of timber. I doubt whether there are many traces of it left. Archaeologists have found the remains of a rectangular building about the same size as the schoolhouse. They say there may be evidence of an early field system behind that and there are a couple of smaller round huts close by. I think these were all originally enclosed inside a boundary wall. Nobody seems to know for sure, but they may date back to the time of the original monastery."

"That's really interesting because the very earliest religious foundations normally only consisted of one or two small buildings or cells. Beth leaned forward with her elbows on the table. "I've done a bit of reading up on St Cadfan. He seems to have come from the nobility. Apparently he came over from Brittany with a number of other high-born and saintly Celts who'd been driven out by the invading Franks. He must have been incredibly charismatic to persuade others to join him in establishing the abbey on the island and, of course, it soon became an important place of pilgrimage. It was just as important in those days as St David's."

"Hence Ynys Enlli becoming known as 'The island of 20,000 saints'" Harry said. "They must have come in boatloads! I can't imagine what a terrible crossing so many of them must have had. Goodness knows how the monks managed to feed them all and provide them with accommodation."

"They would have lived here very simply, feeding off the sea and the land. You've just called the island by its proper Welsh name Ynys Enlli. I believe it means 'Island in the Currents'?"

"Yes, that's how it translates into English and it's an appropriate enough name for it. But there are other theories about the origin of the name. It's been said that Ynys Enlli could be a corrupted form of Ynys Fenlli, or Benlli's Island. He was some kind of Irish warlord who's supposed to have invaded Llŷn and other parts of North Wales."

"So what's the origin of the name 'Bardsey'?"

"I'm not sure we really know. Some say it's named after a Viking invader called Bard. But I like to think of it as the 'Island of the Bards'. After all, Anglesey, and the whole of this far corner of North Wales, is where the Celtic druids made their home. There are some very old legends about the island being the last resting place of Merlin."

"Now this is where it becomes particularly interesting to me." Beth said, her eyes lighting up with enthusiasm. "I'm wondering what stories you may have heard about this, stories, perhaps, that have been passed down the generations."

"Let me see now. I remember my grandfather telling me about Merlin coming here to die and bringing with him the 13 treasures of Wales, although I can't remember what they all were or why they were so important."

"That's something I do know about" Beth said, excitedly rubbing her hands together. "According to manuscripts that were written much later, in the fifteenth and sixteenth centuries, the treasures were all supposed to have magical qualities. There was the white hilted sword of Rhydderch Hael 'The Generous' which was rejected by everyone who was offered it because it would burst into flames the moment it was drawn. There was the hamper of Gwyddno Long Shank which, when filled with food for one man, would feed a hundred men when it was opened again. There was the Chariot of Morgan the Wealthy which bore anyone who rode in it at great speed to wherever they wished to go. And then there was a horn and a halter and a cauldron and a coat and a crook and several other items all of which had magic qualities and all of which were supposedly brought here by Merlin."

"Why did Merlin bring them here?" asked a wide-eyed Rhiannon.

"I suppose he wanted to be sure they'd be safe. The story goes that he collected the thirteen treasures and kept them in a glass tower where he slept beside them and where they were to remain forever or until such time as King Arthur returns."

"It's a great story and good for tourism but it all sounds a bit too fanciful for me." Harry said, scratching his head. "I mean, why a glass tower and could they even build such a thing in those days? And what happened to those thirteen treasures? I can't think of anywhere they could have been hidden. Mind you, I wouldn't mind digging them up one day when I'm out ploughing, that would be something!" He laughed out loud at the thought and everyone joined in.

"Well, I know it all sounds a little far-fetched these days, but behind most old legends there lies an element of truth. Our difficulty, as historians, is always the same. We have to separate the truth from everything that's been embroidered around it. I know the idea of a glass tower may sound straight out of a fairy story. But think about it for a moment. Don't forget that glass had been around since Roman times. Not the clear, see-through glass as we know it today, of course, but certainly a material which light could shine and which the heat of the sun could penetrate. I don't think it's beyond possibility that the monks may have constructed some kind of primitive greenhouse to propagate their vegetable seeds. That, in itself, would be something of a wonder to anyone who saw it at the time. And it might not be all that long before it grew into something much more mystical in their imagination, like a glass tower. The legends about the Isle of Avalon suggest that Merlin built the tower himself. Some of them also suggest that, when the wounded Arthur was carried to Avalon, he was placed in a glass chamber. In those days the sun was considered to have powerful healing properties."

"I love lying in the sun" Rhiannon said "When I close my eyes, it makes me feel all warm and sleepy and safe. It's like my whole body is floating in a huge great big cuddle. But can the sun really make you better if you've been hurt?"

Rhiannon didn't get an answer to her question because her mother intervened.

"Excuse me for butting in" she said "but I have an apple crumble in the oven and I need to ask whether you'd prefer it with cream or with custard."

"Apple crumble, one of my favourites" Beth said "I think I'd prefer custard if it's not too much trouble."

"No trouble at all, Harry always prefers custard, don't you dear? Rhiannon, perhaps you'd like to make it while I serve up the crumble. She makes the best custard you'll ever taste, don't you sweetie?"

Rhiannon stood up with a proud grin on her face and enthusiastically set about her task. Meanwhile Beth watched Mattie remove a large earthenware dish from the oven.

"That smells wonderful" she said. "Those aren't the famous Bardsey apples are they?"

"I'm afraid not" Mattie replied "There may have been a time, many years ago, when there was a proper Bardsey apple orchard on the island. But now we're down to a single tree. You may have seen it. It's right next door to you."

"I must look out for it" Beth said.

"There's been quite a lot of interest in the Bardsey apple recently." Harry said "Do you know, they've taken cuttings from the original tree and are now growing them on the mainland? Our tree must be quite old. It was probably planted when the house was built back in the 1870s. The apple is sometimes called Merlin's apple, so there's another connection for you."

"Fascinating" Beth said.

"You should see the blossom in the spring" Mattie added, "it's almost pure white."

"What's it like to eat?" Beth asked.

"It's actually rather good. It has a bit of a lemony flavour but it's quite sweet. I'm told it makes very good cider, quite strong though"

"It's certainly sweet" Mattie said "I never need to add sugar when I cook them."

"I suppose it's possible the original Bardsey apple goes all the way back to the foundation of the monastery. The monks would have wanted to include fruit in their diet." Beth said. She sat back and watched Rhiannon pour hot milk from a pan onto the custard powder and stir it vigorously.

"Don't make it too thick dear, not everybody likes it that way you know" Mattie said.

"Don't worry about me" Beth said "my Mum used to make it so thick you could stand a spoon up in it. I used to like eating the skin off the top."

"Just as well!" Mattie said.

Soon the bowls of apple crumble had been passed round and Beth helped herself to custard. "Delicious!" she said "and the custard is as good as I've ever tasted!"

Rhiannon looked suitably pleased having scored another hit with her new friend.

"I'd like to return to my research project, if I may. We've talked about Merlin but what about Arthur and his possible connections with Bardsey? Perhaps I can tell you a bit about what we think we know about Arthur. The earliest written historical references to him are rather confusing. They come from early medieval material, a mixture of Latin chronicles, old bardic poems and Christian texts. In them, he's sometimes portrayed as a noble Christian warrior and sometimes as a somewhat tyrannical ruler. But then, somewhere in the middle of the twelfth-century, along comes Geoffrey of Monmouth who reinvents Arthur as a heroic figure. This heroic Arthur is romanticised by later writers and becomes the chivalric Arthur with his knights of the Round Table and the beautiful

Guinevere as his queen. There's little doubt Geoffrey was pretty free with his imagination. But it isn't always easy to know which parts of his story are invented, rather than based on older narratives. And, of course, we can't be certain that we know all Geoffrey's sources. Some may well have been lost over time. What I am particularly interested in is his description of what happened to Arthur after the battle of Camlan."

They had all been listening intently up to this point but then Harry shifted forward in his chair.

"That's all very interesting" he said, "But what I want to know is whether there is any evidence to suggest the so-called battle of Camlan took place near here?"

"It depends what you mean by evidence" said Beth. She went on to tell them about her visit to the ancient battlefields of Cadlan Isaf and Cadlan Uchaf, along the coast from Aberdaron. "They're only just a short way along the coast from Aberdaron. "Of course, there's nothing conclusive in all this and I expect there were plenty of skirmishes between local tribes in these parts in those days. But I've been impressed by some of the arguments presented in a recent book *Journey to Avalon*. Indeed, that's what really brought me down here. The story goes that Arthur left his nephew Mordred in charge of the kingdom while he went over to Ireland to settle a dispute over the payment of tribute with the Irish warlord Llwch Wyddel. While Arthur was away, Mordred decided it was an opportune moment to seize power. As soon as Arthur heard the news, he hurried back with his army from Ireland to put down the rebellion and fought Mordred at the battle of Camlan. Barber and Pykett, the authors of *Journey to Avalon*, argue that the Llŷn Peninsula was an area which Mordred had strong family connections with. They suggest it would have made sense for him to choose to do battle with Arthur on his home territory. They point out there's a place called Porth Cadlan, or 'battle place harbour,' just along the coast from Aberdaron."

"We've been there!" said an excited Rhiannon, who until then had been sitting quietly, listening to Beth and chewing her finger. "It's a funny place for a battle, it's all cliffs and things."

"You're a clever girl!" said Beth. "You see, I don't think anyone is suggesting that because it's called battle place harbour, a battle actually took place there. If you look at the map, Porth Cadlan is almost directly below Cadlan Isaf and Cadlan Uchaf. These two names translate as lower and upper battle place and are much more suitable places for a battle. When I went there the other day and looked down the cliffs to Porth Cadlan, I could see how Arthur and his army might have landed there and scaled the cliffs to meet Mordred's army up above."

"That makes sense." Harry interjected.

"And then there's another interesting thing. You know that large rock sitting out there just off the coast from Porth Cadlan?"

"What, do you mean Maen Gwenonwy?" Harry asked

"Yes, Maen Gwenonwy. Well you know who Gwenonwy was don't you?"

Harry shook his head. "I've always known it as Gwenonwy's rock but I never thought to ask who Gwenonwy was."

"Well, Arthur's sister was called Gwenonwy. She married Gwyndaf Hen, son of a local noble. It was their son Saint Hywyn who established the church at Aberdaron. You can imagine how the rock might have been named after Gwenonwy in memory of the battle her brother fought on the hillside above. Living locally, as she must have done, she might even have watched the battle or at least have seen Arthur's army arriving from across the sea."

"Uhmmm" said Harry, rubbing his hand over the rough stubble of his chin. "That's all very interesting. But I'm not sure I'm altogether convinced and I don't suppose we'll ever know the truth."

"The period of history between the Romans and the Norman Conquest isn't called the Dark Ages for nothing" Beth replied with a smile. "Very little was recorded in writing until several centuries after Arthur. We simply don't know all the true sources of historical writers like Nennius and Geoffrey of Monmouth. It's impossible to know how much may have come from written sources that have been lost, how much is based on stories handed down from father to son, or how much is speculation or pure fantasy. It's generally accepted that the first monastery on Bardsey was established by Saint Cadfan between 516 and 546 AD. This means it would most likely have been up and running at the time of the battle of Camlan. Don't forget that in those days monks specialised in offering herbal remedies for illnesses and injuries. If the battle took place just across the water, it would have been the obvious place to bring a wounded warrior like Arthur. But here, I'm afraid, the story of what actually happened becomes very confused. In Geoffrey of Monmouth's *Life of Merlin* it isn't the monks who attend to Arthur but the Lady Morgan."

Harry raised his eyebrows at the mention of the Lady Morgan.

"Now you're bringing back memories. I'd forgotten about Morgan. I think it must have been my Granddad who told me about her when I was a boy. Didn't she have a lot of sisters?"

"She did, indeed. There were eight of them altogether. Morgan herself is described as being the most beautiful of them. She was the most skilled in her power of healing. She knew all about herbs and plants and how to use them. She is also described as having a good knowledge of science and mathematics. But, as if that isn't enough for a woman of her time, she has another incredible gift, she can change shape and fly!"

"That makes her sound like a bit of a witch to me!" Mattie said with a chuckle.

"Well, at the time that Geoffrey of Monmouth was writing, people really believed in such things. Not all women with extraordinary powers were considered to be the archetypal evil witches who were persecuted a few centuries later. But to continue Geoffrey's story, Arthur was carried across the water by Merlin and the poet Taliesin to the lady Morgan. When they arrived, they were given a warm welcome. Arthur was laid in Morgan's own chamber where she tended to his wounds and told Merlin and Taliesin that she would be able to heal him if they left him in her care."

"It's a great story." Harry said "but if there's any truth in it, I can't quite get my head around a family of beautiful young women living here on the island alongside a community of monks."

"Yes, that does pose a bit of problem doesn't it?" Beth said. "There are plenty of stories of badly behaved monks, but not here on Bardsey I'm sure.

But then some of Geoffrey of Monmouth's other claims about the island of Avalon are equally fantastic. He says that the island produces crops entirely naturally and that everything grows in abundance. He also claims that men who live here reach the age of a hundred years or more."

Harry burst out laughing "If only it were true" he said "I can tell you, it's damned hard work growing anything here on this island!"

"So, it looks like we must put some of Geoffrey's claims on one side as pieces of historical fiction. But that still leaves the real possibility that Arthur could've been brought here to be cared for by the monks." Beth said.

"Did Morgan make Arthur better?" Rhiannon asked, looking rather puzzled.

"I'm afraid we don't know. You see some say that Arthur was so badly wounded that he died soon after the battle. But there are many stories of Arthur recovering, crossing over to France and having lots of adventures there and living into his old age too. There were even those who believed Arthur would return again one day to be a great ruler. But I think that, perhaps, those are stories for another day" Beth said, looking at the clock. "Goodness me, look at the time, it's nearly ten o'clock and I really mustn't overstay my welcome. I expect you all have to be up early in the morning with the farm and everything. I've had a lovely evening, most interesting, and I'd like to hear more about what life on the island was like when you were a young man, Harry."

"I'm sure that can be arranged" Mattie said "Harry isn't quite so busy now that lambing's over and he loves a good chat about old times, don't you Harry?"

He nodded "I certainly do."

"Beth, there's just one thing I'd like to ask you, if you don't mind. As I mentioned earlier, Harry and I have to go over to the mainland tomorrow. I wonder whether you'd mind just keeping a bit of an eye on Rhiannon while we're away. I wouldn't normally ask because she's such a responsible girl. But, what with my mother being so poorly and more bad weather on the way, well, I'd feel much happier if I knew that she could call on you if she needs to. It's only the one night we'll be away and I'm sure everything will be fine, but just in case, if it isn't asking too much?"

"It will be a pleasure, no trouble at all." Beth replied

"And perhaps Beth will have time to tell me more about what happened to King Arthur and Merlin?" Rhiannon said with an excited gleam in her eyes.

"I don't see why not" Beth replied "and perhaps you can show me where the old hut circles are. I couldn't find them when I went to look this afternoon."

"I can make a picnic" Rhiannon said

"Just hold on a moment young lady. Remember you have to look after your Nan and there won't be time for picnics until we get back." Mattie said. "Now Beth, I do hope you'll be able to see your way up the lane, it's pitch black outside. I'm sure Harry wouldn't mind... "

"Thank you but I'll be absolutely fine. I've brought my torch with me. It's been such an enjoyable evening, thank you again, and have a safe trip across tomorrow. Rhiannon, I shall pop down tomorrow afternoon to see how you're getting on."

"Goodnight Beth" Mattie, Harry and Rhiannon all said in unison as she walked out into the night. All was still outside and there wasn't a breath of wind as Beth made her way round the back of the farmhouse. When she reached the track to Llofft Plas, she heard a violent fit of coughing from somewhere in the upper reaches of the house. She turned to look back and saw a light go on in one of the bedrooms and a figure pass by the window. She assumed it must be Mattie. And then all was quiet again and she continued on her way.


### THE ISLE OF APPLES

*'The isle of Apples, which is called the blessed, has gained this name for its nature, since it produces all things spontaneously. It needs no farmers to till its soil: its only cultivation is that provided by nature. Untended, it bears rich crops, grapes and, in its woods, apples born of precious seed. Its soil freely produces everything like grass. The people on it live for a hundred years or*

*more. Nine sisters rule there by right of birth over those who come to them from our lands. Their leader is more skilled in healing and more beautiful than her sisters. She is called Morgan, and has learned the properties each plant has to cure sick bodies. She also has the power of changing her shape, and of flying through the air on strange wings, like Daedalus. She can be at Brest, Chartres or Pavia whenever she wishes, or glide from the skies onto our shores. She is also said to be learned in mathematics according to her sisters, Moronoe, Moroe, Gliorn, Glitonea. Tythonoc, Tythen and Tithen, famed above all for playing the lyre.*

*'After the battle of Camlan we took the wounded Arthur to their island, led by Barinthus who was familiar with the sea and stars. With our ship under his direction, we arrived there with our leader and Morgan received us with due honour. She placed the king on golden coverlets in her bedchamber and herself exposed his wound with her noble hand. After examining it for a long while, she said that he might eventually recover his health, if he remained with her for a long time and was willing to submit to her care. So we joyfully entrusted the king to her and returned with a following wind to our sails.'*

*Geoffrey of Monmouth from 'Life of Merlin'*

# CHAPTER FORTY-ONE

Tom put aside Tillich's *Shaking of the Foundations* and sat for a while in quiet contemplation. If asked, he would have had difficulty putting into words exactly how he felt. The main thrust of Tillich's argument had come as a revelation. It was one of those rare moments when he no longer felt that he was staring at God through a glass darkly. He and Beth had gone to bed late the previous evening. This, combined with the mental effort of such challenging new ideas, was enough to cause him to drift off into a deep sleep. When he woke, he looked at his watch. He was surprised to see that it was already late in the afternoon. He was stiff from sitting for so long and his mouth was dry. But he felt more at ease with himself than he had for a very long time.

He stood and stretched his arms above his head. Looking out of the window, the sun was low above the horizon and there was a build-up of dark clouds in the far distance. He closed the window, went over to the kitchen and lit one of the rings. He always thought more clearly after a cup of coffee. While he waited for the kettle to boil, he found himself thinking about Beth. He wondered where on the island her research might have taken her. Looking back on the previous evening, he could hardly believe they could have shared such intimacy, especially when he remembered how awkward and reserved she had been when they first met. The Beth of last night could hardly have been more different. She had been relaxed, amusing and very much more self-confident. It was almost as if they had switched roles, with Beth becoming the sympathetic listener while he unburdened himself of his troubles. It was the first time he had felt able to talk about Martha's death with anyone outside his immediate family.

His thoughts were interrupted by the loud whistle of the kettle. A few minutes later, clutching a mug of coffee, he stood in front of the window and watched the sun sink lower in the sky. Soon it would disappear altogether, taking with it the last light of day. It perfectly reflected his current state of mind. He had struggled for so long to come to terms with Martha's death. But now his long period of mourning must come to an end.

He closed the window, lit a lamp and sat back down in the armchair, nursing his coffee mug. He smiled when he thought of the moment Beth arrived at his doorstep the previous evening. With the water dripping from her long dark hair there had been something of the water nymph about her. There had also been a beguiling light in her eyes when she smiled at him across the threshold. Her wild and unkempt appearance had, if anything, only added to her natural beauty. He realised now that this was the moment when his long-standing resistance to embarking on a new relationship finally crumbled.

Since Martha's death, Tom had chosen a celibate life. He had believed that to do otherwise would be a betrayal of his love for her. But now, to his surprise, he wasn't harbouring the least bit of guilt over his feelings for Beth. There had been others who had courted his affections since Martha had died. But they had been unable to penetrate his defences. His feelings for Beth were altogether different. She was so unlike the other women who had tried to pursue him. They had either felt sorry for him or had ambitions of filling Martha's shoes as the wife of the vicar. He was sure that Beth's feelings for him were not based on pity and the very thought that she might see herself as a vicar's wife brought a smile to his face. There was nothing calculated about her approach to life. Nor was there any reason for either of them to feel guilty because there was nothing selfish about how they felt for each other. The more he thought about it, the more certain he became that Martha would have approved of this new adventure. She would have understood his need to have someone he could trust and confide in as he battled with his faith and his future.

It was too soon for him to fully understood Beth's expectations. When she snuggled up to him during the night, he hadn't quite known what to make of it. And then it became clear. All she wanted was to be close to him, to seek his reassurance and to express her affection and concern.

When he first arrived on the island, he expected to spend many weeks battling with his faith. That first day on the beach had further diminished his remaining optimism and he had been close to despair. He could only marvel at the transformation that had taken place since then. Tillich had guided him towards seeing his relationship with God in a different light. He was also beginning to accept his need to be close to another human being. For what is life if there is no-one to share it with? He laughed out loud when he thought of Bishop George and what he would make of this unexpected turn of events. But then if anyone was likely to understand it would surely be Bishop George.

While he could delight in his relationship with Beth, there was still much to do if he was to be reconciled to God. The joy of being with Beth was already bringing light and hope into his life. He might no longer need to blame God for his past suffering, but would this be enough to rekindle his faith and commitment?

He had placed a small pile of books on the chest next to his seat. These included a collection of poems by R S Thomas he had purchased from the church bookstall in Aberdaron. He had only glanced through it at the time, but remembered that it included a remarkable poem in which Thomas had tried to describe his relationship with God. Appropriately, it was a poem that Thomas had written about his pilgrimages to Bardsey. Reading the poem again, Tom was astonished to find how close it came to expressing the nature of his own relationship with God.

> *"There is an island there is no going*
> *to but in a small boat the way*
> *the saints went, travelling the gallery*
> *of the frightened faces of*
> *the long-drowned, munching the gravel*
> *of its beaches. So I have gone*
> *up the salt lane to the building*
> *with the stone altar and the candles*
> *gone out, and kneeled and lifted*

*my eyes to the furious gargoyle*
*of the owl that is like a god*
*gone small and resentful. There*
*is no body in the stained window*
*of the sky now. Am I too late?*
*Were they too late also, those*
*first pilgrims? He is such a fast*
*God, always before us and*
*leaving as we arrive.*
*There are those here*
*not given to prayer, whose office*
*is the blank sea that they say daily.*
*What they listen to is not*
*hymns but the slow chemistry of the soil*
*that turns saints' bones to dust,*
*dust to an irritant of the nostril.*

*There is no time on this island.*
*The swinging pendulum of the tide*
*has no clock; the events*
*are dateless. These people are not*
*late or soon; they are just*
*here with only the one question*
*to ask, which life answers*
*by being in them.  It is I*
*who ask. Was the pilgrimage*
*I made to come to my own*
*self, to learn that in times*
*like these and for one like me*
*God will never be plain and*
*out there, but dark rather and*
*inexplicable, as though he were in here?"*

He turned to the window. There was little to be seen in the fast-failing light. In a voice drowned in emotion, he repeated the last lines "and for one like me God will never be plain and out there, but dark rather and inexplicable, as though he were in here".

# CHAPTER FORTY-TWO

SATURDAY LATE EVENING

It was a little after ten o'clock when Beth set off on her way back to Llofft Plas. She had enjoyed her evening in the warm and hospitable company of the Evans family, even though Harry had been unable to contribute anything of much significance to the scant information she had already gathered about the island and its Arthurian connections. She had to assume that her search for further solid evidence was likely to be in vain. As she walked back up the track, her thoughts returned to Tom. She wondered how his day had gone. She hoped he hadn't misunderstood her reason for leaving before he had woken that morning. At the time, she had been sure he would understand, but now she was less certain. She considered calling at Carreg Bach but decided against it. She was too tired, it was late and he would probably have already gone to bed.

Although it had managed not to rain during the day, there was a heavy bank of threatening cloud across the night sky. The feeble light from her torch only just penetrated the darkness. The day's chill wind had strengthened and it was bitterly cold. So she was relieved to arrive back at Llofft Plas.

She shone her torch along the top of the dresser, searching for the matchbox she had left there earlier. But when she found it she was holding it upside down so that, when she slid it open, the matches dropped onto the floor. She cursed under her breath. The matches were scattered all over the place. She picked up as many as she could see and hurried over to light the oil lamp on the kitchen table.

It had been a long day and it was almost as cold inside the cottage as it had been outside. She decided she would be warmer and more comfortable in bed. So she put the kettle on to boil, filled a hot water bottle and made her way upstairs. She was soon tucked up in bed, clutching the bottle to her chest. She had been so engaged with her research that she had hardly given Tom a thought all evening. It had never entered her head that she might meet someone to whom she was attracted during her trip. And yet, it was only a few hours since she had spent the night with a man she had known for less than a week. She smiled when she thought of how shocked her father would be if he knew. There were a thousand and one things that she and Tom had yet to discover about each other, but that was just a matter of time. She was already positive that he was different to all the others. He was kind and considerate. She had never felt so safe and secure in a man's company. It helped that he was battling with his own demons. The last thing she wanted was a one-way relationship. He needed her as much as she needed him.

She was ready for sleep now. She turned the oil lamp down and sunk further into the bed. She pulled one of the pillows round until it was lying against her chest and wrapped her arms around it. She imagined it was Tom lying beside her and pulled the pillow even more tightly to her. She was glad that they hadn't yet made love. She hadn't been quite ready for that. But a quiver of anticipation ran through her body when she thought of how much she wanted it to happen. She would call at Carreg Bach first thing in the morning. If the weather was fine, perhaps they could walk down to the beach to see the seals. She pressed her lips into the soft cotton pillowcase, kissed it tenderly and said 'goodnight Tom, goodnight.'

# CHAPTER FORTY-THREE

SUNDAY MORNING

"Now dear, are you listening to me? I've just popped in to see your grandmother and she's fast asleep, but don't forget to go up to see her after you've fed the chickens. She'll want her cup of tea when she wakes up, you know how thirsty she gets."

"Yes Mummy, I promise." Rhiannon said as she cleared away the remains of the breakfast that she and parents had just shared. Mattie watched her daughter turn on the hot tap and pile the dishes into the washing up bowl.

"You're a good girl Rhiannon. We're very proud of you. I don't know what we'd do without you. Your Daddy and I will only be away the one night and I'm sure you'll manage fine. There's a casserole in the fridge I've prepared for you and Nan's tea. I thought you might like to do scrambled eggs on toast for your lunch." She looked up at her husband who was standing by the front door with a large canvas bag over his shoulder. "Is there anything I've forgotten, Harry? It's all been bit of a rush this morning."

"No, I can see that you're as wonderfully organised as usual." He laughed. "And, judging by the weight of this bag, you've packed enough clothes to last us a week."

"Well, you know how I like to be prepared for any eventuality and you never know what the weather's going to bring. Besides, I've packed one or two things for Gwen's little ones, and there's that nice little set of pottery cups and saucers we don't use anymore. I thought Gareth might find a use for them in his new home."

"No wonder it weighs a ton!" said Harry grinning "Are you sure you haven't packed the kitchen sink as well?"

Mattie cast her husband a well-rehearsed look of disapproval before turning back to her daughter. "One last thing dear, don't forget, if you have any problems, your new friend Beth has kindly said she'd help. But mind, don't trouble her unless you really have to."

"OK Mummy, I'm sure Nan and I'll be fine."

"Come along Mattie. Alun's waiting down at the harbour and he'll want to be on his way," Harry pleaded with his wife, after giving Rhiannon a final hug.

Mattie followed suit, affectionately trailing her fingers through her daughter's golden hair. She kissed her and gave her hand a gentle squeeze. "See you tomorrow then sweetie and take care of yourself."

Rhiannon stood at the kitchen door waving to her parents as they made their way round the back of the farmhouse. She had rarely been separated from them since leaving school. She felt a lump in her throat as she turned towards the back yard where the chickens were waiting to be fed. But, full of pride at the responsibility with which she had been entrusted, she managed to suppress the tears that had been welling up in her eyes.

When she reached the farmyard she was soon surrounded by hungry chickens, each of which she knew by name. She called to them individually as she scattered the feed on the ground. She counted them to make sure that they were all there, then stood back and watched while they greedily pecked up the grain. She loved the way they walked, jerking their heads backwards and forwards. She had to separate two of the older hens as they greedily fought over the last scraps of feed.

It was when she was putting the hens back in their shed that she heard someone knocking on the back door of the farmhouse. She wiped her hands on her pinafore and hurried back to the house to see who it was.

There were two people standing there. When she got closer she saw that it was Bert and Joan.

"'Hello there Rhiannon, is your Mum in?" Joan asked.

"No, just me" she replied. "I'm here all on my own looking after my Nan. Mummy and Daddy have gone to Pwlhelli to visit our Gareth and Gwen and the little ones."

"Oh, I see" Joan said looking somewhat taken aback. "Well the thing is, Mr Cartwright and I, we've run out of eggs. We was hopin' you might be able to find us half a dozen for our tea, if it's not too much trouble, of course."

Rhiannon smiled. "I've got plenty fresh this morning. They're in the shed. I can go and get them for you now if you like."

"Thank you so much dear, we'd be ever so grateful."

After Rhiannon had left, Joan turned to Bert and said "Such a nice girl and ever so pretty. But I can't help wonderin' at her folks leaving her in charge, all on her own, I mean. After all she ain't the brightest button is she? It's plain obvious she's not quite all there."

"There's somethin' missin' I grant you" her husband replied, "but I guess her people knows what they're doin."

"Well, it's obvious she's eleven pence halfpenny short of a shillin'. I'd be thinkin' twice before leavin' her in charge, if she was my daughter!" Joan added. She was in full flow by now but was cut short by her husband. He was standing behind her and had seen Rhiannon re-emerging from the yard. "Watch what you're sayin' Joanie, she's headin' back this way. We wouldn't want to hurt the poor little thing's feelin's would we?"

"Blimey no, Bert, that we wouldn't" Joan whispered. She smiled at Rhiannon who was carrying a basket of eggs over her arm. "That really is most kind, my dear." She looked down into Rhiannon's basket and added "My goodness, what beauties. They're so big and such a lovely brown colour. You don't get nothin' like that in the supermarket back home."

"That you don't" Bert said. He felt in his pocket for some loose change. "How much do we owe you my darlin?"

"You can settle up with Mummy when she gets back. You can borrow this basket if you like. I've got another one"

Bert and Joan thanked her and set off on their way back to the observatory. Rhiannon watched them make their way up the track until she could no longer hear the sound of Joan's non-stop prattle. When they were no longer in sight she turned to go back into the kitchen. She had a puzzled look on her face. Although they didn't realise it, she had overheard every word of the conversation between Bert and Joan. She wondered what Joan had meant when she said that she wasn't the brightest button.

She was even more bewildered by the other thing Joan had said, 'What was it now? Something about eleven pence halfpenny short of a shilling. What on earth could that mean?"

# CHAPTER FORTY-FOUR

The sun had only just risen above the mountain and Llofft Plas, and the other houses that lay along its lower reaches, remained in shadow. Beth was sitting on the low stone wall that skirted the lane. She had woken early after a good night's sleep, and had come out with a mug of tea to smoke her first cigarette of the day. The sky was full of birdsong welcoming the onset of spring. When she had woken that morning she had still been clutching the pillow that, in her imagination, had anthropomorphised into Tom.

It was now 24 hours since she had last seen him. It had been 24 hours of mixed emotions where doubt and certainty had been in constant conflict. This morning her mind was as clear as the pale sky above. She must put the painful memories of her past behind her. She could trust Tom, of that she was sure. She could only hope that he felt the same way about her. She would have to do battle with her innate lack of self-confidence. The unexpected circumstances that had brought them together added to the poignancy of the situation. Neither of them had set out in search of a relationship that was the extraordinary thing. There were no hidden agendas and no questionable motives. But she had to know for certain that he felt as she did. And there was only one way to find that out.

She looked at her watch. It wasn't yet eight o'clock, too early to call on Tom. She would have to sit out her anxiety for a little longer. Although she wasn't particularly hungry, she would fill the time with breakfast. It would help to give her strength for the challenge ahead.

An hour later, she closed the door behind her and set off on the short walk up to Carreg Bach. Looking up at the mountain now drenched in sunlight, it was impossible not to feel a sense of exhilaration. On the lower levels, there were so many different varieties of wild grasses and spring flowers. She was amazed by the remarkable range of their colours and textures. Even the rocky outcrops higher up were covered in green and yellow moss and lichen. It was a wild and beautiful scene and did much to raise her spirits.

When she reached Carreg Bach, she paused for a moment, before unlatching the small iron gate. She saw smoke rising from the chimney. "Well, he's up" she muttered to herself. She was only part way up the path when the front door opened and there was Tom, standing in the doorway, dressed in an old pair of jeans with his shirt hanging out. They stood looking at each other, neither knowing quite what to say. Then they both began to speak at the same time, there was a sudden rush of words and they burst out laughing. Tom waived aside Beth's apologies for disturbing him so early and invited her inside.

She had intended to explain why she had left so early the previous morning, but, as it turned out, this proved unnecessary because Tom immediately brought the matter up himself.

"My dearest Beth" he said, clasping her hands, "you have no idea how much I've missed you over the past 24 hours. When I woke up yesterday morning to find you'd gone, I couldn't help wondering what I might have said or done to upset you. I was afraid you might feel that everything was happening too quickly. It's so very difficult to know what may be going on inside someone else's head, especially when it's someone you're only just getting to know. And... well... it's so long since I have done this sort of thing..."

"Oh Tom, how could you know? I've been through just the same tangle of doubts myself. I spent much of yesterday, and every minute since I woke up this morning, thinking about you and what I was going to say when I saw you. The truth is, I'm not entirely sure that I know why I left when I did. I was so happy lying there next to you and felt so safe. Do you know I lay awake for a while, half-hoping you'd wake up and make love to me? And yet, there was a part of me that wasn't ready for that, not then or, it was too soon. But you should know that it took an unbelievable amount of self-control for me to keep my hands off you."

She looked up anxiously into his face, searching for any suggestion that she might have shocked him. What she saw was a slight movement in the creases at the corners of his mouth as his face broke into a smile. He stepped closer, put his arms around her and held onto her so tightly that she almost cried out. And then he relaxed his hold and raised his hand to caress her cheek. He buried his lips into her hair and whispered affectionate words into her ears. She saw that his eyes were moist with tears. He put his arms around her waist, pulled her up until she was standing on tiptoes and kissed her full on the mouth. She closed her eyes and parted her lips. A shiver ran through her body. With a gasp of pleasure, Tom took a step back. He stretched out his arms and rested his hands on her shoulders. Her face was glowing with excitement. She moved closer and slid her fingers through an opening in his shirt. He brushed his fingers through her long strands of her hair. And then, holding her head firmly between his hands, he looked directly into her eyes, grinned, and said:

"Well, what has the tide washed up this morning? Shall I call you Flotsam or Jetsam?"

"Thank you for that" she said with a chuckle, "but if anyone looks like they've been washed up by the tide, you might care to take a look at yourself, standing there in your bare feet, with your shirt half undone and your hair looking like a gull's nested in it overnight!"

"Well, what do you know, a woman with a sharp tongue and a sarcastic turn of phrase."

"You're the one with the sharp tongue" she said, rubbing her finger over her lower lip "You should try using it as a tin opener!" They both laughed.

"Being serious for a moment, that was a pretty remarkable way to welcome in the new day. But I'm dying of thirst. I haven't even had a cup of tea yet, let alone anything to eat. Do you think we might possibly manage to contain our feelings for each other until a little later in the day?"

"You mean there's more to come?" she exclaimed "I didn't think that you men of God got up to that sort of thing!"

"Ah well, you see, I'm strictly non-monastic. No vows of poverty, chastity and obedience for me which, I hasten to add, doesn't mean that I'm totally devoid of any concept of morality."

"Well, that sounds encouraging. Look, how about you finish getting dressed and washed and whatever else you have to do, and I'll make you some breakfast."

"Won't you join me?"

"Some of us get up a little earlier than this particularly disreputable representative of the Church of England standing before me. I've already had my breakfast, but I'll join you for a cup of tea."

"Actually, all I want is a couple of slices of toast, if you can get that grill to work. It was a bit dodgy when I tried to light it yesterday. There's some honey on the sideboard and the butter's in the fridge. The tea bags are in that pot, on the shelf."

"Tea bags, how common! But I suppose on a clergyman's pay..."

"Nothing to do with poverty" Tom called from halfway up the stairs "I fear that standards have dropped since I've been living on my own. I've become a bit of a lazy slob around the house. I got fed up washing out the tea pot."

"I can see that you have sunk very low indeed. I shall have to take that as a challenge."

Beth listened to Tom shuffling about upstairs while she prepared his breakfast. When he came back down, he stood watching while she cut two thick slices of bread and placed them under the grill which she had lit without difficulty. She turned to him and said.

"Did you know that Harry and Mattie had lost a son?"

"Goodness me no, I thought their son was living on the mainland. Isn't he a carpenter or something?"

"Yes, that's Gareth. But they had another son who was Rhiannon's twin. He was called Dafydd. He died tragically quite a few years ago. They think he must have had an accident and fallen into the sea, but they never found his body. Mattie told me all about it last night, before Harry came in. She didn't want to talk about it in front of him. Apparently he still hasn't come to terms with the loss. He feels responsible in some way. He and the boy must have been very close. Rhiannon talks about Dafydd as if he's still alive. I suppose it's understandable. They were very little when the accident happened and you know how close twins can be."

"She must get pretty lonely out here on the island, especially in the winter when there are no visitors. You can understand why she keeps her brother alive as an imaginary playmate."

"I agree. I have to say that he seems very real to her."

Beth gestured to Tom to sit down at the table. He noted she had already begun her campaign to raise domestic standards. A dark green teapot sat in the middle of the table. Although it contained tea bags rather than fresh leaves, it was a step in the right direction.

When she bent down to pull out the grill pan, her head was bathed in a shaft of golden sunlight. Once again, he was astonished by her exceptional beauty. Her hair was a delightful deep brown with coppery flecks. They stood out as exquisite natural highlights that an accomplished hairdresser would be hard-pressed to imitate. But it wasn't just her physical beauty that was so striking for it was matched by the grace of her movements. But this wasn't some kind of show that she was putting on. Tom was in no doubt that it was natural and totally unselfconscious.

"At last, I think it's done" Beth said, taking the toast out from under the grill. "If you'd like to pour us a cup of tea, I'll bring it over."

"The sad tale of Dafydd apart, how did you get on with the Evans' last night?" Tom asked.

"Oh, they're a lovely couple and they made quite a fuss of me. The only thing is that, to be honest, I didn't really learn anything much that will help with my project. They were very forthcoming about life on the island and that sort of thing, Harry especially. But he didn't have anything to say on the subject of Bardsey's Arthurian links that isn't common knowledge. To be fair, he did remember his grandfather telling him about Merlin and the 13 treasures of Wales and he'd also heard of the Lady Morgan and her sisters. But, the funny thing is, he didn't seem all that interested in the subject which I find rather odd. I mean, wouldn't you want to know all about it if you lived on the island? Apart from anything else, it's wonderful stuff for all those tourists. It isn't as if everywhere has such a fantastic story to tell."

"Perhaps they like the island as it is and don't want to encourage too many people to come here." Tom suggested.

"That's possible I suppose. You know, the only time his eyes really lit up was when he was telling me about the Bardsey apple."

"The Bardsey apple? I haven't come across that before. There's hardly a tree on the island, never mind an orchard."

"I know, it's odd isn't it? It seems there's only one tree left on the island. It's in a crevice on the side of Plas Bach, you know, the house next to my stable. Harry says they've taken cuttings from it and got them growing successfully somewhere on the mainland. But here's where it gets interesting. Apparently, the fruit was sometimes referred to as Merlin's apple. What's more, I've done a bit of research and discovered that on this side of the mountain, almost directly above Plas Bach, there's a small cave which they call Merlin's cave. The story goes that Merlin was buried on the island in a glass house, with the 13 treasures of Wales, to wait for the return of Arthur. It's all rather confusing, but perhaps there's some connection between the glass house and the cave."

"That sounds a little far-fetched to me" Tom said, raising his eyebrows "a glass house! Did they even have glass in those days?"

"Oh yes, they most certainly did, the Romans in particular. Rhiannon has shown me the cave. You must promise not to tell her that I've told you as she's sworn me to secrecy. As far as she's concerned, nobody else knows about it except her and Dafydd. The cave isn't all that easy to find. The only way in is on your hands and knees. It's actually quite small and poky inside. Rhiannon told me there's also an inner chamber. I haven't seen it though because the only way in is through a very small opening."

"It doesn't sound like there would be much room for Merlin's treasures, whatever they were."

"Well no. But putting the treasures aside for a moment, the whole point about myths is that they're often founded on real events. The facts get embellished over the years as they're passed from one generation to another. This could so easily be what's happened here. Forget all that stuff about stone castles, knights in armour and Merlin with his long white beard holding court as a wise counsellor to the king. Imagine instead Merlin as a wild man of the woods. He's adopted by a roaming warlord called Arthur and acts as his kind of private soothsayer. Arthur is seriously wounded in a fight with cousin Mordred and Merlin brings him over here to recover. After that, everything is clouded in mystery. Does Arthur survive, recover and retire to the continent, as some have claimed, and there's some interesting evidence to support that theory. Or, do you follow the more accepted line that Arthur's wounds are fatal and that he dies after Camlan? If you go with the former argument, then you can see Merlin remaining on the island, living on in the hope and expectation of Arthur's return one day. If you take the latter argument, then perhaps Merlin's hermit-like existence on the island should be interpreted in a more mystical sense, as he awaits the 'second coming' of his hero who he believes is the future saviour of Wales."

"Hmm" Tom said "interesting, the reference to a 'second coming' has a parallel to the Christian Gospel, of course."

Beth looked at her watch.

"Just look at the time. Tom, this is really interesting but would you mind if we take it up again a little later? I don't think I mentioned it, but Mattie and Harry have gone off to the mainland. I promised Mattie that I'd keep an eye on Rhiannon while they're away. I really ought to pop down to Ty Pellaf now to make sure everything's under control."

"Of course I don't mind" said Tom "would you like me to come with you?"

"No, you stay here and finish your breakfast." Beth said, heading for the front door. "How do you fancy going to see if we can spot those seals when I get back? I shan't be long. It's such a lovely morning. It would be good to get some fresh air."

"That sounds like an excellent plan to me. Seeing as it's Sunday, I'd like to say Morning Prayer while you're away and then I'll see what I can find to pack up for a picnic."

"Perfect, and then, well I don't wish to be presumptuous, but, perhaps we can come back here again later on. You never know but you might just be able to persuade me to stay the night again. It's my turn to cook. If we call at my place on the way back, I've got eggs and bread and things, and I seem to remember there's still half a bottle of brandy sitting on your sideboard."

"What are you trying to do, turn me into an alcoholic?"

"You're the one who brought the brandy!" Beth said with a flirtatious smile as she left through the front door.

# CHAPTER FORTY-FIVE

"Everything all right at Ty Pellaf?" Tom asked as he and Beth strolled down towards the harbour.

"I think so. Mrs Davies seemed a little short of breath but Rhiannon says it's something that comes and goes. There was one thing though. I may have just imagined it, but Rhiannon seemed a bit subdued. I can't quite put my finger on it but, somehow, she wasn't quite her usual cheery self. You know how enthusiastic she normally is about everything? Well, not today, or at least much less so than usual."

"Do you think she's finding it difficult looking after the old lady on her own?"

"No, I don't think it's that. She seems to be coping well. No, it's more as if something or someone has upset her."

"Perhaps she's just missing her Mum and Dad?"

"I'm sure she is but I sense there's more to it than that. I asked her if anything was wrong but she just shook her head. If there is something, she doesn't appear to want to share it with anyone or, at least, not with me."

"If you're worried about her, we can always call again on the way back, just to make sure?"

"Yes, I think I'd like to." Beth replied. By now they had reached the slipway where a couple of old fishing boats lay above the waterline. They were both much the worse for wear. One of them was lying on its side like a beached whale, exposing the weathered timbers of its belly to the elements.

They didn't see anyone else on their way to the harbour. From where they were standing, the lighthouse on the promontory beyond them looked solid and dependable as if guarding the headland from some long-awaited adversary.

"I wonder where the best place to see the seals is?" Beth said. "I meant to ask Rhiannon but stupidly forgot. I'm pretty sure it's somewhere down this end of the island."

"I'm afraid I don't know either" Tom said. "But, I tell you what, it's damned cold standing here in the full force of the wind. There's a much more sheltered spot on the other side of that narrow spit of land leading up to the lighthouse. I've been there. Why don't we head over there to take a look? If nothing else we'll be able to find somewhere to sit down for our lunch without being blown to pieces."

"Sounds like a good idea to me" Beth said, taking hold of Tom's hand. "Come on, let's get a move on, I'm absolutely frozen."

They hurried across the windswept terrain to the opposite side of the island. From her map, Beth identified the beach that Tom had referred to as Porth Solfach. They dropped down off the bank and soon found the place where Tom had found shelter before. The narrow strip of white sand leading down to the sea looked infinitely more inviting than it had on his previous visit.

Beth unrolled her mat and they sat down and huddled together, gazing out beyond the rocks in search of their first seal. They watched the gulls swooping down in search of their prey. They saw a tiny crab struggling across the sand in front of them. But there wasn't a seal in sight.

"Perhaps it's too early in the year?" Tom said "I'm not exactly sure when they mate but I think I read somewhere that they have their pups quite late on, September or October."

"I expect they'll show up if we're patient" Beth said, rubbing her hands between her knees to keep them warm. "I tell you what; I wouldn't mind some of that coffee and a sandwich."

Tom unpacked the sandwich box and thermos flask. "Pretty simple fare I'm afraid but I didn't want to spoil that gourmet supper you've promised me."

"Very funny. Can you please get a move on with that coffee before I turn into a lump of ice."

"I haven't exactly pictured you as an ice-maiden!" Tom chuckled, unscrewing the thermos. Beth held the mugs while he poured the coffee.

"That's better" she said "You'll be glad to hear that this particular ice-maiden is finally beginning to thaw out, from the inside... " but she was interrupted by Tom who suddenly stood up and pointed excitedly out to sea.

"Look, do you see it? There, just beyond that large flat rock sticking out of the sea at a crazy angle. Oh, hang on a minute, it's gone again. It must have dived or something... hang on a minute... there it is again, can you see it?"

Beth stood up and tried to work out where he was pointing. "I can't see a thing. Where do you mean? Oh there, yes, I see it, or I can see something bobbing up and down between the waves, it looks like a head... yes I'm sure it is... and look, there's another, further out, do you see it?"

"Yes, and isn't that another one over there to the right?"

There were now several seal heads bobbing up and down in the open sea. While they watched the comings and goings of the seals, the sun came out from behind a dark cloud and lit up the whole of the bay. Until that moment, the rocks, the sea and the sky had been various muted shades of grey. Now, the minute particles of sand glittered in a host of different colours and there were several large patches of blue sky. The wind too seemed to have dropped and Tom and Beth were able to sit down again in relative comfort.

"Fancy a sandwich?" Tom asked "I can offer you egg and tomato or tomato and egg if you would prefer."

"I'm spoiled for choice, that's for sure. Yes please, and I wouldn't mind some more of that coffee, if there's any to spare."

They were so absorbed in their lunch and watching the seals that they hardly spoke. When they had finished eating, Tom packed away the remains of the picnic. He sat back against a large rock and stretched his legs out.

"Do you know, the last time I was down here I pretty nearly hit rock bottom, if you'll forgive the pun."

Beth turned to look at him. She was saddened when she saw the pained expression on his face. "I'm so sorry" she said.

"Yes, it was a particularly low point in my search for spiritual reawakening. It was rather odd. You see, when I first came down here I was feeling relieved at being away from all the normal pressures of life. I had my little book of Bible extracts, poems and favourite quotations with me. You know, all those bits and pieces that have meant something to me over the years. I started to thumb through the pages, not entirely sure what I was looking for. After a while I found that extraordinary poem by Emily Dickinson. I wonder if you know it. I can't remember it all, but it begins 'Exultation is the going of an inland soul to sea, past the houses, past the headlands, into deep eternity!' It seemed to be describing just what I saw and felt as I looked out towards the distant horizon. The more I thought about it, the more I could to see how stupid I'd been to question God's existence. But I was also overcome by a terrible realisation. It wasn't that God didn't exist. No, it was something much more frightening than that. I felt that the God I had tried to serve, over so many years, had abandoned me! How else could I explain Martha's death?"

Beth put an arm around Tom's shoulder."Oh Tom, I can see how much this has been troubling you. I wish I could help you to find some answers."

"My dear Beth, how kind and understanding you are. But don't fret for me because I believe the worst may be over. I've done a lot of serious thinking since then. It'll take time but I'm slowly learning to stop blaming God, or indeed anyone else, for the travails of this world and for my own loss. Sitting here with you now I feel none of the despair that I felt on that last visit."

He took old of Beth's hand and raised it to his lips. He would have embraced her had it not been for the sound of distant whistling. The whistling grew steadily louder and it was clear that they would not be alone for much longer.

"What a pity!" Beth said as Tom withdrew his hand and looked up.

"I'm afraid that normal services will have to be resumed later!" he chuckled "and look who it is, your old friend from the observatory, Bert what's-his-name if I'm not mistaken?"

"I hope you're into birds" Beth whispered, "I think you may be about to get one of his lectures on the greater spotted something or other." She stood up, waved, and with a welcoming smile called out "Hello there Bert. What brings you down here?"

"Hello Beth" Bert replied cheerily. "Just takin' a bit of a stroll. Joan's got one of her wretched migraines, poor thing. She's best left to get over it in peace and quiet as I've learned over the years!" He turned his attention to Tom "I don't think we've been introduced, although I've seen you about. Joan and I are stayin' up at the observatory. We come here every year for the birds, have been doin' for as long as I can remember."

"Good to meet you Bert. I'm Tom." They shook hands.

"Nice beach this isn't it, what with all that lovely white sand? It's one of the few places on the island where you can get some proper shelter at this time of year."

"We've been watching the seals" Beth said, pointing out to sea.

"Yes, there's lots of fish out there so I reckon they swim round when they're hungry. Mind you, if it's the seals you've come to see, you'd do better over the other side at Henllwyn, you know the rocky beach by the harbour. On a fine day like this, you'll see them lazin' around, stretched out full length, sunbathin' on the rocks."

"I'm sorry to confess that I don't know all that much about seals" Tom said.

"Well there's more than one kind of course. These ones are Grey Atlantics. You'll find them on both sides of the Atlantic and as far up as the Baltic. Ynys Enlli is one of their favourite breedin' grounds. In the summer as many as 200 have been recorded here."

"Is that when they have their pups?" Beth asked.

"No, that's later on, in the autumn."

"It's difficult to tell from here because they're so far out, but I was wondering how big they are?" Tom asked.

"I reckon you'll be surprised at how big some of them can be. You'll see for yourself if you stroll over to Henllwyn. The males can grow as long as seven or eight feet. Do you know, their pups can weigh as much as 25 to 30 pounds?"

"Good Lord!" Tom exclaimed "that's some baby."

"One of the things I find fascinating is how long they seem to be able to stay underwater" Beth said "I mean, I've been watching and sometimes they don't seem to come up at all or else they come up so far from where they first dived that you can't be sure it's the same one."

"Well that's another remarkable thing about them seals" Bert responded. He was clearly enjoying showing off his expert knowledge. "They can stay under for much longer than you might imagine, up to 20 minutes in some cases."

"That's amazing" Beth said, catching a knowing smile on Tom's face from out of the corner of her eye.

Bert looked at his watch."Cor blimey, is that the time? I'd better be gettin' back to see how the missus is doin'. Strange things them migraines, but once she starts comin' out the other end, you can be sure she'll start demandin' scrambled eggs and a cuppa. Nice to talk to you folks and, don't forget, if you want to see the seals nice and close, you'll find plenty of them over by the harbour."

"Thanks Bert, it's good to have met you" Tom said.

"I hope Joan's on the mend when you get back to the observatory" Beth called after Bert's retreating figure. She grinned. "I think that may have been a lucky escape, his having to get back to Joan. He means well, but he's not one of the easiest people to get away from when he's in full flow!"

Tom put his arms round Beth "Before we go to take a closer look at our submersible friends, how about resuming where we left off before we were so rudely interrupted!"

# CHAPTER FORTY-SIX

A little later, Tom and Beth followed Bert's advice and made their way over to Henllwyn. They were not disappointed. There they came across a score or more of the magnificent creatures flapping around playfully in the sea or stretched out on the rocks, basking in the warm sun. Further out, others showed off the grace and speed of their waterborne skills which were such a striking contrast to their ungainliness on land.

They would have lingered longer but for the dark and threatening clouds sweeping in across the sea. They had only just passed through the field gate on their way back to Ty Pellaf when they felt the first drops of rain. Although they had planned to call on Rhiannon on their way back, Beth had come out without her coat so Tom suggested she went straight back to Llofft Plas to avoid another soaking while he called at Ty Pellaf to check on Rhiannon and her grandmother. They agreed to meet back up at Carreg Bach later on.

Tom found Rhiannon to be unusually subdued. At first, he thought this was because she was worried about her grandmother who, she told him, had been coughing incessantly all morning. He offered to go upstairs to check on the old lady, but Rhiannon persuaded him not to as she had only just fallen asleep. He sat with Rhiannon in the kitchen for a while. He was surprised at how little interest she showed in anything he said, even when he told her about their visit to see the seals. By the time he set off on his way back to Carreg Bach, he felt sure that there was something troubling her. It was a pity that it had been he rather than Beth who had called on Rhiannon. After all, she had established such a strong bond with the young girl.

In the meantime, Beth managed to get back to Llofft Plas before the heavens opened. She spent the rest of the afternoon reading her notes, curled up in the armchair in front of the heater. She was disappointed that she had discovered virtually no new evidence to support the island's Arthurian claims, but not altogether surprised.

She laid the notes aside and closed her eyes. She thought of Tom and the time they spent together that afternoon. She chuckled when she remembered their encounter with Bert. She could still see the wicked smile on Tom's face during Bert's attempt to impress them with his knowledge of the life and times of the Grey Atlantic Seal. It had been a wonderful afternoon, not least because Tom appeared to have cast his gloom aside. From the moment they met, she had recognised his generosity and capacity to show compassion for others. What was now beginning to emerge was his passion and delightful sense of humour.

When she re-opened her eyes, she saw the rain clouds had passed over and the early evening sun cast a shaft of silvery light through the window. She was excited at the thought of the evening that lay ahead. She had believed she understood the nature of love when she had embarked on her affair with Bill Matthews. But it had never felt like this. Looking back now, she could see how flawed that relationship had been. It was inevitable that it should end in disaster. Bill had been good company and she had been impressed by his sharp intellect. But she could see now that he was a selfish man with high ambitions and very little concept of loyalty. She had been overwhelmed with self-pity when they had broken up. This had been as much to do with the pain and indignity of his callous rejection as with any true sense of loss. But Tom, dear Tom, he was surely something else. She felt that she could tell him anything and he would be neither shocked nor dismayed. She was determined to be completely frank and open and to hide nothing from him. It would take all the courage she could muster, but he deserved an honest explanation of her odd behaviour that night in Aberdaron. It spoke much of his sensitivity and understanding that he had not pressed her on it. For far too long, she had suppressed her yearnings for a relationship in the mistaken belief that men were really only after one thing and that every relationship was bound to end in some form of betrayal. But she was fairly certain that Tom was different.

Her thoughts were interrupted by a repeated tapping on the window. She looked up and saw a small bird was intent on trying to force its way through the glass. She stood up and waved her arms about, hoping to scare the bird away. She banged on the window and shouted "Go away you silly bird, you'll hurt yourself, go on, shooo!" To her relief, the bird finally flew off and settled on the wall by the footpath.

It was darker now and soon she would need to change before going up to Carreg Bach. There was just time to go outside for a cigarette. Beyond the lighthouse, the sun was sinking fast in the western sky and the wisps of cloud were bathed in a radiant orange glow. She shivered in the chill evening air, stubbed out her half-smoked cigarette and went back inside.

An hour or so later, when Tom opened the front door, the figure on his doorstep couldn't have offered a more dramatic contrast to the rain-sodden creature who had stood there two evenings before.

"You look wonderful" he said "I don't know how you do it, you've hardly a hair out of place." She was wearing a pure white Afghan sweater that hung down over the top of her faded blue jeans. Her hair was neatly tied back and shimmered in the evening sunlight. He stood, staring at her, not wanting the magic of the moment to be broken. There was something delightfully enchanting about the happy smile that lit up her face. Then her smile turned into a broad grin.

"It's a bit nippy out here you know, I don't suppose you were thinking of inviting me in, were you?"

Tom stepped aside "I'm so sorry. I'm not sure what's come over me. It's just that... forgive me, I'm not usually at a loss for words... it's just that you look so irresistible. Here, let me take that basket"

"Thank you kind sir" she said as she handed over the wicker basket in which she had carried up their supper. "I'm afraid there's nothing very exciting in there, just some pasta, cheese, an onion and a little bacon. I thought I might try my variation on macaroni cheese out on you. Oh, and there's a bottle of red wine. The only thing I couldn't lay my hands on is mustard."

"As it happens, I think you may be in luck. I'm pretty sure I saw a tin of Colman's in one of the cupboards in the dresser."

"Well then, you can prepare yourself for a true gourmet evening. But, hang on a minute, seeing as you find me so utterly irresistible, don't I get a welcoming kiss?"

Tom looked admiringly at Beth. Her Afghan sweater was loose-fitting but it didn't disguise the seductive rise and fall of her breasts. Above its low neckline, he could see the soft brown skin above her breastbone. He stretched his arms out and pulled her gently towards him. She stood on her toes so she could reach up and clasp him round the back of his neck. He lowered his head until their lips touched. She closed her eyes. She could feel Tom teasing her lips with his tongue. She opened her mouth wider and their tongues touched and then, with a deep and satisfied sigh, she pressed a finger into his lips. She reached up further to plant a light kiss on his forehead. She was laughing now.

"That'll do for starters" she said. "I don't know about you, but I'm absolutely ravenous. It must be all that sea air. How about I get started on supper?"

"Sounds good to me." Tom said "I'll set the table and perhaps I can open that bottle of wine."

Beth rooted in her basket for the bottle, handed it to him and emptied the rest of the contents onto the table.

"Anything else I can do to help?" Tom asked, laying knives, forks and two tumblers on the table before turning his attention to the wine.

"No thanks, I'm pretty much under control thanks, but here, you might need this. I brought it with me just in case" She handed him a corkscrew.

"Just as well you did" Tom said "I certainly haven't come across one." He pulled out the cork, poured out some wine and passed one of the tumblers to Beth.

"Here you are, this should warm you up nicely."

"Nicely for what, may I ask" Beth said, with a coy expression on her face.

Tom grinned and then glanced at the fireplace "And, talking about warming up, I'd better pop round the back to bring in some more wood for the fire. It feels like it's going to be another cold night."

By the time Tom returned from more than one visit to the woodshed a large pile of wood was neatly stacked by the fire.

"I'm amazed at how much wood they manage to collect. They must depend almost entirely on the driftwood that gets washed up on the shore."

"I know" Beth said "The islanders are nothing if not resourceful. Harry was telling me the other night about how he and Rhiannon make regular trips out with the tractor to forage for whatever they can find. Some of the pieces that get washed up are so big that he has to take a chain saw to them. You can't help wondering where it all comes from in the first place!"

Tom lit a fire and then, standing with his back to it, he watched Beth cooking. After the initial preparations, everything went into a large dish, was sprinkled with grated cheese and put in the oven.

"Well, that should be ready in a few minutes. I find it so much tastier when you brown it on top. And now I can savour the wine you've kindly poured out for me." She said, sitting down.

"Actually it's rather good." Tom said "I can't imagine you bought this in the local shop in Aberdaron."

"As it happens, you couldn't be more wrong. They have a surprisingly good wine selection in there."

"Well I never, I'm quite impressed."

They chatted on for a while about nothing in particular, with Beth checking the oven now and again. When she was satisfied that it was sufficiently browned on top, she took it out of the oven and placed it on the table. Tom topped up their wine while Beth served out the food.

"Tom, I've been meaning to ask, how did you get on at Ty Pellaf?"

"Well, I think everything's all right. Rhiannon says her grandmother's cough's got rather worse. I offered to go up to see her but Rhiannon said she had only just fallen asleep."

"What about Rhiannon herself, how did she seem to you?"

"There's the thing. There's nothing I can put my finger on but she did seem a bit low. I don't know, it may just be that she's more worried about her gran than we realise. But I couldn't help feeling that something else is troubling her."

"We'd better keep a close eye on her until Harry and Mattie get back tomorrow. I'll pop down there in the morning to check her out and to see if there's anything she needs."

"That would be kind. She's such a lovely young girl but she may be just a little bit more vulnerable than most youngsters of her age."

"Yes, I can see that" Beth said, sitting back in her chair. "It seems so unfair, doesn't it? That Rhiannon should have this particular handicap I mean. She's got so much going for her and yet, I imagine, it will always hold her back to some extent. I really feel for Harry and Mattie too. It must be very hard for them, especially having lost her twin brother so tragically."

"I agree. But you know, such awful experiences can be the making of some people and I suspect Mattie and Harry are a perfect example of that. Look at how well they all get on and at how cheery they always seem to be. They've been through the hardest of times and yet the sun still radiates out of them."

"You're right, of course. You must forgive me but I always tend to see things from a rather negative perspective. I can't help it. I think it must be deeply embedded in me from childhood. My father was such a narrow-minded puritan. He always went out of his way to blame people for their misfortunes as if they were being punished for their shortcomings."

"Don't worry, I've come across plenty of people like that!" Tom said with a smile "But from what I know of you, I certainly wouldn't put you in that category. I'm sure you have a dark side, we all do as I've found out for myself. But the other you, the you I'm getting to know, isn't like that at all. That you, is a laughing, happy, caring you. It's also a dangerously seductive you! There's nothing in the least bit gloomy or negative about that you and that's the 'you' I find so irresistible."

"You certainly have a gift for making this particular me feel better about herself." Beth said. She looked at Tom's empty plate. "That seems to have gone down rather well. There's plenty more if you're still hungry."

"Thanks, but I'm absolutely stuffed. How about you?"

"No, like you, I'm full to the gills. I wouldn't mind another glass of wine though."

"Of course. Shall we take it over to the fire? We'll be more comfortable over there. It isn't exactly tropical at this end of the room."

They rose from the table. Beth put their dirty dishes in the sink while Tom took their glasses and the wine bottle over to the fireside. Before sitting down, he refilled their glasses and placed another large piece of wood on the fire.

"Don't wash those things up now Beth, I'll do them later. Come and sit down."

"All right, but do you want a cup of coffee or anything?"

"I'm fine for the moment, thanks. I'm enjoying this excellent wine and, don't forget, there's a drop of brandy waiting for afters."

Tom watched Beth as she made her way across the room. She sat down in the other armchair and he noticed how supple she was when she crossed her legs, brushing her hands down her thighs to press out the creases in her jeans. They didn't talk at first but sat there sipping their wine and enjoying the warmth from the fire. Tom thought he detected a flicker of concern pass over Beth's face. Something appeared to be troubling her. What if she was having second thought about their relationship and where it might be leading? He wanted to ask her if anything was the matter but held back. He felt sure she would bring it up sooner or later. As it happened, he didn't have to wait very long. She had already made up her mind that if she didn't share her secret with him now, she never would.

"Tom" she said, tentatively sitting forward with her hands clasped tightly together, "Tom, there's something I have to tell you. I've wanted to all along and I'm sorry it's taken me so long, but I haven't known how to find the right words, and I had to be sure that I could trust you."

She looked at Tom and was encouraged by his tender smile. She could see that he was wanted for her to continue. He exuded such kindness and sympathy and she felt that her task was not going to be as difficult as she had feared.

She began by telling him about her former lover, Bill Matthews, and of the callous way in which he had ended their relationship. She told him that he had left her feeling used and abandoned. She told him how lonely and depressed she had subsequently become and of how the experience had made her feel pathetically inadequate when it came to relationships. As a result, she said she had lost her self-confidence and had shunned approaches from other men which they had interpreted as being indicative of arrogance or frigidity.

Tom reached forward to clasp her hands.

"Poor Beth. I can hardly believe you can have been so misunderstood."

"But there's more, I'm afraid" she said, with a crack in her voice. "You see, after a while I couldn't stand the loneliness any longer. I made the stupid mistake of accepting an invitation to attend a college function with one of my fellow lecturers. I didn't know him all that well but he'd always been friendly on the few occasions we had met in the Senior Common Room or about college. It had been so long since I'd gone out with anyone that I felt I ought to make an effort to try to be a little more sociable. In any case, I asked myself, what could possibly go wrong at the college summer ball? Well it was fine to start with. I have always been rather a good dancer and I enjoyed dancing with my host and some of my other colleagues. The refreshments were fantastic and there was plenty of decent wine."

"We partied well into the night. It all finally came to an end around five in the morning when they served up the usual end of summer ball breakfast, you know, bacon and eggs with a glass of Buck's Fizz. I suppose I must have been pretty sloshed by then and I was certainly very tired and ready to go home. My host, who was equally merry, offered to walk me back to my flat. When we arrived at my place, like an idiot, I invited him in for coffee. As soon as we got upstairs to my flat, he waived the offer of coffee aside and produced a half full bottle of red wine he'd somehow managed to smuggle out from the ball. I went into the kitchen to fetch a couple of glasses. When I returned, he was busy rolling a joint. I'd never smoked pot before, but I was so far gone that I sat down on the sofa next to him and accepted his offer of a smoke without really thinking about what I was doing. I don't remember much about what happened after that. I know we must have finished the wine and I can remember him lurching over and kissing me and trying to fondle my breasts. But after that I must have passed out. The next thing I remember is waking up with the most God-awful headache and an excruciating pain between my legs. I was still lying on the sofa but I was almost completely naked. My ball gown was in a heap on the floor. My knickers were halfway down my legs and my bra was hanging off my shoulder. I was still feeling incredibly muggy but it slowly dawned on me what must have happened. I ran to the bathroom and was violently sick. When I had finally finished throwing up I ran a hot bath and I scrubbed my body from head to toe. I was desperate to get rid of every last trace of what had happened to me. But scrub as I might, I couldn't seem to get rid of the odour of unwanted sex. I have never felt so utterly violated and betrayed in my whole life."

Tears were pouring down Beth's cheeks as she recounted the details of her terrible ordeal. Tom could do nothing but listen intently and continue to hold her hands. Soon she was sobbing so hard that she could no longer speak. He would have wrapped his arms around her but feared that she might recoil from physical contact. She raised her swollen eyes to look at him and moved forward to kneel on the floor in front of his chair.

"You are a dear sweet man" she said, still sobbing "I... I'm so sorry to burden you with all this. But it's something you must know if you are to understand me."

"There's nothing to say sorry about. I can't imagine how difficult it must have been for you since that dreadful night. If you feel that you can, please tell me what happened after that. Clearly you had been sexually assaulted. Did you report it to anyone?"

"Don't let's mince words, I was raped. I didn't go into college the next day, I couldn't face anyone. But I did pluck up enough courage to go in the day after that and I found the bastard who had attacked me talking to a couple of his friends in the Senior Common Room. When he saw me come in, he grinned at me as though nothing had happened. I was so angry, I couldn't control myself. I ran across the room, grabbed him by the collar and accused him of having raped me. He put on a good act of looking shocked at my accusation and, of course, fervently denied everything. He said that we'd both been very drunk and he hadn't done anything that I hadn't encouraged and been willing to go along with. He even went so far as to say that, if anything, I'd led him on. I couldn't believe it. How could he lie so? I appealed to his colleagues but they just looked away. It was obvious they didn't want to get involved. I was even angrier by now and started shouting at him and beating him with my fists. But all he did was to back away, grinning, while one of his friends grabbed me and pulled me off him. I felt utterly humiliated. When I saw that no-one was prepared to believe me, I stormed out of the room. I went to my study where I spent the rest of the morning crying my eyes out. It was bad enough having been raped. You can imagine how I felt now that my accusation was out in the open but had fallen on deaf ears. I felt that I would become the laughing stock of the college."

"But surely, you didn't let the matter rest there, did you?"

"Actually, I am afraid I did. You see I felt such a deep sense of shame at what had happened that I couldn't bear the thought of sharing it with anyone. I could imagine what the bastard who raped me would tell everyone, if I did. No doubt half the college would soon believe that, at the very least, I couldn't hold my drink and, no doubt, there were some who would be happy to believe I was the college tart! And, of course, the more I thought about it, the more I began to doubt myself and wonder whether I'd been more responsible for what had happened than I wanted to accept."

"From what I know about these sorts of situation, I am afraid that's very often the case. The victim is inclined to take on all the shame and guilt. I can understand why you didn't want to take the matter further. But tell me, it must have been hard to carry on as if nothing had happened in such a small community, how did you manage?"

"Oh, to start with I couldn't bear the thought. I even drafted a letter of resignation. But, to my immense relief, I heard on the grapevine that my assailant had got a new job at a college somewhere in the West Country and wouldn't be coming back the following term. That, plus the fact that the whole of the long summer vacation lay ahead, persuaded me not to hand in my resignation after all."

"I don't think you told me when this all took place."

"It was in July the year before last."

"So, not all that long ago. How did you feel when you went back to college the following term? It can't have been easy."

"To be honest I was incredibly apprehensive. But the strange thing is it was as if nothing had happened. Nobody said a word about it. I didn't get any odd looks, even from his friends who'd been there when I attacked him in the Common Room. Mostly, I felt a sense of relief. But, there was still a part of me that wanted to shout at those who had witnessed my distress but chosen to dismiss it."

"I bet there was. The trouble is, I don't think we men fully understand how a woman must feel when she's been violated. I find it equally difficult to imagine how any man could get pleasure out of subjecting a woman to such an ordeal."

"You're not doing too badly on the understanding front." Beth said, wiping her eyes with a tissue. "But, you know, what's much worse than the act itself is everything that follows afterwards. It's that horrible feeling that you can't really trust anyone. You become fearful of relationships. But, for me, the very worst thing is how I keep waking with the same nightmare. I'm being pursued by someone who I'm sure is going to attack me. It's night and so dark that I can't see anything except the indistinct shape of trees and undergrowth as I try to run away. I can't see who's following me but I can hear him. He's not far behind and he's getting closer and closer. And then I wake up in a cold sweat and it all comes back. I remember the full horror of having been raped, not in the forest of my nightmare, but in my own flat, on my own sofa by someone I thought was my friend!"

"My poor dear Beth. How often do you get these nightmares?"

"Not as often as I used to. But sometimes, when I go to bed, I lie awake for hours, terrified that I'm going to drift off back into the same nightmare all over again."

"Have you talked to anyone about this, a counsellor or someone who might be able to help? I mean, it sounds to me like you're suffering from some form of post-traumatic stress?"

"I'm sure I am but, the thing is, I don't have much faith in that sort of thing. We've got a department of psychiatry attached to college but, to tell you the truth, the people I've met from there all seem to me to be pretty loony themselves, if you know what I mean?"

"Yes, but there are some excellent counsellors out there. I've worked with some of them. You know, people who mainly listen. It's one of the things that the Church is taking very seriously these days, the 'ministry of listening.'"

"Well, if you're anything to go by, the good old C of E is right on track. I can't help thinking that talking to you is doing me more good than talking to a professional counsellor could ever do." Beth gazed up into Tom's eyes."Kiss me, please kiss me" she pleaded, pulling him towards her with a sudden burst of passion. When they drew close he saw that she had closed her eyes. Her lips were parted, quivering in anticipation. Their mouths touched and he felt her slide her hand inside his shirt.

"Are you sure Beth, are you sure?" he asked.

"Shhh" she replied "no more words!" She silenced him by parting his lips with her tongue. He slid his hands under the bottom of her sweater. Her felt her body shiver with pleasure as he slid them over the soft curve of her stomach. He guided his hands slowly up over the arch of her lower ribcage and then up, still further, until he reached the cleft between her breasts. He slipped his fingers inside her bra. Her nipples were rigid with excitement and she let out a soft moan of pleasure. She pulled away from him and slid her sweater over her head. She smiled and slowly began to undo the buttons of his shirt. The touch of her cool hands sent shivers through his body. They kissed again with renewed passion. Her hands were locked around his back. She pulled him towards her, moving slowly backwards until he slid out of his chair. They sunk down onto the rug in front of the fire where they soon lay, side by side, exploring each other's naked bodies with a lingering passion. There was nothing hurried about the lovemaking that followed and when it was over, they were hardly able to believe that so much love could have come out of so much grief.

# CHAPTER FORTY-SEVEN

There had been a sharp change in the weather overnight, the sky was heavily overcast and a bitterly cold wind billowed around Beth **as she** made her way down towards Ty Pellaf. But, however unfriendly the elements, Beth had never felt so happy. In a single night, she felt that her life was moving from one of disappointment and bitterness to one of hope and expectation.

After they had made love the previous evening they had not gone upstairs to bed. Tom had brought down a couple of blankets and they remained huddled together on the rug in front of the fire. They had not stirred until the first glimmer of daylight had begun to show through the cottage windows.

She had been surprised to discover how good a lover Tom was. She had enjoyed sex before but never imagined that anyone would take such care in satisfying her physical yearnings. He had brought pleasure to every part of her body. Her natural inhibitions soon melted away and she found herself responding with equal passion. She, too, had taken pleasure in discovering those parts of his body that were most sensitive to her touch. They had both cried out in the final throws of orgasm. And when it was over, they had lain together whispering words of affection in each other ears.

As she walked down to Ty Pellaf, Beth found it difficult to think of anything else. And yet she knew that she must turn her mind to the needs of Rhiannon and her grandmother. When she drew near to the farmhouse, she saw smoke rising from the chimney. She was pleased that Rhiannon had had the good sense to light a fire on such a cold morning. She knocked at the back door. When Rhiannon let her in, she saw everything in the kitchen was neat and tidy and that a basket of clean washing was waiting to be hung out. She put her arms around the young girl and gave her a hug.

"I see you've been busy around the house" she said, "your mother will be pleased. How's your Nan this morning?"

"I think she's much better. She's eaten all her breakfast and she wanted a second cup of tea. Would you like to come upstairs to see her?"

"Yes, I'd like that very much, if you don't think she'll mind."

"Mummy told her you'd be calling to see us. Nan said she'd like to meet you. I've told her all about you and your search for King Arthur."

Rhiannon led the way up the narrow staircase and across to the room in which the old lady lay in bed waiting for them.

"Nan, this is my new friend Dr Davenport, I've been telling you all about her." And then she added proudly "she says I can call her Beth 'cos we're special friends."

"It's lovely to meet you Mrs Davies" Beth said, crossing the room and taking the old lady's hand. "I hear you've been rather poorly. How are you feeling this morning?"

"Oh, I've felt worse, thank you for asking" the old woman croaked. "It's this wretched congestion on my chest. I just don't seem to be able to get rid of it. It makes me wheeze and cough something rotten."

"Oh dear, that doesn't sound so good. Is there anything I can do for you?"

"Thanks, but I've got my medicine and it isn't too bad if I sit up. As for my chest, well, it's always worse at this time of year what with the cold and the damp."

"Well, hopefully the warmer weather shouldn't be too far away now that we're well into spring."

Rhiannon straightened her grandmother's eiderdown which had slipped to one side and the old woman reached forward to take her hand.

"I don't know what I'd do without my precious little granddaughter. She's such a godsend you know. Nothing's too much trouble for her." Then, with a big smile on her face, she continued "I understand you've been telling Rhiannon all about King Arthur and Merlin. I haven't seen her so excited for a very long time."

"Well, she's so interested and asks so many sensible questions. It's a pleasure to share it all with her. I wish some of my students showed half her enthusiasm!"

"She's always been the same you know. Once she gets her nose into something she simply won't let go. I'm sure she's got lots of other questions she'd like to ask you and I'm feeling a little tired. Rhiannon dear, perhaps you'd like to take Dr Davenport back down to the kitchen. You could make her a nice cup of tea. Thank you for coming up to see me. I hope you enjoy your stay on the island."

Mrs Davies squeezed the young girl's hand affectionately, leaned back into her large pile of pillows and closed her eyes.

"It was so nice to meet you Mrs Davies. I hope you're feeling much better soon." Beth said, but saw that the old lady was already drifting off to sleep. "Come on then Rhiannon" she whispered, "let's go down and get that kettle on, shall we?"

When they arrived back downstairs, Beth sat at the table while Rhiannon set about making the tea.

"Fraid we haven't got any cake but would you like a biscuit? They're gingers, Mummy made them yesterday."

"Yes please, I'm particularly fond of ginger biscuits, especially when they're homemade."

"I can't 'member, do you take sugar?"

"No thanks, just a little milk."

Soon Rhiannon joined Beth at the table and asked "Do you think Arthur really got well again when he was brought here after he'd been hurt?"

"Well, of course, it was all such a long time ago that we don't really know. But, I think there could be some truth in those early stories that suggest that he recovered."

"When you told us about Arthur being healed, you said he was put in a glass room or something. Was that the same place where Merlin put all the treasures?"

"My goodness, you do have a good memory and that's a very good question. As I've already said, we don't really know what happened. There are so many different stories. For instance, that little cave you took me to, you know, your secret place? Well, when I saw all those shiny bits of stone in the walls and roof, I couldn't help thinking that it looked a bit like a glass chamber. It would certainly have been a safe place for Merlin to hide the 13 treasures. And then there are the stories about Arthur being healed by the Lady Morgan and her sisters. I would have thought that they would have had somewhere much more suitable than a cave in which to attend to Arthur's wounds. One of the most interesting stories about Arthur, written a long, long time ago, perhaps going back more than a thousand years, is called *La Folie Tristan*. It tells of how Morgan, the Queen, lived in a chamber of glass in which all the rays of the sun converged."

"It's all very comlificated if you ask me" Rhiannon said, scratching her head. "But why was it 'portant that Arthur was put in a glass place, I mean could it really help him to get better?"

"Well, of course, it would have taken more than just the sun to heal him because he'd been so very badly wounded. But, in those days, they did believe that the sun had special therapeutic powers. In fact, a lot of people still believe that today too. You see, when the sun shines through glass, it gathers extra strength. That's why we grow so many things in greenhouses."

"I know" Rhiannon said excitedly "my sister Gwen has a little greenhouse in her garden. It's ever so hot when I go in there. What does thera... thera putic mean, I don't know that word?"

"Oh I'm sorry. Therapeutic, well it just means something that's able to heal, to make you better, you know, like a medicine."

Beth was delighted that Rhiannon was showing so much interest. It never crossed her mind to ask herself why or to put it down to anything other than a child's love of a good story. But this was something she would remember later.

They chatted on for a while until Beth felt she had answered all the girl's questions and it was time to return to Tom.

"I promised Tom I'd pack a picnic and take it up to the old chapel before lunch" she said. "He's up there doing some spring cleaning. Apparently, they used to do that when he came here on those pilgrimages when he was a young man."

"Can I come? I used to help Nan clean the chapel until she got her 'thritis. Nobody does it very often now."

"It's very kind of you to offer, but I think that Tom will have more or less finished by the time I get up there. And, in any case, don't you think you ought to stay here to look after your grandmother?"

"S'pose so" Rhiannon said, looking disappointed. "P'raps I can come with you when Mummy and Daddy get back. We could pick some wild-flowers and put them in a jam-jar, like I used to with Nan."

"Yes, that's a lovely idea. Now listen Rhiannon, I know your Mum and Dad will be back later this afternoon, but don't forget, in the meantime, you only have to come and ask if you need anything."

Rhiannon followed Beth to the kitchen door where she threw her arms around her and said. "Thank you for coming to see Nan and me and for being my special friend."

Beth gave the girl a warm hug. "Goodbye my special friend and take care."

She set off down the path. When she looked back, Rhiannon was still standing on the doorstep. They waved to each other and Beth felt a tide of emotion sweep over her. It was impossible not to be captivated by her sweet and touching innocence.

# CHAPTER FORTY-EIGHT

"*W*ell done everyone that went much better this time. Ieuan, you look the part, you sound the part but you absolutely must learn your lines. I know we've only got three days and you've got a lot more to remember than the others, but everything and everyone hangs on you knowing your lines."

The tall, lanky, dark-haired young man to whom this was addressed looked thoroughly dejected. He knew how much the others were depending on him. He had been thrilled when Tom first cast him to play the role of St Francis. But now, he wasn't so sure. He hadn't realised how difficult it would be to learn all his lines by heart.

"I know Tom. I'm doing my best, but it's really difficult you know."

"If you'd like me to run through them with you again, you've only got to ask." Tom suggested.

"Perhaps a little later on? Emyr and I want to climb the mountain this afternoon."

"Sometime before supper then? Why don't you come up to Ty Capel? Half past five shall we say?"

"OK then, that's fine by me, see you then."

Tom watched Ieuan and Emyr make their way past the chapel to the foot of the mountain. Most of the others were also setting off, in twos or threes, to explore different parts of the island. Soon, only Tom, the Franciscan brothers Mark and Andrew, and two of the younger boys, Gwylim and Huw, remained It was one of those steaming mid-August afternoons when only butterflies and bees seemed keen to be active. They sat down to chat on the long grass beneath the ancient abbey tower.

Tom couldn't remember when he had last felt so content. Ieuan's memory lapses aside, the play was coming on well. He was confident they would be ready to give their first performance in Aberdaron in three days time. But *it was the joy of being on the island that brought Tom his greatest happiness. He had always been attracted to remote and barren places. As a child, it had been the mountains and fells of the Lake District, the windswept hills and moors of Derbyshire and the less accessible cliff-tops of Anglesey that he had most loved. But Bardsey, by virtue of the three miles of treacherous waters separating it from the mainland and its sparse population, appealed to him more than anywhere he had ever visited. It was easy to understand why St Cadfan had chosen to build his monastery here and why the island had become such a special place of pilgrimage over the ensuing centuries. He could think of no greater joy than to be in such a magical place sharing the convivial company of the Franciscan brothers and his fellow young ordinands.*

*"Much as I'm enjoying sitting here and doing nothing, I've got a date with a bucket, a mop and a feather duster" Mark said. "Can I can persuade any of you sun-loving layabouts to get off your arses? I could do with a hand. I'm going to give the old chapel a bit of a going over. It doesn't look like anyone's touched it for a while."*

*"You can count me in" Tom said.*

*"What about you two young 'uns, want to give us a hand?" Mark asked, addressing Gwylim and Huw.*

*"Don't see why not" Huw said, standing up with a grin on his face "Come on Gwily. As my Mam always says, cleanliness is next to godliness."*

*Tom heard Gwilym mutter something in Welsh to his young friend, which he took to be an expression of his somewhat reluctant consent.*

*"All right then boys," Mark said "here's what I suggest. Go back to your respective lodgings and pick up whatever you can find in the way of cleaning materials, you know, buckets, mops, sponges, cleaning cloths, polish, dusters, that sort of thing. We've got water on tap at Ty Capel, right next door to the chapel. So, let's meet up there."*

*In less than 20 minutes they had all arrived at the chapel, armed with an impressive array of cleaning materials.*

*"Ok lads" Brother Andrew said, looking at Gwilym and Tom, both of whom had come armed with long witches' broomsticks, "The first thing we need to do is to get those cobwebs down off the ceiling. Tom, you're the tallest,*

I reckon you should be able to reach up to the top if you stand on that pew. We can move it along when you've done the end near the door. You won't need it at the far end because you can to stand in the pulpit."

"That's great, Tom" Huw interjected. "You can preach us a sermon while you're up there."

Tom laughed. He looked at the enormous pulpit that dominated the east end of the chapel. "I'm not sure I'd be quite up to the job. I bet some pretty powerful stuff has been delivered from up there. I can imagine the islanders quaking in their seats as they listened in to some black-robed minister, pointing at them accusingly, and telling of the eternal damnation that was awaiting them if they didn't mend their ways!"

"It's certainly one of the most impressive pulpits I've ever seen" Brother Andrew said.

"Well, it's what chapel has always been about in Wales." Gwilym said. "I was brought up Church of Wales but most of our neighbours were chapel folk. God's Day for them, is all about dressing up in your Sunday best, walking to chapel, listening to sermons that go on for ever and, of course, singing your heart out."

"OK boys, that's enough chatter, let's get on with the job." Brother Mark said and soon they were all busily occupied with their different tasks. Once Tom and Gwilym had managed to brush down the worst of the cobwebs, the others set about dusting and polishing the pulpit, the bookcase in which the red hymn books were stored, the wooden altar, window sills and pews. When they had finished, Tom swept the accumulated pile of dust and cobwebs out through the chapel door. Brother Andrew and Huw got down on their hands and knees and began to scrub the floor, while Gwilym made his way back and forth to Ty Capel to provide them with a regular supply of clean water. Brother Mark, meanwhile, had climbed into the pulpit, armed with a tin of Brasso and a cleaning cloth, and was polishing the impressive candle holders on either side of the pulpit. It was at this point that Brother Andrew began to sing John Bunyan's hymn 'He who would valiant be', filling the chapel with his rich baritone voice. Soon they had all joined in, singing the last four lines with particular conviction:

'Then fancies flee away!
I'll fear not what men say,
I'll labour night and day
To be a pilgrim.'

The cleaning done, they took it in turns to choose their favourite hymns and songs. They had just finished an enthusiastic rendering of 'Bread of Heaven' when Father Beuno appeared, looking very pleased with their handiwork.

"Well, I am impressed. You've done a fantastic job. I was sitting on the wall by the abbey and I heard you all singing away. But I didn't realise you were actually giving the chapel the once over. I understand the minister is coming over from the mainland to take a service here on Sunday week. He'll be chuffed to bits. There doesn't seem to be anyone with the time to look after the place properly these days. Of course, it would have been a different matter when there were 60 or more souls living on the island. But nowadays, well, that's all in the past. Seeing as you've put in such an effort, can I suggest that we celebrate our Eucharist here on Sunday? What do you think??"

"Oh yes!" they all responded enthusiastically.

"So, Father, are you going to give us a song?" Brother Andrew asked.

"Well, if you insist, I suppose I could" he replied, clearly pleased to have been asked. "You Welsh boys will know this one, I'm sure. It's one of my favourites. The story it tells goes back a very long way." Propping himself up against the end of one of the solid mahogany pew ends, he raised his head, closed his eyes and in a mellow, light tenor voice sang in Welsh 'Dafydd y Garreg Wen'.

They were all so moved by Father Beuno's singing that nobody spoke a word after he had finished. It was Tom who eventually broke the silence.

"Father, that was truly beautiful. What a haunting melody. Of course, I hardly understood a word of it. What's it's about?"

"Well, it's a sad tale. In English, it translates as 'David of the White Rock'. It tells the story of how David asks his wife to bring him his harp so that he can play one more tune before he dies. He asks her to help him to lift up his hands so that he can reach the strings. On the previous night, he had heard an angel say to him 'David, come home and play through the glen'. He bids farewell to his harp and asks for God's blessing for his widow and his children."

"What a sad tale. But who is this David?" Tom asked.

"Oh well, you see, it's David Owen the famous harpist and composer. He lived near Porthmadog during the early part of the 18th century. He was known locally as Dafydd y Garreg Wen because 'The White Rock' was the name of his farm. He was only 29 when he died. It's a traditional Welsh folk tune. The words were added much later by the poet John Ceiriog Hughes."

Tom looked out through the open door. He saw that the sun had disappeared behind a large black cloud. A flurry of wind rattled the chapel windows, followed by a sudden and unexpected shower of heavy rain.

"I can hardly believe the weather has turned so quickly" Brother Mark said. "Small wonder they can't always get across from the mainland."

"Perhaps we'll get stranded here for a few days" said Huw, hopefully.

The rain pounded down and they could hear the wind gusting outside. They were grateful to be safe within the solid stone chapel. Never one to miss an opportunity to amuse the assembled company, Brother Andrew launched into song and soon they all joined in:

'Eternal Father, strong to save
Whose arm doth bind the restful wave,
Who bidst the mighty ocean deep
It's own appointed limits keep:
Oh hear us when we cry to thee
For those in peril on the sea.'

The rain stopped almost as suddenly as it had started and soon the sun came out again. Tom stepped outside and looked down the length of the island towards the lighthouse and beyond to where the sea lay glittering in the gold of the early evening sun. He had never felt so content or so certain about his vocation.

# CHAPTER FORTY-NINE

Tom and Beth were in need of a breath of fresh air. They had toiled away all afternoon, scrubbing clean the floor of the old chapel. They decided to make their way down to one of the island's wilder and rocky stretches of coastline, near Bae Rhigol. While they had been working, they had been unaware of a change in the weather. Now, as they stood looking down at the turbulent sea below, they had to lean heavily into the wind to stay on their feet. The sky was overcast and a blanket of even denser black cloud was heading in from the north. Through the one remaining gap in the clouds, a shaft of sunlight lit up the rearing heads of the waves as they ripped across the channel. There had been bursts of thunder and lightning all afternoon from out over the Irish Sea. But the storm was getting much closer now. From the firm way she was gripping his arm, he sensed Beth shared his strange mixed feeling of apprehension and excitement. The waves crashed into the rocks below them, sending up enormous showers of spray.

"I think we'd better move a bit further back" Tom shouted at Beth, pulling her away from the edge of the cliff.

They found a flat piece of rock where they were able to sit, sheltered from the worst of the storm.

"Just look at how the sea's got up in the short time since we came down." Beth shouted back excitedly. She pointed at a small fishing boat, far out in the storm-tossed sea that was struggling to make its way back to the safety of the harbour. "My God, I wouldn't want to be out there in that." She said "What a life!"

The heavy black clouds had now moved much closer. A sudden flash of fork lightning lit up the sky, shortly followed by a loud rumble of thunder.

"Phew, that was a bit too close for comfort. I think that's our cue to head back" Tom said. Not waiting for an answer, he stood up and grabbed Beth's arm. The wind tore into their backs as they hurried across the fields towards the abbey ruins and the cottage beyond. While Tom was fumbling with the key, there was another blinding flash of lightning directly above them, followed by an ear-splitting crash of thunder. They only just made it inside before the heavens opened and the island was drowned in sheets of driving rain.

Tom slammed the door shut behind them. "My goodness, that was a close one."

Beth laughed. "Well, it isn't the first time you've rescued me from the perils of the rain. At least, this time you won't have to spend the rest of the evening helping me dry out."

"More's the pity. You should know by now, I rather enjoy ministering to rain-drenched maidens. You have no idea how sexy you looked standing there dripping on my doorstep!"

"I can always go out and come back in again, if you prefer me that way!"

There was another flash of lightning followed by an even louder crash of thunder.

"Perhaps not, under the circumstances. Rain-drenched is one thing, but a pile of cinders, that has considerably less appeal!" They laughed. Tom drew Beth towards him and kissed her on the cheek. She put her arms round him and snuggled up closer.

"I'm falling in love with you Tom, do you know that?"

"Yes, that's how I feel too, my little mermaid." He ran his fingers affectionately across her lips.

"Who would have thought it possible?" she whispered.

"Wasn't it Arthur Conan Doyle who said that when you have eliminated the impossible, whatever remains, however improbable, must be the truth."

"Do you believe that? How can we be sure that we aren't deluding ourselves? Is it really possible for two people to fall in love when they've known each other for barely a week, and under the oddest circumstances?"

"I don't know whether that's a genuine question or a simple statement of disbelief."

"Oh Tom, it isn't either of those. It's just... it's just that I can hardly believe what's happening."

"Beth, dear Beth" Tom said, stepping back and holding her firmly by the shoulders. "When I arrived on this island, I felt as though my life was as good as over. I had lost my wife and I had lost my faith and nothing seemed to have any meaningful purpose any more. I came here expecting to face weeks of agonising soul-searching. It was my last desperate attempt to see if I could salvage something from the wreck of my life. The only love I came in search of here was the love of God, which seemed to have altogether deserted me. And then what happens? You come unexpectedly into my life and in the blink of an eye, everything has changed."

"It hasn't been all that different for me you know" Beth said. "The truth is that I've been just as troubled. I've only managed to keep going by burying myself in my academic life. I think we've both been travelling along a very lonely road. You lost your faith in God; I lost mine in my fellow men and women. It seems so extraordinary that one chance meeting should have changed everything so completely."

"I know and isn't it wonderful? And, do you know what? I don't think we should waste another moment questioning the hows and whys. We're here in the now and I don't feel the need to know why. They say that you can tell everything from looking into a person's eyes. And what do I see when I look into your eyes? I see love and compassion and hunger and kindness and gentleness and just a little fear, and it makes me want to hold you tight and never let go."

Beth allowed herself to be pulled gently into the warmth of Tom's arms. They continued to offer each other words of comfort until Beth finally pulled away.

"What is it Beth, what's the matter?"

"It's all right Tom." she said "It's just that with this awful storm, what if Mattie and Harry haven't been able to get back? What if Rhiannon has to look after her grandmother all night on her own? I promised Mattie I'd keep an eye on things. I won't be able to fully relax until I know that Rhiannon is all right."

"But you can't go out in this dreadful storm! Why don't I go?"

"That's all very chivalrous and manly of you but no, I'll go. I'll be fine. It sounds as though the wind's dropped a bit anyway and it's almost stopped raining. The thing is, Tom, it was me that Mattie asked and, let's be honest, I'm probably in a better position to help if help is needed."

"Well, I can't argue with that" Tom said "but why don't I come with you?"

"No, you stay here. There's no point in us both exposing ourselves to the elements. In any case, somebody needs to cook our supper and keep the fire stoked up."

Tom could see that Beth had made her mind up and there was little point in arguing. He helped her on with her coat, gave her a final hug and watched through the window as she hurried down the garden path.

# CHAPTER FIFTY

Tom stood by the cooker, watching the kettle slowly come to the boil. He could hear occasional movements from upstairs where Beth and Rhiannon were tending to the old lady. But most of the sounds were drowned by the constant high-pitched howling of the wind and the incessant pounding of the rain against the farmhouse windows. The storm that had temporarily abated was now back in full force and appeared to be set in for the night.

He felt sick inside, overwhelmed by a strong sense of guilt. How could he have said what he had said? How could he have been so unbelievably pious and selfish and stupid? How could he have allowed his own pathetic doubts and fears to come before the desperate needs of the old lady who was dying upstairs?

He stared across the room at the mahogany-cased marine clock that was slowly ticking the time away on the mantelpiece. He wished he could wind the hands back to before the moment when Beth had returned to Carreg Bach with the news that Mattie and Harry had not returned, and that Rhiannon's grandmother had taken a serious turn for the worse. When she had gone upstairs to see Mrs Davies, she had found her steeped in a heavy fever and barely conscious. There had been a brief moment when the old lady had opened her eyes and looked up at her imploringly. She had just managed to croak the words 'minister, fetch a minister', before falling back into unconsciousness. The old lady had been so earnest in her request that Beth had rushed straight out into the storm and run all the way up to Carreg Bach to fetch Tom. And what a fool he had been. Instead of immediately agreeing to go back with her, he had indulged in a raft of pious excuses. How could he minister to the old lady when he was so unsure of his own faith? Wouldn't this be an act of gross hypocrisy?

He continued to plead his pathetic excuses until she finally went down on her knees, with tears streaming down her face, and literally begged him to come with her.

It was only then that he had finally succumbed. With his mind in turmoil, he reluctantly nodded his assent.

"I mean now, this very minute" she shouted at him. "I don't think that she's much time left, don't you understand? She needs you and she needs you now."

Shocked into action, he hurriedly put on his coat, picked up his prayer book and ran with Beth through the driving rain down to Ty Pellaf. When they arrived, they went straight upstairs where they had found Rhiannon kneeling by the side of her grandmother's bed. Through tear-stained eyes, the young girl told them that her grandmother had not regained consciousness. Beth had taken one look at the old lady, turned to Tom and said in a hushed voice:

"There's nothing you can do here for the time being. Why don't you go downstairs and make us all a cup of tea. I'm sure that Rhiannon could do with one and I certainly could. I'll let you know if she wakes up."

He made his way meekly down to the kitchen, feeling like a schoolboy who had been severely admonished. What was wrong with him? How could he have been so selfish? For the first time since they had been together he felt his relationship with Beth was hanging by a thread.

It all happened so quickly. And now, here he was, listening to the seconds tick by while he waited for the kettle to boil. Well, if nothing else, he was doing something useful. He wondered if Beth understood. Would she ever forgive him? They'd been so happy and now he'd spoiled it all. There was a hiss of steam from the kettle. He spooned tea into a large brown teapot and filled it with boiling water. He left it to stand while he looked for mugs and sugar and milk then put everything on a tin tray and made his way upstairs. Through the bedroom door he could hear the muffled sound of voices in low conversation. He tapped on the bedroom door which Beth opened for him.

"How is she?" he asked.

"It's not looking good I'm afraid. She's really struggling with her breathing. She came round again briefly, while you were downstairs, but then had such a dreadful coughing fit that she went quite purple in the face. I really thought the end had come. I feel so helpless Tom. I honestly don't know what to do for the best. What she needs is a doctor or a trained nurse."

"There's fat chance of that I'm afraid, well not until this storm has passed and goodness knows when that will be". He turned to look at Rhiannon who was sitting next to her grandmother's bed, tenderly wiping the old lady's face with a damp facecloth. "How's Rhiannon bearing up do you think?" he whispered.

"She's amazing. She's so kind and thoughtful. There's nothing that's too much trouble to her. Mind you, I'm not sure she fully understands how poorly her Gran actually is."

"Well, with any luck, this storm will pass over during the night and Mattie and Harry will be able to get back in the morning. We'll just have to hope she doesn't get any worse."

"It's so frustrating that there's no way we can get hold of them in the meantime. Although, even if we could, I suppose all they could do would be to worry themselves silly."

"Yes, perhaps it's better that they don't know, under the circumstances. Look, let me pour the tea before it goes cold. Do you know if Rhiannon takes sugar?"

Rhiannon looked up when she heard her name. "Two sugars please and lots of milk."

Tom smiled "I can see that you love your grandmother very much."

"My Nan's the best Nan in the world." She replied proudly.

"I'm sure she is and I'm equally sure that she couldn't wish for a kinder and more loving granddaughter." Tom looked at Beth. There were dark shadows under her eyes and she was deathly pale. He could see that the strain of the situation was getting to her. "Beth, you look all in. Let me take over for a while."

But before Beth could reply, Rhiannon called out excitedly "look, she's woken up again. She's trying to say something. What is it Nan, can I get something for you?"

Tom and Beth hurried across to the bedside. The old lady's eyes were open and she was attempting to raise her right hand. She seemed to be trying to attract Tom's attention. Her lips were moving but it was impossible to hear what she was trying to say.

Tom stooped down and put his ear close to her lips. At first, all he could make out were the words 'bless' and 'dying' which she kept repeating. And then, with a supreme effort, she managed to croak "I know I'm dying. I need your blessing. Please, pray with me."

He took her hand. "Of course. We can all pray together. Rhiannon, would you fetch my prayer book from the chest of drawers. Yes, that's right, it's that thick black book next to the glass bowl." He gestured to Beth and Rhiannon "come and join me. We can all kneel by the side of the bed." He turned to Rhiannon "Do you know your Nan's Christian name?" he asked.

"Yes. It's Mary, like Jesus' Mummy." Rhiannon replied. Beth put an arm around her shoulders and knelt down on the floor with her, on the opposite side of the bed to Tom. He, meanwhile, had turned the pages of his prayer book until he reached the Order for the Visitation of the Sick. He placed one hand over the old lady's and began to say the Office in a strong and reassuring voice:

"My children, we are gathered here together in the presence of God to bring comfort to Mary in her final hours. Mary, you seek God's blessing before your leave this life and enter into the presence of God. I ask you if you confess your sins of thought word and deed and seek God's mercy. If you do, just squeeze my hand." Tom felt a slight movement of the old lady's fingers. He continued:

"Our Lord Jesus Christ, who hath left power to his Church to absolve all sinners who truly repent and believe in him, of his great mercy forgive you your offences: And by his authority committed to me, I absolve you from all your sins, in the name of the Father, and of the Son, and of the Holy Ghost." They all joined in the "Amen".

Tom made the sign of the cross above the old lady's head. Her eyes were open and he was sure that he detected the trace of a smile in the creases around her mouth.

"Unto God's gracious mercy and protection we commit you. The Lord bless you and keep you. The Lord make his face to shine upon you, and be gracious unto you and give you peace, both now and for evermore." The old lady had closed her eyes again but Tom sensed that she was still aware of what was happening. He continued "Unto you, O Lord, we commend the soul of your servant Mary that, dying to the world, she may live to you; and whatsoever sins she has committed through the frailty of earthly life, we beseech you to do away by thy most loving and merciful forgiveness; through Jesus Christ our Lord."

Tom looked across at Beth. She was still holding Rhiannon firmly around the shoulders. Tears were streaming down the young girl's face as she tried to comprehend the enormity of what was happening. "Shall we say The Lord's Prayer together?" Tom said and when he began Beth and Rhiannon both joined in. The old lady had opened her eyes again and was staring blankly in front of her. When they reached the end of The Lord's Prayer, Tom felt her fingers relax and he knew that she was on the point of death. He raised his head and in a loud voice proclaimed:

"I am the resurrection and the life, saith the Lord: he that believeth in me, though he were dead, yet shall he live: and whosoever liveth and believeth in me shall never die."

He reached across the bed, took hold of Rhiannon's hand and placed it over those of her grandmother. "Rhiannon, you see that smile on your Nan's face. She's smiling because she's at peace and because she's so happy that you are here with her at this last precious moment." And then the smile slowly faded from the old lady's face and all was quiet.

"Has my Nan gone to heaven" Rhiannon asked, looking anxiously up at Tom.

'Yes', said Tom "she is at rest now." He gently closed her grandmother's eyes.

Rhiannon stared for a moment at her lifeless body and then turned to Beth and said:

"Now that my Nan's with God, is it all right if I cry?"

"Of course it is my darling" Beth replied. "It's the most natural thing in the world."

# CHAPTER FIFTY-ONE

"Poor girl, I do hope that she manages to get some sleep, she must be exhausted" Tom said, looking at Beth across the kitchen table at Ty Pellaf.

"I think she may have reached that point where she has literally run out of tears, if you know what I mean." Beth replied, nervously fingering the handle of her empty mug.

"To be perfectly honest, I didn't really know what to say to her. She loved her Nan so much. Having to cope with all this without her Mum and Dad seems so incredibly unfair."

"Actually, I thought you were pretty fantastic." Beth said, reaching across the table and taking hold of his hand. "You said those prayers in such a strong and positive voice. It must have been wonderfully reassuring for the old lady. Do you know, it is the first time I've actually seen someone die? I found it all so immensely moving, if you know what I mean, rather beautiful in fact."

"Yes, death can be beautiful, especially when the person who's dying isn't afraid of death."

"I think Rhiannon understood that. In her uncomplicated way, she seems to have accepted the inevitable. Her tears were for her own sense of loss and not so much for her grandmother." Beth paused and then gripping Tom's hand more firmly she took a deep breath and said:

"Tom, I'm so sorry. I feel I owe you an apology for earlier on. I don't think I was very kind to you and I know what a struggle this must have been for you. I can see now that I expected too much. Can you forgive me?"

"There's nothing to forgive. I'm the one who should be apologising. I've spent far too long wallowing in self-pity."

"No, you haven't. It's just that you aren't ready to return to the priesthood yet, I can see that. But, tonight, you were magnificent. You have such an exceptional gift. I suppose you'd call it a true vocation. I so much want to help you to give strength to that vocation. I believe in you and I can see that you would be wasted doing anything else."

She felt Tom tighten his hold of her hand. His eyes were moist with tears.

"I shall never forget this night, Tom. Who would ever have thought that death could have so much meaning?"

"Oh, I've seen scores of people die. It isn't always so peaceful, I can assure you. The ones who really suffer are those who are left behind. It's not easy to accept losing someone you love, especially if they're taken before their time. When Martha was killed, the worst part of it all was not being there when it happened, not being able to say goodbye." There was a catch in Tom's voice. He closed his eyes and Beth sensed the pain that his memories were bringing back. She wanted to hold him close but held back. She could see that, for now, his thoughts were for his lost love and not for her. She sat quietly waiting for him to regain his composure. It was an awkward moment during which neither of them spoke. The silence was only broken by the sound of Tom's heavy, uneven breathing. Finally, he opened his eyes, took out a handkerchief and blew his nose.

"I'm so sorry Beth. It's stupid, I know, but I still can't deal with Martha's death, with the pointlessness of it all. It doesn't make any sense to me, it never has."

"If only I could do something."

"But you are. You have no idea how much you fill me with hope. I know I can't go on living in the past. I've done that for far too long. I love you Beth. Whatever life may have in store for me in the future, I want it to be with you if you'll have me."

"Oh Tom, do you really mean that?"

"Yes, I most certainly do, with all my heart. It may seem entirely the wrong moment to say so but that is how I feel and that is what I want."

"If only you knew how much I want that too. How extraordinary the last few days have been. I can hardly believe what's happening to us. It's almost as if..."

"As if in some way, it was all intended?"

"Yes, that's exactly what I mean. It's like someone's grabbed hold of our lives and brought us together when neither of us thought that anything so wonderful could ever happen again."

"Do you know, that's just how I feel. You might expect the priest in me to pronounce that 'God works in mysterious ways'. But it would be presumptuous to assume that the hand of God has anything to do with the events of the last few days. For what it's worth, I couldn't give a tinker's cuss as to how or why it's happened. I just want us to share the joy of every minute of every hour of every day that we spend together."

"Are you frightened it won't last?"

"I suppose I am, just a little. It's all happening so very quickly."

"Do you think it's wrong for us to be talking about such things when poor Mrs Davies is still warm in her bed and her granddaughter is probably lying awake crying her eyes out?"

"We can't help how we feel. And, you know, it's at such moments, when your emotions have been completely caught up in the absolutes of life and death, that you're most likely to discover other truths about yourself."

"Tell me honestly, Tom, did it feel strange, slipping back into your role as a priest?"

"Well, I think I must have switched on autopilot and it all just happened. But, to answer your question, no, actually it didn't feel particularly odd."

"That's good, isn't it? Doesn't it suggest that it'll be all right in the end?"

"I don't know Beth, I really don't. What's more, I'm feeling so tired now that I doubt whether my thoughts on the matter are likely to be all that coherent."

"It sounds as though the worst of the storm is over. It's certainly stopped raining so hard and from the sound of it, the wind's dropped too. Why don't you go back to Carreg Bach and get a few hours sleep? There's going to be such a lot to do in the morning. Hopefully, the sea will have calmed down by then. One of us can stay here with Rhiannon while the other goes down to the harbour to wait for Mattie and Harry to break the sad news."

"Yes, but what about you? You must need some sleep too. I think I'd rather curl up in one of those armchairs for an hour or two. Why don't you do the same? It seems to be quiet upstairs for now, so I reckon Rhiannon must have fallen asleep. If she wakes before morning we can take it in turns to be with her."

Beth nodded her agreement and, after a quick embrace, they curled up in the armchairs either side of the fireplace and were soon sound asleep.

# CHAPTER FIFTY-TWO

Despite being exceptionally tired, Beth woke up several times in the hours before dawn. She found it impossible to put aside her memories of the previous evening. When she finally gave up and tiptoed across the kitchen to look out of the window, she was pleased to see that the sky had almost cleared. The ground outside was still sodden and dotted with large puddles. She looked over at Tom. He was still sound asleep, curled up in the armchair with his head cradled in his arms. She poured herself a glass of milk and sat down at the kitchen table to focus on the challenges of the day ahead.

Her first concern was for Rhiannon. She hoped she had managed to get some sleep. And then, what about Mattie and Harry? What a terrible homecoming it was going to be for them. While she had lain awake she had wondered whether there was any way they could get a message to them. There were no telephone lines to the mainland but she assumed the lighthouse people must have some means of communication in case of emergency. The problem was that she had no contact details for Mattie and Harry's son and daughter-in-law and she didn't want to wake Rhiannon. The girl needed all the sleep she could get. In any case, she assumed that Mattie and Harry would probably have returned to Aberdaron in the hope of being able to make the crossing the previous afternoon. No doubt they would have put up somewhere overnight. She looked out of the window again. Although she was getting to know the island, it was hard to believe that there could be such dramatic changes in the weather.

She heard the sound of footsteps descending the stairs. When she saw Rhiannon, her heart went out to her. The girl's face was ashen, except for the red blotches around her tear-stained eyes. Her hair was in disarray and seemed to have lost its natural lustre. Instead of her usual bright smile, she met Beth's welcoming "hello" with downcast eyes.

"My poor wee thing, you look so very sad. Did you manage to get any sleep? Can I get you something to drink?"

Rhiannon threw herself sobbing into Beth's arms. She hugged the girl tightly to her chest, gently stroking the back of her head.

Tom had woken when Rhiannon had come down the stairs. He stood with his arms stretched out in front of him as if in some form of supplication. He was still half asleep.

"Tom, do you think you could put the kettle on? I'm sure we could all do with a hot drink."

"Of course," Tom said, suppressing a yawn.

After a while, Rhiannon's sobbing began to subside. Beth took out a handkerchief and wiped the girl's eyes. She kissed her on the forehead and led her across to the kitchen table, where they sat down next to each other.

"You're a very brave girl Rhiannon. Your Mummy and Daddy will be very proud when we tell them how brave you've been."

"But I've cried and cried like a baby. That's not very brave."

"On the contrary, as I said to you last night, it's the most natural thing in the world to cry when you lose somebody you love. What really matters is that you were able to say goodbye to your Nan. She knew you were there and it must have meant a great deal to her."

"She's in heaven now, isn't she?"

"I'm sure she is," Tom said, from over by the cooker. "Your Nan was a good person and God always has a special place for good people."

"I wish Mummy and Daddy were here."

"I know, sweetie, and soon they will be. They'll be so sad when they hear what's happened. It's such a pity that we haven't been able to get in touch with them." Beth turned to Tom. "During the night, I wondered whether we should have tried to get a message across via the lighthouse people, but then I realised that we didn't know where they would be staying."

"Yes, I had similar thoughts myself." He looked out of the window. "At least the storm has died down so they should be able to get across today. Rhiannon, what time does Mr Price usually make his first crossing?"

"He only comes over once a day, 'cept in the summer. Sometimes he doesn't come at all. When he does come he tries to get here round 10 o'clock, 'cos then we all know when to 'spect him if he's got anything for us. When there's been a storm, like last night, it can take ages for the sea to calm down. He won't come unless it's safe."

"I suppose that means he could come at any time or he might even not come at all" Beth said looking anxiously at Tom.

"The only way to tell is to go down to the harbour to look at the sea. You can't tell from here." Rhiannon said.

"Well, let's have that nice hot cup of tea Tom's just made and then perhaps we can all walk down to take a look. Do you think you'll be able to tell, Rhiannon?"

"Spect so. Daddy says I'm use'ly right. I got a 'stinct for that sort of thing."

They sat round the table together, drinking their tea and eating some digestive biscuits Tom found in one of the cupboards. They plied Rhiannon with questions about life on the island, in the hope of distracting her from thinking about her grandmother's death. As soon as they had finished their tea, they put on warm outdoor clothing and set off for the harbour with Rhiannon clinging firmly onto Beth's hand

As they approached the harbour, a pale sun was struggling to emerge through a layer of thin white cloud hanging like a shroud across the sky. Rhiannon pointed out to where white-crested waves were relentlessly rolling in towards the island.

"Oh dear, that doesn't look too promising." Beth said

"That's nuffing" Rhiannon said "Mr Price comes over when it's much worse than that."

"Well it's still quite early" Tom said. "If he comes at all, I don't suppose he'll set off for another hour or two, will he?"

"It'll prob'ly take him a bit longer than usual 'cos he'll have to go further up the coast before turning for the island. That's so's he doesn't have to come through so much choppy water."

"You certainly seem to know your stuff" Tom said, smiling down at

Rhiannon. He was pleased to see her smile back at him. She seemed to be coping with the situation much better than they might have expected.

"So, what shall we do then?" Beth asked. "I think one of us should wait down here to break the news to Mattie and Harry. I don't like the idea of them not finding out until they arrive at the farmhouse."

"I'm more than happy to do that" Tom said. "But, as they're unlikely to get here for another couple of hours, why don't we all go back to get some breakfast and then I'll come back down and wait for them."

"Can I come too?" Rhiannon asked pleadingly.

"I don't see why not." Tom said, turning to Beth. "It's probably the best thing she can do under the circumstances. It'll give her something to do."

"I agree" Beth said. "But I think I ought to stay up at Ty Pelaf, I don't like the idea of them coming back to an empty house. Besides, I can make sure the kettle's on, ready for them, and tidy up a bit more in the meantime."

They walked back up to Ty Pellaf. As soon as they arrived, Rhiannon went off to feed the chickens. Beth dreaded the thought of returning to the bedroom where the old lady's dead body lay as they had left it the previous evening. However, she was determined that the Evans should find the bedroom as tidy as possible when they returned so she made her way tentatively upstairs. Tom meanwhile set about preparing boiled eggs, toast and a pot of coffee for breakfast.

A little over an hour later, while they were all still sitting at the kitchen table, Rhiannon remembered that the two dairy cows needed to be milked. Tom offered to help but she insisted this was something she was quite capable of doing on her own. As soon as she had gone out, Beth turned to Tom.

"Do you think she's all right? I mean this is quite something for her to cope with."

"I know, but what else can we do? I think we're agreed that the best thing, for the moment, is to keep her as busy as possible. She needs her Mum and Dad and hopefully they'll soon be here."

"But what if they can't make it? What shall we do then? That sea still looked pretty scary to me. I wouldn't be at all surprised if they don't get back today!"

"Let's wait and see." Tom looked at the kitchen clock. "It's nearly half past nine. As soon as Rhiannon gets back from milking, we'd better be off down to the harbour. Beth, I'm wondering, don't you think it might be better if you came with us? There really is nothing more you can do here and you and Rhiannon get on so well. I'm sure she'd prefer you to come."

"I suppose you're right. I think perhaps I was being a little selfish in that I didn't want to be the one to break the awful news to poor Mattie and Harry."

"I know. It's not going to be easy. But surely, the most important thing is to give Rhiannon all the support we can. After all, we may be waiting for the ferry all day, and even then they may not make it back today."

"You're right. Look, it was seriously nippy down there. While we're waiting I'll make some coffee to take down with us. I spotted a thermos under the sink and I can pack some biscuits and things."

Tom left Beth in the kitchen and went out into the farmyard in search of Rhiannon. As he approached the milking shed, he heard the sound of metal scraping on stone and Rhiannon emerged carrying a shiny silver milk bucket.

"Hello Tom. I've nearly finished. Ruby's been very naughty today. She's just kicked my milk bucket and nearly knocked it over."

"Is she usually naughty?" Tom asked

"Yes, she's high sp'ritted. Daddy says she's so frisky that he's s'prised her milk doesn't come out as butter!" They both laughed.

"Are you nearly ready to go, Rhiannon? We must be on our way as soon as we can. Beth's just preparing a hot drink to take down with us."

"I use'ly take the milk round to people now. Shall I do that before we go to meet Mummy and Daddy?"

"I don't think there's enough time Rhiannon. It'll have to wait until we get back."

"All right then but I've got to put the cows back in the field. I won't be long."

Tom watched Rhiannon leading the cows out through the farmyard entrance, her golden hair glowing in the early morning sunlight. He thought how pretty she looked. There was something of a past era about her, Hardy's Bathsheba Everdene perhaps?

It wasn't long before they were all standing on the slipway. The air had been relatively still up at the farmhouse but there was quite a stiff breeze where they were now standing. Rhiannon suggested they sheltered in front of the boathouse.

When Tom looked out beyond the creek he was relieved to see the sea was looking much calmer.

"That's extraordinary" he said, "who would have thought that the sea could have settled down so quickly."

"It'll be rough round the headland," Rhiannon said "that's where you get the really big waves."

"But don't you think it's looking a little more hopeful now?" Beth said, trying to keep Rhiannon's hopes up. But she needn't have worried, for she was now pointing excitedly out to sea:

"Look, look, there's a fishing boat. Can you see it?"

"I can't see anything" Beth said.

"Look, it's out there, bobbing up and down. Can you see it Tom?"

"I'm not sure where you mean. Oh, over there, yes, I can see something. He's quite a long way out, isn't he? That must be a good sign. He wouldn't have come out unless he was pretty sure it would be safe."

"Yes Tom, I'm sure you're right" Beth said. "The local boys will know every trick of the weather along this coastline. They won't take unnecessary risks."

"So, there must be a good chance that Alun Price will make it today."

Meanwhile, Rhiannon had scrambled over the rocks on the beach immediately below. She reached down to pick up something that she was carefully examining.

"I wonder what she's found?" Beth said "Thank goodness, she seems much happier than she was earlier."

"Let's hope we can keep her spirits up, at least until Mattie and Harry get back." Tom said. Meanwhile Rhiannon had begun to make her way back. She was waving excitedly, clutching something tightly in her hand.

"Look what I've found" she said, opening her hand up to reveal a tiny golden pendant on the end of short gold chain.

"Let's see" Beth said, taking hold of Rhiannon's hand. "Well I never! You see what it is, don't you Rhiannon?"

"Yes" Rhiannon replied, with a broad grin. "It's a dragon. I think it's the red dragon, like the one Merlin showed the king, the one that scared off the bad Saxon dragon."

"You've got a good memory. Do you know what, I think you may be right. After all it's only the red dragon that you'd expect to find here in Wales."

"I wonder how it got here?" Rhiannon said, turning it over to look at the other side.

"It wouldn't float, so it can't have been washed up. I expect someone must have dropped it by mistake, perhaps one of the children who visited here last summer."

"Perhaps it came here by magic."

"Well, of course it could have done. Maybe that's why you've found it because you believe in magic, don't you Rhiannon?"

"Oh yes. But you mustn't tell Tom our secret, 'member, you promised."

"Yes, I promised."

"And what secret would that be?" Tom asked, raising his eyebrows.

"Don't be silly. We can't tell you, else it wouldn't be a secret anymore, would it Beth?"

"No it wouldn't. I'm sorry Tom, but you'll just have to remain in the dark I'm afraid. After all, a secret's a secret."

"We dance round in a ring and suppose, but the secret sits in the middle and knows." Tom proclaimed.

"And what on earth has that got to do with anything?" Beth asked.

"I'm not quite sure, it's just something that came into my head and I thought I'd throw it in anyway. Nothing like a bit of Robert Frost on a chilly morning like this."

"Talking of which, who'd like a nice hot cup of coffee?" Beth asked, taking the thermos out of a shopping bag she'd borrowed from the Evans' kitchen.

"Yes please" said Tom.

"Me too" Rhiannon said. "Tom, do you think this is real gold?" She held the pendant up and Tom took hold of it to examine it more closely.

"It's hard to tell, it's so dirty." He took a handkerchief out of his trouser pocket and began to rub one side of the pendant vigorously to remove the dark deposit from its surface. At first, he had assumed that it was an inexpensive child's keepsake, probably purchased from a tourist shop on the mainland. But when he felt the weight of the pendant and saw its glittering surface, he was not so sure.

"Do you know what? I reckon this really could be gold. And look, now that I've managed to clean it up a bit you can see that it's exceptionally well-crafted. Rhiannon my dear, I think you may well have stumbled across a real piece of treasure!"

But Rhiannon was no longer listening. She was jumping up and down and pointing excitedly out to sea "Look. It's the ferry. It's coming round the headland. And look, there's my Mummy and Daddy!"

# CHAPTER FIFTY-THREE

TUESDAY EVENING

Tom was woken by the sound of someone knocking on the door. He yawned, sat up in bed and stretched his arms above his head. He couldn't remember when he had last slept so well. When he reached for his watch, he was surprised to see that it was approaching seven o'clock in the evening. He heard the sound of the front door opening and closing and Beth's voice calling out "Tom, are you awake? It's me, Beth."

"Come on in" he called back down. I'm afraid I'm not up yet. I fell asleep as soon as my head hit the pillow. Thanks for waking me, I need to get up or I'll never sleep tonight. Give me a minute and I'll be right down."

"I thought you'd be hungry when you woke up. What with one thing and another, neither of us has eaten properly since breakfast. I've brought some eggs with me. They'll go nicely scrambled with some of that smoked bacon I spotted in your fridge the other day."

"Yes, I'm starving and you're a saviour. I'll give you a hand if you hang on a minute."

"There's really no need, I can manage fine. Coffee or tea?"

"I think I'd prefer tea if that's OK with you. I've got a devilish thirst. I'm not used to sleeping in the daytime, but, after last night..."

"There's no need to justify it. I've had a good nap myself back at Llofft Plas. I tell you what you can do when you come down, you can light a fire. I reckon it's going to be cold again tonight."

"Of course, I was going to do that anyway."

Tom dressed quickly and appeared downstairs clutching a flannel and a toothbrush.

"I hope you don't mind but I simply must run a flannel over my face and I'd like to brush my teeth. It'll help me to wake up. I'm afraid I'm feeling rather growdy."

"Growdy? That's a new one on me. What precisely does it mean, may I ask?"

"Actually, it's a word I made up years ago. It describes how you feel when you're slightly hung-over and your teeth are all furred up."

"I know that feeling!"

"Well you would wouldn't you; it's all those fags, filthy habit. But I mustn't be too pious. I used to smoke the occasional cigarette myself, but never got seriously hooked."

"Lucky you!" Beth said, "I don't think I could get by without them. I've tried to convince myself to give up because of all the money I'd be able to save to pay for a new car or a wonderful holiday or something. But then, I imagine myself sitting in a café, looking out over a beautiful beach with a gin and tonic in one hand... but there's the rub. That's the very moment I'd want to reach for my cigarettes!"

"No will-power, that's your trouble! OK, I'm finished here now" Tom said stepping away from the sink, "you can make a start on the eggs and bacon."

The wood was dry and Tom soon had a bright fire blazing in the hearth.

"There's something particularly comforting about an open fire isn't there" Beth said, looking across at Tom who was kneeling on the floor, staring into the flames. He didn't reply. She could see that his mind was on other matters so she left him to his thoughts.

Tom was experiencing an odd mixture of emotions. He was troubled by the dramatic events of the day. It wasn't so much the old lady's death that concerned him, for there had been something rather reassuring about the peaceful way in which she had slipped away. He wasn't concerned about Rhiannon either. She had seemed to be coping with everything remarkably well. What he couldn't get out of his head was the look of despair on Mattie's face when they first broke the news to her. He knew that look. He had seen it on the faces of so many others. He felt it himself, still felt it to this very day. It was that feeling of guilt at not having been there when it happened, at not having been there to offer comfort in those final hours and minutes, at not having been able to say goodbye.

It all came flooding back. Would he ever be able to overcome his own guilt at not being there when Martha died? And where had he been at the time? At some wretched meeting of the Mother's Union at the other end of the parish.

It was at that moment that a log that had been perched precariously on top of the fire chose to roll down. Tom only just managed to kick it back before it fell onto the fireside rug where he was kneeling.

"That was a close one!" Beth said. She had been watching him out of the corner of her eye. "At the risk of interrupting your thoughts, supper's on the table."

When Tom looked up, Beth saw the look of despair on his face.

"What is it Tom? What's troubling you? It's been a hell of day for all of us, but is there something else? You aren't angry with me, are you? Is it because of last night, because of the pressure I put on you? I know how difficult it must have been for you. I know you're not ready yet to..."

"Stop Beth, please stop! It's not that, I promise you, it's nothing you've done. You were right. It was me who was being selfish and cowardly. No, what's been bothering me was that look on Mattie's face when we first told her. I know that look only too well and it's been haunting me ever since. I know what it's like not to be there when you lose someone you love. It took me back to when the police called at the parish hall to tell me the dreadful news. I could see how Mattie was weighed down under the intolerable double burden of grief at her mother's death and guilt at not having been there. She'll come to terms with her mother's death, given time. It's the guilt that never seems to go away."

"Thank goodness she's got Harry. Don't you think he'll be able to reassure her? He's as solid as a rock. I was so touched by the way he took charge of the situation with such tenderness. I almost cried when he wrapped his arms round Mattie and Rhiannon and hugged them so tight. He'll be a wonderful support to them both."

"I'm sure you're right. He may be a man of few words but he certainly showed remarkable sensitivity." Tom said, making his way over to the kitchen table. "Anyway, I have to confess, I'm starving."

"It's nothing very much."

"Simple's often the best and, right now, it's just what the doctor ordered."

"Tom, I've been wondering. After we've eaten, do you think that one of us ought to go down to Ty Pellaf to see if there's anything we can do to help?"

"Frankly, no, I don't Beth. I think they'd probably prefer to be left alone tonight. But tomorrow's a different matter. I overheard Harry having a word with Alun Price. It sounded like he was making plans to return to the mainland in the morning. He has to arrange for the doctor to come over to sign the death certificate and I expect he'll want to call on the vicar to make the funeral arrangements and, of course, he needs to let the rest of the family know."

"Of course. It's quite a business isn't it, making all these arrangements, especially when you live on an island."

"Yes, it's complicated enough without that extra challenge. But, the truth is it helps to be kept busy at such times. All the paperwork and planning can be a bit of a blessing."

"Yes, I can see that. I suppose the funeral will take place in Aberdaron."

"Actually, I'm not so sure. There's that little graveyard up by the abbey. I've noticed that some of the graves are quite recent. I assume it must still be consecrated so she may well be buried here on the island. I imagine that's what Mrs Davies would have chosen herself, wouldn't you?"

"I'm sure she would. I can't think of a more peaceful place to be buried."

"Anyway, going back to your original question, I suggest one of us calls at Ty Pellaf in the morning. It would probably be better if it were you. You know them much better than me. We could both go, of course, but I don't think we should swamp them."

"I think you're right, Tom. I'm happy with that. To change the subject, I've been thinking. It's been a shattering last 24 hours. I'm going to go back to Llofft Plas tonight so that we can both get a good night's sleep."

Tom smiled, leaned across the table and took hold of Beth's hands. "My own thoughts exactly, but I didn't know how to suggest it without sounding as though I had gone off you or something."

"Dear Tom, do you have so little faith in what I feel for you? I love you." She stood up and walked over to where her coat hung by the front door. She turned once more to smile at Tom, blew him a kiss and headed out under the darkening skies.

# CHAPTER FIFTY-FOUR

"Mind you, it wasn't all plain sailing with her you know" Mattie said, smiling. "She could be as obstinate as an old mule and she had quite a fiery little temper if she didn't get her own way."

"Had she been living with you for long?" Beth asked

"It was soon after my Dad died. That was nigh on 10 years ago, back in 1977. He had chronic asthma you know, he'd suffered with it all his life. She nursed him, on her own, over the last few years. He was very poorly most of the time. He should probably have gone into a home but she wouldn't have anyone else look after him. She was devoted and took it very hard when he was taken from us."

"Were they living here on the island?"

"Oh, good gracious no, I wish they had been. The sea air would have been good for him and I could have done more to help. Harry and I tried to persuade them to come and live with us. After all we had plenty of room. But my mother wouldn't hear of it. She said he needed his friends around him. She said she could make him more comfortable in their little bungalow in Nefyn and that he'd be much happier there than he would ever be over here. She had a point because he did have a lot of good friends who called on him regularly, blokes he'd got to know down at the 'social'. The other thing, of course, was that being so poorly for much of the time, she never knew when he might need the doctor and we're pretty cut off over here."

"Your father must have been quite young when he died."

"Yes, he was. He passed away just before his 65th birthday. He was two years younger than my mother."

"I hope you don't mind me asking about them at this difficult time" Beth said.

"Goodness no, dear. I don't mind at all. In fact, it's doing me good to talk about them. There's no point in sitting around moping all day is there? After all, poor old Mum had been poorly for such a long time and was getting worse by the day. We knew it was only a matter of time and she'd had a pretty good innings. Of course, it was a terrible shock coming back yesterday to find it had happened while we were away. I feel ever so guilty at going away when we did, leaving poor Rhiannon on her own. Thank the Lord you two were around, that's all I can say. You've both been so kind. I can't say how sorry I am to have caused you so much trouble."

"You mustn't concern yourself about that, you really mustn't. I'm glad we were able to help. One thing I will say, you should be very proud of your daughter. She couldn't have been more loving and caring in those last few hours. She was so very grown up in the way she coped with it all. We could see how much she loved her Nan. I found it all very moving." Beth paused briefly before asking "how is Rhiannon by the way?"

"She's been very quiet since we got back. I think she's finding it difficult to take it all in. She cried quite a lot at first. But, in her own way, she seems to be coming to terms with what's happened. She'll miss her Nan, there's no doubt about that. They were very close, very close indeed. They say, don't they, that youngsters often have a special bond with their grandparents and those two got on like a house on fire."

"It'll take her time to adjust, of course. It's a big thing for any young person to have to deal with."

"I suppose we all cope in different ways. After we got back home, Harry and I sat down with her and she told us all about what had happened. After that, we shared memories of things we all used to do together. We talked about when her grandfather was still alive, and about time she spent with her grandmother and the things they used to do together, before she became so poorly. And then she asked, if we minded if she went out for a walk. She seemed to want to be on her own for a while. So, I said 'of course not, you must do just what you want'. When she'd gone out, Harry said he thought that she'd be all right now, that she'd got over the worst."

"Mattie, I'd like to know more about your mother and father if you don't mind? Were they both originally from this part of Wales?"

"Oh no. They didn't come down to Llŷn until my father retired through ill health. That was when he was in his mid-fifties. Before that, they'd lived all their lives in Wrexham, I don't know whether you've ever been there?"

"I've passed through a couple of times, but I can't say I really know the place. I did stop to take a look inside the parish church once, rather a fine building."

"Yes, isn't it? It's the largest parish church in Wales you know."

"So I believe. How did your mother and father meet?"

"Well, there's a big house in Wrexham called Erddig. You may have heard about it. It was in the news quite a lot in the 70's. Philip Yorke, he was the last surviving member of the family you know, well, he had a bit of a struggle trying to persuade the National Trust to take it over. It was in a terrible state and there was no money left. Anyway, that's another story. When my father left school, just after his 14th birthday, he was taken on there as an apprentice gardener. The house was still in its prime in those days and the gardens were beautifully laid out. There was a team of six working under the head gardener and they had their work cut out I can tell you."

"When Dad first started, he wasn't allowed anywhere near the formal gardens. He had to learn everything he needed to know to tend the flowers and shrubs. There were some very rare ones from around the world. For the first year or two he spent most of his time doing the heavy digging and planting in the walled garden, and visited the greenhouses to learn how the young plants were nurtured. It was backbreaking work in those days, but my father stuck to it, despite his asthma. The doctor said the fresh air would be good for him. He was never one to be shy of hard work. The head gardener at the time was strict but also very kind, especially if you were prepared to put the work in."

"Did your father live in at Erddig?"

"Oh no. There was accommodation above the stables for some of the unmarried staff and cottages around the estate for those who were married.

But my Dad's parents, my grandparents, lived on the other side of town, so he chose to carry on living at home. He had to get up at half past four in the morning to walk the two miles to work to be ready to start at six."

"Those were the days!" said Beth, clapping her hands together. "I can't imagine what my students would make of it. It takes them all of their time to get up for their ten o'clock lectures, and they've only got to walk a couple of hundred yards across the park from their halls of residence!"

"I know, they have it pretty easy these days, don't they? Anyway, I've been going on and what you actually wanted to know was how my Mum and Dad met. Like I said, at first my Dad's work was mostly in the walled garden and vegetable plots. This continued until after his 16th birthday. But one day he and another lad who'd been taken on at much the same time were taken aside by the head gardener. He told them their help was needed up at the house. The family was holding a masked ball that very evening and it was all hands to the deck. My Dad soon found himself helping to carry tables and chairs from an outbuilding in the stable yard. It had rained during the night so the steps down to the big lawn where a marquees was being erected, were quite slippery. He never understood how it happened, but somehow my Dad lost his footing. He went head over heels down the steps and landed in a heap on the path below. He couldn't have timed it better because, just at that moment, old Mrs Yorke, the mistress of the house, was passing by to check on how everything was going."

"Poor lad, he must have felt so embarrassed" Beth said, putting her hand up to her mouth.

"Oh, don't worry" Mattie said, seeing Beth's vain effort to suppress her laughter "we've all had a good chuckle about it over the years. Anyway, to finish the story, you can guess how my Dad felt. He was lucky he hadn't really hurt himself. He was just a bit shaken up, that's all. He thought he'd be in for a real roasting from Mrs Yorke. He'd never met her before, but he knew she had a reputation for being very strict. You can imagine how surprised he was when, instead of giving him an earful, she took a white handkerchief out of her sleeve, knelt down in front of him and pressed it gently against the palm of his right hand which was bleeding from where he'd grazed it when he'd fallen. She told him how sorry she was and sent him off to the house with one of her young maids to get properly cleaned up and bandaged. As it turned out, that maid was to become my Mum."

"What a lovely story. But they were both very young then, how long was it before they got married?"

"They took to each other right away and started courting. Unlike most of the other maids at Erddig, my Mum didn't live in. She was a local girl and lived with my grandmother in the town. My grandfather had been killed in the Great War and the two of them had to work hard to scrape a living together. Anyway, to cut a long story short, my Mum and Dad got married as soon as he reached his 18th birthday and she was just short of 20. For the first few years they lived with my grandmother in her terraced house in Trevor Street. My Dad carried on working at Erddig until he was called up in 1939. He'd shown a gift for repairing machinery on the estate, so, when he was conscripted, they sent him to serve with the RAF in the aircraft maintenance team. He was moved all over the place, mainly working on the bigger planes, you know, Wellingtons and Lancasters."

"What about your mother?"

"Oh, she gave up her job at the house soon after they were married. An opportunity came up to work in the local telephone exchange. It was better paid and much less hard work. And, of course, with the start of the war it became very important work and she had to do a lot of extra training."

"What happened after the war?"

"My Dad never went back to work at the big house again, although they promised to keep a job open for him. Truth is, he'd learned a lot of new skills in the RAF which were much in demand. Also, like so many country houses after the war, Erddig wasn't the place it used to be. Folk simply weren't prepared to go on doing the menial jobs they used to do, and who can blame them. There were so many new and better opportunities. My Mum carried on working for the Post Office for a while and my Dad went into business with one of his mates from the air base. They persuaded the bank to lend them enough money to set up a small farm machinery shop and repair business."

"That sounds quite adventurous."

"It was, and quite risky too. But it turned out that my father had a good business head as well as engineering skills and his partner was pretty smart with the sales patter. It wasn't long before they were doing a roaring trade. My Mum gave up working when I was born. I think she'd have liked to carry on but you know what it was like in those days. My grandmother died when I was ten. With my mother being an only child, she left everything to her. My Mum and Dad sold the house in Trevor Street and moved into a larger place, just out of town. That's where my brother and I were brought up. Dad's business continued to grow and soon they had quite a big workforce. He did a lot of travelling, all over North Wales and even across the border into England. But sadly, his asthma gradually got the better of him so he decided to retire early. His business partner bought him out and they moved to Nefyn, where they bought a bungalow overlooking the sea."

"It must have been tough for him, giving up a job that he enjoyed so much."

"I think it was, but it had all become a bit of a strain with his poor health, you know. After he retired, he became less and less able to get about. Fortunately, he was a keen reader and found great comfort in his books. Quite a little library he built up."

"What did he like reading?"

"Oh, I don't know, a bit of everything. I do remember he had a fascination for science. He always wanted to know where everything came from and how it all worked."

"It sounds like he was quite a character. What did he make of you and Harry settling here on Bardsey?"

"I'm sure he thought we were crazy at first. He'd always got on well with Harry and I think, secretly, he was rather pleased I'd chosen to marry a farmer. Mind you, that didn't stop him from continually telling me we'd never have any money. Farming out here on the island, well it didn't make any sense to him. But that all changed after he and Mum came to visit us, for the first time. Sadly, as it turned out, it was the only time he managed to come here because soon after that his health really began to let him down. But the thing is, on that one time he did make it, he fell in love with the place. He'd always been keen on wildlife. He used to sit all day watching the birds through his binoculars."

Beth saw there were tears in Mattie eyes.

"I can tell you were very close to your father, weren't you?"

"Yes, very close indeed. He was a wonderful Dad when I was little, used to take me everywhere with him, spoiled me rotten. What I loved most about him was his passion for life. He never did anything by halves. His enthusiasm was infectious. I'm sure that's why their business did so well. Poor Dad, it was such rotten luck that he suffered so much from his asthma. My one serious regret is that he died before Rhiannon was old enough to understand what a remarkable man he was. If he'd lived longer, I'm sure that they would've become very close."

# CHAPTER FIFTY-FIVE

The path Tom took up the mountain was not especially steep or difficult. Nevertheless he found that the long pull up to the top quickly sapped his energy and he stopped several times to draw breath. He was fairly sure it was the very route he had taken all those years ago, when he and a couple of his fellow pilgrims had raced each other to the top. They had hoped to be able to see across to the mainland. They even thought they might be able to make out the Irish coast. He remembered how disappointed they had been when it had started to rain and just as they had reached the summit the distant coastline had been swallowed up. They could hear the boom of the waves down below but could hardly see more than a few feet in front of them.

But this was a crystal-clear morning with a pale blue sky. The view from the summit was nothing short of spectacular. Across the channel, between the island and the mainland, the cliffs rose majestically above the rock-strewn shoreline. Tucked into the steep hillsides the occasional white cottage shone out in the dazzling sunlight. There was hardly any wind and wisps of smoke rose almost straight up into the sky from more than one of the cottages. Spring might have arrived but there was still a chill in the air. It was not yet time to abandon the warmth and comfort of an open fire.

He sat down on a soft patch of mossy ground. When he closed his eyes, he could hear the wild shrieks of the gulls. It was pleasantly warm in the bright spring sunlight. He had slept well the previous night and felt more able to reflect on everything that had taken place over of the last few days. His mind was clear and uncluttered.

Inevitably, his first thoughts were of Beth. What a remarkable person she was. He had seen so many different aspects of her nature in the space of little more than a week. His early impression had been of an intense and withdrawn career-driven academic. But it hadn't been long before he had discovered the other Beth, the compassionate listener who had supported him with sympathy and understanding. She had readily become his confidante and subsequently his passionate lover. And now he had discovered yet another Beth, the strong and clear-sighted young woman who had shamed him into putting aside his own unresolved doubts and fears to minister to the old lady in her last hours.

It was for this last act that he owed her the most respect. She had fought so hard to overcome his initial resistance and knew precisely what she was doing. She had recognised that it was a situation that might help him rediscover his vocation.

He was so lost in his thoughts that he jumped when he felt a light touch on his shoulder.

"Oh, it's you Rhiannon. You took me completely by surprise, I never heard you approaching. What are you doing up here? I thought you'd be with your Mum and Dad."

"Mummy said I should come out to get got some fresh air, otherwise I'd get under her feet. She's busy tidying up before Daddy gets back with the doctor. He's coming to sign the death 'stificate you know. And Beth's helping too."

"Well, come and sit next to me. You can tell me how you're feeling this morning."

"I'm all right. I cried a bit at first, when I woke up and 'membered that my Nan had died. I wanted to see her again and Mummy said I could. We went into her bedroom together. She looked just like she was sleeping. I wanted to kiss her but Mummy said that she wasn't really there any more; it was just her body lying there. I said you'd told me that Nan was in heaven now and she said yes, she was sure she was. We both cried and then we went downstairs again, and Mummy made a cup of tea and I felt better. That's when Beth arrived and Mummy sent me out."

"I thought you were a very brave girl last night. I could see how much your being there meant to your grandmother."

"I loved my Nan. She taught me lots of things."

"Yes, she was a very special person. I'm sure of that."

They sat in silence, looking out across the sea. Tom felt Rhiannon snuggle up to him and he put his arm around her. It was warmer now that the sun had risen higher in the sky.

"Tom, can I ask you something?"

"Of course you can."

"Do you think that God can make you better if you're sick?"

"That's quite a question Rhiannon. The Bible tells us that God made everything and that includes all the herbs and chemicals and everything that we've learned how to turn into lots of different medicines. So, yes, in that way he helps us to get better when we're poorly."

"That's not what I mean" Rhiannon said, frowning. "What if you're sick in a way that medicines can't help, can God make you better then?"

"Well, there are lots of stories in the Bible about Jesus making people better. There was the man with leprosy and another who was born blind. And there are some wonderful stories about people who were very poorly who recovered because they believed in the power of prayer and that God could help make them better. But, of course, it depends rather on what's wrong with you. If you lose a leg or an arm in an accident then God isn't going to give you another one, not a real one anyway."

"What about me? Do you think that God can make me better?"

Tom had wondered what was behind Rhiannon's original question and now he knew. How he could he answer her in a way that she would both understand and accept? And what had prompted all this? Surely not just her grandmother's death, there had to be more to it than that.

"I think that God loves you just the way you are. You are quite the sweetest, kindest, brightest young woman I have met for a very long time."

But there was something about the look on Rhiannon's face that told him that there was more to her question than he had been able to fathom.

# CHAPTER FIFTY-SIX

Wednesday midday

Tom arrived back at Carreg Bach around lunchtime after his unexpected meeting with Rhiannon. He was hungry after the walk and cut himself two thick slices of bread which he filled with cheese and pickle.

When he had finished eating he decided to fill the time before Beth's return by washing some of his dirty clothes. He was outside, hanging out the washing in the garden to the rear of the cottage, when he heard the sound of voices approaching. He recognised Beth's voice at once but couldn't place the others. He put the clothes basket down and went round to the front of the cottage to satisfy his curiosity.

"This is Tom's place", he heard Beth say "It looks tiny from outside, but it's bigger than you'd think and it's got stacks of character."

His face lit up as soon as he saw that Beth's two companions were none other than the young couple who he had last seen down at Porth Meudwy on the day he had caught the ferry. Beth saw Tom standing in the garden and waved.

"There you are. I gather you know these two already. They've just come across on the same boat as Harry and the doctor."

"Welcome to Bardsey! I'm so glad you decided to take a look at the island." He opened the gate and went to greet them. "I don't think you'll be disappointed. It's good to see you both again. They may not have told you, Beth, but these two as good as saved my life a few days ago. They dragged me back from the edge of where I'd stupidly decided to have a nap! How are you both and how did that fishing trip go, Max?"

"We've been having a great time thanks" Max replied "and the fishing trip was amazing, although I was out for such a long time I think Kate got a bit fed up."

"It was unbelievably cold on that beach, hanging around waiting for you all morning, that's why" Kate said.

"I thought you'd appreciate a bit of peace and quiet. You're always saying I never stop gabbling!"

"Too damned right, you should hear yourself sometime." And then seeing the crestfallen expression on his face she said "Come here you great big softy, I love you really!" She gave him an affectionate hug. Then she turned her attention back to Beth and Tom. "I'm very keen to see the abbey ruins. I'd like to take some photos while the light's still good. I think we'd better get on our way if you don't think us terribly rude."

"Of course not" Tom said "but why don't you call here on your way back, I'll have the kettle on if you've time for a cuppa."

"We'd love to" Kate said. "I say, would you mind awfully if we left our rucksacks with you? They're getting rather heavy."

"No problem," Tom replied, "just lean them up on the other side of that wall. They'll be perfectly safe and it doesn't look like it's going to rain, for a change."

"That's really kind" Kate said, as they stacked their rucksacks. "Come on Max, let's go and take a look at where those monks used to hang out."

They watched the young couple disappear up the lane. When they were out of hearing, Beth said:

"Tom, can I make a suggestion? Max and Kate want to stay on the island for a couple of days. Harry's told them that several of the holiday lets up near the abbey are available. But they need a good clean before anyone moves in because they haven't been occupied since last year. Mattie normally looks after that sort of thing. Understandably, he's a bit concerned. It's hardly a good time to ask her."

"Yes, I'm afraid you're right, it certainly isn't, under the circumstances."

"I've been thinking. What if I were to move out of Llofft Plas? Kate and Max could stay there for a day or two."

"What, and move in here with me?" Tom said grinning, "I couldn't have come up with a better idea myself!"

"Do you think Mattie will mind?"

"What, if you and I shack up together? I don't think so for a moment. Neither she nor Harry strike me as being particularly narrow-minded. I don't think she'd think it any of her business anyway."

"Actually, I get the impression she's rather tickled by the thought that you and I have fallen for each other."

"Well I suppose it brings a bit of romance to the island."

"If you're OK with the idea, I think one of us had better have a word with Mattie right away. Otherwise they'll have to catch the ferry back to Porth Meudwy in a couple of hours."

"I think it should be you rather than me, if you don't mind. I have an instinctive feeling she'll take it better coming from you."

"Coward!" Beth said, chuckling "but why this reluctance on your part? Are men of the cloth banned from publicly engaging in romance or something?"

"Not in my view, as I'm sure you've already discovered. But there are an awful lot of folk around who'd be only too happy to express their disapproval."

"How sad! Anyway, don't let it worry you any further. I'm quite prepared to run the risk of having myself labelled a harlot and seducer of the Godly. I'll pop down now. Perhaps you wouldn't mind tidying the place up a bit. I have no intention of moving into a slum!"

He laughed and she reached up and ruffled his hair. He watched her set off at a jaunty pace down the track before going back inside. When he looked round the living room, he was amused to note that the majority of the items scattered untidily around were hers not his. It didn't take him long to complete his task. When he'd finished, he filled the kettle and set the tea things out on the kitchen table while waiting for them all to return. He couldn't remember when he had last felt quite so content.

# CHAPTER FIFTY-SEVEN

"I can't say how incredibly grateful we are" Kate said, putting the heavy box down on the kitchen floor. It was full of Beth's books and food supplies which she had just carried up from Llofft Plas. "To be honest, we didn't think there was much chance that we'd be able to find somewhere to stay here on the island, at such short notice. When Harry told us his mother-in-law had just died, it hardly seemed like the right moment to ask."

"As it happens, Kate, you're doing us a good turn. Tom and I want to be together anyway, and I'm beginning to get fed up with traipsing backwards and forwards between our two places whenever I need a change of clothes."

"How romantic. I mean you and Tom falling for each other like this. I thought it only happened in novels."

"Frankly, so did I. I certainly didn't come here with any such expectations."

"That was something I was going to ask you, if you don't think I'm being too nosy! What did bring you out here to Bardsey?"

Before Beth could answer, Tom and Max came in through the front door, carrying the remainder of Beth's belongings.

"Thank you so much Max. If you put the rucksack on the table, I'll take this stuff upstairs." Tom said.

"I think that's the lot. Did you bring my coat from the hook by the back door?"

"Yes, it's on the chair there." Tom said, making his way upstairs.

"Why don't you two sit down while I put this stuff away?" Beth said "By the way, while we're on the subject of food, I hope you've brought some provisions over with you. You can get fresh eggs and milk, on the island, and fresh fish sometimes. But that's it, I'm afraid."

"Yes, we bought a few things in the village shop before coming over, just in case." Kate said. "We only plan to be here for a day or two. We've got bread, cheese, butter, a few tins of beans, some fresh fruit, biscuits, you know, the bare essentials."

"It sounds like you won't starve then." Beth said. She turned to Tom, who had just come back down from the bedroom. "What do you say Tom? Don't you think it would be rather fun if these two joined us for supper tonight. It won't be anything too exotic I'm afraid. I've got a couple of tins of stewing steak, so we could easily knock up a casserole, if you fancy coming over a little later."

"That's a great idea" Tom said. "It'll give us a chance to get to know you both a little better."

"That would be lovely" Max said. "But only if it isn't too much trouble."

"But you've already been wonderfully generous, letting us move into Llofft Plas. We really don't want to be a nuisance" Kate said, looking embarrassed.

"Nonsense" Tom replied. "It'll be good to have your company, and, in any case, it's a way of saying thank you for saving my life."

They all laughed.

"Well, if you're absolutely sure, we'd love to, wouldn't we Max? You'll be pleased to hear we managed to squeeze a couple of bottles of wine and a few cans of beer into our rucksack."

"It sounds like we shall have quite a party then" Beth said. "I expect you'll want to go back to Llofft Plas to settle in and things. What say you come back up here at around half past seven?"

"That sounds perfect. Come on then Max, let's give these good people a little time to themselves and we'll see you back here later."

"What a nice couple" Beth said as she watched them disappear down the track. "You didn't mind me asking them to join us for supper did you Tom? It seemed a bit mean not to."

"Actually, I think they'll prove to be rather good company. Let's face it we could both do with something to take our minds off the events of the last 24 hours."

"I couldn't agree with you more" Beth said, standing on tiptoes and reaching up to kiss him. "We've a good hour before we need to start preparing supper. I wonder how we can fill it?"

# CHAPTER FIFTY-EIGHT

Beth had insisted they dine by candlelight, "so much more romantic than that stinky old oil lamp!" she had said to Tom earlier on. And now, looking across at the young couple on the opposite side of the table, she thought how attractive they both looked in the flickering light of the candles. Max was a well-built young man, tall and handsome in a rugged kind of way. Kate was tall too but, by contrast, had the softest of features. With her long golden hair glittering in the candlelight she reminded Beth of a fairy tale princess.

"Are you both at university" she asked.

Max had his mouth full at the time so Kate answered for them both.

"Yes, we are. I'm only in my first year, I'm reading English. Max is a year ahead of me battling with media studies."

"I assume you're at the same university?"

"Yes, Sussex. You know, the place where all the posh kids go who don't make it to Oxbridge." Kate said grinning.

"And is it really like that, I mean full of young men and women from wealthy homes?" Kate asked.

"Well I think it used to be more than it is now. But we still get our fair share of Hooray Henrys and bright upper-class gals straight from private school."

"And how about your courses, are you enjoying them?"

"I'm not sure that enjoy is quite the right word" Max butted in. "The problem is, I don't really think I'm cut out to be a journalist or film maker or anything like that..."

"Nonsense" Kate interrupted, "You write well and that film you made, you know, the one about the restoration of that church in Wiltshire, I thought that was pretty damned good."

"I suppose so. But it's such a competitive world these days. I'm not sure I want to spend the rest of my life battling to stay on level terms with all those ambitious wankers who see themselves as the natural successors to Tati, Fellini and Preminger. There's not a lot of natural humility to be found amongst my fellow media students I can tell you. They nearly all think they're on the pathway to an Oscar or a BAFTA!"

"But surely there are lots of opportunities in television these days, aren't there?" Tom said.

"Yes, and the media industry is branching out into a lot of new areas. It's just that, well, it's just that I don't really like the people all that much. They all seem far too self-satisfied for my liking and, talk about mutual admiration clubs; they're all so desperately in love with each other it makes me sick!"

"So, what will you do if you decide against a career in the media?" Beth asked, pouring them all another glass of wine.

"Well that's just the point; I haven't really got a clue. But, something'll turn up I suppose."

"And what about you Kate, what do you plan to do with your English when you've completed your course?" Tom asked.

"Oh, that's easy. I want to teach. I've always wanted to teach, ever since I started secondary school. My parents are both teachers, so I suppose it's in the blood."

"What age do you want to teach, primary or secondary?" Beth asked.

"It's A-level stuff for me. I've never fancied teaching little'uns and I don't think I'd be very good at coping with less able kids. I'm afraid I'm not a very tolerant person when it comes down to it. I suppose that sounds rather awful, but it's the truth."

Beth thought she saw a look of surprise and possibly disappointment on Tom's face and so she quickly interjected:

"I think I know what you mean. It's really a matter of horses for courses. If you're not cut out to deal with the less bright youngsters, it's better to face up to it and do what you're good at. I get a great deal more satisfaction out of my seminars and tutorials with the brighter students than I do from my day-to-day lecturing."

"We were wondering what you did, Beth. Max thought you might be an academic. What's your discipline?"

"I lecture in early medieval British history. You know everything after the Romans and before 'The Conqueror.'"

"Wow, that sounds interesting. Where do you teach?" Kate asked.

"UCL, you know, that 'godless institution in Gower Street' as they call us!"

"You can blame my nineteenth-century forefathers at King's for that unkind but accurate description" Tom said with a grin.

"Well, I could hardly expect you not to remind us of that. All you Kings' theologs are the same." Beth said

"Gosh, a theologian in our midst" Max exclaimed. "I trust that you've learned the error of your ways. I mean, you're not still a believer are you? Frankly I find the whole religion business impossible to swallow. It's all so out of step with the late twentieth-century. I simply can't come to terms with it all."

"Well, it's certainly not easy, that I can tell you. But I think I'd better lay my cards on the table. I've been an Anglican clergyman for the past 30 years. It hasn't always been without a struggle, I grant you that. Maintaining one's faith is far from straightforward in this day and age. Actually, if you really want to know, that's why I'm here." Tom said with a flicker of emotion.

"There you go again Max, putting your foot right in it." Kate said, addressing her companion sharply. "I'm so sorry Tom, I'm afraid Max has a habit of mouthing off without considering the consequences."

"Please don't worry on my account. Sticks and stones and all that kind of thing! I can assure you I've had to put up with far bigger challenges to my faith. So, tell me Max, out of interest, what is it that you don't believe in?"

"Well, seeing as you ask" Max said, leaning forward earnestly "I just find the whole concept of a divine creator to be a bit primitive. I can see why, in earlier times, man needed to find an explanation for his existence. But, it seems to me that over the centuries, religions have become a convenient tool for the powers that be, a means of controlling us by proclaiming that whichever God we serve demands unquestioning obedience. Rather convenient don't you think? And just look at all the terrible things that have been done in the name of God. Even today, whether you're talking about Ireland, the Middle East, South America or Africa, religion is still being used as a justification for the most unbelievable acts of violence and hatred."

"I see where you're coming from, but I fundamentally disagree." Tom said "It is undoubtedly true that man has often chosen to misinterpret the basic tenets of his religion to his own advantage. But to lay the blame for this at the door of God is ridiculous. Nothing that man does challenges my belief in the eternal goodness of God."

"I think Tom has a point there, don't you Max?" Kate said. She saw that he was still frowning and added: "Anyway Max, what's made you such a sceptic?"

"Oh, I don't know really. I suppose that five years at public school, with chapel twice a day and three times on Sunday, having religion constantly rammed down our throats may have had something to do with it. What's more, our school chaplain was such a hypocrite. One day he'd be preaching the value of Christian love from the pulpit and the next he'd be out on parade in his cadet force army major's uniform, showing us how to use a bayonet. 'Don't forget' I can hear him saying, 'you don't just stick it in, you twist it!'"

"That's horrible" Beth exclaimed.

"Yes, I can see how that might put you off." Tom said.

"And another thing" Max continued with rising passion "Don't you think there's something rather feudal about the concept of prayer and worship? All that going down on bended knees and saying thank you for this and thank you for that and, by the way, if it isn't asking too much, could you be so kind as to help us to win the rugby match on Saturday!"

Tom couldn't help laughing. "I have to admit there is a certain amount of that kind of thing around."

"I'm sure it must be something you've been asked a thousand times before" Kate said, "but what I can't understand is why God allows the awful things to happen in this world. You know, earthquakes and floods, the spread of HIV, wars and tribal massacres in Africa and all that kind of thing. If there is an all-knowing and all-powerful God, why does he just sit back and watch? Isn't it all rather sadistic? And then there are all those simple human tragedies like cot deaths and being born with a disability, and dreadful accidents and things. Wouldn't a loving God take more care of us?"

Beth could see the subject was getting a little too close for comfort as far as Tom was concerned. She quickly came to his rescue. "Look, I'm sorry to interrupt, but, shall we give it a rest for a while, who's for coffee?"

Grateful to Beth for her considerate intervention, Tom got up to make coffee while Beth and Kate cleared away the dinner plates and the conversation moved on. Soon they were all sitting round the fire discussing Max and Kate's plans for the following day.

# CHAPTER FIFTY-NINE

"I thought it always rained for funerals" Beth said, looking out of the window at where the drops of overnight dew were glistening in the honey pale light of an early morning sun.

"Not in my experience" Tom replied "you've been watching too many movies. You know, the ones where they all gather round the graveside in their black overcoats under black umbrellas for the funeral of the gangster who's been killed in a shoot-out with a rival gang! There's nothing like a bit of rain to add to the sombre atmosphere."

"Well, it looks like we're set for a fine day today. Do you think Mattie and Harry really want us to join them for the funeral, or were they just being polite?"

"No, I'm sure they meant it. Mattie was adamant it was what the old lady would have wanted and I don't suppose there'll be all that many people on the invitation list, apart from the family that is."

"I've no idea what to wear. I hardly came here expecting to go to a funeral."

Tom looked across to where Beth was standing in front of the window. Her freshly washed hair was hanging limply down over her shoulders. Unaware that she was being watched, she tossed her head back and ran her fingers through the thick dark tresses. They glistened as they caught the light from the sun. "I cannot imagine you wearing anything in which you will look anything other than the epitome of loveliness!"

"You old flatterer you, but that doesn't really help. After all, this is hardly a beauty contest. What on earth shall I wear?"

"If you take my advice you'll put on something warm. I reckon it'll be pretty chilly up by the abbey. There's quite a breeze blowing today. It looks like a jeans and thick sweater day to me."

"That's all very well but I haven't got anything in the least bit sober. My jumpers and things are all rather bright and breezy."

"I don't see that as a problem. Anyway, you'll be wearing your coat won't you? Mattie and Harry will understand. They know we haven't got many clothes to choose from."

"Well, I suppose there isn't much I can do about it now anyway. What time do you think we should aim to get up to the chapel?"

"The actual service is at half past ten. They've got to come right past our front door on the way up from Ty Pellaf. Mattie said we should just look out for them and tag along behind. But I think it might be better if we make our own way up to the chapel. It'll save them having to introduce us to all the other members of their family. There'll be plenty of time for that later. So, I suggest we set off from here at ten if you can be ready by then."

"No problem, and that was very thoughtful of you Tom. I'd better get a move on then" Beth said, looking at her watch.

It was just after ten when they set off up the track towards the chapel. As Tom had predicted, there was a cool stiff breeze blowing in from the west. As they neared the chapel, they were surprised to see that a considerable number of people already gathered outside.

"Look, there's Bert and Joan, I thought they'd be here. I wonder where all the other folk have come from. Surely they can't all be family members?" Beth said.

"Just look at what Bert's wearing!" Tom whispered in Beth's ear. He was hardly able to suppress a chuckle at the sight of the amiable twitcher, garbed from head to foot in a bright orange oilskin. "And you were worried about what you were going to wear!"

"Well, there's no accounting for taste. I suppose we should go over and have a word with them?"

But before they could do so they heard the unmistakable voice of Alun Price, calling out to them from behind:

"Hello you two. Harry's been telling me what a wonderful help you've been. My goodness, what a bit of luck it was that you were around when the old lady passed away. I don't know how poor little Rhiannon would have coped otherwise, I'm sure."

"She's a very remarkable young lass." Tom said. "She and her grandmother were so close. It must have been a terrible ordeal for her. But, do you know what; she never seemed to think of herself for a moment, at least not until Mrs Davies finally died."

"I know Harry and Mattie will always be grateful for your kindness."

"Well it's good of you to say so, but we only did what anyone would do under the circumstances." Tom said. "But tell me, there's a good number of folk gathering here for the funeral, are they mostly family members?"

"Oh no, Gareth and Annie and their kids are all coming up from Ty Pellaf with Harry, Mattie and Rhiannon. There's a cousin of Mattie's down there too I believe. They'll be making up the funeral procession with the vicar and the undertakers. Most of the people up here are old family friends and there are one or two folk who used to live on the island. The old lady over there, the one with the white hair talking to the tall fellow wearing a cloth cap, that's Mrs Jenkins. She used to be the schoolteacher here on the island, you know, before people moved away and they closed the school."

"How on earth have they all managed to get here?" Beth asked.

"Oh, I've been backwards and forwards with a boatload a couple of times and Jim Talbot brought a load over too in his fishing boat"

"It's just as well the weather's held then" Tom said.

"Yes, it was a bit choppy, but nothing to worry about. But you must excuse me, I'd better go and have a word with Mrs Jenkins or she'll never forgive me."

"What a nice man." Beth said. "I tell you what, I wouldn't mind a word with Mrs Jenkins myself before the day's out. I've hardly put a thought to my research over the last few days. If anyone is able to throw further light on Bardsey legends it will surely be her."

"Good thinking" Tom said.

They looked up as the chapel bell began to toll. It was a sad, mellow sound that marked the sombre nature of the occasion. Someone said "look they're coming" and everyone turned to look down the track. The approaching group of mourners was led by a tall, impressive figure in full mourning dress, wearing a top hat and carrying a long silver- topped cane. He was followed by the Reverend Hugh Pritchard. The vicar was dressed in full clerical garb and Tom thought his rotund figure looked even more monk-like than when he first met him in Aberdaron. A short distance behind came the coffin, borne by Harry, a tall, good-looking young man, who they both assumed must be Harry and Mattie's son Gareth, and two black-suited undertakers. Next came Mattie, holding tightly onto Rhiannon's hand, followed by a small grey-haired woman who bore a strong resemblance to Mattie, no doubt the cousin to whom Alun Price had referred.

The procession turned off the main track towards the chapel. Hugh Pritchard began to intone the familiar words from the Order for the Burial of the Dead:

"I am the resurrection and the life, saith the Lord: he that believeth in me, though he were dead, yet shall he live: and whosoever liveth and believeth in me shall never die." Tom was surprised to hear the English language being used. No doubt it was in recognition of the non-Welsh-speaking guests who were present.

By now the small procession had reached the entrance to the chapel. The bell ceased tolling and the mourners moved in to encircle the funeral party. Everybody bowed their heads. After a short pause the vicar continued:

"Neither death, nor life, nor angels, nor principalities, nor powers, nor things present, nor things to come, nor height, nor depth, nor any other creature, shall be able to separate us from the love of God, which is in Christ Jesus our Lord."

When Beth looked into the faces of Mattie and Rhiannon she felt a lump in her throat. Neither of them had been able to hold back their tears. She turned to look at the mahogany coffin, resting on the shoulders of the four bearers. Its brass handles gleamed in the bright sunlight. It was decked with a simple arrangement of pure white lilies. The coffin was then carried slowly forward into the chapel where it was laid carefully down on a trestle in front of the pulpit. The mourners filed quietly into the rows of seats and remained standing while the vicar climbed up into the pulpit. He stood for a moment, with his head bowed, and then continued:

"The Lord is my shepherd: therefore can I lack nothing. He shall feed me in a green pasture: and lead me forth beside the waters of comfort... "

Tom could see Beth was close to tears. He took her hand and gently squeezed it. He had officiated at countless funerals, but there was something especially poignant about this particular occasion that was beginning to affect him too. He saw Rhiannon was shaking with emotion and Mattie firmly wrapped her arm around the young girl's shoulders. At the conclusion of a reading of the twenty third Psalm, they were invited to join in singing the first hymn, 'He who would valiant be'. When they reached the last line of each verse 'To be a pilgrim', Tom remembered that day, all those years ago, when he and his fellow pilgrims had joined in the very same hymn here, after they had cleaned the chapel.

Meanwhile, Beth found herself thinking that it must have been like this, when there were more people on the island and they had gathered for their regular Sunday worship.

When they reached the end of the hymn, Harry stepped forward to read from the New Testament:

"I saw a new heaven and a new earth: for the first heaven and the first earth were passed away; and there was no more sea..." He read in a quiet but determined voice. He paused between each sentence in an effort to retain his composure. He began to struggle when he reached the words "And God shall wipe away all tears from their eyes; and there shall be no more death, neither sorrow, nor crying, neither shall there be any more pain: for the former things are passed away" and finally, his voice cracked. Mattie and Rhiannon were standing just a few feet in front of him. Harry saw that they were having difficulty holding back their tears. He paused, cleared his throat and bravely continued on to the end.

Tom was impressed by the short address that followed. Hugh Pritchard chose to dwell on the gift of life and its transitory nature. From the warmth of his many references to the good life which the old lady had embodied, it was evident he had known her well and had held her in great respect. This all brought home to Tom what a close-knit community there existed in these remoter corners of Wales. It offered a stark contrast to the urban parish community he was used to serving. How many times had he officiated at the funeral of someone he had hardly known? How often had he been entirely dependent on members of the family to gain any insight into the nature and achievements of the person he was burying?

At the conclusion of the vicar's address, Gareth stepped forward. He was holding a guitar which he must have brought up to the chapel earlier that morning. At a nod from the vicar, he began to strum the unmistakable melody of the hymn 'Guide me o thou great Jehovah'. They all stood up. Tom took in a deep breath, ready to join in, but then closed his mouth again when he realised that those around him were singing in Welsh 'Arglwydd, arwain trwy'r anialwch'. It was one of his favourite hymns but he would just have to stand and listen. But he wasn't to be disappointed. The chapel was soon full of the sound of voices raised in a great outpouring of spirit. Yet again, he couldn't help reflecting on the contrast between the joyous singing of this small Welsh congregation and the mumblings of his own congregation back home.

At the end of the hymn, Gareth leaned his guitar up against the wall and took up position with the other bearers. They raised the coffin onto their shoulders and, led by the vicar, processed out of the chapel, followed by Harry, Mattie, Rhiannon and Mattie's cousin. The rest of the congregation followed on, making their way in silence towards the freshly dug grave in the nearby cemetery. When they had all gathered by the graveside, the vicar clasped his hands in front of his chest and recited the opening words for the burial in a subdued monotone:

"Man that is born of woman hath but a short time to live, and is full of misery. He cometh up and is cut down like a flower; he fleeth as it were a shadow, and never continueth in one stay."

Beth whispered in Tom's ear "What dark words... 'Full of misery'... I'm not sure about that, I'm really not."

"I know" Tom whispered back to her "they're hardly the most reassuring words for those of us left behind."

When the coffin had been lowered, one by one the family members each cast a handful of earth into the grave.

"Earth to earth, ashes to ashes, dust to dust; in sure and certain hope of the resurrection to eternal life through Our Lord Jesus Christ" the vicar intoned. Tom looked across the grave to where the bereaved family were standing together, a close and loving family drawn even closer by their shared loss.

They all recited The Lord's Prayer and other prayers were said in Welsh, followed by 'The Grace'. What happened next took Tom completely by surprise. For, raising his arms, Hugh Pritchard looked directly at him and said:

"I want you to welcome into our midst the Reverend Tom Gregory who is on retreat here on Bardsey. It was he who was there to minister to Mrs Davies in her dying moments, to pray with her and to bring her comfort at the very end. He and Dr Davenport, who is also with us today, were both there to provide love and support to Rhiannon in the unfortunate absence of her Mum and Dad. Mattie and Harry have asked me to call upon him to give us the Lord's blessing before we depart."

Tom looked around at the assembled company who had now all turned to look at him. He raised his right hand to make the sign of the cross and proclaimed in a strong and resonant voice:

"The blessing of God Almighty, the Father, the Son and the Holy Spirit be with you this day and for evermore". With Beth standing beside him, the bereaved family facing him and the small community of friends all around him, he felt closer to his fellow man and to his God than he had felt for a very long time.

# CHAPTER SIXTY

Tom and Beth had only just finished clearing away their lunch when they heard voices outside in the lane. When Tom opened the front door he saw it was Mattie and Max. They appeared to be in earnest conversation. Mattie's face was flushed and she was frenziedly waving her arms around.

"Mattie" he called out, hurrying down the path "Is everything all right?"

"Oh, it's you Tom. I was just asking Max if he happened to have seen Rhiannon. She went out first thing this morning. She wouldn't touch her breakfast, said she wasn't hungry, and that's not like her at all. She said she wanted to go for a walk, that there was something she had to do. I couldn't get any more sense out of her. 'Well', I said, 'that's probably for the best, there's not much point in your moping about here'. It's going to take her such a long time to get over her Nan's passing. I suggested she might like to call by her Nan's grave, you know, to see if any of the flowers needed fresh water. People were so kind and thoughtful bringing them over in pots so they'd last longer. I told her to be sure to be back by lunchtime. And it's nearly three o'clock now and not a sign of her. We always have our lunch at midday as Harry's always starving from being out on the farm so early in the morning. I don't know what's got into her; she's never been this late back before."

"I expect she's just lost track of the time" Tom said, "I'm sure she'll turn up soon."

"Would you like me to pop up to the cemetery to see if she's there?" Max asked, seeing that Mattie was far from reassured.

"Oh, that would be so very kind. I called at the observatory on the way up here to see if Bert or Joan had seen her, but there was no-one there. They must be out bird watching somewhere."

Max set off at a run in the direction of the abbey ruins.

"Is there anywhere else you can think of where she might have gone?" Tom asked. "Beth and I were planning to go out for a walk this afternoon. If there's somewhere in particular you'd like us to look I'm sure..."

"That's just the problem" Mattie interjected. "She has so many places she likes to go, I really don't know where to start."

"Well, let's wait until Max gets back. If he hasn't had any luck up at the abbey, perhaps Beth and I could go down to Trwyn y Gorlech and make our way round the coast to Porth Solfach. We can come back via the harbour? If she's anywhere out that way, we should spot her easily enough."

"Oh, I'd be ever so grateful. But I don't want to put you to any trouble. As you say, the silly girl probably doesn't realise what time it is."

"It won't be any trouble at all. We'll call in at Ty Pellaf on the way back whether we've found her or not, just to let you know. Hopefully she will have made her own way back by then, anyway."

"I really appreciate your help Tom, it's ever so kind of you. Well, if you'll excuse me, I think I'd better get back home, in case she's already there."

As soon as Mattie had left, Beth appeared at the front door wondering what had kept Tom so long.

"What was all that about?" she asked, joining him by the gate.

"Rhiannon's gone missing. Apparently, she went out for a walk this morning, promising to be back by lunchtime, but she hasn't returned. Understandably, Mattie's quite worried because she's usually so reliable. What with her grandmother's death and everything, I expect the poor girl simply wants some time on her own. Max has gone to see if he can spot her up by the graveyard. I told Mattie we were going out for a walk this afternoon. If Max doesn't find her, I suggested we could do a round trip along the coast from Trwyn y Gorlech round to Porth Solfach and back by the harbour. If she's anywhere on that side of the island, we shouldn't have too much difficulty spotting her. It's fairly open and flat down there."

"Well, let's not hang about then. We've got to go up by the abbey anyway. We can check with Max on our way."

They met Max on his way back from the cemetery. He told them that he had drawn a blank. He was fairly sure Rhiannon couldn't have visited her grandmother's grave, as the flowers looked in need of a good watering. He then hurried off, down the hill to Ty Pellaf to report back to Mattie.

They had passed the abbey and were on their way across the fields towards the coast when Beth surprised Tom by saying:

"It may sound a bit odd, but I think there's something up with Rhiannon. I know she's missing her Nan and she's bound to be very upset, but I think there's something else, something more than that. You know how bright and cheery she usually is. Well, I couldn't even get a smile out of her when we were all down at Ty Pellaf after the funeral. She was incredibly subdued."

"It's hardly surprising, she was devoted to her grandmother."

"Yes, but there was another thing. It was while I was having a chat with Mrs Jenkins. Well, out of the corner of my eye, I saw Bert and Joan heading towards Rhiannon. It was clear they wanted to have a word with her. But, when she saw them approaching, she turned on her heels and headed straight for the kitchen."

"Perhaps she hadn't seen them?"

"Oh, she'd seen them all right. She'd have had to be blind not to. What's more, you could tell from the peeved expression on Joan's face that she suspected Rhiannon was avoiding them."

"I don't altogether blame her, do you? They are an exceptionally tedious couple" Tom said, chuckling.

"Can't you be serious for a moment?" Beth said sternly. "I tell you, there's something very strange going on there. When I saw Rhiannon making a run for it, I could tell something was up. Anyway, I made my excuses to Mrs Jenkins and followed Rhiannon through to the kitchen, but she wasn't there. Then it crossed my mind that she might have gone out to feed the chickens, and that's where I found her, out in the yard. She was sitting on the ground with her knees pulled up to her chest. She was staring blankly in front of her and tears were pouring down her cheeks, poor girl. She must have heard me approaching, but she didn't look up at first. It was only when I asked her what the matter was that she managed a pathetic little smile. She said she was sorry to be such a cry baby. I told her not to be so silly, that I knew how much she had loved her grandmother and that it was perfectly natural for her to be sad. 'But it isn't that' she said, 'my Nan's in heaven now and she won't be poorly any more'. 'Well, what is it then?' I asked, but I couldn't get any sense out of her to start with. So, I sat down on the ground next to her and put my arm round her. She stared at the ground for a while and then frowned and said 'I hope they've gone now, they don't like me very much'. 'Who?' I asked. 'Bert and Joan' she said 'they think I'm stupid.' 'I'm sure they don't' I said, 'what makes you think that?' I could tell she was quite angry by now. 'It's just something they said. But you wait, I'll show them!' she said 'when I'm better, I'll show them!' It seemed such a strange thing for her to say. I wanted to ask her what she meant. But, just at that moment, Mattie called out for her and we had to go back inside."

"How odd!" Tom said, looking puzzled. "And there's another thing. I don't think I've told you this. When I went for that walk up the mountain I bumped into Rhiannon. She asked all sorts of questions about God and whether he could cure people. They were really quite intelligent questions and I wondered where this was all coming from. And then she came right out with it. Did I think God could cure her? I can tell you, that rather put me on the spot!"

"But that must be it. Somehow, she's got it into her head that she can be cured. What on earth did you say?"

"Well, I'm afraid I probably rather disappointed her. I told her she was such a dear, sweet thing that God loved her just as she was. I certainly didn't want to mislead her into believing that there was some miraculous way in which she could overcome her disability. I don't understand. Where has this sudden awareness of her condition come from? I suppose she may have been teased about it at school. Kids can be very cruel to anyone who's different. But, even if she was, it must have been quite a while ago. And where do Bert and Joan come into it? We both know they can be a bit of a pain in the arse, but they seem well-meaning. I can't imagine either of them would intentionally say anything to upset her."

"No, I agree" Beth said "I can't say that I really take to them, but I don't see either of them saying anything like that." Suddenly, she put her hand to her mouth. "Oh dear. I think I can see where this is all leading and I think I may be responsible for setting it off!"

"Setting off what?" Tom asked but, he was only half listening because he had just caught sight of someone in the distance. "Hang on a minute, speak of the devil, isn't that Bert down there looking through those binoculars? And look, I'm sure that's Joan sitting on top of that rock. Let's find out if they've seen Rhiannon."

However, their enquiries were met with blank expressions. Bert told them that they had been there all morning but 'hadn't seen a soul'. "We spend a lot of time down here. It's a good place to look out for oystercatchers you know. But you'd best ask Joan. She's got a better view up there. She'll have seen her if she's been down this way."

Joan was equally unable to help, but promised to keep an eye open and to send Rhiannon 'right back home' if she came their way."I'm not sure as I'd let that girl roam around on her own if I was her Mum, what with her not being quite all there, if you know what I mean."

Tom saw a look of disgust pass across Beth's face and grabbed her by the arm before she had a chance to articulate her anger.

"Come on Beth, no time to waste. We need to get on with our search. Thanks anyway, you two, and please do keep your eyes open."

They were hardly out of earshot before Beth vented her fury "I take back my previous remarks. Actually, I think there is something quite malicious about those two, well, about her anyway. They didn't seem to care a toss about what may have happened to Rhiannon and they obviously think she's a complete moron. No wonder the poor thing gave them the cold shoulder yesterday. God, what awful people they are."

"I think you may be exaggerating just a tad, but I know what you mean. Sadly, it isn't all that long since young people like Rhiannon were locked away in asylums for the rest of their lives. There is nothing so dangerous as ignorance. Hopefully, most of us are rather more enlightened these days."

"There you go again, ever anxious to explain everything with your bucket loads of understanding. I'm sure you're right. But it won't stop me from despising people like that."

"I do love you when you get angry! You have such a generous heart and you have every right to be dismissive of such blind prejudice. But less of this. We need to get a move on; we've a long way to go."

§

"Phew, I'm feeling quite puffed" Tom said, as they passed the old boathouse by the harbour. "Do you mind slowing down a bit, I'm not quite as fit as I used to be and I can't keep up with those young legs of yours."

"Come on, it's not far now. I'm really anxious to know whether Rhiannon has found her way back."

"We're lucky the sun's been out all day. Can you imagine what it would have been like if we'd had to trudge through the pouring rain?"

"Yes, at least that's one good thing." Beth stopped to allow Tom to catch up. She put her hands on his shoulders and looked up at him. "Tom, I'm really worried. What if she hasn't returned, what do we do then?"

"Don't you think that we should wait and see? She's probably back home by now and tucking into a one of Mattie's homemade cakes."

"Yes, but what if she isn't?"

"Well, that's really up to Harry and Mattie. But, I suppose we'll have to organise a proper search party and tackle those parts of the island we haven't yet covered."

"You know what that means, don't you Tom? It means the mountain. It'll be getting dark soon and you can imagine how dangerous that could be. That's why I want us to hurry back. If we have to go out again, we shall need all the daylight we can get."

"Heaven forbid that it should come to that. But I see what you mean. OK, let's get a move on."

§

When they arrived at Ty Pellaf, the front door was wide open and they could hear someone crying inside.

"Oh dear, it doesn't sound good." Tom said, standing apprehensively on the threshold.

"I'm afraid it doesn't" Beth said, pushing past him "we'd best go in and find out the worst."

There were no lights on in the kitchen and they were only just able to make out the figure of Mattie. She was weeping, crouched over the table with her hands clenched tightly together. She looked up hopefully when she heard them enter. But as soon as she saw that they didn't have Rhiannon with them, she began to cry again.

"I'm so very sorry" Tom said "we must just keep looking. We can't give up hope. There must be lots of places where she could still be."

"Do you really think so?" Mattie said. She stood up, putting a hand on the table to steady herself. "I'm sorry... I know... I must pull myself together... I'm no good to anyone like this. It's just that, well... it's just that I can't believe this is happening to us, all over again, just like it was with Dafydd."

Beth swallowed hard to hold back her own tears. She put an arm round Mattie.

"We'll find her, I'm sure of it" she said.

"She's normally such a sensible girl. I don't know what's got into her head, to stay out like this. What if she's fallen and hurt herself. She could be lying out there somewhere, calling for help, desperately hoping that someone will hear her."

"Well, if that's the case, I'm sure we'll find her" Tom said. "Don't worry, we'll search every inch of the island if we have to."

"You're so kind, all of you. Do you know, that young boy Max and his girlfriend, I can't remember her name... what is it? Kate, yes, that's it. Well, they've gone off with a bunch of keys to search the empty houses we let out on behalf of the Trust, just in case, you never know. You see, sometimes she likes to go and play at housekeeping and pretend she's got her own little

346

home to look after. Harry was going to go, but he's got a couple of late ewes in labour, and they kindly offered. Ever such a nice young couple. I wanted to go myself only Harry said that someone needed to stay here in case she makes her own way back, and that it would be best if it were me."

It was at that moment that the front door swung open and Harry appeared. He looked around anxiously in the hope that his daughter might have returned. But from the dejected look on their faces he knew at once that this was not so. He bent down, put his hands on the kitchen table and let out an audible moan.

"Max and Kate are on their way back down," he said. "They only had one more call to make. I'm afraid it looks like they've drawn another blank."

"Oh Harry!" Mattie wailed, "What are we going to do?"

"I was just about to ask Mattie if she could think of anywhere else Rhiannon may have gone," Tom said, "you know, somewhere we haven't thought of looking. We can organise one or more search parties as soon as Max and Kate get back, and set off before it gets dark."

"Well, I've left it to last because, to be honest, I didn't think that she'd go there. But we've looked everywhere except the mountain. It'll be tough going, I'm afraid, especially as it will be getting dark in an hour or so."

"So, how do you suggest we tackle this?" Tom asked.

"If everyone is willing to lend a hand, I think we should split into two groups. Perhaps I can go with Max and Kate. We can take the path up by the chapel and search the far end of the mountain and then make our way back along the top. Tom, perhaps you and Beth could start this end. You can take the path up behind the farmhouse here. If, when you get to the top, you start heading towards the other end, we should meet up somewhere in the middle."

"How do we let each other know if one of us finds her? I mean we'll want to bring her straight back down, won't we?"

"Yes, of course. I'm afraid there isn't much we can do about that. If we don't meet each other on the top, all I can suggest is that we carry on and come down the same way the other group went up. At least, that's likely to mean she's been found and brought back home."

"That sounds like a good plan to me" Tom said. "I'm sure Max and Kate will want to help."

"Tom and I can take in Merlin's cave on our way up, just in case. I was up there with Rhiannon the other day and I know the way," Beth said.

"That makes sense" Harry said. "We'll set off as soon as Max and Kate get back. Mattie, dear, I think it best if you stay here. She may still make her own way back."

"Will you be alright here on your own, Mattie? One of us can stay with you if you like?" Beth asked, seeing how distressed she looked.

"Don't worry about me. It's more important that you're all out looking for her. It'll likely get very cold later on. Max and Kate could do with something to keep them warm and dry. I'll see what I can dig out" Mattie said, hurrying towards the door at the bottom of the stairs.

"Yes, and we'll need torches too once it gets dark" Harry said. "There's one on that shelf there and there's that fisherman's lamp Alun gave me a while back. I last saw it in the shed. I'll go and look for it."

Left alone in the kitchen, Tom and Beth exchanged looks.

"What do you think?" Tom asked. "Surely, there must be some hope, mustn't there? After all, she's only been gone since this morning. I keep expecting her to walk in through that door."

"I'm with you, Tom. She'll either just turn up as if nothing's happened or we'll find her somewhere out there. She knows the island like the back of her hand. I've been up the mountain with her a couple of times. She knows every rock and every stone. I can't believe she'll come to any harm. At the very worst, she may have slipped and hurt herself. If that's the case, we'll find her all right. But there's something I've been trying to work out, it's been bothering me all day. You see, I think I may know what this is all about. I'm just trying to make sense of it."

"Sense of what?" Tom asked, looking puzzled.

"I'll explain when we're on our way. I don't want to talk about it in front of Harry and Mattie. You'll understand why when I tell you. But listen, isn't that Kate and Max I can hear outside?"

Mattie heard their voices too. She hurried back into the kitchen, clutching an assortment of waterproofs which she dumped on the table. From their dejected expressions when they came in through the kitchen door, closely followed by Harry, it was evident that they had not found Rhiannon.

There was nothing for it. They would have to search the mountain.

§

A few minutes later, with Beth leading the way and Tom following on behind, they began the steady scramble up the lower reaches of the mountain on the path towards Merlin's cave. There was just enough light from the sinking sun for them to see their way. The only shadows on the treeless landscape were those they cast themselves. The wind had dropped and there were few sounds apart from the loose stones they disturbed as they passed by.

They reached the top of a particularly steep incline and stopped to recover their breath.

"So, come on Beth, what's this theory of yours?"

"Well it's still all a bit muddled in my head. But it's connected with what I was telling you about this morning, before we bumped into Bert and Joan. You remember me saying that Rhiannon seemed to go out of her way to avoid talking to those two after the funeral. When I challenged her she told me that they thought she was stupid. When I asked her why on earth she should think that, she intimated that it was just something that they'd said. But it was what she said next that has started me thinking."

"What was that?"

"She said something like... what was it now... oh yes, that's it, she said 'but just wait, I'll show them when I'm better.'"

"What, in heaven's name, do you think that she meant by that?"

"Don't you get it? When I'm better, when I'm cured! It's all my fault. I'm the one who filled her head with stories about Arthur being laid in a glass tower, and about the healing properties of the sun, and all that stuff. And then Bert and Joan must have inadvertently made some reference or other to her disability, which I'm sure she wasn't supposed to hear. And then she's asking you about God, and whether he can cure people. You only have to put two and two together to see that, in her sweet and simple mind, she must believe that somehow she can be cured."

"So, what if I buy that? How's that going to help us? What is it that we're looking for? A glass tower? On this island? I haven't seen so much as a greenhouse never mind a mystical glass tower."

"I know, and that's what's been puzzling me too. But I think I may have the answer. You see, soon after I first arrived and before you and I had met up again, Rhiannon and I went for a walk up the mountain. For some reason, she latched on to me and seemed keen to take me to visit what she called 'our secret place'. This turned out to be a small cave, where she and her brother Dafydd used to play. I didn't know it at the time, but I've since realised that this must be the cave that is commonly known as Merlin's cave. I have a hunch we may find her there. It's not much further on from here. So, if you've got your breath back, can we please get going again?"

"Of course" Tom said, following Beth up the path "but, I still don't get it. A cave, that hardly sounds like a glass tower."

"Ah, but wait until you see inside." Beth called back over her shoulder "The walls of the cave are covered in shiny bits of mica that reflect the light so it almost looks like glass."

§

By the time they reached the cave, the sun had dropped below the horizon. However, Tom was just able to make out a small opening to one side of a large slab of rock. From where they were standing, it was pitch black inside. Beth asked Tom to pass her the torch Harry had lent them. She crouched down on her hands and knees and began to crawl slowly forward, under the rocky overhang. Cautiously, Tom followed behind. The bright beam of the torch lit up the walls of the cave with a warm, yellow light. Tom ran his fingers over the surface of the rock. It was mostly rough to the touch, but there were a number of places where the crystals glistened like glass, just as Beth had said.

She shone the torch to the far end of the cave and called out Rhiannon's name. But there was no reply and nothing to suggest that anyone had been there.

"I'm afraid it doesn't look as though your theory holds up" Tom said.

"Hang on a minute. There's another small inner chamber through that hole over there. I need to check she hasn't squeezed through."

Beth pushed her head and an arm through the hole and shone the torch around. But there was nobody there either. She pulled herself back out and sat down on the floor.

"I'm so sorry Tom. I really thought she might be here. What on earth do we do now? Oh God, this is such a nightmare, I can hardly believe it."

"There's only one thing we can do" Tom said. "We just have to go on looking until we find her. Come on, there's no point in sitting here any longer. We'll have to take extra care climbing up from here, but we've got the torch. Come on Beth, let's get going.

§

When Tom and Beth finally met up with the others on the top of the mountain, it was only to discover that they too had had a fruitless search. It was well after ten o'clock by now. The night air was cold and damp, and Harry was beside himself with worry.

"We've searched everywhere up here and there's not been a trace of her" he said. "There's nothing for it. We'll have to go back down to Ty Pellaf and think again. To be honest, I don't know where else to look. Oh, you stupid child where are you?" he cried out into the night, with tears in his eyes.

"Well, surely it's a good thing that we can rule out the mountain." Max said, trying to introduce an element of cheer into the sombre atmosphere.

"But what if she's fallen and hurt herself? She could be lying unconscious, stuck on a ledge somewhere halfway down the mountain, for all we know." Harry said.

"Don't let's jump to conclusions" Tom said, "surely there must be somewhere else she could be?"

"I can't think of anywhere" Harry said, forlornly shaking his head.

"But we've been assuming that wherever she's gone, she's stayed in that same place. What if she's been moving about too? We could easily have missed her altogether" Kate said.

"Of course, we haven't thought of that" Tom said. "Anyway, there's no point in hanging about up here. Let's get back down. She may even have returned home by now. If not, we'll just have to go on looking."

"She's a sensible girl, Harry. I seriously don't see her doing anything that would put her life in danger" Beth said. "I agree with Tom, she could well be back home by now, let's go down."

They made their way down the mountainside, as quickly as they were able, stretched out in single file behind Harry. They were grateful for the additional light from the pale moon which emerged from behind the clouds soon after they set off. They were so busy concentrating on the difficult descent that nobody spoke. At last, the path levelled out and they were able to make out the dark shape of the chapel. Even when they reached the main track and were heading down towards Ty Pellaf, they continued in silence. Nobody knew quite what to say.

Harry began to run when they were nearing the path to the farmhouse, and the others hurried after him. They were all desperately hoping to find that Rhiannon had returned. Harry had already gone inside when the rest of them arrived outside the back door. They could hear Mattie wailing with grief and Hurry's faltering voice trying to console her. They knew at once that their search would have to continue.

"We can't give up yet" Beth said. "Harry and Mattie need a little time on their own, but we should start planning what to do next."

"I agree" Kate said.

Hand in hand and deep in thought, Tom and Beth walked to the corner of the house from where they could see right across the island. The moon had disappeared behind a cloud. The island lay stretched out in front of them, shrouded in darkness save for the regular flashing of the beam from the lighthouse. Beth found herself counting the flashes that came with each rotation of the light. One, two, three, four, five she counted and then, after a short pause, there they came again, one, two, three, four, five flashes. And then it suddenly dawned on her. Of course, there was just one place where they hadn't looked, one place where it would make complete sense for Rhiannon to have gone...

"I know where she is," she blurted out, excitedly, "she's in the lighthouse, I'm sure of it."

"But, surely that can't be possible. I thought the lighthouse was automatic and unmanned these days. It must be locked up securely, mustn't it?" Tom said, looking far from convinced.

"Yes, it would be, normally that is. But I remember Alun Price telling me on the way across that a maintenance crew was due over in the next day or two. And I'm pretty sure I saw someone up there when we passed by the harbour yesterday afternoon."

"Well, I suppose it is the one place that nobody's looked."

"But don't you see? It's the most obvious place of all. It has to be Rhiannon's tower of glass."

"I get where you're coming from and there's only way to put your theory to the test. But what are we going to say to Mattie and Harry? They've had enough disappointments already. We must be careful not to raise their hopes too high."

"Look Tom, believe me, I feel just the same way as you. But, I'm certain I'm on the right track. It all adds up, please trust me."

"All right, we'd better go and share your theory with the others."

# CHAPTER SIXTY-ONE

Tom, Beth, Max and Kate all sat on the floor of the trailer, clinging to its sides as it lurched and swayed its way towards the harbour. They had no choice but to suffer the unpleasant fumes pouring out from the tractor's battered exhaust. It had been Harry's suggestion that they should take out the tractor. They were all exhausted, and he wanted to get to the lighthouse as quickly as possible. The tractor's dim headlights hardly lit up the track ahead of them, but Harry knew every hole and bump and kept his foot flat down on the accelerator. It wasn't long before they passed the harbour and made their way up to the narrow peninsula leading up to the lighthouse.

Tom watched the beam from the lighthouse as it passed over their heads, illuminating the swirling wisps of sea mist sweeping in from the ocean. It reminded him of how the light from the cinema projector used to shine through the clouds of cigarette smoke in his youth. It was approaching midnight and was much colder under the clear night sky. He could feel Beth shivering next to him so he pulled her closer and wrapped his arms round her. She managed a weak smile of gratitude.

"What if I'm wrong Tom? Harry and Mattie will never forgive me!"

"But you were so certain, Beth. Don't despair now. The more I think about it, the more sense it makes. We're nearly there and we'll soon know."

"And there's another thing. You realise how dangerous it must be to expose yourself to the full glare of that lamp up there. I'm worried she may have been blinded by the light. What if she's fallen down the steps or, even worse, gone out onto the gallery and fallen over the edge."

"Hush Beth. You're letting your imagination get the better of you. We need to stay calm, for Harry's sake."

They were interrupted by the grinding of the tractor's heavily worn gearbox as Harry attempted to change down. After a final, violent, lurch to one side, they drew level with one of the lighthouse's outbuildings and came to a stop. They climbed down from the trailer and joined Harry, who was standing in front of the tractor, staring up at the lantern chamber at the top of the tower.

"Do you really think she's up there?" he said turning to Beth with a doubtful expression.

"Well, there's only one way to find out. Come on, let's go take a look" Tom said, heading off past the outbuildings and towards the entrance to the tower. Harry left the tractor engine running to power its lights and they were just able to make out the broad red and white bands painted round the solid square tower. When they arrived at the entrance, as Tom had half feared, they found it was firmly locked. In desperation, Harry began to pound on the door with his bare fists, shouting out "Are you there Rhiannon, are you there? It's your Daddy. Please answer me if you're there, please Rhiannon, please answer me!" Soon they had all joined in, shouting out her name, but there was no answer.

A door slammed shut somewhere behind them and suddenly they were caught in the glaring beam of a spotlight. A deep and angry voice growled "What the hell do you think you're all up to? You realise, I suppose, that you're trespassing on the private property of Trinity House?"

They turned to see who had addressed them and found themselves looking up at immensely tall and thickset young man with a bushy beard. It was clear they had disturbed him from his sleep, for the bottom of a pyjama shirt could be seen sticking out from under his navy-blue sweater.

"You must be a member of the maintenance crew" Tom said. "We didn't know you were still here. We're so sorry to have disturbed you in the middle of the night like this. The thing is, we urgently need to get inside the lighthouse. It's a long and complicated story but we think there's a young girl in there and we're desperately worried that she may be in danger."

"Impossible!" the young man replied. "As you can see, the door is always kept locked. No-one can get in without the key."

"But surely, you must have been in and out during the day. I don't imagine you lock the door every time."

"Not when I'm actually on site, no. But I'm the only one here at the moment and I'm always within earshot. It is exceptionally unlikely that anyone could get in without my knowing about it."

"Yes, but what if someone really wanted to, without being seen I mean?" Beth interjected.

"As I just said, it's most unlikely that I wouldn't see or hear them."

"But not impossible?" Beth challenged.

The young man shrugged his shoulders. "I suppose not" he said.

During this brief exchange, Harry had stood back from the rest of the group, clenching his fists in frustration. Now he stepped forward to look the young man full in the face.

"We haven't met before. You must be new to the job and you don't know me from Adam. I can understand you're suspicious. But look, I'm Harry Evans, I've farmed this island since I was a boy. I have a 17 year old daughter. She's very young for her age, a simple soul, if you understand what I mean. Well, she went out early this morning and she hasn't been seen since. We've searched every inch of the island and we can't find her anywhere. My wife and I are worried to death. This is the only place we haven't looked. Dr Davenport here believes there may be a good reason why she's come here. So, I beg you, can you please unlock the door, it's our only remaining hope of finding her?"

"But why would she come here?"

"I can explain all that later" Beth said in despair. "Please, don't waste any more time. If she's where I think she is, she could be in very great danger!"

"All right then" the young man said resignedly. "I think it's a waste of time and thoroughly irregular, but I suppose there's nothing to be lost". He unhooked the key ring hanging from a belt round his waist, selected the largest key and inserted it into the lock. He opened the door and they all followed him inside. He flicked a switch to turn on the lights on the staircase that led up to the lantern chamber. "Well, there's no-one here" he said, looking round the empty ground floor of the lighthouse.

"No, not down here. If she's anywhere, she'll be up in the lantern chamber." Beth said as she began to climb the concrete steps.

"Hang on a minute. You can't just go up there, it's far too dangerous. You could be blinded by the light if you don't know what you're doing. Hang on, let me go first."

The young man pushed past Beth and began the steep climb up the steps, closely followed by Beth and Harry. "The rest of you stay down there" he shouted to the others.

When they reached the top of the stairs, the young man raised his hand to caution Beth and Harry to stay back. "You two wait here while I take a look, we don't want any unnecessary mishaps." He climbed a further two or three steps until his head was above the floor level of the lantern tower. He couldn't see anything at first and then, as the lighthouse beam rotated and illuminated the floor of the chamber, he let out a stifled gasp. "Oh my God!" he cried.

"What is it?" Harry asked, climbing up beside him. He had to wait for the lantern to complete yet another revolution before he saw her. She was lying on her back with her arms stretched out above her head. Her eyes were closed and she lay there as still as death.

"Rhiannon!" Harry cried. He attempted to push his way forward into the chamber but the young man put out a restraining arm to stop him.

"You must stay down below the light unless you want to be blinded" he said. "We'll have to crawl on our hands and knees. Come on, follow me, but for Christ's sake stay down and whatever you do, don't look directly at the light."

Beth climbed up higher to see what was happening. Her knuckles turned white as she gripped the top rail of the staircase and stared into the chamber. The young man was the first to reach the prostrate figure. Beth saw him lean forward to put his ear close to her mouth and listen. The seconds ticked by and then he turned to Harry, smiled and said "It's all right, she's still breathing, but we need to get her out of here and fast. She must have passed out with the heat from the lantern." He motioned to Harry to take hold of Rhiannon's ankles while he reached under her armpits to raise her up.

As they half carried, half dragged Rhiannon across the floor to where she was waiting, Beth could see the tears of relief pouring down Harry's face. She called down to the others "we've found her, she's alive, but she's unconscious. We need some more help up here to get her down. Max, you're the strongest, could you come up please?"

The staircase was steep, narrow and awkward to negotiate. It took a full 15 minutes for them to make the descent. Harry went first, holding onto the railings and climbing down backwards, ready to help anyone who might trip or fall. The young man followed a few steps behind, holding Rhiannon under her shoulders and bearing the brunt of her weight in his strong arms. Max came next, holding her legs and Beth brought up the rear.

When they reached the bottom of the staircase, they laid Rhiannon carefully down on the floor. She was still unconscious. Harry knelt down next to her. He gently raised her shoulders off the ground and cradled her in his arms. He kept saying "You're safe now, my little darling, you're safe now, you're safe."

"She must be pretty dehydrated after lying up there in that heat" Beth said, turning to the young man. "I'm really sorry but I don't know your name."

"It's Marcus."

"OK, Marcus. You've been a great help. You couldn't possibly fetch some water could you? She'll need it when she comes round. Oh, and if you've got a spare one, could you bring a towel?"

"Of course, I'll be right back" he said and hurried off across the yard towards the former lighthouse keeper's quarters.

"Thank God we found her!" Tom said. "You were right about the lighthouse Beth, who would have guessed it?"

"How did you know she'd be here?" Kate asked. Neither she nor Max had been told about Beth's theory and were both looking puzzled.

"I think that had better keep until tomorrow." Beth replied "It's a long story and I think this young woman needs our full attention right now."

In no time at all, Marcus returned with a large enamel cup and a jug of water which he put down on the floor next to Beth. He handed her a small white towel which had been draped around his neck. "Sorry, it's the best I can do" he said.

"Thank you, it'll do fine" she said. She poured a little water onto one end of the towel and proceeded to bathe Rhiannon's face. "We need to cool her down" she said. "Her forehead's burning, like it's on fire!" She half-filled the cup with water and raised it to Rhiannon's mouth. She dipped her fingers in and moistened the young girl's lips. Harry, meanwhile, continued to cradle his daughter in his arms while the rest of them anxiously looked on.

It was Kate who first spotted a slight fluttering of one of Rhiannon's eyelids. "Look, did you see that? I think she's coming round."

They all stared at the young girl's face, searching for any further sign that she might be regaining consciousness. And then, as Beth dipped her fingers into the cup of water once more, Rhiannon's lips began to part, just a little at first, and then still wider. Beth dabbed more water onto her lips. Rhiannon opened her eyes and blinked in the bright light. She looked up at the anxious faces staring down at her. From her puzzled expression it was clear that she was trying to understand where she was and who all these people were.

"Thank God she's coming round" Beth said.

"Thank God indeed" Tom replied.

# CHAPTER SIXTY-TWO

TWO WEEKS LATER

It was two weeks since the day Rhiannon had gone missing. Tom was sure that he would never forget the look of relief on Mattie's face when they arrived back at Ty Pellaf. As Beth had suspected, Rhiannon's main problem had been dehydration and, to everyone's intense relief, she had almost completely recovered by the following day.

At first, Beth blamed herself for filling Rhiannon's head with stories of miraculous cures. She had been equally concerned about how Rhiannon would react once that she knew that no such cures existed. But she needn't have worried. When she and Tom called at Ty Pellaf the following day, Rhiannon threw her arms around them both and thanked them for bringing her safely back home. "Mummy and Daddy say they love me just as I am" she said. Beth hugged her tight, kissed her and told her that she was indeed quite the sweetest, kindest and most lovely young girl she could ever hope to meet.

During the days that followed, Tom and Beth spent much of their time continuing to explore the island, more often than not, accompanied by Max and Kate, of whom they had become extremely fond. On several of their excursions, Rhiannon was their guide, proudly introducing them to her favourite island haunts. The one place to which she didn't take them was Merlin's cave. This she continued to regard as her special secret place which no-one apart from Beth would be admitted to. Beth had long given up any hope of uncovering further clues relating to the Bardsey's Arthurian connections on the island itself. But at least the evidence was strong enough to ensure that the island's claims had been worth investigating. The evenings Tom and Beth kept mainly for themselves. They passed the time reading by the fireside and talking into the small hours. Needless to say, the nights they spent wrapped in each other's arms.

And then the day came when Beth had to leave the island to return to London to present a paper to an international conference. Tom walked with her down to the quayside to wait for the arrival of Alun Price. At the first sound of the ferry approaching, Beth clutched hold of Tom.

"Tom, O Tom" she said through her tears "I do so hate partings. This isn't the end is it? Promise me you mean it when you tell me you love me and you want us to be together?"

"Beth, how could you doubt it? No, this isn't the end, this is the beginning!"

Beth laughed. "Only you could make a declaration of love sound like a line from the Bible." Tom joined in her laughter, pulled her towards him and kissed her on the lips for one last time. When the boat finally arrived and her luggage had been stowed on board, they said their farewells once more. She climbed aboard and smiled down at him from the open cockpit, wiping away the occasional tear.

And now it's Tom's time to return to life on the mainland. Two more weeks have passed and it's his turn to take an emotional leave of Mattie, Harry and Rhiannon. They beg him to return to the island before too long and Rhiannon throws her arms around him and cries. But leave he must, for now he feels secure enough in his faith to return to his duties.

Standing for one last time on the deserted beach at Aberdaron, he smiles with childlike pleasure. He sends a small stone skimming across the calm surface of the sea and watches it skid and bounce and skid once again until it is finally enveloped by an incoming wave. He has an appointment to see Bishop George on his return. He wonders what his old friend will have to say when he tells him that he has found rather more on the island than he was looking for.

# About the Author

Chris Green has worked in the cultural industries for forty years. He was Popular Events Director of the City of London Festival (1978-1991), Director of The Poetry Society (1989-1993) and Chief Executive of the British Academy of Songwriters, Composers & Authors (1998-2008). He contested Hereford and South Herefordshire for the Liberals (Liberal Democrats) in 1979, 1983 and 1987 when he came within 1200 votes of winning. He is married to Sheila and lives on the Welsh border in rural Herefordshire. He has two grown-up sons Damien and Jonathon. He is chair of the Education Charity 'Learning Skills Research', a board member of Hereford's Courtyard Arts Centre, a member of the newly formed Herefordshire Cultural Partnership and chair of the Francis W Reckitt Arts Trust. He is a Fellow of the Royal Society of Arts and a Freeman of the City of London. He was awarded the BASCA Gold Badge of Merit for service to the Music Industry in 2009. 'The Swinging Pendulum of the Tide' is his first novel.

# Further Reading

*The Accidental Pilgrim*  Maggi Dawn  (Hodder & Stoughton)

*The Ancient Celts*  Barry Cunliffe  (Oxford University Press)

*The Ancient World of the Celts*  Peter Berresford Ellis  (Constable)

*Arthur and the Lost Kingdoms*  Alistair Moffat  (Weidenfeld & Nicolson)

*Arthurian Romances*  Chrétien de Troyes  (Dent)

*Bardsey*  Christine Evans  (Gomer Press)

*Bardsey Bound*  Enid Roberts  (Y Lolfa Cyf)

*Celtic*  T W Rolleston  (Senate)

*Celtic Pilgrimages*  Elaine Gill and David Everett  (Blandford)

*The Celts*  Frank Delaney  (Harper Collins)

*The Celts Life, Myth and Art*  Juliette Wood  (Duncan Baird)

*Celtic Mythology*  Written and published by Geddes & Grosset

*Exploring the World of King Arthur*  Christopher Snyder  (Thames & Hudson)

*Folklore of Wales*  Anne Ross  (Tempus Publishing)

*The Four Ancient Books of Wales*  William F Skene  (Forgotten Books)

*History of the Britons*  Nennius  (Lightning Source UK)

*History of the Kings of Britain*  Geoffrey of Monmouth  (Penguin Classics)

*Holy Ways of Wales*  Jim Green  (Y Lolfa Cyf)

*The Journey Through Wales*  Gerald of Wales  (Penguin Classics)

*Journey to Avalon*  Chris Barber & David Pykitt  (Blorenge Books)

*The Life of Merlin*  Geoffrey of Monmouth  (Readaclassic)

*The Mabinogion*  translated by Sioned Davies  (Oxford)

*Le Morte D'Arthur*  Sir Thomas Malory  (Modern Library Giant)

*Myths and Legends of the British Isles*  Richard Barber  (The Boydell Press)

*Pilgrimage*  John Ure  (Constable)

*The Shaking of the Foundations*  Paul Tillich  (Pelican)

*Tales of the Celtic Underworld*  John Matthews  (Blandford)

*R S Thomas  Collected Poems*  (Phoenix Giants)

*Wild Wales*  George Borrow  (Collins)

28078149R00222

Printed in Great Britain
by Amazon